THE PLEASURE AND THE PRICE

Lilah Conway had wondered what life in the fast lane was like ever since she had abandoned her dreams, and accepted banking tycoon's Ben Conway's wedding ring.

Now Lilah had her once-in-a-lifetime chance to have it all. The spotlight. The applause. The adulation. Everything that stardom could be.

Until she met legendary male movie star Craig Kimball—and was entangled in the clutches of this man's fearful sexual power and perverse desire to make a woman like Lilah his victim and his slave . . .

"Fast-moving and glitzy!" —*Library Journal*

"Intriguing . . . fun to read" —*Chattanooga Times*

Selected by the LITERARY GUILD

LIVING COLOR

Kate Coscarelli

AN ONYX BOOK

NEW AMERICAN LIBRARY

PUBLISHER'S NOTE

This book is a work of fiction. Names, characters, places, and incidents either are the product of the author's imagination or are used fictitiously, and any resemblance to actual persons, living or dead, events, or locales is entirely coincidental.

NAL BOOKS ARE AVAILABLE AT QUANTITY DISCOUNTS WHEN USED TO PROMOTE PRODUCTS OR SERVICES. FOR INFORMATION PLEASE WRITE TO PREMIUM MARKETING DIVISION, NEW AMERICAN LIBRARY, 1633 BROADWAY, NEW YORK, NEW YORK 10019.

For information address New American Library.

Living Color previously appeared in an NAL BOOKS edition published by New American Library and published simultaneously in Canada by The New American Library of Canada Limited.

 Onyx is a trademark of New American Library.

SIGNET, SIGNET CLASSIC, MENTOR, ONYX, PLUME, MERIDIAN and NAL BOOKS are published by NAL PENGUIN INC., 1633 Broadway, New York, New York 10019

First Onyx Printing, April, 1988

1 2 3 4 5 6 7 8 9

PRINTED IN THE UNITED STATES OF AMERICA

*This book is dedicated with love
to my husband, Don, who makes
things happen for us all,
and to our grandchildren,
Makena, Andrew, and Katelyn,
who have made our world
a better place to be.*

ACKNOWLEDGMENTS

I would like to thank the following people for their expertise, their advice, and their responsiveness to my questions.

Daniel S. Schag, Ph.D., Associate Professor, California School of Professional Psychology

Cyndie C. Schag, Ph.D., Research Psychologist, Veterans Administration and Department of Psychiatry and Biobehavioral Sciences, University of California School of Medicine

Linda Dobbs, M.S., Genetic Counselor, University of California Medical Center

Robert E. Sparks, M.D., Head of Genetics Department, University of California School of Medicine

My agent, Joan Stewart, who counsels me to write to please myself

My editor, Maureen Baron, who keeps me from verbosity

And to the memory of Janice Bradley, who saw beauty everywhere

By convention there is color,
by convention sweetness, by convention
bitterness, but in reality there are
atoms and space.

—DEMOCRITUS, 460(?)–370(?) B.C.
Fragment 125

1

WHY is it, Lilah wondered, that when the telephone is ringing on the other side of a locked door, it always stops as soon as the door is opened? Sure enough, even though it had rung only four times before she could get inside the house, drop her groceries, and snatch up the receiver, she was too late. The impatient caller had hung up. Feeling frustrated, and annoyed at Stella, who was probably watching her soaps and pretending not to hear it ring, Lilah hurried back to the car to get the other bags and close the garage door. March winds roared across the lake, penetrating the very bricks and mortar of her large comfortable home.

She shivered and slammed the door closed, not that it would make much difference to a force that the heaviest weather stripping couldn't seem to keep out. She had always hated the winters of Illinois, even though she had lived all of her life there.

"Stella, I'm home. You can put the groceries away and start dinner now. Mr. Conway will be home early this evening." There was an answer from the maid's room that sounded very much like, "In a minute," but she couldn't be sure. Stella was given to grumbling under her breath, loud enough to let everyone know she wasn't happy but not intelligible enough to get her into trouble.

Lilah started to knock again and complain about her

not answering the telephone but thought better of it. There was really no reason to take out the day's irritations on her housekeeper and risk the retribution of an overdone piece of meat or lumpy gravy.

As she walked toward the closet in the foyer to hang up her coat, suddenly the sight of the new arrival in the house caught her eye, and a small gasp escaped her. She had forgotten that it was going to be delivered today! Dropping her coat onto a chair, she hurried into the living room to the large bay window where her childhood friend stood. The beauty of the Steinway grand piano, gleaming in its bright ebony finish, was startling. Hesitantly she ran her fingers along the curve of the case, and memories of her youth came crashing down on her like the opening chords of a Rachmaninoff Concerto. Suddenly Lilah was twelve again, and it was a warm summer day with the sun filtering through the window screens as Grandma smiled proudly at her brilliant little prodigy.

"Grandma," she whispered, and her eyes were filled with tears. "I'm so sorry I failed you . . . and I miss you so much."

Brushing away the tears and the memories, she concentrated on the instrument. The man who had refinished the case had done an excellent job on the old piano. A rare Model A, it had been built in 1905 and was a treasure she had promised to keep with her all of her days. She had called it her Black Beauty, and it had been her pet, her playmate, her best friend until she was twenty years old, and now that it was again sharing her house, she would have to deal every day with the guilt she felt for having banished it from her life.

Lilah started to pull the bench away to sit down but hesitated. Instead she looked inside at the newly gilded harp and the bright new red felt pads. Tears began to puddle in her eyes again. Gently she touched the keys to check the tone, to see if they had done as good a job on the inside as they had on the outside, and the beautiful, resonant sound filled the room like the ghost of her childhood. Quickly she withdrew her hand from the keyboard. It was too painful.

Her grandmother had died almost a year ago, and when the old mansion was sold and the furnishings auctioned off, Lilah realized that she could not break her promise to the woman who had been the most important person in her childhood. She had to make a place in her home for the piano, even though it would be a silent testimonial to her failure.

Lilah walked up the stairs, past the family portraits on the wall and the grandfather clock that her aunt had given her and Warren as a wedding gift twenty years before. In the large bedroom with its tiny blue-flowered Laura Ashley cotton print fabrics, she took off her shoes and threw herself across the coverlet on the four-poster bed and closed her eyes. Would the sorrow of losing her grandmother ever go away?

The telephone rang, and she sat up quickly, catching it in the middle of the second ring. She was eager for some diversion from the gloom that had overtaken her. The operator asked for Mrs. Lilah Conway, and when she responded, she was told to hold for a call from London.

Lilah's spine straightened in surprise. Who could possibly be calling her from London? There must be some mistake. A few moments later a woman's voice said, "Hello, is this Lilah Conway?"

"Yes."

"This may sound a bit mysterious, but I need to know if I'm talking to the right person. By any chance, was your maiden name Greer?"

"Yes, it was. Who is this?"

"My name is Rose Wilkins, and I have something very important to discuss with you. I'm flying to New York next Thursday. Would it be possible for you to meet me there at the Plaza Hotel?"

Lilah was puzzled by the audacity of the request. "New York? Heavens, no! Who are you, anyway?"

"I've rehearsed this conversation a million times, but I just can't seem to get it right. Forgive me for being abrupt, but I've learned from a very reliable source that we're closely related."

"I don't know who you are, but there's got to be some kind of mistake. My only living relative was my grandmother, and she died last year." Although the woman's voice was cultured, Lilah was beginning to suspect that this might be some kind of a crank call, and she knew she ought to hang up.

Evidently sensing her suspicions, the caller hurriedly tried to reassure her. "Believe me, I know how peculiar this must sound to you, but you have nothing to lose by listening to me. You see, I have every reason to believe that we're sisters."

"I think you've got me mixed up with somebody else. Really, you have. I have no sisters," Lilah protested.

The woman's voice was silky, her tone reasonable. "Perhaps you're right, but it's important to make absolutely sure. Weren't you born on November 12, 1945? And your grandmother's name was Ellen Simpson. Is that correct?"

"Yes, but that's not exactly classified information."

There was a slight chuckle of amusement as the voice said, "Well, I'm glad to know you're not easily conned. Mrs. Conway, I know this is going to be a terrible shock to you, just as it was to me, but I've been told that you and I are twins."

"That's the most ridiculous thing I've ever heard! Where did you ever get such a preposterous idea?"

"This story just can't be told over the telephone. Look, Mrs. Conway, the only way for both of us to find out if it's true is for us to meet. When we see each other, we'll know, right?"

Twins! The idea that there was another person living and breathing who looked and talked just as she did and who had the exact same blood coursing through her veins was overwhelming, but because of the mysteries surrounding her own life, the possibility was not to be completely dismissed.

"Where did you get your information?" Lilah asked, but her curiosity was growing as rapidly as her heartbeat had accelerated, and she needed to know more.

"Lilah, I know just how you feel. What you're experiencing right now is exactly what I went through when I found out about you. It's taken me months to come to terms with it and call you, so I shouldn't expect an immediate agreement from you. I don't want to press you too hard. Take a day to think it over and I'll call you again tomorrow."

Suddenly Lilah was afraid that the woman would hang up and disappear forever. "Wait, no, please, I must know who told you this."

"The woman who raised me, my—our—father's sister, was a loving and honest woman, and she told me the entire story on her deathbed. She was intelligent and lucid and very religious." The caller paused as if to gather strength and went on, "She said it was important that she clear her conscience before she died and met her Maker. You see, she believed with all her heart that there was a heaven . . . and a hell . . . and I'm quite sure that if there's a God, she's with Him. She was a wonderful woman."

The sincere emotion of the woman's responses, layered on the outrageousness of her claim, gave the entire conversation a surreal, dreamlike quality. "Wh-what was her name?" Lilah asked.

"Geneva Wilkins, and her brother's name was Harry . . . Harry Wilkins. He died in an automobile accident shortly before we were born. Look, we have to meet and talk. I would be more than happy to pay all of your expenses to New York. In fact, I'll have your plane ticket sent to you—"

Lilah interrupted her. "No, absolutely not. I couldn't possibly go to New York, but I'd be more than happy to meet with you here in Chicago to lay rest to your ridiculous claim."

"For reasons that you'll understand when we meet, it is extremely important to keep this just between us . . . at least for now. In fact, under the circumstances, I think it would be wise not to tell your husband about this call, either."

"Why not?" Lilah asked.

"That's another matter that we need to discuss in person. Now, before you say no, think about it overnight, and I'll call you tomorrow at the same time."

"No! I just don't see any way that I could come to New York," she protested, but her voice had begun to lose most of its conviction, and the caller sensed it.

"Think it over, Lilah. Can you really stand the thought of never knowing whether it's true or not? I can't, although God knows I've tried to put it out of my mind for six months now. I'll call you at the same time tomorrow. The decision is yours now."

There was a click, and Lilah realized that the call had ended. She lay down on the bed again and closed her eyes. Good Lord, was she hallucinating? Did that call really happen, or had she dozed off and dreamed it? Her father's name was William Greer . . . but Geneva? Where in the dim recesses of her childhood memories had she heard that name before? Geneva?

That evening at dinner, Lilah had trouble concentrating on the conversation. Matt and Mary Ann, her twin son and daughter, were having a dispute over a dent in Warren's car. Both disclaimed any knowledge of it and blamed it on each other. Warren was unhappy about the piano, and there was a frown on his handsome, tanned face.

"I don't understand," he complained, ignoring the children's bickering. "The only reason I agreed to have that hardware dominate the living room was that I thought you were going to have it refinished in a nice walnut tone to match the furniture. But it's black and shiny and stands out like a sore thumb."

"I know we talked about changing the color, Warren, but when it came right down to doing it, I couldn't.

Wood-tone pianos are pieces of furniture, a black grand piano is a musical instrument," she explained patiently, feeling unusually remote from his annoyance.

"But I really liked having my chair at the window where I could look out and watch the squirrels. Now you've pushed me over to a corner where the light is terrible, and I probably won't be able to read at all without the lamp on," he continued.

"Well, I think the piano looks neat, Mom," Mary Ann assured her.

Matt added his approval too. "Yeah, so do I, but why won't you ever play for us? Grams used to tell us how terrific you were." Both twins were eager to get off the subject of the car.

"Maybe someday I'll play again, now that Black Beauty has come home."

"Too bad Black Beauty, as you call it, isn't a horse. At least Mary Ann could ride it," Warren remarked dourly.

The conversation drifted toward graduation. The twins had applied to different colleges and would be facing the first separation of their lives. As she watched them Lilah's mind was filled with thoughts of her own twin sister and was amazed that she had begun to accept the reality of it all. Did she want it to be true? She remembered the poignant longings of her childhood as she grew up alone in that big house with her grandparents, curious about her dead parents, wishing for a brother or a sister to play with, always feeling slightly unfinished, as if there were some part of her that was missing.

After the twins had left the table and gone upstairs to do their homework, Lilah found herself asking Warren a favor.

"Dear, let's fly to New York next week for a couple of days. We could see a few Broadway shows, and I could shop for some new spring clothes."

"New York? Afraid not. I've got too much going on right now. Besides, if I did have time to get away, I'd much rather go to Florida or Arizona where we could play golf and enjoy ourselves. I'd never go to New York if I didn't have business there. What's wrong with the stores on Michigan Avenue? They're as good as anything New York has to offer."

"But I'd like to go, anyway. Couldn't you arrange to do a little business and take me along?"

"Not for the next month or so. I have to go to Milwaukee on the third for a meeting, and I wouldn't even go there if it weren't absolutely essential to talk personally with Carl Hatfield." Warren unfolded his tall, trim frame from the chair and headed toward the den. "Going to watch TV with me?" he asked. "There's a basketball game on. The Bulls are having a great season."

"No, I don't think so. I'm reading a good book, and I'm anxious to get back to it." She picked up the plates and carried them into the kitchen where Stella was cleaning up.

"That was a delicious dinner, Stella," she remarked to the woman at the dishwasher. Before she turned to leave the room, Lilah asked, "Stella, do you have any sisters or brothers?"

"Yes, ma'am, you could say I do. Five brothahs and three sistahs. Had fo', but one died givin' birth," Stella replied.

"Are you close to them . . . your sisters, I mean?"

"Used to be, not much now. They's still back in Mobile. I ain't been back there in a long while." Stella was delighted to be involved in a conversation. It wasn't often that her employer talked to her about personal things.

"Do you miss not seeing them?"

"Yeah, sometimes. We used ta fight a lot, but we allus stuck togetha against the brothahs. They give us a hard time, for sure."

"Would you like to spend next Christmas in Mobile with them, Stella? I could give you an extra week off then, if you'd like," Lilah offered in a burst of generosity.

Long experience had taught Stella to be cautious about gifts that might cost more than they are worth. "Well, ma'am, I'm not rightly sure I can affo'd that much time off 'thout gettin' paid."

Lilah smiled. Stella was a cagey woman. "I meant that you'd get your pay, too, Stella. Time off without pay is unemployment, not a vacation. I know that."

"Well, thank ya, ma'am, I do 'preciate the kindness. Don't know if I got enough fo' the fare, though."

"We'll work something out," Lilah replied, and left the kitchen. If she stayed any longer, Stella would probably talk her into airfare and a new wardrobe so she could go home in style.

While her husband was watching the game Lilah poked through the box of old photographs that she had found in her grandmother's chifforobe after the funeral. For two hours she examined every snapshot and photograph in detail, hoping to find some clue to her background . . . some thread of affirmation or denial of the existence of Rose Wilkins, but she found nothing.

After the eleven o'clock news Warren came upstairs to find Lilah already in bed. "Are you feeling all right?" he asked.

Startled out of her reverie, she replied, "I'm fine . . . just a little tired."

Warren unbuttoned his shirt and smiled wickedly. "Too tired?" he asked, his gray-green eyes bright with desire.

"No, not really," she replied, too preoccupied with her secret to be very enthusiastic but also feeling guilty about keeping the information from him.

As Warren climbed into the bed beside her he slipped his arm under her waist and pulled her close to him. For a long time he kissed her gently . . . on the eyes, the nose, the cheeks, the mouth, and then he softly stroked her. As she felt herself becoming aroused,

Lilah was again entranced by the change that came over Warren when they were in bed. He was the gentlest, most patient, most considerate of lovers, so different from the cold, formal businessman others knew.

Gradually, as Warren felt her begin to respond, he became more passionate and aggressive, and when he finally entered her, she welcomed him with abandon. In her fantasy she saw their lovemaking as a tiny bud that rapidly grew amid the warmth and moisture until suddenly it bloomed into a bright red, fragrant flower at the instant when they reached the peak of their emotion together.

"You're so beautiful," Warren whispered as he held her close and continued to caress her.

"How can you tell with the lights out?" she teased, brushing her lips across his.

"I don't need my eyes to see you . . . my fingertips tell me . . . my mouth tells me . . . and especially my cock tells me," he whispered.

"It's a good thing nobody but me ever hears you talk like that. What would people say about the proper president of the bank using such words?"

"Well, I guess I'd better let you get some sleep," he replied, and suddenly her lover was gone. Lilah was surprised. It was not like Warren to turn away so abruptly. Usually, on the nights they made love, she went to sleep cuddled in his arms. A wave of guilt washed over her . . . did he suspect that she was concealing something from him? Nonsense. She wasn't doing anything wrong. She had the right to some private thoughts, and besides, she would tell him all about it later.

When Lilah awakened the next morning, the previous day's telephone call seemed more unreal than ever. Wrapping herself in a heavy wool robe, she went down to the morning room to oversee breakfast. Warren was alone at the table, drinking his coffee.

"Aren't the twins down yet?" she asked. "They'll be late for school."

"They've already gone, ma'am. They didn't want no breakfast," Stella informed her.

Without looking up from his paper, Warren commented, "Well, you were really sound asleep this morning." There was no hint of the passionate man who had made love to her the night before.

She sat down and took a sip of coffee, feeling ridiculously guilty. She had never been very good at being secretive. "I guess I was. I was awake most of the night and didn't drift off until after three."

"Want some oatmeal, ma'am?"

"No thanks, Stella. I'm really not hungry. Just some more of this delicious coffee."

"You like that, ma'am? I got the recipe from Talley, who works over at the Trentons'. It's got a bit of chicory and vanilla in it."

"Tastes the same to me," Warren commented.

When he had finished his usual bacon and eggs and was ready to leave, Warren reminded Lilah that he needed his tuxedo for the stag dinner at the club that evening.

She kissed him good-bye at the door, as she did every morning, and then stopped to look at her reflection in the foyer mirror. She and the woman on the other side of the glass appraised another. Each saw a tall, slim woman with broad shoulders and olive skin that looked sallow in the winter but golden in the summer from days on the golf course.

"Rose, when I look at you, will it be just like looking in a mirror? Do you think the same things, dream the same dreams as I do?" she whispered. Lilah leaned closer to inspect her hair. The blond streaks were half grown out, and the dark roots were much too dominant. She'd call the beauty shop that morning and see if Mabel could work her in for touch-up this week.

Early in the afternoon Lilah found herself back in

her bedroom. She had tried to pay attention at the endless club meeting she was obliged to attend as the bank president's wife, but it was impossible. The impending call from Rose Wilkins was all she could think about. Finally she had excused herself and hurried home to wait for the telephone to ring. It did twice, but both calls were from friends, and she was almost rude about cutting them off. She didn't want the line tied up. When the phone rang for the third time, her heart pounded as she again heard the gentle voice from London.

"Hello, Lilah, this is Rose. Have you made a decision yet? Are you going to meet me in New York?"

She heard her voice answering as if it were outside her body, making the decision for her. "Yes, I can be there in the late afternoon of the third . . . will that be all right?" Good God, what was she saying?

"Wonderful. I knew you'd come. We're a set, Lilah, you and me . . . and it's time we got put back together again."

"Why do I believe you? You're just a voice," Lilah said faintly, feeling herself caught in a web of fascination that she was unable to resist.

"Because you know I'm telling the truth. I'll never lie to you, Lilah. And I can't tell you how pleased I am that you believe me and trust me. I want it always to be that way."

"So do I, Rose. I think I believe you because I want you to be real."

"I'm real, all right, honey, and life is never going to be the same for either of us. I'll be at the Plaza all day on the third waiting for you. Call me when you arrive. Ask for Ben Frost's suite."

Suddenly the spell was broken. "Ben Frost? Who's he?" Lilah asked suspiciously.

"My friend and my manager. I'm an entertainer, sister, dear."

"An entertainer? Are you anybody famous?"

"I'm getting there, Lilah."

"I still don't understand why we can't meet here in Chicago. Why does it have to be New York?"

"Believe me, it's in *your* best interest that we meet in New York. You'll understand then. Trust me, Lilah."

When the conversation was over, Lilah threw herself into a chair and wailed in disbelief, " 'Trust me,' she says. 'Trust me'! Good grief, have I lost my mind?"

2

ROSE put down the telephone and walked to the bar in her room. She knew it was not wise to drink under stress, but the conversation had almost undone her. She held up her long, slim hands with their long opalescent rose nails and saw that they were shaking. It had taken her six months to get up the courage to make that telephone call the previous day, and today's hadn't been much easier. It was positively ridiculous for her to complicate her life right now when everything was going so terrifically well, but the compulsion to see Lilah Greer Conway had grown unbearable. Ever since Geneva's death Rose had been haunted by the specter of what might have been, and she was afraid that if she didn't lay it to rest, it would destroy her.

Pulling open the door to the small refrigerator, she inspected the shelves. Damn, there was no champagne left. She must have drunk the last bottle. She called room service to order some more. Only one more interview, she sighed, and then she was free to do as she pleased for three whole days before her flight to New York and her triumphant return to the U.S.

Room service at the Savoy was efficient, and within fifteen minutes a chilled bottle of Taittinger champagne was delivered and opened. As Rose lifted the crystal flute so that the light from the window caught the wine's sparkle, she murmured a toast that was both exultant and apprehensive. "To my dear, long-lost twin sister . . . and to our reunion . . . at last."

She lifted the glass to her lips, but before she could drink, the telephone rang. A familiar voice said, "How's my lovely lady?"

"Benjie . . . it's so good to hear your voice. Are you still in New York?"

"Sure am. It hasn't been easy getting the details on the contract ironed out. I told them you weren't going to set foot on American soil until everything was signed, sealed, and delivered."

"And they believed you? *C'est folie*. Are you crazy, Benjie? Anybody with a grain of intelligence would know that I wouldn't miss those Academy Award ceremonies . . . I might win the damn statue!" she protested.

"Now look, baby, cut out that 'win' stuff. You already won by being nominated. The rest isn't important, and I don't want you getting your hopes up for something that's not gonna happen, understand? This job is worth a lot more than a damned trophy. I want you on that little screen every damn week, not just for thirty seconds of breathless thank-yous. That's why I want this deal set up right now. That nomination isn't worth beans after the awards are made. Nominees are only hot for a month, remember that. We're planning for the long run."

"Are there any problems?" she asked nervously. She was afraid the deal was going to fall through, as so many had in her career.

"Nothing major, just little things that I'm sure they're going to agree to . . . like hotel bills, limos, and a security guard when you travel."

"Benjie, for God's sake, don't lose the deal for a few frills. I don't need a security guard, you know that."

"Kiddo, these aren't frills. We want them to make concessions that will acknowledge you as the star of this show."

"Who're you kidding? That show has been doing well in the ratings. If it keeps on as it started, everybody in the cast will be a star."

"But none of them was anybody before *Broadway*. This show is tailor-made for you. You're an international singing star, and you'll be a smash in the role of a Broadway legend. You're a living legend yourself, and I want you treated properly. You know the standards we establish now will set the course," he declared.

"I know, I know. Don't lecture me, and don't give me that international star stuff. I'm a legend only in your own mind. Let's face it, most people in the States had never heard of me until I got the Academy Award nomination for that supporting part I did in Louis's film," she protested, and took a long swallow of champagne. If there was one thing she had learned, it was that it was okay to kid everybody else, but it was important never to believe the crap yourself.

"Sweetheart, leave it to me. Wasn't I the one who talked you into doing that film? Wasn't I the one who said it was time you started to act and soft-pedal the singing? Come on, give me a break."

"Okay, okay. You do it, honey. I trust you, and I sure miss you. This hotel room is getting pretty lonely."

"Is everything okay there? How's the service?"

"It's beautiful, baby. The room is gorgeous, the bathroom looks like a concert hall, and room service is terrific. It only took 'em fifteen minutes to replenish my supply of bubbly just now," she replied.

"Go easy on that stuff, will you?"

"You worried about me getting drunk, Benjie?"

"No, but you know it kills your appetite, and I worry about you not getting enough to eat. You're way too thin as it is."

"Benjie, baby, don't you know you can never be too rich or too thin?"

"Yeah, but if you ruin your health, you're not gonna have a chance to enjoy being rich. Have you had anything to eat yet today?"

"Sure . . . I had croissants and jam and a big glass of orange juice," she lied.

"Yeah, sure, I just bet you ate some jam. Now, after you hang up, I want you to have room service bring you a decent meal. Don't do that interview without some food in your stomach, you hear? And be careful what you say. I hear that reporter from the *Telegraph* is a real ball-buster. She'll sweet-talk you and try to be your best friend, and then she'll skewer you with her typewriter."

"Don't worry. I'm getting good at this stuff. They all ask the same questions, anyway."

"You know I love you, don't you?"

"Yeah, sure, I know. I love you, too, Benjie. Do you think it would be okay if I rented a car and drove out to the countryside? I could use a little time away from the big city before I head for New York."

"No problem, but get a driver. You're a valuable piece of property, and I don't want anything to happen to you."

"Well, I'm a good piece, that's for sure."

"You're a lot more than that. As the song says, you're my special lady."

Rose put down the telephone and finished the glass of champagne. Then she called room service to order a chicken sandwich, then the concierge to request a car and driver for the next day.

Moving over to the window, she stood looking down at the Thames and tried to sort out her feelings. Why wasn't she hysterical with joy? For twenty years she had sacrificed everything to make it in show business, and now she was hot, really hot, but the emptiness inside her was still there. It was as if a cold, tight fist of hunger squeezed her at the center of her soul, and the feeling had been with her all of her life. She had always called it ambition, but now she wasn't certain, not certain at all.

She had expected success to make everything okay: satisfy the hunger, quench the thirst . . . fulfill her.

But it hadn't happened. The void was there. Would seeing Lilah Conway make it better . . . or worse?

When the interview was over, Rose closed the door behind the woman and let out a deep sigh. Jesus, the last thing she had wanted was to get into a philosophical discussion. Why couldn't the pretentious bitch have just asked about her taste in clothes and men? She just hoped she had been successful in diverting the reporter. Rose's politics had been a little radical at one time in her career but not anymore. Now, for God's sakes, she wanted that old stuff buried. She needed to be loved by all America.

Rose called out, "Sheila!" and a woman in a maid's uniform hurried in from the bedroom. "Yes, mum?"

"Sheila, I've got to get out of this place for a little while. You haven't packed all my wool slacks yet, have you?"

"I can unpack a pair, quick as a wink, I can. No trouble. Would you like a heavy jacket and a pair of brogues?"

"Please. I need to take a walk and get some fresh air."

"It was a longer interview than usual, wasn't it, now?" Sheila asked.

"I feel like I've been put through a bloody wringer."

"Well, I'm sure she'll write a nice article. She seemed like such a sweet, gentle lady."

"Whoa, no way. That lady is tough. Benjie warned me about her, and I could tell from the way she was asking questions that she was looking for a hook to hang me on in the headline."

"Would you like a cuppa tea, mum? I could fix it right up?"

"Tea won't do it. I'm going to take a long walk, and if I come across a pub, I might just stop in and give them some business," Rose replied as she headed for her bedroom to change out of the cream silk lounging pajamas she had donned for the interview.

When, half an hour later, Rose left her suite, her tall, thin frame was covered by a pair of Kenzo's heavy brown tweed slacks, a matching jacket bulkily lined with sheared beaver, and flat-heeled boots. Her wild mane of curly hair was wrapped in a wool turban, and her large, kohl-rimmed amber eyes—which the press referred to as her "tiger eyes"—were hidden behind oversize tinted glasses.

After she emerged from the elevator at the hotel's lower level, she walked out the back door, through the garden, and down to the riverbank. Pulling on heavy gloves against the chill, she strode in the direction of the Houses of Parliament, which loomed farther down the historical river, and she felt suddenly free. As her stride lengthened and her pace quickened, her breath and her blood seemed to flow more freely. God, it felt so good to move.

As she walked, she worried about what life had in store for her. Would she ever be happy living in the United States again? Did she really want to be a celebrity there . . . hounded by newspaper and maga-zine reporters, unable to walk the streets of the city without being assaulted by people who liked her and even some who didn't? No. But she desperately wanted the power that came with success, a power that had eluded her all these years, and the money, of course, the money. She had had quite enough of artistic integ-rity, thank you. Integrity didn't pay the bills for the kind of life a star was supposed to lead.

Most of all, however, she wanted to be accepted in the country where she was born . . . at last. It had been a long time coming, and for that she would have to carry some of the blame, but America owed her something, and she intended to collect.

Now she had another reason to want to go home. Her twin sister. She wondered if life had been any easier for Lilah Conway, or had she, too, suffered? Rose shivered, not from the chill of the wind across the water but from wonder at the power that fate exerted on one's life. The babies were supposed to be identical. What, then, had compelled Geneva to keep her and give her sister away? Was it random chance that had decided their fate? What would her life have been if things had been different . . . if she had been the one chosen to be raised by her grandmother? How far could she have gone, how much faster, if she hadn't had to start with nothing . . . nothing at all? When she saw Lilah, would she hate her for what she was or would they love each other?

An hour later Rose returned to the hotel. She had not stopped into a pub because she needed to be alone, and she was glad to see that Sheila had gone.

As she was undressing, the telephone rang. It was Benjie calling from New York. "Baby, I've got great news! They bought the package . . . gave me damn near everything I asked for."

"Benjie, don't mess with me . . . is it true?"

"It's true. My God, I don't believe it, either. When Trask, the attorney for the network, called me, I thought, 'Uh-oh, I'm in for a fight now,' but all he said was, 'Mr. Frost, we've got a deal . . . but only if that contract is signed and in our hands within twenty-four hours. We're getting sick and tired of your asking for more every time we talk.' "

"Jesus, I hope you signed the damned thing!" she exclaimed.

"Honey, you know you're the one who has to sign it . . . not me. So I called Pan Am and made a reservation for you on the next flight. If I've got it figured right, that's just three hours from now. Are your bags packed, sweetie pie?"

"I'm supposed to have a couple of days' vacation," she protested, but very weakly.

"You can take it here in New York . . . with me. Get on that plane, baby. You hear me?"

"I hear you, Benjie . . . loud and clear."

Rose changed into a lightweight pale gray wool pantsuit by Giorgio Armani, with a matching high-necked

silk blouse and gray shoes and hose. She ordered a
limousine to take her to the airport, and tossed the
rest of her clothes in the partially packed suitcases.
When the porter arrived for her luggage, she pulled a
full-length lynx coat around her shoulders, being careful to let her thick, curly black hair cascade down the
back, and followed him out the door.

At the front desk she left an envelope with cash and
a note of thanks and farewell for Sheila, tipped everyone generously, and then swept dramatically through
the Art Deco doors out into the long black limousine.
From now on she intended to be the epitome of glamour. After all, Lady Rose was going home a star.

3

IT was on her mind constantly, and nothing she could do would put it from her. Rose Wilkins, Rose Wilkins. The name was like a pulse beating inside her body, throbbing at her wrists, her temples, her heart, her mind. Lilah tried to divert herself with telephone calls to her friends, the latest best-selling novel, lunch at the club, but the name was always there. Sometimes the awareness of Rose Wilkins's existence was frightening, calling forth the dangers of the unknown. At other times it was a thrill to imagine another being, another soul, closer to her than any other person could ever be, closer even than her own child. Lilah had become a woman possessed with the possibility that there were two of her.

Even in her dreams she thought about the moment when she would come face-to-face with her mirror image. Somewhere in the recesses of her mind lurked the notion that it might all be a hoax, but whenever it emerged, she banished it. Rose Wilkins was her sister. Her heart knew it, her unfinished soul knew it, and when she got to New York, she would prove it to her eyes and to her mind, because she wanted it to be so.

Lilah dared not tell Warren about her sojourn because he wouldn't believe it, not for a single minute. Warren was too pragmatic and down-to-earth to get caught up in such an improbable fantasy. Not only would he disbelieve Rose Wilkins's claims, but he would also deem it necessary to impose his doubts on Lilah, and she didn't want that to happen. As the days passed, she came to realize how much she wanted it to be true, and if Warren were to argue against the trip, prevailing with reason and logic, as he almost always did, she would never find out for sure about Rose. She had to go to New York.

Working out the logistics of the journey was dependent on getting the schedule for Warren's trip to Milwaukee. Rather than arouse his suspicions and have him ask questions, Lilah called his secretary.

"Sandra, this is Lilah. Is my husband there?" she asked, knowing full well that he would have already left for the club luncheon.

"You just missed him, but if it's important, you can call him at the club."

"No, no. It's nothing important. I was just wondering what flight he was taking to Milwaukee next Thursday. I forgot to ask him."

"I'm not sure. He made his own plane reservations, but I did arrange to have a limousine pick him up here at the office at ten."

"Great, I wanted to make a luncheon date that day if I didn't have to take him to the airport. Is the limo picking him up when he returns on Friday?"

"Yes, late in the evening."

"Of course. Sandra, don't mention that I called. I forgot that he told me there was something or other on Friday evening that he was going to."

"No problem, Lilah. Call me anytime."

The only problem Lilah could foresee was that Warren might call her on Thursday evening. He hadn't done that lately when he was out of town, but he used to, and if he should happen to call, she would need some sort of a cover. God, she felt like a character in a spy movie.

She decided to call her friend Florence Bennett and ask for her help. Lilah had known her for years, and although they weren't as close as they had been when

Florence's husband was alive, they still talked on the telephone at least once a week. She called her and invited her to lunch. Just as she put down the receiver, the phone rang, and she was startled to hear Rose Wilkins's voice again.

"Rose, what a surprise. I just arranged to fly into New York next Thursday morning."

"Wonderful! I wanted to let you know that I was here. Did you tell your husband . . . about me?" Rose asked.

"No, I haven't told him. Is that important to you?"

"Not in the least, but it might be very important to you. Once we've met and know the truth, you can make the decision whether or not you want him to know about me."

"Why wouldn't I want him to know if it's really true that we're twin sisters?" Lilah asked.

"Don't you enjoy having little secrets?" Rose asked.

"Not really," Lilah replied uncertainly.

"Don't change your mind, Lilah. I'm in the Plaza Suite, all right?"

Lilah assured Rose that she'd be there, then put down the telephone, feeling again the sense of loss that engulfed her whenever she stopped speaking to the strange yet intimately remembered voice. It was like speaking to herself on the telephone. Rose Wilkins's voice was her voice . . . she was sure of it.

4

Rose sat looking at herself in the mirror of her dressing table and wondered if the time spider had begun to weave its tiny web around her sister's eyes too, when Ben walked into the room.

"Whatcha doin', baby, looking for wrinkles again?" he asked as he walked toward her and put his hands on her bare shoulders.

She looked up at his handsome face and felt a strong urge to tell him about Lilah Conway. "I'm so excited, Benjie—" she began, and he interrupted her with a kiss on her lips, followed quickly by his response. "I know you are, and so am I. That's the best damn contract I ever negotiated. I haven't been able to sleep for the past couple of nights. Jesus, what a deal."

Rose closed her eyes for a moment of thankfulness that her manager's enthusiasm had saved her from making a mistake. A lifetime of lost illusions and disappointments had made her extremely cautious about sharing information with anyone . . . even the man she loved and trusted above all others. She had been with Ben Frost almost three years now, and he had brought a measure of order and focus and success to her life that she had never known before.

Whenever his arms were around her, she felt safe

and loved and warm. "Benjie, I love you," she whispered.

"I love you, too, my sweet lady. Now, I promised we'd go to the reception at the Museum of Modern Art tonight, because we need to be seen around town—a lot. The word is out, so you'll be hot copy for the society columns and the fan magazines. Have the furs arrived yet?"

"Yes, they were delivered an hour ago, but they're a little extreme, don't you think?"

"Try 'em on and let me see."

Rose got up and went to the closet and pulled out a long garment that was covered with pale blue silk. She ripped off the cover and slipped her arms into a blond leather coat that had hundreds of small matching fox-tails sewn on it in a crosshatch pattern. It was Revillon's idea of a fun fur. She paraded across the room for Ben, who had seated himself on the kingsize bed to watch. She twirled and lifted the large swirl of leather and fur in an arc as she moved. "So, what do you think?" she asked.

Ben shook his head. "No good. The color doesn't do a thing for you. It's too yellow."

"You're right. It's beautiful, but not for me. Benjie, you've got the best eye for color. You should have been an artist. Now shut your eyes while I put on the other one," she said playfully.

Ben did as he was told and lay back on the pillow to wait. Rose hurried into the bathroom but before donning the second coat, she slipped out of her negligee. Then she called out, "Open your eyes, here I come," and she swept toward the bed wrapped in a cloud of white mink. Lifting the wide shawl collar so that it stood up at her neck and formed a halo behind her cloud of black hair, she posed and smiled coquettishly.

"That's it . . . you look sensational. Wear it over that white-beaded cocktail dress and you'll knock 'em dead."

"I think you'll like what I've got on under this coat right now much better," she said suggestively, and slowly opened the fur to reveal her nude body underneath.

Ben grinned and put his hands behind his head. "Yeah, maybe you ought to wear that out tonight. I'll bet we'd even make the eleven o'clock news."

Rose drew the coat around her again and replied, "You'd like that, wouldn't you? The ratings on my first show would probably be astronomical with people wonderin' how much Lady Rose was going to take off."

"Well, when I was negotiating, I did tell 'em that your presence on the tube would add at least three points to their ratings. We might have to do something extreme to deliver."

"Ben Frost, I ought to strangle you."

"I'm up for a little abuse. But first, take off that coat and set it down carefully. We have to return it in perfect shape tomorrow, you know."

Insolently Rose opened the coat and let it slide slowly from her shoulders and sink gently into a heap on the floor. Not taking her eyes from Ben's, she walked toward the bed, swaying her hips. Languidly she kneeled on the bed and swept her leg across his body, straddling his hips with her naked thighs. She began to unbutton his shirt. "You're fresh, you know that, Benjie," she whispered. "Someday, somebody's gonna put you in your place."

"How about puttin' me in your place, baby," he said as he began to feel the warmth of her body through the thin wool of his trousers. Slowly he put his hand under her and lifted her vulva slightly so that he could unzip his fly and release his growing hardness from its constraints. As soon as he was free, she encircled him with her warmth, moving slowly and gently.

Her movements increased in speed and intensity as she sensed her partner's climax nearing. "Oh, honey," she groaned, "you're fantastic." And within moments she felt the sudden thrust upward that told her that it was almost over. She stopped moving immediately and let her slender body melt over his bulky one. She tucked her head into his neck and closed her eyes, thinking that this was the best part of sex. They were still joined in warmth and relaxation, but the huffing and puffing was all over.

Rose wished she could enjoy sex as much as Benjie did. She loved him so much that she wanted to respond, but something inside her seemed to withdraw when they were making love, and she couldn't focus on the joy she felt in his arms. Even on the rare occasions when she succeeded in reaching a climax, she wondered what all the fuss was about. She was sure people made much more of orgasms than they were worth.

Even if she could do without sex, Rose couldn't do without Benjie. For the first time in her life she had a man who loved her, took care of her, and placed her welfare above his own. He had even given up his own promising career as an actor to concentrate on hers. He had told her she could be great but that he'd never be more than mediocre. Even so, she was sure that success eluded him only because there were so few good parts available to him. Ben was smart, handsome, and funny. When she was down, really down, he could always find something to make her laugh. That's why she initiated sex so often. Benjie liked it, he liked it a lot, and she loved making him happy.

Suddenly Ben was ready to get moving. "Better take your shower, sweetie pie. The makeup lady will be here at six to do your face, and Teddy's going to comb your hair out at seven." He rolled her reluctant body off his and stood up. Looking down at his pants, he groaned, "Jesus, another pair of pants for the cleaners." He winked at her. "Man, it's expensive living

with a hot bitch. You gotta quit rapin' me like that,
sugar."

Rose pulled the sheet up and covered herself. The
smile on her face had turned to a dark frown. *"Sacré
bleu!* Don't ever call what we just did 'rape,' Benjie.
You don't know anything about that unless it's happened to you, and believe me, it's not sex."

Detecting the sudden frozen anger in her voice, he
sat down on the bed beside her and put his hand softly
on her cheek. "Sorry, baby, I didn't mean it that way.
You know that."

"I know you didn't, but I get sick and tired of
people making jokes about it. Every time I hear the
word, I remember everything . . . every little detail
. . . every miserable moment of pain and humiliation
. . . and degradation and . . . *la souillure,"* she said,
lapsing into French, the language that had dominated
the past twenty years of her life. She would have gone
on with her litany of grievances, but Ben had heard
them all before. "Stop it, do you hear me . . . stop it!
The next thing we know, you'll work yourself up to a
crying jag again, and your eyes will be red and swollen.
Now, you're going to forget it, remember?"

Rose buried her head in the pillow and mumbled,
"I'll never forget it, never," but the stridency had
gone from her voice and the crisis was over. Ben
leaned down and kissed the top of her head. "Take a
little rest while I shower. You've got half an hour. I'll
wake you up when Marja gets here."

He sat caressing her for a few moments until her
breathing became soft and regular, and he was sure
that she had fallen into a deep sleep, as she always did
after an emotional reliving of the experience that had
marked her so deeply. It was almost as if an evil beast
of a memory slept inside her, and when it was awakened, it ripped and clawed at her. The only way she
could escape it was to go to sleep.

Ben got up from the bed carefully and lifted the
telephone off the hook. Silently he tiptoed out into the

sitting room and called the desk to tell them to hold all calls for half an hour. Then he went into the bathroom to get ready.

As he shaved, he talked to an unseen presence.

"One of these days I'll make you pay, you bastard. I don't care who you are, I'll get you for what you did to her."

5

FLORENCE Bennett got into her car and started the engine. It was a cold, wintry day, and the sky was overcast. As she drove the Oldsmobile out of the garage she shivered, but it was not from the chill outside. She had been emotionally frozen and filled with dread since yesterday when her old friend Lilah had called her and insisted they have lunch together at Spiaggia's in the city, saying she had something important to talk about.

Stopping the car for a traffic light, she took a quick glance at herself in the mirror. She saw a woman in panic and was sure that anyone, even a stranger, could look into her eyes and see the fear within. God, what would happen in the next few hours? Would she be able to handle it, or would she collapse in hysteria at the moment of accusation?

The light changed, and she moved the car ahead slowly, at every street corner seriously considering the possibility of turning back, going home, of calling the restaurant and telling them to notify her friend that she had suddenly fallen ill . . . had broken her leg . . . died. But she went on.

Forty-five minutes later she arrived at the restaurant, which was located in the exclusive shopping area on Michigan Avenue. She walked through the Palladian facade, past the kitchen displayed behind walls of glass, and was seated in a booth, elevated so that she had a clear view through the tall windows of the city and Lake Michigan. She looked around appreciatively at the subdued richness of the plum, rose, and celadon-green room with its postmodern decor and tried to relax. After all, she mused, she didn't get to dine in places like this often nowadays, so she should at least try to enjoy herself, although it was a lot like standing in front of a firing squad and trying to enjoy a cigarette. She ordered a glass of wine and sipped on it nervously until suddenly it was gone. Quickly she ordered another. She needed every bit of strength and courage that alcohol might give her to weather the coming tornado.

Lilah breezed in ten minutes late, as usual, and as she strode confidently across the room Florence felt a familiar envy well up inside her again, poisoning everything she saw, felt, heard, or tasted. It was unfair that one woman should have been blessed with so much. Lilah was beautiful in her own unique and complex way. Her blond-streaked hair accentuated her tawny skin and her eyes . . . those strange amber eyes that looked as if they might glow in the dark. Lilah's tall, lithe form seemed never to have an extra ounce of flesh on it, and she moved as gracefully as an antelope. Florence recalled how, when they were girls, her parents had dragged her to Lilah's endless concerts and recitals, forced her to endure hours of Lilah pounding the piano, always to the ecstatic admiration of everyone. She was to be Chicago's Van Cliburn, everybody said. What a joke that had turned out to be.

For once, just once, Florence's prayers had been answered. Lilah had failed, not in a miserable, picayune way but in a grand, spectacular fall. She had gone to Moscow as a contestant in the Tchaikovsky Competition, and she had not only failed to win it, she had been ignominiously disqualified in the first round. Florence had gotten more than she had asked for, however. With her usual flourish Lilah had returned home, airily declared she was giving up the piano forever, and had thrown herself into preparations for her immediate marriage to Warren Conway, the most desirable and eligible bachelor in town, and Florence's secret passion.

Florence's mother had always said, "Be careful what you ask for, honey, you might get it." Well, she had prayed that Lilah would lose the competition. Every night she had asked God to give that perfect little princess a taste of failure, and her prayers had been answered. How many nights had she lain awake wondering what would have happened if Lilah had won that damn competition? Would she have gone on to fame and glory and forgotten Chicago and Warren Conway? Would Florence Bennett now be Florence Conway? Would it be Florence who was now married to the handsome and successful bank president and mother of two beautiful children? Or would she still be as she was: widow of a sterile man who was destined to die too young . . . childless . . . alone.

"God, I'm so sorry I'm late, Flo. I had a million errands to run this morning, and the traffic was awful. Say, you look terrific. What are you doing to your hair?"

Florence reached up to smooth her newly tinted blond-red hair and then quickly returned her hand to her lap. She was nervous and didn't want Lilah to see her hand shaking.

"Nothing much. Just a little rinse to bring out the highlights—" she began.

Lilah finished it for her. "—and cover the gray."

Florence's laugh was hollow. "You look good, Lilah, what's going on in your life? You sounded so mysterious on the phone."

Lilah asked the waiter to bring her some wine, and then she responded. "Florence, I need your help. I'm going to New York on Thursday, and I don't want Warren to know about it."

"You're what?" Florence asked in disbelief.

"Wait a minute," Lilah protested, laughing. "It's not as bad as it sounds. Don't worry, I'm not having an affair. You know better than that. Warren and I would never cheat on each other. Our marriage is much too good for anything dumb like that."

" 'And love is a thing that can never go wrong, and I am Marie of Romania,' to quote Dorothy Parker. So, if it's all so innocent, why the secrecy?" Curiosity had replaced apprehension.

Lilah had considered telling Florence the truth, but her sense of loyalty to her husband precluded that. After all, if she couldn't tell Warren, she certainly would not tell anyone else.

"You're probably going to think I'm silly, but I just want to do something for myself. It seems that everything I've done for the past twenty years has been for someone else . . . Warren, the twins . . . you know. I just decided that for once I wanted to do something all on my own . . . and all by myself. Does that sound selfish?"

"You should be thanking your lucky stars that you've got a husband and children to think about. Being all on your own isn't exciting. It's damn miserable," Florence said petulantly.

Lilah sipped at her glass of wine and listened. She did feel sorry for Florence, but dear heaven, did the woman have to be such a damn martyr all the time? Even when her husband was alive, Florence always found something to complain about.

"Well, maybe it is a silly idea, Florence. I'm probably just tired of all the bad weather. I wanted Warren to go with me, but he's got some old business thing in Milwaukee. I'm not telling him because I know he'd veto the whole thing, and I don't want a fuss. It's not worth it."

"Well, it's really none of my business, anyway. Sure, if needed, I'll be happy to cover for you. What you are going to do in New York that's so mysterious?"

"Nothing much. I'm just going to shop a bit, and I thought maybe I'd call one of my old friends—uh, uh, uh, my dear, don't get that suspicious look on your face. Marcy is a woman . . . and an old friend from my Juilliard days."

Florence smiled. This was going to make an interesting story to tell. "Okay, so what do you want me to do?"

"In case it's necessary, just stick to the story that you and I drove into town for dinner and a show and that your car broke down and we decided to stay here in this hotel for the night. Okay?"

"What about the children? What are you going to tell them?"

"Neither of them will be at home. Matt's going down to St. Louis on Wednesday to stay with friends and look over the campus at Washington University. He's very partial to that engineering school because his best friend, Jeff, has applied there. Mary Ann is going with him to spend the weekend with an old friend who moved to Webster Groves last year when her father got a job with McDonnell Aircraft."

"Well, that's all very convenient."

Lilah laughed. "Yes, I'm surprised at how easily I've slipped into a life of deception and intrigue."

Florence patted her hand. "Well, you can count on me. And as your oldest and closest friend, I can only hope that you have as good a time as you think you'll have."

Florence enjoyed every bite of her carpaccio and pasticcio di spinaci, and she ordered a rich tiramisu for dessert with very little urging by her hostess. After two cups of cappuccino they said good-bye and went their separate ways. On the drive back home Florence talked gleefully to herself, and it wasn't because of the two glasses of Pinot Grigio. It was just that lunch had turned out to be a giggle instead of a fiasco. Lilah must think Florence was a fool to tell her that stupid story. All by herself . . . what a bunch of nonsense! She obviously was having some kind of rendezvous. Lord, she could hardly wait to tell darling Warren. Now, with just a little pressure, she might be able to convince him to spend the whole weekend with her for a change, instead of one of those one-night quickies.

THE plane took off on schedule, and Lilah sighed in relief. So far, so good. Even if the whole thing turned out to be a hoax or a mistake, she fully intended to enjoy the experience, and so far, that was the way it was working out. Her life had become entirely too well ordered and predictable, but Rose Wilkins' telephone calls had certainly changed all that. Sitting on the plane, she felt freer than she had felt in years, and she began thinking about her grandparents, who had raised her after her mother and father died. They had been concerned about her occasional tendency toward wildness and unladylike behavior. How scandalized they would be if they could see her now.

Taking the cup of coffee offered by the stewardess, Lilah declined the breakfast and gazed bemusedly out over the clouds. Was it possible that the people who had brought her up to be honest, truthful, and ladylike at all times had themselves been guilty of deceit? If she really did have a twin, why had they been separated? She shook her head, and the nagging suspicion that this had to be a wild-goose chase came back again. There was just no way that Clark and Ellen Simpson could have been guilty of lying. It was against their principles, against their faith, and against their whole way of life. They had, in fact, been loving and giving, but the security she felt with them had not kept her from wondering about her dead parents.

not have approved of her deceiv-
grandfather had taught her never to
om an issue and always to seek the truth
wasn't that exactly what she was doing now?
thought back to the day of her wedding to Warren
and how pleased everyone had been. Grandpa Simpson had presented her with the deed to the property
on which they had built their house, and her grandmother had given her the small diamond watch that
had been her mother's.

She thought again of all the times she had asked
questions about her father, but there had been so few
details forthcoming. And no pictures. No photographs,
no snapshots of him. Nothing. It had been a small
wedding, they said. The war, you know. He died
overseas. That was all. She had been told that her
mother had some kind of blood pressure problem, that
she died a few days after giving birth to the tiny,
three-pound baby girl. It was a miracle that she had
lived.

In their taciturn way her grandparents had made it
abundantly clear that talking about it was painful for
them . . . always . . . even years later. Lilah never
wanted to hurt them, but in her natural child's way she
insisted on asking, again and again, always hoping that
someday the answers would be fuller in information,
richer in details, but they never were.

And that, she supposed, was why she was here,
winging her way to New York. She was looking for
answers to questions asked by the child she had been
many years ago. Questions which had never been answered.

7

THE pile of dresses on the bed had grown higher with each gown that was tried on and discarded. It was after eleven, and Rose still hadn't found the look she wanted. Her hands were shaking, and her heartbeat accelerated with each rejection. Damn, damn, damn. She had a closet full of new designer dresses, and they all seemed too theatrical . . . too gauche . . . too . . . too much.

One by one she slid the hangers back and forth, looking for the right one, but there was nothing there. Nothing simple, understated, and elegant. Too much Bob Mackie, not enough Chanel. Suddenly her hand touched the rich white silk pants, and a thought occurred to her. She didn't have to wear a dress, for heaven's sake! She'd wear this beautiful white outfit designed by Claude Montana. Quickly she pulled the hangers out of the closet and stepped into the softly pleated pants and pulled the horizontally gathered bustier into place. She wrapped the wide green leather belt around her waist and buckled it loosely so it would slide down and rest on her sharp hipbones. As she pulled the emerald-green silk blouse on, she sidled over to the mirror to observe her reflection. Not bad, actually. Would the matching white, long jacket be too much over the blouse and the bustier? She tried the jacket and was satisfied with the layering. The silk was heavy but fine, and her bone-thin figure carried all the fabric easily because of her height.

At the dressing table she brushed a little green powder over her eyelids to enhance the effect the green would have on her eyes, which seemed to take on any strong color she wore. She tried a pair of large faux pearl earrings but quickly took them off. No fake jewelry for this encounter. It might be stylish, but it just wasn't appropriate for today.

Rummaging in the closet, she found a pair of white silk pumps with flat heels and stepped into them. Again she returned to the full-length mirror to observe herself. How close to her image would the woman be? How much had environment and upbringing influenced the appearances of two beings who had sprung from the same cell, emerged from the same womb, traveled through the same tunnel of love minutes apart? How much would they resemble each other in face, voice . . . voice? Voice? Her mind stumbled on the word. Good God, could this other being sing with the same richness and mellowness as she did? Were there actually two voices with the identical depth and range that critics all over Europe had praised? If so, why had her twin never sung? Why, in fact, had one remained an unknown Midwest housewife while the other was on her way to being an international star?

Perhaps . . . perhaps Geneva—darling, beloved Geneva—had made a mistake. Perhaps in the last moments of extremis she had imagined it all, and the poor woman who was traveling all the way from Chicago would have been duped.

Ridiculous. Geneva was incapable of making such a mistake. She had spent her life as a hardworking, pragmatic woman who found satisfaction and contentment in serving others. The confession she had made on her deathbed had come with great difficulty.

The telephone rang. When Rose answered it, the woman's voice said simply, "Rose, I'm here."

She replied, "Thank God. Please come right up."

8

LILAH put down the house phone in the bustling and busy lobby of the Plaza Hotel and walked toward the elevators. Now that the moment of truth was at hand, she wasn't sure she wanted to go any farther. For one brief moment she considered fleeing. It would be so easy to walk back out the door, get into a cab, and return on the next flight to Chicago. She would put Rose Wilkins away, store the memory of her voice and her wild ideas in an airtight place in her mind, and never take her out again. She would go back to being the one and only Lilah Greer Conway, mother of Mary Ann and Matthew, wife of Warren.

Even as she speculated, her feet kept moving her relentlessly toward the assignation. Lilah had no real intention of leaving the Plaza Hotel without confronting Rose Wilkins face-to-face. Stranger-to-stranger. Sister-to-sister. Twin-to-twin.

As the elevator carried her upward she placed her hand on her chest. Her heart was beating so hard and so fast, it must surely show through the fabric of her clothes.

When the elevator stopped, she walked purposefully toward the door of the suite and rapped firmly on the door. It opened almost immediately, and standing before her was a figure she had seen before. She gasped. "Oh, my God!"

The tall woman in the exquisite green-and-white

clothes took her arm and pulled her inside. "Shush,
Lilah. If you're going to have a heart attack, do it
inside where my public can't see you."

"My God, I've . . . I've seen you . . . your picture
. . . you're . . . you're . . ." She groped for the name,
but it eluded her. Rose patiently waited until Lilah
finally made the proper connections. "You're Lady
Rose! I read about you in *People* magazine. You can't
possibly be my twin sister."

Rose raised her eyebrows and said through tightly
clenched teeth, "Oh, really? Then come over to the
mirror and have a look for yourself."

With her fingers pressing into Lilah's arm, Rose
pulled her over to the mirror and forced Lilah to look
at the two of them, side by side. "Lilah, open your
eyes and look at us. Look at the cheekbones . . .
they're the same. Look at the figures . . . broad shoulders, skinny, tall." She grabbed her hand and held it
beside hers; the long pink fingernails on Rose's hands
could not hide the sameness of the knuckles, the contour, the size and shape of the fingers.

"Now look at my eyes," Rose commanded. "You've
been looking at those same golden-amber eyes in the
mirror for almost forty years. Isn't that true?"

Lilah closed her eyes. She didn't want to look at
Rose and see what she knew was there, but Rose
would not be denied. "Lilah, look at me, damn it . . .
look at me!"

Lilah opened her eyes, and the exact same eyes that
she had been viewing the world through were now
blazing into hers and forcing her to see things she had
not considered possible.

"We are sisters, Lilah Conway. You cannot deny
me, nor I you, and it is something we must both come
to terms with. We exist, you and I, and even if no one
else ever knows, we can't escape the truth, and we
must not try to fool ourselves."

Lilah turned away. "We can't be twins. It's some

kind of strange coincidence . . . some weird trick of nature," she insisted.

Rose raised her eyebrows. The nervousness was over. She had found the answer to the question that had plagued her ever since the night Geneva had revealed her secret. She let go of Lilah's arm and turned her back to her.

"Come in and sit down, and you'll hear the whole story of our birth and our separation. I have it all on tape in the words of the woman who lived it, just as she told it to me. I think you'll find it quite interesting."

She turned and looked at Lilah, who seemed immobilized. "But before I turn on the recorder, I think you should have a stiff drink. It must be quite a shock to find out that your twin sister is a black woman . . . or do you still think of us as Negroes?"

9

Geneva's Story

"**D**ADDY was such a good man. Oh, he'd get mad once in a while and take a swing at us, but he'd be sorry right away, and he'd reach into his pocket and find a penny to give us. He'd never come right out and say he was sorry, but Harry and I knew he loved us.

"He was a good-lookin' man too. Tall, skin the color of honey, and eyes so bright and big that Harry and I used to think they could see right into our souls. We weren't afraid of him, but we respected him a lot, and we always felt sorry for him because he was so sad. Every Sunday he'd dress us up neat and fine and take us into town to the First Baptist Church. After services he'd walk us around the neighborhood where we lived when Momma left. He'd stop and talk to people, askin' questions, but people just shook their heads. You'd think he'd give up hope of her ever comin' back, but he didn't, not once in his whole life.

"Daddy had pictures of Momma that he kept in a cigar box on a table beside his bed. She was a beautiful white lady, with long blond hair that she did up in a braid. Daddy met her when they were both workin' for a rich family in a big house on the South Shore. She came over from Norway and didn't speak any English. Daddy said she was always gettin' into trouble because she didn't understand what folks was sayin' to her. He was the chauffeur, you see, and he'd sit in the kitchen late at night and teach her the language as best he could.

"One thing led to another I guess, and she got pregnant with me. They got married, but they didn't tell nobody. When she started to get big, she left her job and lived in a roomin' house. Daddy would visit her on his days off, and I guess they were happy together, at least for a while. She got pregnant again pretty quick with Harry, and Daddy quit his job to work as a janitor in one of the high schools, just so he could be home with her every night. It wasn't nearly as nice a job as takin' care of that beautiful big Packard car, but he was so in love with his wife and so proud of his beautiful children that he didn't care.

"Harry was two years old and I was three when Momma left. I guess she finally learned enough English to realize there was no future for her bein' married to a colored man in America. Or maybe she just found somebody else. I don't hardly know. Anyway, one day she was just gone. She took what little clothes she had and left us.

"Daddy didn't hardly know what to do. He didn't make enough money to pay the rent, feed us, and pay somebody to watch us, too, and we were too little to be left on our own. But, like I say, Daddy was a good man. He hustled around, and he found the Simpsons. They were real wealthy and nice too. Had a big house on a lot of ground way out in the suburbs. Mr. Simpson needed a chauffeur and a handyman, so he took Daddy on. He let him have a little shack on the grounds for us to live in, and even if he didn't pay Daddy much money, it gave us a place to live and be together. There was always good food on the table, and we had lots of space to roam around and play in. Mr. Simpson kept horses too. His wife loved to ride. She was a real sweet lady. She always saw that we had shoes to wear that fit.

"We had a pretty nice life, at least we thought so at the time. Kids don't hardly know the difference between rich and poor. The Simpsons had a daughter just our age. She was our best friend. Of course, she went to a private school, and Harry and I went to a public school, but we still managed to spend a lot of time together. Bein' a year older than Harry, I bossed him around a lot, but he and Peggy would always stick together. The older they got, the closer they got, it seemed. I guess maybe the older folks should have guessed that there could be a problem, but nobody did. It was all so natural that we should have fun together.

"Harry grew up to be the most beautiful man I ever saw. He didn't look nothin' like me. He was tall and strong. His skin was a pale caramel color, his hair was thick and curly and brown, and he was smart, really smart. He had a big dimple on his left cheek and teeth so big and white and fine that they sparkled, just like his brown eyes did when he laughed, which was often.

"Peggy used to buy us presents all of the time out of her allowance. Nice things. Once she bought Harry a beautiful red cashmere sweater, but we had to hide it from Daddy because he didn't like us taking things that we didn't earn.

"Peggy tried to talk her parents into lettin' her go to college in Chicago, but they said no. Her mother had gone to Wellesley, and so would Peggy. She stopped arguin' when she found out that Harry was plannin' to go into the Army. If Harry wasn't going to be there, she didn't want to be there, either. I should have known we were in for trouble.

"It was just around the time when it looked as if the war was goin' to be over when the ax fell on top of all of us. Dumb old me was struttin' around, happy as a clam now that Harry wouldn't have to go off and fight and maybe get killed. We were sittin' out near the stables under a beautiful old oak tree on a bench Daddy had made when Peggy and Harry told me that

Peggy was pregnant. Jesus Lord, I hardly knew where babies came from myself, I was so ignorant, but I knew enough to know we were in a terrible fix. But the worst part of it all was that those two silly kids didn't have sense enough to realize how much trouble they were in. They acted as if God had blessed their union by giving them a baby. Somehow that baby meant that nobody or nothin' was ever going to separate them.

"But they were smart enough to realize that they had to leave town and get as far away from the Simpsons as they could. Peggy knew that she and Harry could never again be together if anybody found out, and being with Harry was the most important thing in her life.

"Did I tell you Harry was beautiful? He was. Peggy was a pretty little thing, all pale blond and blue-eyed with freckles on her nose. She was so tiny and delicate next to Harry's big golden body. He loved to sweep her up into his arms and carry her across the yard with her yellin' and kickin' and screamin' to be put down. When I think back to those times, I wonder what those Simpsons were thinkin' of. Did they feel safe havin' us together so much because we were black and didn't really count?

"Anyway, Peggy and Harry cooked up this plan. I didn't want any part of it, but in the end I went along. I couldn't stand the thought of havin' them leave me behind. At night Harry worked on an old Ford that had been put up on blocks during the gasoline rationin'. During the days he worked at a gas station as a mechanic and tried to save every cent he could. I had a job stockin' shelves at the local grocery store. We put away what we could, and Peggy started stealin'.

"I guess it wasn't exactly stealing. Yes, it really was. Day after day she'd take a little money from her mother, a piece of jewelry here, a small knickknack there. She was very careful not to take anything that might be missed. If it was, she'd find it immediately so that none of the folks who worked there could be blamed. She'd give them to Harry, and he'd take 'em into town and sell 'em at a pawnshop.

"We didn't have as much time as we thought, either, because Peggy started growin' out of her clothes awful soon. She made a big deal about eatin', even though she would rush upstairs and vomit in secret after every meal, and then she'd complain about getting fat.

"Well, anyway, as soon as Harry had that Ford runnin' good, we left. Harry left first and waited for us in downtown Chicago for three days. Peggy didn't want anybody to know we were leavin' together, and it was just as well. I left second, telling Daddy I was going to find Harry. When Peggy left, she wrote a note to her parents tellin' 'em that she'd fallen in love with a young man she had met at a dance and they were runnin' away to get married. She told 'em he was a fine, upstandin' person from a good family and that she'd telephone them frequently and keep them posted on her whereabouts. I supposed they believed it because they wanted to.

"We drove across the country, headin' for California. Peggy and Harry decided to begin a new life out there. They got the notion in their heads that there wouldn't be any prejudice or anythin' out there on the Coast, and they'd be able to live and work in peace, like normal folks. Talk about people believin' in fairy tales.

"We were on the road for a long, long time. The car kept breakin' down, and we'd have to stay in one town for weeks at a time, workin' at odd jobs to earn enough money to keep on goin'.

"Like I say, Peggy seemed to get too big too fast. It was almost like somebody was blowin' her up with a bicycle pump. Her hands swelled, her ankles swelled, and her face got all bloated-lookin', and she felt sick most of the time. The only thing she could stomach was ham sandwiches on rye bread with dill pickles.

"She was about in her eighth month when we crossed into Arizona. We got lost on one of those desert roads when suddenly there was one of these storms, and water by the tons came washin' down the mountain. Harry tried to keep that car on the road, but he just couldn't handle it. I was lyin' down in the backseat when it happened. The car went into a skid and rolled over. My pretty Harry's head got smashed like an eggshell, and little Peggy got thrown through the windshield. I was knocked out, and my arm was broken in two places, but that's all. The highway patrol found us and rushed us to the hospital. They kept Peggy alive long enough to save her babies . . . beautiful, tiny twin girls.

"They told me at the hospital that she probably wouldn't have survived the pregnancy even if she hadn't been in that accident. She had some kind of poisoning . . . toxemia, they called it. You know, she never would go to see a doctor. She said we had to save our money for a doctor when she really needed one.

"I had Harry and Peggy laid in the same grave out there in Arizona. I don't rightly remember exactly where, it was so long ago, but it doesn't seem to matter much. I know they're in heaven together, and I want to make sure I join up with them someday.

"I know I didn't do right, separatin' you girls like I did, but I just felt at the time that the good Lord had given me two girls so that Peggy's family could have part of her and I could have part of Harry. When you babies were big enough to take out of the hospital, I called Mrs. Simpson, but I never told her there was more than one child. She and Mr. Simpson came right out to Arizona. They thanked me and gave me some money to go to California and start a new life, and they asked me not to tell anybody. You see, I never told them it was Harry's child. I just said that Peggy had got herself in trouble and asked us to help her since we were good friends. I made up the name

William Greer. Said he was the father. They might have suspected the truth, but they never let on.

"Less than two years after he lost Harry, Daddy died, probably 'cause his heart just broke. I always felt bad that I never told him the sweet little grandchild of the Simpsons was his granddaughter too.

"I'm right sorry to drop all of this on your doorstep, honey, and go off and die and leave you with it, but the truth has been too long comin'. I loved you more than if you had been my own. You were the little lady who made my life worth livin'. And I'm so proud of you.

"If someday you and your sister meet up, tell her I loved her too."

10

ROSE got up from the couch and walked over to the tape recorder and snapped it off. Her eyes were glistening with tears. She turned and looked defiantly at Lilah, who was sitting in a chair by the window, numb with shock.

"Now do you believe that we're twins?" Lady Rose asked.

"How long before she died did you make that recording?" Lilah asked without looking at Rose. After the first astounded appraisal she had difficulty looking at the woman who was quite obviously her sister.

"About two weeks. Geneva had a fast-growing cancer that started in her colon. They did a colostomy, but it was too late. She managed to live until her birthday. She died at midnight." Rose turned away and concentrated her eyes on a picture she had placed on the mantel of the fireplace in the suite. "She was a saint. She did her best to raise me right, but it was hard. The only work she could do was housework, and it never paid much. I used to go with her on Saturdays when she cleaned offices and helped her so she could get home earlier, but she hated to have me do that. She always wanted me to get an education and be a teacher, but I hated school. All I wanted was to sing."

Lilah was not yet ready to focus on the life of Lady Rose; she needed to know more about the woman

61

who had decided her fate. "Where was she living
when she died?"

"California. San Pedro. Near the ocean. She used to
go up into the hills on the Palos Verdes peninsula and
clean the big homes that looked out over the sea
toward Catalina. She would never leave that area. I
had her buried there."

"You must have loved her very much," Lilah said
softly.

"Not enough, and *je le regrette beaucoup*. I left this
country almost twenty years ago, and I didn't come
back very often . . . or stay very long. I've been living
in Europe . . . France mostly. They don't have quite
as many prejudices about race as we have here, but of
course, you wouldn't understand about that. You're
white." The last words were said with a touch of irony
in her voice.

At last Lilah looked up, and their eyes met for the
first time since her arrival. "Why did you tape her
story?" By concentrating on peripheral details Lilah
was able to avoid dealing with the major revelations.

"She asked me to. She loved gadgets and all the
new technology. For her age and education she was a
remarkably modern woman. She said I might need it
to convince you . . . and she wanted us to be reunited.
She said we both needed to know our history, because
she had recently realized that most women—especially
blacks—had been denied their history, and she felt it
was a sin."

"But why did you wait six months?"

"*Il y avait beaucoup de raisons.* I suppose because it
took me that long to stop being jealous of all you had
growing up—money, family, position—but I didn't want
to hate you. You're the only relative I have now. I
haven't got children or a husband. Oh, I've been married, *certainement*, but it didn't last . . . and he doesn't
count. Can I fix you another drink? The ice is all
melted in that one."

Lilah looked down at the untouched glass in her

hand and shook her head. "No, no thanks." She set it down on the table and turned her head again to look out the window toward Central Park. It was a cold day, but the sun was shining, and her life had been turned upside down. She no longer knew who she was or what she was.

Rose sat down in the chair opposite her. "Are you upset because I've told you that your father was black?" she asked gently.

After a few moments Lilah nodded her head. When she spoke, her voice was heavy with dismay. "Yes, Rose. I've never been much good at lying. Yes, I'm extremely upset, but not for myself, you understand . . . not just for myself. I have two children."

"You're worried that the world will label them black because they have a grandfather who was part black, aren't you?"

"Yes, does that upset you?"

"Dear Jesus, no. I didn't come into your life to disrupt it. It's not important to me what you choose to tell your family. Let's not tell anybody. Our relationship can be our secret. We don't need anybody else to know, do we?"

"I don't know."

"In fact, if you want to walk out of this room and never contact me again, I'll understand. You know that, don't you?"

"I don't want that. I've known from the moment you called that you were my sister. In fact, all through my life I've sensed your existence. Does that sound too dramatically mystical?" Lilah asked.

"Not really. I felt an emptiness, too, but I blamed it on my race. And I must admit, I felt some resentment when I found out that I had a twin sister who was white."

"You shouldn't resent me, Rose. After all, I'm just a dowdy little housewife from Illinois, and you're a big star."

"I don't resent you, Lilah . . . not anymore." She

got up and walked to the telephone. "I've ordered lunch. Shall I have it sent up now? I think we need a recess, don't you?"

"Yes, by all means," Lilah agreed.

"I hope you like champagne," Rose said, "because I've ordered a magnum of Dom Perignon."

Lilah smiled. "That sounds perfectly wonderful. I love it, but my husband says champagne's far too expensive to drink except on special occasions."

"I believe in drinking it only on special occasions, too . . . and I consider lunch a very special occasion," Lady Rose declared emphatically. "Especially this one."

11

ROSE and Lilah talked for hours, drinking the champagne and becoming increasingly relaxed and uninhibited as they tried to put the pieces of their two separate lives together. It wasn't long before they began to deal with their emotions and reactions to the events in their lives. Lilah was the first to venture into delicate territory.

"The biggest single event in my life was Moscow, Rose. I know that when I first mentioned it, I glossed over it as if it hadn't mattered all that much, but it was such a magnificently grand failure that I still haven't come to terms with it twenty years later. The hurt is just as excruciating now as it was the moment they read the names of those who were going on to the next round and my name wasn't called."

"But just one little competition shouldn't have thrown you. Didn't you want to keep on trying?"

Lilah shook her head and sipped her wine. "No, I didn't. Because I didn't know how to fail. I hadn't had any practice. I'd gone through life on a cloud of privilege. Everything went my way. I was attractive, bright, and very popular, not because I was such an adorable person but because I was so dedicated to my music that everyone treated me as if I were a genius. My grandparents thought everything I did was perfectly marvelous. Every day after school I'd hurry home to the Steinway and practice. That piano made me feel terribly special, and I pitied all my friends who had to poke along without having this wonderful, magical talent to set them apart . . . and above everyone else."

"Nothing ever came easy for me except my music," Rose said. "I started out singing in the church choir when I was just a little girl. I had a big voice, but there were a lot of beautiful voices in that church and nobody thought mine was very special except Geneva. Have you ever sung? Your voice should be the same as mine."

Lilah smiled. "Yes, as a matter of fact, it was my singing in Sunday School that convinced my grandmother I was musical. To her, being musical meant playing the piano. Obviously I should have kept singing."

"But you must have been good to have gotten as far as you did," Rose protested.

Lilah shook her head. "No, the talent, I suppose, was just never there. I had become technically skilled through sheer persistence and determination. The first time somebody saw through me, I faced up to it."

"What do you mean, you faced up to it, honey? *Caved in* would be a better description. Don't you know you have to fight constantly to make people appreciate you? All my life people have been putting me down, but I always believed I was good, no matter what anybody said," Rose protested.

"I just accepted reality, Rose. I haven't touched a piano since that day."

"*Mon Dieu*, what a waste. How could you take all those years of your life and flush them down the toilet like that?"

"The disappointment . . . the feeling of failure was more than I could handle. I never wanted to set myself up to be knocked down again, Rose, so I did what all my friends were doing. I got married and settled in as a housewife."

"*Merde*. You turned chicken, *ma chère*, and ran

away, that's what you did . . . just like I did. You know, we really are alike."

"What did you run from, Rose?" Lilah asked, curiously, eager to know everything about her sister.

Just as Rose began to answer, there was a knock at the door. "That must be **Benjie**. Now don't say anything about our being twins. Let's see if he notices the similarity, *c'est bon?*"

Lilah nodded. "This should be interesting."

Rose got up from the couch and hurried to the door. When she opened it, a tall black man who looked to be in his late forties stepped inside and swept her into his arms. "Hi, sweetie pie, didja miss me?"

Rose kissed him lightly and then pulled away. "Not now, Benjie. We've got company."

Looking surprised, the man moved toward Lilah, his hand outstretched. His skin was very dark, his eyes were large and bright, and he had a deep dimple in his cheek when he smiled, which he was doing very cordially.

"Well, so we do. Hello, I'm Ben Frost," he said.

"Benjie, this is Lilah Conway. She's an old friend from Chicago. Lilah, this is my manager . . . and my roommate."

Lilah got up from the chair to say hello, but as she reached out to shake hands there was a sudden stillness, and a crackle of tension charged the air. Ben Frost, now close enough to look into Lilah's eyes, was staring as if he had suddenly been turned to stone. His jaw went slack as he stared into a face that was so strangely familiar to him.

"Jesus Christ!" he murmured, and he had never been a man to take the Lord's name in vain.

"What's wrong, Benjie?" Rose teased. "You look like you just saw a ghost."

Slowly he turned and looked again at Rose's smiling face and then again back to Lilah's. "Who are you?" he demanded.

"Who do you think she is, Benjie? Does she look familiar to you? You think you might have met her before maybe?"

"I'm Lilah Conway, and as you've probably guessed, I'm Rose's twin sister . . . long-lost, I might add."

Rose pulled the bottle of champagne from the ice and poured him a tall glass. "Here, honey, drink this and sit down. We'll tell you the whole story."

Mutely Ben sat on the couch, and as Rose filled him in on the details, his eyes never wavered from Lilah's face, so intrigued was he by both the similarity and the difference in their appearances.

When they were finished, he shook his head. "What a story this will be. My God, the magazines will lap it up. Say . . . suppose we put together a similar story line and let Lilah here make a guest appearance on the show—" he began excitedly, the promoter in him already making use of the situation.

"Stop right there, Benjie! Right there. Nobody is ever going to know about this except us. Lilah's got a family, and they're all white—*c'est tout dire.* It's our little secret, understand?" she declared forcefully, and then turned to Lilah. "Don't worry, Lilah. Ben's the most trustworthy person I've ever known. He wouldn't betray you. Right, Ben?"

Ben looked over at Lilah and reluctantly put the scheme away. "Right, honey . . . right." He sighed.

Suddenly Lilah was afraid. She didn't know this man at all, and now he was privy to a secret that threatened her family. The exciting lark on which she had embarked had turned into a nightmare. "I hope you'll understand, Mr. Frost, the need for secrecy. If word of our . . . relationship should ever be made public, it would ruin my children's lives."

A slight sneer appeared on his face and in his voice. "Call me Ben, Lilah. And, of course, I understand. Better than you can imagine. Naturally, now that you know your lily-white blood is tainted with color, it's important to keep it a secret. You must be pretty upset about the whole thing yourself."

"Ben!" Rose exclaimed, wanting him to stop, afraid he would offend her sister and drive her away.

Lilah was stung by his words, but all she could manage to ask was, "Do you have children?" She hoped to find some common ground.

"Yeah," he replied, "but I don't see 'em much."

"You never see them, Ben. Tell the truth," Rose interjected.

Lilah's hopes of appealing to his fatherly instincts began to fade. He probably didn't give a damn about his children.

"Don't make me out to be a bad daddy, damn it, Rose. I never see them because my ex-wife turned them against me, not because I don't want to. Besides, she got married again, and there's no room in their lives for me."

As he spoke, his eyes were fixed on Lilah's, determined to convince her that he loved his sons, and she saw in him both hurt and anger, as well as resignation. Hopefully she tried again. "Ben, I'm not at all ashamed of the color in my background; in fact, I'm proud to have a sister so talented and successful, and I envy her accomplishments. As a matter of fact, she's probably disappointed in me. I've never really done much except be a good mother. My children have always come first, even before my husband. I brought them into this world, and it's my responsibility to do everything I can for them. And right now, at this point in their lives, I don't want to burden them with anything more. Rose agrees with me, don't you?"

Rose nodded her head vehemently. "As a matter of fact, Ben Frost, it was my idea—not hers—to keep it a secret. Besides, my career is going great now. I don't need to complicate it with anything . . . you understand?"

Ben heard the urgency in her voice and sensed a

desperate need in her for him to make peace with her sister.

Smiling at Lilah, he reached over to take her hand in both of his. "Will you forgive me, Lilah? I want to be your friend . . . because I love your sister a whole lot."

Relieved, Lilah smiled back, reassured that Ben Frost was a man who could be trusted. "Of course I do. Well, I'd better get busy and get myself a room in the hotel."

"You can stay right here . . . in Benjie's bedroom. He never sleeps there, anyway," Rose said slyly.

"Absolutely. But first let's go over to La Grenouille for dinner. I'm starved. I missed lunch," Ben said.

"Are you crazy, Ben? Lilah and I can't go out together. Look how quickly you saw the resemblance between us," Rose protested.

"Yeah, yeah, but that's because I know you like the back of my hand, sweetie pie. Nobody else would know. Look at her, for God's sake . . . she's white and her hair's blond."

"Come on, Benjie, cut it out. Just look at those eyes. Haven't you seen them before . . . in my face?"

Benjie smiled. "She can wear a pair of your dark glasses."

"Benjie, just order dinner from room service," Rose retorted, and poured more champagne into her glass. "And tell them to send up another bottle of this. We're celebrating."

Ben's face showed disapproval. "If Lilah wants it, I will, but you've had enough. You know you can't sleep when you drink too much, and you need your rest. You've got an appointment with Scavullo tomorrow afternoon, and he won't be able to do a good job photographing you if you look wasted."

"Not for me, please," Lilah said quickly. "I've really had more than I should."

Staring defiantly at Ben, Rose said, "Don't poop

out on me now, sister, dear. We've got to stick to-gether. After all, this is a big occasion."

Lilah's eyes met Ben's, and she detected a plea for support. "No, really, I've had enough. Let's look at the menu and decide what we want to eat."

Haughtily Rose slammed down the glass and headed toward the bathroom. *"Zut alors!* I thought I was getting a sister to stick up for me, but all I got was another damn mother telling me what to do."

Ben smiled at her retreating back. "Don't worry, Lilah. She's not mad . . . and she's not a drunk, ei-ther. I just worry because she's so damned skinny, and when she drinks, she won't eat."

"Funny. I have a great appetite, but I never gain much weight, either." She paused and looked appre-ciatively at Ben. "She's lucky to have you, Ben."

Ben smiled back into the burnished amber eyes he knew so well and wondered if they, too, gave off flashes of gold when she was angry or excited. No, it was not possible. This one was too cool, too reserved. She looked like his Rose, but she was another woman altogether. He picked up Rose's glass. "You, too, Lilah. I think you're gonna be good for her."

12

"**W**ARREN, where have you been? I've been calling and calling," Florence's voice demanded as Warren picked up the telephone in his hotel room.

"I just this minute got in," he lied.

"Poor baby, did you have a busy day? Well, I'll make you feel better. We've got a reservation at the Versailles at seven. Meet you downstairs in ten minutes."

Warren started to protest, but it was futile. Florence had already hung up. Jesus, what a mess he'd made of things. For almost six months now, he had been carrying on a stupid charade of an affair with his wife's oldest friend, and he hated it. God knows what had happened to him, because he certainly didn't. He had never even particularly liked Florence, much less been attracted to her physically, until that dratted Fiesta Night at the country club, when they were dancing together . . . Jesus, it embarrassed him even to think about it. She had moved her body sensuously against him, and like some stupid teenage kid he'd gotten an erection. God, he would never forget the words she whispered into his ear. "You want me, don't you, Warren? I can feel that beautiful big cock of yours. Mmmm, if you put it inside me, it'll be better than anything you've ever had before."

He must have had too much to drink . . . or he was suffering male menopause or something, but he suddenly found himself waltzing her toward the door. Holding her body close to his so that no one would see the bulge straining at the zipper on the tight caballero pants of his costume, he waited until no one was watching and then pulled her with him, out the door. They hurried along the cart path of the golf course, and when they reached the huge old oak tree at the second tee, they did it, yet he couldn't even remember kissing her. All he could remember was pressing her body against that tree trunk and ramming his penis inside her again and again as she wrapped her legs around his waist and gasped, begging him to do it harder, faster, until she came with a loud, wild moan that brought on his climax too.

Just thinking about it brought beads of perspiration to his forehead. He splashed some cold water on his face and then dried it. It must have been all those margaritas he had drunk that had sent him clear out of his mind. Too bad the subsequent couplings with her hadn't been as exciting as the first one. At least he would have gotten some enjoyment from being in a predicament that he detested. Through some strange combination of time, circumstances, tequila, and hormones, Florence Bennett had gotten him exactly where she had always wanted him, and she had made it clear that she was not about to let him go. Every time he tried to disengage, she would hint that if he did, she would tell his wife everything, in dirty detail. Like a fool, he had allowed her to lead him around by his cock, because he was afraid of losing Lilah, his marriage, and his children's respect. Warren's smooth, well-ordered life was careening out of control.

As Warren got off the elevator and headed into the lobby, Florence felt the old familiar flutter she always experienced when she saw him. He was so tall and strong, and the years had made him even more attractive than ever. The gray-green eyes were still startlingly deep, and the light brown, wavy hair was touched with silver. Stupid Lilah didn't have the sense to know what she had. "Warren, what a pleasant surprise to see you here," she said loudly, deliberately making a sham of their subterfuge.

Quietly he took her arm and propelled her to the door. "Just get in the cab, Florence, and don't make a silly scene."

"Don't be so edgy, darling. We're going to have a good time tonight. I have something fascinating to tell you."

"And just what is your exciting news?" he asked when they were settled in the taxi.

"Well, I'll just give you a little hint now," she said coquettishly. "It's about Lilah."

"What about her?" he asked warily. It had not taken him long to find out that Florence was extremely envious of his wife, with good reason.

"I suppose you think she's sitting at home waiting for you to come back like a good little housewife. Well, she's not. She's in New York."

Warren didn't believe her. Lilah would never do anything without telling him. "Where did you get that information?" he asked skeptically.

"Now, now, I've really got you going, haven't I? Well, my lips are sealed. After all, she is my best friend."

"Florence, you know how I hate games."

She smiled secretly and whispered, "I promised her I wouldn't tell, but maybe you can beat it out of me in bed tonight, but be prepared, you'll have to get it up real good . . . and hard." Seductively she ran her fingers along the inside of his leg.

Warren sighed and turned away to look out the cab window, thinking that it was amazing that he could get it up with her at all.

13

LILAH sat at the piano watching the rain splatter mammoth drops of water intermittently on the bay windows surrounding her. She had taken an early flight from New York and had gotten home just minutes ahead of the storm that was brewing. The cold light of morning, without benefit of wine and excitement, had thrown her into a state of panic, and now, looking out into the dark, wet night, she was depressed and confused.

She had left the hotel in New York early, leaving a note for Rose, telling her that she would call her soon, that she needed to get home before her husband did. It was the truth, but it was a lie, too, for she simply could not face Rose feeling as she now did. After a night of tormented sleep she had arisen to wrestle with the problem that had seemed so easy to dismiss the day before. How could she go on living with Warren without telling him the truth? For the first time in their marriage she felt unsure of their relationship. She wanted to share everything with him—the joy she felt at finding her twin sister, the pride she had that someone identical to her had achieved so much—but she was afraid.

She rested her head against the edge of the piano and gently caressed the keys. Twenty years ago she had turned to Warren when she had failed, and he had given her love and security. They had a good marriage, but some difference in their personalities kept them at an emotional arm's length from each other. She realized that not once in all those years had Warren ever turned to her in distress, asking for comfort or emotional support. He was a tower of strength and reason, of rectitude and propriety, and she was afraid to tell him about her family. It was a deplorable comment on their relationship.

The truth was supposed to set one free, Lilah reflected bitterly, but it had managed to put her into a cage of deceit.

Walking over to the mirror in the foyer, she studied herself. It was the same face that had been hers for almost forty years, but now it also belonged to Lady Rose. She shook her head and turned away. How could she expect to know how her husband would feel when she didn't really know herself?

She was sitting on the piano bench again, staring off into space, when Warren arrived home from his trip to Milwaukee, on schedule. Warren did everything right on schedule.

They greeted one another tentatively, each preoccupied with secrets and wary of revealing too much to the other.

"Hi, dear," Lilah said. "Did you get wet?"

"No, I didn't. The driver was waiting for me. How are you doing? Anything happen while I was away?"

"You were only gone overnight," she replied evasively.

"You hear from Matt or Mary Ann?"

"No, but I thought I'd wait till you got home to give them a ring. I was sure you'd want to talk to Matt after he had a chance to look around the campus."

"Good idea. Think I'll run upstairs and take a quick shower. Why don't you make us both a drink, and I'll build a fire?" he said as he picked up his bag and headed for the stairs.

"All right. If you're hungry, I can fix you a chicken sandwich. Stella has already gone to bed," she replied.

"Fine. I'll be down in fifteen minutes."

In the kitchen Lilah fixed them a snack and then went to the bar in the family room and mixed a martini for Warren and a gin and tonic for herself. She checked to be sure there were logs in the wood box.

When Warren came downstairs, she was watching the late news on television. He made the fire, and they sat together, side by side, not touching or talking as they stared at the tube, but nothing, not the hunger, nor the murders, nor the threats of war seemed half as important as the thoughts and secrets churning in their minds. Their secrets weighed heavily, and although they felt an urgent need to unburden themselves, both were too afraid of the consequences to do so.

That night, after they had eaten and talked to their children long-distance, Lilah and Warren lay beside each other in their king-size bed, awake, afraid to touch for fear that any kind of emotion would flush out information neither was prepared to reveal.

14

BEN waited impatiently in the hallway of the house they had just leased in Beverly Hills. Dressed in a tuxedo that had been tailored especially for him at Bijan's, he was pacing nervously. Finally he shouted up the stairs, "Rose, for God's sake, we're going to be late if you don't get down here right now!"

Their new housekeeper, Mae, came to the head of the stairs. "She's almost ready, Mr. Frost. She asked me to tell you to stop shouting at her. It's making her extremely nervous."

"Well, will you please tell her that she's making me extremely nervous? If she doesn't hurry up, we'll miss getting on the pre-show, and they might not even seat us until after the opening."

"Yes, sir. I'll tell her what you said."

As the middle-aged woman turned away, the door to Rose's room burst open, and she strode out into the hallway. Standing at the head of the stairs, she whined, "Oh, God, Benjie . . . I look awful. Do you think I ought to call in sick?"

Ben looked up at the vision of the woman he loved and whistled, a long, low, appreciative sound. "No way, baby. You're going to make every other woman there look like a guy in drag."

"You think so?" she said, reassured, as she began her descent. She was dressed in an unadorned heavy white crepe gown, cut high in the neck and very low in the back, with long sleeves fitted close to her wrists. It had been created especially for her by Bob Mackie for her appearance at the Academy Awards that night, and he had designed it to show off her slim, broad-shouldered, narrow-hipped figure. Her long hair, which was held back from her face by a thin circlet of platinum and sapphires, billowed behind her like a great froth of black cotton candy. She wore sapphire-and-diamond earrings and a huge sapphire ring on her hand. All the jewels were loaned to her for the occasion by Fred Joaillier. Hurrying behind her, Mae carried a white fox cape, also loaned for the occasion by Somper Furs of Beverly Hills.

Ben whisked Rose out of the house into the limousine, and finally they were on their way downtown to the Music Center, where the annual tribal rite of alternately elevating and then trashing selected members of the movie industry was about to get under way.

"I've told the driver to hurry, baby. I want you to get out of the car in time to be interviewed by Army Archerd. Be sure to mention that you just started filming the last two episodes of *Broadway* and that you've recorded a new title song for the show. Also, don't forget to say that you love being back here in the States. Okay? Don't throw in any of those French phrases, understand?"

"I don't do that intentionally, Benjie. It's just a habit. After all, it was my primary language for—"

"But not anymore, and it makes you sound arch and snooty. Now, when the nominations for supporting actress are announced, sit up straight and smile enigmatically. Stay cool. And when somebody else is announced as the winner, look pleased and in control. Applaud with enthusiasm . . . but not too much, or it won't look genuine."

"And if I win, master, then what do I do?" she asked sarcastically.

Ben looked away impatiently. "You're not going to win, damn it . . . you won just by being nominated.

Get that into your head, will you? And let everybody know that you feel that way. You won't get the hardware, but it's only a piece of metal. It really doesn't mean a damn thing to anybody. It's an illusion."

"Why are you so sure I'm not going to win?" she asked haughtily.

"It can't happen, my dear. It just can't happen. First of all, you've got too much competition, and your role was too small, and it was in a picture that wasn't a studio picture. Believe me when I tell you that you're not going to be a dark horse . . . not tonight."

The limousine pulled into the circle at the Music Center. It was late afternoon, and the setting sun had cast a golden glow over the pool of glistening water that surrounded the Water Department building across the street. Fans jammed together behind ropes to cheer and watch the celebrities adorned in glitter get out of their long limousines and hurry across the plaza, past the Lipschitz sculpture and the reflecting pool and into the mirrored and marble halls of the Dorothy Chandler Pavilion with its gigantic crystal chandeliers.

Army Archerd, the perennial Hollywood reporter, was waiting with microphones and television cameras to greet the important stars. Ben and Rose were just approaching him when Archerd caught a glimpse of Ann-Margret and her husband Roger Smith behind them. Archerd was just about to pass Rose by when Ben thrust his hand forward and said, "Hello, Army. How are you? I think you're getting younger every day."

His attention momentarily distracted and his access to Ann-Margret successfully blocked by Ben's imposing figure, Archerd did a quick recovery and replied, "Fine, just fine. And here we have the lovely Lady Rose, who is one of the nominees for best supporting actress for her role in *Daphne's Rain*. Tell me, Lady Rose, how does it feel to be back working in the United States again?"

"It's wonderful, Army. It's so good to be home, especially now that I'm involved in *Broadway*."

"Have you started work on it yet?"

"Yes, as a matter of fact, I was on the set for the first time yesterday, but I've already recorded a new title song for the show. It will be played over the credits, beginning with the first episode I'm in."

"Terrific. And how do you feel about tonight? I guess this nomination was a dream come true. Are you going to win?"

"But I've already won, Army. Just being placed in the same category with all those talented actresses is more than I ever hoped for, and I'm so grateful to all the wonderful members of the Academy whose votes put me there, as well as to my manager, Ben Frost here, who guides my career." She smiled sweetly and walked away.

As they headed toward the Dorothy Chandler Pavilion Ben laughed. "Well, at least you got to make your acceptance speech on television, after all, didn't you?"

"Damn right," she replied, waving her hand toward the fans.

Throughout the telecast of the awards show Lilah had been glued to the television set in the bedroom. She had told Warren that she was going to bed early because she was exhausted, and she hoped he would fall asleep on the couch in the den so she could watch the proceedings alone. She had no desire for him to see her sister's face in close-up on the screen and perhaps notice the similarity.

Ordinarily she and Warren would not watch the award program, which was meaningless to them since they had stopped going to movies years ago when the children were small. Now, because of her sister, she had become fascinated by the world of show business, to the extent that she even had begun to read movie magazines at the beauty shop.

The show was a long one, but Lilah was engrossed.

Every time the camera panned into the audience, she searched for her sister's face. When she saw the pre-show interview and heard Rose's comments, she was glad that she had turned on the videocassette recorder so she could replay it. She hoped her husband wouldn't notice.

To her dismay, Warren appeared in the bedroom at nine o'clock, just as the supporting actress nominations were about to named.

"I thought you were going to bed early?" he asked.

"I couldn't go to sleep, so I thought I'd watch the Academy Awards."

"Really? What for?"

"It's kind of fun watching to see how everyone is dressed," she replied a bit too hastily. She felt guilty and exposed, and quickly she thrust the remote control toward him. "It really doesn't matter to me. Here, you can switch it if you want to see something else." Just as long as that recorder kept going, she wasn't concerned about missing the show.

Warren shook his head. "No, I'll watch this with you for a while. It looks kind of interesting. Besides, I think that Johnny Carson is pretty funny. I hear he plays golf."

Rose's name was announced, and her face appeared on television. She looked marvelous, Lilah exulted, and clenched her fists. God, she hoped Rose would win!

Warren was not watching the screen. Instead his eyes were fastened on his wife, and he was curious about her behavior.

The name of the winner was read by Kathleen Turner, and it was not Lady Rose. The camera immediately switched to the winner, but not before Lilah saw the briefest wisp of disappointment brush her sister's face. Rose recovered instantly and smiled confidently with her chin in the air. Lilah, however, sagged back on the pillow in bitter disappointment. Poor Rose, she must be devastated, Lilah thought, remembering that awful moment in Russia when her name had not been called. There was another brief shot of her sister smiling and applauding enthusiastically as the winner made her way to the stage.

"You're really into this, aren't you?" Warren asked curiously.

Lilah felt like a child caught playing doctor. "What do you mean?"

Warren smiled. "I was watching your face when the name was announced. The person you wanted to win didn't . . . right?"

Lilah shrugged her shoulders. "Why would it make any difference to me?"

15

My dear Rose,

Please forgive me for not calling you on the telephone, but it is so much easier for me to write and not have to justify an enormous telephone bill to my husband. I love talking to you, and I'm eagerly looking forward to seeing you in New York when you return there to film in November. Through some kind of miracle I've gotten Warren to consent to a trip to Europe, and I've arranged for us to come through the Big Apple on our return and stay for two days, November 15 and 16. I say *miracle* because Warren is usually content to stay home by the fire, and to get him out of Illinois just for a vacation, especially out of the country, is a monumental accomplishment.

I just love watching you on *Broadway*. To say you're sensational may sound self-serving (we are twins, you know), but you really are. I've taped every show so far, including the final two episodes of last season, and when I'm at home alone, I play them again and again, fast-forwarding through all the scenes without you, of course. I was thrilled to see that the season's first episode, featuring you, shot to the top of the ratings and that the show has stayed there. Hurrah, hurrah.

Life here goes on pretty much the same. I'm

doing all right at golf, I guess, since I wound up as the women's club champion this year, but it just doesn't seem to be that interesting anymore. Your life is so glamorous and exciting in comparison to mine.

Warren has changed somehow. I don't know if it's just in my mind or what, but he seems to be easier to get along with than he has ever been. He actually suggests going out to dinner often in spite of the fact that he used to profess to hate restaurants, and lately he's insisted that I go along on all his business trips. Last week we went to Scottsdale, Arizona, for three days and had a great time.

I do know that he misses the children terribly now that they're away at school, perhaps even more than I do. Warren has always been a man whose greatest contentment was having his family around him. I know he would like to have had more children, but the twins just about did me in. The table seems so empty at dinner now with just the two of us.

Matthew is very happy at Washington University in St. Louis. We went down to see his dormitory room and met some of his friends. Mary Ann, I'm afraid, is not so content at Wellesley. This is the first time the twins have ever been separated, and it's very difficult—for her, especially. Warren doesn't understand why I felt it important for them to go to different colleges, but I wanted Mary Ann to establish an identity of her own and be a bit more independent. She was always too content to let Matthew lead the way.

They are such wonderful children, Rose. How I wish they could meet you and you them. I know you would all love each other, and they would be so proud of you and your achievements. I hope you truly understand why I've hesitated to tell everything to them and to Warren . . . about you and our father. I think about it all of the time, but it's a decision I can't bring myself to make just yet. I feel so grateful for your sensitivity and understanding.

I love you, Rose. Knowing you exist has enriched my life immeasurably.

Lilah

P.S. I'm having a terrible time getting copies of the albums you recorded in Europe. I bought the soundtrack for *Daphne's Rain,* and I've played it a hundred times or more. Your voice is magnificent.

Love again.

16

THE young girl, who looked to be no more than sixteen, rubbed her wrists in pain. "Who the fuck was that creep?" she asked as a young man in a red uniform cut her ankles free from the posts of the bed where she had lain for the past two hours.

"None of your business, kid. Now get dressed and get out of here. Your dough is on the dresser."

"No dice. I want more, you shithead. You never told me the guy was gonna rape me with a goddamn telephone pole. Whatsa matter, can't he use his cock anymore?"

"What are you talkin' about, bitch? You can't rape a whore . . . unless you don't pay for it. And if you tell anybody about tonight, you won't have a body to sell around here, understand? Now take the money and get your little ass out of here before I decide to give it a coupla more whacks," he ordered.

"Yeah, yeah, you don't scare me, you jerkoff. All I wanna know is who the shit is so that I don't ever get caught in bed with him again. Christ, I'm so sore, I won't be able to work for a month! No wonder he insisted on tyin' me up and turnin' out the lights."

"If you wanna keep on working in Vegas, my advice to you is just to forget about tonight. And don't worry about runnin' into this guy again. He only comes around occasionally . . . and he never wants the same dame more than once. He likes fresh meat. Now get your clothes on and get outa here."

The young girl pulled the long sweater over her head, stepped into a pair of leather shorts, and moaned as she pulled up the zipper. "Geez, these are cuttin' me in half. I'll never be able to sit down in the car in 'em."

"Tough shit, baby. Now move it."

As soon as she had closed the door behind her, the young man bolted the door to the hallway. Hurriedly he pulled the sheets with their smears of blood and semen from the bed and stuffed them into a large plastic trash bag along with the stick and the ropes. Quickly he remade the bed with fresh linens so there would be nothing for gossiping maids to talk about, and when the room was in order, he left to deposit the bag in the trash. Moving quickly, he opened the door to the suite next to the room he had just finished cleaning. He hurried across the sitting room and through the bedroom to knock on the bathroom door. "Mr. Kimball? Everything's shipshape. You want me to have room service send your breakfast now?"

"Fine," a deep voice replied.

Quickly the bellman dialed the number and said, "Mr. Kimball wants his breakfast now."

The bellman waited to be sure everything was in order as the waiter rolled in a table covered with white linen, silver, and fine china. The scrambled eggs, toasted muffins, orange juice, and coffee were fresh and inviting. Copies of the *Los Angeles Times*, *Variety*, and the *Hollywood Reporter* and a crystal vase with two deep red roses surrounded the food. Wherever Craig Kimball went, there were always red roses, because the name of the film that had brought him to stardom was *The Red Rose*.

Again the bellman tapped on the bathroom door. "Your breakfast is here, Mr. Kimball," he said softly, and the voice within answered, "Thanks, Al. You can go now. Stop in later this afternoon and we'll settle up."

When he was certain the room was clear, Craig Kimball opened the bathroom door and went into the sitting room to eat. Wearing a white terry-cloth robe, he shuffled across the room in his scuffs, and no one who had ever seen his movies would have recognized the handsome, debonair chap who had been one of Hollywood's most enduring sex symbols.

His eyes were bleary and red, and his skin, long exposed to the sun to maintain its flattering tan, was wrinkled and leathery and now scarred from the surgical removal of numerous small cancers. Although his tall frame, which had worn both tuxedos and Levi's jeans with equal grace and aplomb, was now slightly bent, he still displayed a sense of muscle and power as he moved across the room.

He sat down at the table, and as he picked up his orange juice he winced. He looked at tiny but deep wounds on his right hand. That damn little cunt had sunk her teeth into him good. It would've served her right if he'd smashed her head in with the stick instead of giving her a thrill with it.

The telephone rang. He ignored it until the sixth ring. When he picked it up, he was sorry he had. It was his wife Claire, calling from home.

"Craig, I just got a call from Palm Springs. They want to know if you'll cut the ribbon on the new shopping center at a fund-raiser for the Desert Hospital next month."

"You called me for that? Jesus, I was still asleep. Tell 'em I'll let 'em know later."

Her voice had grown slightly testy to match his.

"They want to know now, dear. If you don't do it, they'll get Sinatra."

"Tell 'em to call Sinatra, then, and let me the fuck alone. You know I don't like you to bother me when I'm here for a rest."

"Sorry, I didn't mean to intrude. When are you

coming back to Los Angeles?" she asked, and her voice was heavy with suppressed anger.

"When I get damned good and ready," he barked, and slammed down the receiver. Where in the shit was Sudsy to field his calls?

Returning to his breakfast, he read the trades as he ate. Then he picked up the *Times,* perused the first page, and turned to the section where entertainment and movie news appeared. When he saw the front page, he knew his day was off to a really bad start. Staring out at him from a large photo was Lady Rose, looking gorgeous, perched on a rock overlooking the ocean at the beach in Malibu.

He swore silently as he read Charles Champlin's interview. He was only halfway through when there was a knock at the door.

"Who is it?" he called.

"It's me, boss. Sudsy."

Carrying the paper with him, Craig got up and opened the door to let the tiny man in. Sudsy Chapman had once been a popular clown on television in its early days, but when his career faded, he had become Craig Kimball's court jester.

"Hi, boss, have a good night?" he asked, and winked broadly.

"Where the hell have you been?" Kimball snarled.

"Hey, it's not ten o'clock yet. I been in bed, where ya think I been?"

Craig Kimball had already returned to his chair and was again immersed in the article about Lady Rose. When he finished it, he threw the newspaper at Sudsy and said, "Read that and tell me what you think."

Sudsy, who was tiny of stature and had eyes so large that they seemed to pop out of his head, picked up the paper and said, "What . . . what you want me to read?"

"The story about that black bitch . . . read it."

Kimball lit a cigarette and walked over to the window to look out at the strip below while he waited.

When Sudsy finished, he looked up and said, "So? The dame's made it big. So what? What's it to you?"

"What's it to me? Look." He approached the smaller man menacingly and, pointing to the scar on his cheek, said, "She's the cunt who did this to me . . . that's who she is."

Sudsy laughed. "Yeah, well, it looks like the dame last night gave you another one on your hand. You oughta quit playin' around with such feisty broads."

"I'm not laughing, Sudsy. I thought I'd finished that bitch's career. Then she gets a goddamned Academy Award nomination and now this."

"I don't know, boss. Are you sure she's the same one? I don't remember no Lady Rose."

"She's got a new name, idiot. But I'm positive that's the chick who sliced me after I gave her a part in *Star Bright.*"

"Geez, boss, I thought you said you never wanted the title of that bomb mentioned again. You said you just wanted to forget you ever did it."

"Yeah, but I believe in retribution, Sudsy. And I want her off that television show," Kimball stated.

"Hey, fat chance. You might still have friends around this town, but ratings are more important than friends, you know, and that show's on the top. The folks at home love her."

"Maybe, but I've got a score to even with that nigger lady." One corner of his mouth turned up in a wicked smile. "I've got an idea. Sudsy, call that lazy agent of mine and tell old Buck I'm thinking about coming out of retirement at last."

"Oh, yeah . . . wait, wait now . . . don't tell me any more . . . let me guess. You've decided out of the goodness of your heart—and to please your millions of fans—that you're going to make an appearance on that glittering, glamorous nighttime soap, *Broadway.* How's that for clairvoyance, eh?"

Craig Kimball smiled the smile that had thrilled millions of women from the great silver screen and replied, "You're a smart little asshole, Sudsy. That's why I like to have you around."

The grin left the little man's face, and he put his hand on the arm of the man who had dominated his life for over twenty years and warned, "Don't do it, boss. Don't do it."

"Why not?" Kimball snarled.

"You don't look the same as you used to. Let 'em see you on the late show."

"Fuck off, you midget."

17

ROSE grabbed the closest thing she could get her hands on, which happened to be a four-ounce bottle of Joy perfume, and hurled it across the dressing room. As it smashed into the tall, freestanding mirror, sending shards of glass and perfume sailing in all directions, she screamed at the top of her lungs, "No! No! I won't do it!"

Ben, who had just told her the odious news, stood helplessly by and watched, making no attempt to restrain her tantrum and, in fact, feeling a similar urge to smash things. "I'm sorry, baby . . . I'm so sorry," he murmured softly, hoping the entire studio hadn't overheard her.

"Don't just stand there mewling that you're sorry, do something! You're my manager. You're supposed to take care of me. Do it!"

"They won't listen, baby. I tried. I threatened. I did everything I could, but the deal's set. Contractually we have no grounds to fight them . . . do you understand?"

"Don't give me that 'contractually' stuff. Suppose I just don't show up. What'll they do about that?" she asked menacingly.

"Baby, all I can tell you is what they said . . . they'll write you out of the show next season. Period. End of television career."

"Can they do that? Would they?" She had finally slumped onto the couch in her dressing room.

"Yeah, I think they'd do it. Craig Kimball's appearance on this show is a very big deal. He's coming out of retirement to shoot the season's last episode, and it's going to be some cliffhanger, I understand."

"But why . . . why me . . . my show . . . oh, God, Benjie, I can't face him. I'm not a good enough actress to cover up all the things that'll be going on inside me. I just can't do it." Her anger was dissolving in tears, and Ben knew that a storm of weeping was about to strike.

"There, there, baby. It's gonna be okay. Maybe the guy has changed. Maybe he wants to make friends with you again after all these years. After all, he did call up the producers of the show to tell them that he wanted to come out of retirement to appear in one episode, because it was his favorite show on television."

"Ben, you don't know him. He's evil. Evil men don't change."

"Yeah, maybe. But even in retirement he's still one of the most powerful in the business, and I don't want you to make the same mistake as before and wind up being banished to Europe again."

"Ben, I wasn't banished . . . I went to Europe of my own accord. I was tired of appearing in bit parts, tired of being cast as a sultry black nightclub singer who looked white. That's why I left."

"Come on, honey. Don't try to bullshit old Ben. After you slashed that billion-dollar face of his I'm surprised you got out of the country alive. You couldn't have gotten a job as a maid in Hollywood after that."

"He deserved it. Do you know the kind of things he made me do?"

Ben tried to stop her. He had heard it all before, and it took too long to calm her down after she talked about the experience.

"I know, I know. Now forget it, will you?"

"Forget it? Never. I don't want to forget it. I'd like to shout it from the rooftops so that every young girl who thinks that sleeping with a star is going to make her career could find out about me . . . and that devil Craig Kimball."

"You've gotta stop thinking about it, do you hear me? It's in the past. Craig Kimball is still one of the world's most popular movie stars in spite of the fact that he hasn't made a movie in almost nine years. Everybody loves him. He's gotten more philanthropic awards than Frank Sinatra and Bob Hope put together. That poster of him outsold Robert Redford and Paul Newman. The president of France gave him the Legion of Honor, and the president of the United States praised him for his outstanding citizenship. Now, tell me, who in the hell is going to believe a little black singer against all that? Jesus Christ, if you don't keep your mouth shut about him, you'll be poison on TV. Am I making myself clear?" Ben's anger was not directed at her but against the situation.

"Yes, crystal clear, but I can't help how I feel, and there's no way . . . absolutely no way I could ever run through a scene with him or touch him without showing how much I hate him."

Ben got up and started pacing the dressing room. He was relieved that he had finally managed to stop the tears and the tantrum, but now he had to find some way to get through to her the necessity of dealing with Craig Kimball.

"Look, let's put this whole thing on the back burner for a while. When we see the script and see what you have to do, then we'll face it, understand? It's highly possible that his part will involve one of the other characters on the show, and you may not have any contact with him at all. Don't go crazy over something that may never happen. After all, the guy is getting close to sixty-five . . . and it's rumored that his heart is bad . . ."

"Huh! He doesn't have a bad heart, he doesn't have one at all," Rose retorted nastily.

"Look, my momma always told me that the trick to surviving in life was to take bad situations and turn them to your advantage. Now let's deal with him in a civilized way and try to lose the bad blood between you. It doesn't help a career to have too many enemies around this town, especially ones with as much influence as he has."

"Benjie, do you think maybe I lost out on the Academy Award because of him?"

"No, but there are an awful lot of people who vote who owe him. He made a lot of movies, and every damn one of them made money—even the schlocky ones—because Craig Kimball was always better than the material. His movies provided a lot of jobs for a lot of members of the Academy. He may be a sadistic son of a bitch with women, but he has an aura about him that can't be denied. Even though it's never been publicly admitted, that scar on his face took a long time to heal . . . and it cost the studio a lot of money. Word gets around."

Rose got up from the couch and went to the door. "Jenny," she called, "will you come in here and clean up a mess? I broke a bottle of perfume." She then turned to Ben and said, "Check to see if they'll need me any more today. I want to get out of here. The smell of that perfume is driving me crazy."

In the limousine on their way home Ben asked if Rose would like to go to L'Orangerie for dinner, but she declined. "No thanks. I've got too many lines to learn for tomorrow. I just want to soak in a hot tub and relax with the script. Do you mind?"

"Not at all, baby," he reassured her, but she could tell that he was getting tired of sitting in front of the television every night. Ben Frost was a restless, energetic person, and she knew that he hated staying at home so much.

"Benjie, why don't you call up Manny or somebody and go out for the evening. Really, I wouldn't mind at all."

"Well . . . if you're sure. I just might cruise around and try to find out what's going on in this town. You know, it wouldn't be a bad idea to get you signed up to do a movie during the show's hiatus . . . if it's a good part."

"Good idea. I need to work as much as I possibly can while I'm hot. You know how fast TV stars cool down."

The limousine pulled up into the driveway of the Tudor mansion they were leasing in Beverly Hills.

"You take the limo and go on," Rose suggested.

"No way, honey. I want to make sure that you're safe inside and locked up for the evening."

"Ben, that's silly. Mae and Clifton are here. I'm not exactly alone."

As he helped her out of the car he insisted, "No problem. Besides, I want to drive the Ferrari. I really love that thing."

Standing in the driveway, Rose suddenly threw her arms around Ben and hugged him. "And I love you. I'm going to buy you another one for Christmas." Then she looked into his eyes and said, "Ben . . . don't ever leave me. Promise?"

He kissed her lightly. "That's the last thing you have to worry about."

When she was in her bedroom alone, Rose looked at the clock. It was almost seven, too late to call Lilah. Warren was undoubtedly home. Well, she'd do it in the morning when she was fairly sure that Lilah would be alone. She needed to get a few things off her chest about Craig Kimball. Surely her sister wouldn't mind listening.

18

LILAH picked up the telephone on the second ring and heard the voice that had become so familiar and beloved over the past few months. Rose had taken to calling her in the early California hours, which worked out nicely, since the calls always came in after Warren had left for work.

"Comment vas-tu, ma soeur?" Rose asked.

"Fine, but the weather is getting chilly. I envy you those wonderful sunshiny days in California."

"Don't. It's overcast and gloomy . . . and so am I. I've got big trouble."

"What's happened?" Lilah enjoyed vicariously living the life that was everyday reality to her sister.

"Craig Kimball is coming out of retirement to appear in this season's last episode of the series."

"My God, that's great . . . I think he's marvelous. I've been a fan of his ever since I was a kid."

Bitterly Rose replied, "Yep, that's exactly it. Everybody loves the son of a bitch except me . . . and that's why I've got trouble."

"Do you know him?" Lilah asked, totally intrigued by Rose's attitude and anxious to hear all the details.

"Have you got time to hear the whole story?" Rose asked. "Because I don't want to give it to you in bits and pieces."

"Sure," Lilah lied, thinking that the women at the

Symphony League would have to have their executive committee meeting without her.

"Good. I'll try to keep it as short as possible, because I've got to leave for the studio in half an hour . . . but here goes."

As Lilah listened intently to the story she found herself pulled into a dark world of brutal tyranny that novels and magazines and trashy newspapers rarely probed. Perhaps because of her close ties with her twin, the story affected her almost as deeply and emotionally in hearing it as it had her sister in the telling, and when it ended, both women were crying.

"That's why I ran away. For years, even in Europe, I was afraid most of the time. I was sure that someday he would track me down and kill me. And, of course, my career in Hollywood ended the day I picked up that decanter and hit him with it."

"Rose, it must have been awful. . . ."

"I never should have come back, no matter what Benjie said. I could have stayed in Europe and continued to live a perfectly normal life."

"But . . . Rose, you're a star now. A big star. Millions of people watch you every week. You've been on the cover of so many magazines and newspapers lately, I can hardly keep up with them. How can you say you shouldn't have come back?"

"God, Lilah, suppose one of those awful papers ever got wind of this. Do you know what they'd do to me?"

"And him, Rose. After all, he was the villain, not you," Lilah insisted.

"Yeah, sure. But those rags aren't concerned with the truth, and I don't play an angel in that series, you know. My character is a combination of JR and Alexis Carrington, with a dash of Caligula thrown in."

"Stop it, Rose. You're getting carried away. I know that what happened was a terrible experience, but it's in the past. You've got to go on and show that bastard who won . . . and you can do it. It's just a part. Learn it as you would any other and try to pretend he's just another actor."

"Listen, Lilah, I didn't call you to get a lecture, because I've got Ben Frost to do that for me, and that's more than enough, believe me. Can't you just listen and sympathize with me?"

"Of course I can, and I *do*. I'm sorry, I really am, and I want you to feel that you can call me anytime to talk. I can't tell you how much these conversations mean to me. I think about you all the time, and I've begun secretly collecting everything that's printed about you," Lilah confessed.

"That's very flattering but dumb. Somebody's going to see that stuff and make the connection one of these days. You know, I think about you, too, and I worry about you. Now that my face is everywhere, aren't you afraid that somebody's going to see the resemblance?"

"I'm not worried about it, so you shouldn't," Lilah replied, trying to keep her voice light, although it was a fear that had taken up permanent residence in her mind.

"I've gotta run. I'm really looking forward to seeing you in New York. They've booked the cast at the Wyndham Hotel on Fifty-eighth Street. It's a small, private hotel. Leave a message at the desk if I'm not in when you call. Give my regards to Paris. Love you, sister."

"I love you, too, Rose."

Replacing the receiver, Lilah got up and went again to the mirror, as she had done so often in the last months. As she stared at her face she thought about the story she had just heard and wondered again at the twist of fate that had made Geneva choose one child over the other to keep.

Two sisters. One was raised poor and black, had suffered abuse and torment, yet rose from it all to the pinnacle of fame. The other, raised rich and white, was protected at all times from care or want or debasement, given every opportunity to achieve, and yet failed ever to rise above mediocrity. Had Geneva held those two babies in her arms and sensed that one was superior? Or perhaps they both had the same potential, yet Rose's spirit was sharpened by adversity while hers had been blunted by comfort and privilege. Would she ever know?

Slowly Lilah walked down the stairs, put on her coat, and got into her car to drive to the Symphony League meeting. As she maneuvered the car through traffic she felt again, as she had so often in the past months, that she had become disembodied and her real self was out there in Hollywood, going to work every day on the set. Without admitting it, she had begun to see her life as dull and unimportant compared to her sister's. And in spite of the story she had just heard, she often wished to taste a little of that fame and glamour.

19

Rose's Story

"**G**ET your little black ass over to Starpoint, baby. They've agreed to test you for the part," Denny Silver snapped into the telephone.

"You kidding me, Denny? That last job you sent me on, they took one look and said no. They wanted a white singer. Are you sure this part calls for a Negro?"

"Yeah, yeah. Believe me. I checked it all out and it's okay. There's not a lot of actin' to do . . . you're just supposed to be this terrific little kid that the guy discovers singing on the street and turns into a big rock star. You can sing rock, can't ya?"

"I can sing anything, Denny, and you know it, but this sounds kinda like the old Judy Garland movie, you know, where the guy walks into the ocean," she said.

"Don't get such big ideas, kiddo. You ain't the star. He's in love with somebody else . . . and he's just trying to prove that he's so hot, he can make a star out of anybody. Got it?"

"Got it." She sighed. "What time should I be there and who should I ask for?"

Two hours later Rose walked through the gates of Starpoint Productions, one of the small, independent movie companies that had become successful in producing low-budget films for television and was now rich enough to embark on the higher-cost theatrical films. She sat in Bert Hankins's office for half an hour before he was ready to see her.

His first words to her were, "You're whiter than I expected, Rosie Wilkins. What kind of experience have you had?"

"Didn't Denny send you my résumé?"

"Yeah, but I don't pay any attention to that crap. I want the truth. Craig Kimball's getting pretty fussy about who gets cast around him, and getting him to do this picture with us is like money in the bank. I want to keep him happy."

"Singin' or actin'? Which?"

"Both." He leaned back in his leather chair in the sparsely furnished office and lit a cigarette.

"Well, I started singin' in church down in San Pedro. Then I got a part in *Showboat* at school, and the director from the Civic Light Opera in Long Beach saw it and told me to take lessons. He said I had great vocal range. I didn't have any money for that kind of stuff, but there was a music teacher at my junior high school who gave me lessons after school."

Bert leered slightly. "Singin' lessons, honey, or something else?"

"She gave me voice lessons. Then I got into a group with a couple other girls. Some guy offered to back us in cuttin' a record, but it didn't work out. I did some singin' with a band in high school, and when I graduated, I moved up here to Los Angeles. I've done a few gigs around, and then Denny agreed to represent me. I've worked in six TV shows, but my part got cut in all of 'em except *Bonanza*—I played an Indian in that—and *Batman*, but with the costume and the makeup you'd never know it was me," she finished.

"Agents don't make stars, Rosie. They just give us producers headaches after their clients make it on their own. Now listen, I'm gonna hear you sing, and if you get past me, you better keep your little story to yourself. If anybody, anybody at all, asks about your background, just tell 'em to read your résumé. Whoever wrote that thing's got a helluva lot better imagination than you have. Now go on over to the recording studio. I'll be there in ten minutes."

Rose was less than halfway through her song when Bert Hankins knew that he had found just what he was looking for. This young chick had a voice so clear and sweet and beautiful that she could bring believability to the story. Excitedly he put in a call to Craig Kimball and announced the news.

When she had finished the song, Bert called over the intercom from the sound booth, "That's fine, Rosie. Be here at nine tomorrow morning. If Craig Kimball approves, you've got the part."

Rose was too excited to sleep that night. It was too much. All of her dreams were coming true. Not only was she about to land a big part, a singing part, in a major feature film, but she was going to be working with, of all people, Craig Kimball . . . a star of stars. And she was still only nineteen years old! This was only the beginning, she vowed. Someday she intended to be as famous as Lena Horne.

The next morning she appeared at the studio on schedule and had to wait for three hours for Craig Kimball to make his appearance. Sitting on the hard chair in the sound studio, the minutes ticked away like hours, and she had begun to think that her dream was just that when there was a sudden commotion and a group of men invaded the studio. Craig Kimball and his entourage had arrived.

Bert Hankins pointed to her and said, "Rosie, I want you to meet our star, Craig Kimball. Craig, what do you think?"

The tall man with the broad shoulders and deeply tanned skin strolled over to her and began his inspection. After a brief moment of appraisal he said, "Bert, I hear she's colored . . . is she?"

"Yeah . . . well, she's a little colored, but it doesn't matter, not really. In fact, I think it's a good idea to cast the part with a Negro. With all this civil-rights stuff goin' on, it makes us look good to give one of them a break, don't you think?"

"Yeah, you've got a point there, but I'll have to chew on it for a while. She's not bad-looking, but those tits'll have to be pumped up a bit. She's too skinny."

Bert rushed in with a response. "But that's the beauty of it, don't you see? She's a poor little waif on the streets with this big voice, and you pick her up and turn her into a star."

Without ever addressing her personally, Craig turned toward the sound booth. "Okay. You've convinced me. Now let's see if she can sing. Sudsy, did you get that bet down on Mile-High in the third?"

Still feeling humiliated from the crude inspection, Rose did not sing as well that day as she did the first, but it was good enough. When Craig and his retinue had departed, Bert announced that she was in. She went home to wait for Denny to finish her contract negotiations. They were completed in two days. They had offered her scale, and Denny took it gratefully. Rose Wilkins, whose voice was to bring credibility to the picture, would be paid the same as any bit actor.

Before shooting started, Rose recorded both of her songs, which would be synchronized with the film later. The first day on the set, she was called to Craig Kimball's large and lavish dressing room.

He was reclining on a couch, dressed only in a pair of boxing shorts and a white cotton T-shirt. Embarrassed, Rose looked away and apologized. "I'm sorry, Mr. Kimball, they told me in makeup to come in here to see you."

"Sit down. We've got to get a few things straight before this picture gets started. You understand?"

Rose nodded her head. Brought up by Geneva alone, Rose had had little close contact or association with older men, but she had been taught to be courteous and polite to her elders, especially white ones.

"I suppose you've never heard the phrase *droit de seigneur,* have you, my little tar baby?"

"No . . . no, sir," she replied, embarrassed, but careful to do nothing to jeopardize her chances.

"Too bad, then I'll just have to explain. You're on this picture because I said you were. If I say you're out, you're out, understand?"

"Yes, sir, and I'll try my best—" she began, but he cut in sharply.

"We'll see. Now go over there and lock that door so that no one will bother us, and we'll begin your lessons," he ordered.

She did as she was told, and then he beckoned her to come near him. As she walked toward him he opened the fly on his shorts and pulled his penis out. She stopped in her tracks, suddenly realizing exactly what the phrase meant. Dear God, all those stories she'd heard about the casting couches in Hollywood must be true.

"Get over here you little black cunt and give me a blow job, and you better make it good and fast. If I don't come in five minutes, you're off the picture."

Rose moved toward him. She really didn't know all that much about sex. A guy had tried to rape her in a hallway once, but she'd gotten away. The only real sex she'd ever had was once when she was dating her best friend's older brother, but it had hurt and hadn't been fun at all, and certainly not worth the three weeks of worrying about being pregnant afterward. She did know what a blow job was. There was a hooker in their apartment house who had described it to her.

Kneeling down beside him, she took the flaccid organ into her hand. God, he didn't even have a hard-on. She'd never be able to do it in five minutes. Quickly she took him into her mouth and began to suck gently.

"Your tongue . . . use your damn tongue," he ordered, but he was beginning to grow hard, and soon her mouth was filled and he was thrusting himself deeper into her throat. He put his large hand on the back of her head and pushed it down until she could barely breathe. She gagged helplessly as he went deeper and deeper until suddenly he shuddered, and his hot, sticky fluid filled her throat, but he did not loosen his grip. "Swallow it!" he ordered, and she did as she was told, trying to close her mind to what was happening so she wouldn't retch.

When it was all over, he released her and smiled. "Not bad . . . a little over five minutes, but I'll be generous since it's your first time. Now sit down. I don't want you to rush out and vomit my precious fluid down some goddamn toilet. Don't you know that there are millions of women who would love a taste of my stuff? Consider yourself honored."

He covered himself up and got off the couch, and she sat quietly, waiting to be told what to do. She tried not to think about what had happened because she had a terrible feeling that her association with Craig Kimball had only begun. As he poured himself a glass of Scotch he said, "Now get your ass out of here. Sudsy will give you my address. I want you at my house at ten o'clock tonight, understand?"

Without a word Rose rushed out and ran toward the small cubicle assigned as her dressing room. As she passed a group of crewmen she heard their comments.

"Looks like Kimball just gave the little nigger the star treatment," one man said, snickering loudly.

"Yeah, she probably loved it. Them black gals start doin' it when they're just kids. She's probably a pro by now," commented the other.

"Maybe, but personally, I wouldn't touch her with a ten-foot pole, especially mine . . . probably get the clap. I think Kimball's crazy to take a chance with a coon. Man, to think of all the beautiful asses he could have . . ."

Rose locked the door behind her. She wanted to shut out the world. Quickly she closed herself into a stall, and holding her head over the toilet, she stuck her finger down her throat, but it wasn't necessary.

The retching started immediately, and within moments all of Kimball's precious bodily fluid was on its way into the sewage system along with the oatmeal she had eaten that morning to give herself energy.

When she was called to the set to do her first scene with the star, she was nervous and had trouble saying her lines and looking into his face. Kimball, however, was generous and magnanimous.

"Look, Bert . . . take it easy on the kid. It's her first day. Let's run through it a few more times without the camera."

After eight takes they finally had a print, and she returned to her cubicle to worry about the evening ahead of her. At lunch she stayed away from everyone and went to the telephone to call her agent. Miraculously he was in and took her call. Thus she learned another of Hollywood realities. Agents always take calls from clients who are working.

"Denny, I got a problem with Craig Kimball—" she began, but he interrupted her.

"You got no problem, kid. Just do as you're told and you'll get along fine."

"Wait . . . let me tell you what he did to me."

"I don't want to hear about it. I got you the job, now do the best you can," he snapped, his voice surly.

Rose was a bright young woman and it didn't take her long to realize that he had known what would happen to her when he sent her to audition for the part. Furious, she screamed into the telephone, "You son of a bitch! Why didn't you tell me about him?"

"Tell you what? That you better not cross him? Everybody knows that. Now concentrate on your work and don't go blabbing everything you know. It isn't good for your career . . . or your health."

"He wants me to be at his house tonight at ten," she said, "but I can't go."

"If you don't make it on this picture, kid, you better look for another line of work."

"Bert . . . he lives in Malibu and I haven't got a car," she said through clenched teeth.

"You got a license?"

"Yeah."

"Then you got no problem. I'll rent one for you. We'll just take it out of your checks. I'll bring it over to you this afternoon."

"Thanks, Bert . . . thanks a whole goddam lot."

She slammed the telephone onto the hook and strode back to her dressing room to wait for the next call to the set.

That evening it took Rose more than an hour to find her way on the darkened highway to the actor's home on the beach. She had decided not to let the man or the system destroy her, and she vowed to endure whatever Kimball did to her. She was determined to survive and triumph.

The little man with the large eyes let her into the beach house, and she followed him through a long corridor to a large room where several men were sitting around talking. They all seemed to be drinking, some were watching the news on television, and there was a sweetish, acrid smell in the room. Kimball was not there.

"Want a drink?" Sudsy asked.

"I'll have a Coke," she replied, and then asked, "Where is he?"

"In bed. You wanna sniff it or drink it?"

"What?" she asked.

"One Coca-Cola coming up," he retorted, and got a bottle out of the refrigerator, opened it, and handed it to her. She sat down on a bar stool and looked around. There was a huge picture window, which she assumed looked out onto the now dark beach. The walls were covered in knotty pine. The room was a mess, with so many newspapers, magazines, and so much junk around that it was hard to tell how the room was decorated, but it wasn't very attractive, which surprised her. According to the movie magazines, all stars lived in glamorous mansions.

The three men sitting in front of the television were

silent, and another man had fallen asleep on the sofa. None of them had given her more than a cursory glance. She sat on the uncomfortable, worn bar stool, drank her Coke, and waited for three hours. At about one A.M. two of the men got up and went into another room, and the other man stretched out on the floor and went to sleep.

She looked around for a bathroom. She had to pee badly, but she was afraid to open any closed doors. God knows what might be behind them. Finally, at one-thirty, Sudsy reappeared.

"Where's the john?" she asked.

He motioned to a door at the end of the room, and she went in and locked the door behind her. She delayed her return as long as possible, and when she came out, Sudsy was gone again. Good God, what was happening?

Instead of perching on the bar stool, she settled down into a deep leather chair and closed her eyes. She was so tired. In a few minutes she was sound asleep.

Suddenly she found herself being awakened by a hand roughly shaking her shoulder.

"Wake up, kid, and get out of here," the voice growled into her ear.

She opened her eyes and saw that it was morning. The ocean was rolling almost up to the window next to her. She jumped to her feet as Sudsy snapped, "Get out, quick. He don't like no dames to be here when he comes down for coffee. Now move!"

Like a condemned prisoner who had just been granted a reprieve, Rose sprinted down the hall, out the door, and into the little Toyota. She felt like singing as she pulled onto the Pacific Coast Highway and headed home.

She barely had time to bathe and dress before she had to get back on the road to the studio. Her heart was light, and she had high hopes that she had passed the test and would now be left alone to concentrate on her work.

The morning shots went well, but when everyone was having lunch, she was summoned to Kimball's dressing room for a repeat performance. When it was over, he smiled and said, "Now, that was better than lunch, wasn't it? Sudsy tells me that you were on schedule last night. That's good. Same time tonight."

That night the actor was talking to four men in the den when she arrived, and he motioned Sudsy to take her into his bedroom. The second part of her nightmare had begun. Sudsy told her to take off her clothes and get on the king-size bed. She waited for him to leave the room, but he just stood there staring at her. Finally she slipped out of her skirt and sweater and sat on the bed, but he said, "Everything." When she was naked, he told her to lie on the bed, facedown. She did but pulled the sheet over her.

"Turn over on your stomach, kid," he ordered.

"What for?"

"It's a surprise," he replied. Quickly and expertly he slipped a silk cord over her wrists and ankles and then tied them to each of the four posts on the bed so that she was lying in a spread-eagle position. She felt helpless and very alone. Suddenly Sudsy pulled the sheet off her, and she yelled as she felt his finger suddenly poking inside her rectum.

"Get your hands off me, you ape!" she gasped.

"Hey, I'm doin' you a favor, kid. Without Vaseline you wouldn't have any fun at all."

She closed her eyes and tried to will herself into a state of suspension where she would feel no pain, experience no humiliation, but suddenly Kimball was on top of her, forcing himself inside. She tried to relax, let go, but her muscles tensed, and as they did, he struck her on the side of the head hard.

"Let me in, you cunt, or I'll feed you to the fish," he snarled in her ear, and the weight of his body fell heavily on her, almost cutting off her breath.

The pounding, the prodding, the poking, seemed to go on for hours, and she felt as if she were being torn apart. When he had at last spent himself and rolled away, Sudsy returned almost immediately, as if he had been watching and waiting for the climax. He untied her and told her to get out as fast as possible, which she did.

Her life became a cycle of abuse and uncertainty. Each night on the long drive she never knew if it would be a night of sleeping in a chair or a night of horrifying brutality and degradation. He rarely abused her in the same way twice. One night, when he did not feel like having her himself, he watched while his friends did it to her.

Rose began to lose all sense of self and reality. He gave her no rest, and always there were the threats to destroy her. Never was a word of kindness spoken to her in private, although he was magnanimous in his praise of her performance on the set.

Rose knew, however, that she was not doing well. She could see it in the eyes of the crew and the director. She was moving like a zombie, not feeling or seeing, and she began to dream about death—peaceful, restful death. The first Sunday that she was not working, she drove down to San Pedro to see Geneva.

She tried to put on a smile, but the evil that was crushing her spilled out of her voice and her eyes, and Geneva, who felt that her God had deserted her, was frightened.

"Honey, please don't go back. Don't let the devil have your soul without a fight. No career is worth it. Please baby. You're sick. I can see it."

Geneva's words haunted her, and she began to awaken from the cruel and submissive coma that she had forced herself into. Life wasn't worth living if it was going to be like this, but what was she going to do about it? She knew that if she quit, it would be the end of all her dreams and there would be nothing in her future but a life of drudgery like Geneva's.

The next evening she got into her car and drove to the beach as usual, but it was not to be an ordinary night of debasement. Kimball was extremely agitated, and she suspected he had taken some kind of drug, for his eyes had a particularly evil glitter in them. She felt her heart pounding as he circled the bed, watching her lie there, naked, tied with her arms and legs spread wide, totally vulnerable. Suddenly his eye caught the half-empty Coke bottle on the table where she had left it, and he grabbed it and poured the contents into her face. Then, with a laugh, he threw his leg over her and sat on her knees, and with a thrust he rammed the bottle inside her as hard as he could. She yelled in pain, but he pressed his large hand over her mouth and did it again and again.

She struggled and pulled, but he was enjoying her pain and kept on. Suddenly the cord on her left arm pulled loose, and her hand was free. She clawed at him, but he was too strong, too frenzied to be stopped. Desperately she groped around until her hand touched the glass decanter of brandy on the bedside table. She clutched it, and with one wild and lucky stroke she smashed him on the side of the face, splitting the skin on his cheek.

He screamed and clutched his face as blood spurted everywhere. Sudsy appeared instantly, and the commotion was like the sounds of the damned in hell.

The lucky stroke had suddenly given Rose back her spirit. Quickly she untied herself and leapt from the bed. She had to get out of there before somebody decided to kill her. Grabbing her purse with the car keys, she ran out of the house totally nude, covered only by blood, her own below and his on her arm. She got into the car and drove as fast as she could through the darkness of the night, not stopping until she got to San Pedro.

20

New York

THE moment Warren stepped out of the hotel room, Lilah picked up the telephone and called the Wyndham Hotel. It was close to seven in the evening, and she hoped that Rose would be in. Ben answered the telephone.

"Lilah! Where are you?" he asked.

"In the Waldorf Towers. I tried to get Warren to make reservations at the Plaza or the Park Lane, which is much nearer to your hotel, but he insisted on staying here. Is Rose there?"

"No, she's not. They're doing some night shots in front of a theater over on Broadway. I don't expect her back until late. She'll probably be here all day tomorrow sleeping. I just came back to the room to make some calls and pick up some medicine for her. She's fighting a cold. This rotten weather is getting to her. How was the trip?"

"Nice. I was alone in the daytime, but I went to a lot of museums, did some Christmas shopping at Harrod's in London, and gained several pounds eating in Paris. Do you think it would be all right to drop in tomorrow afternoon? I don't know what time. It depends on Warren . . . when he leaves."

"Lilah, she'll want to see you anytime you get here.

She's really down in the dumps, and I'm hoping you can cheer her up a bit."

"I hope so, too, Ben."

The next day Warren insisted that Lilah accompany him to the luncheon meeting at Le Cirque, since the host had invited her. She tried to look interested in the conversation, but her mind kept drifting toward the afternoon. At two she excused herself by saying she was on her way to a concert and left the two men to talk business. It was a chilly, overcast New York day, and the wind was blowing.

When she arrived at the Wyndham, she was startled to find that the lobby door was kept locked. The doorman admitted her, and she was soon knocking at the door to her sister's suite. Her heart palpitated with excitement. Over the past months their relationship had grown deeper and closer in spite of the miles between them.

The door was pulled open, and Rose stood there with arms outspread, ready to envelop her only living relative. They hugged each other amid tears and laughter.

When they had separated and were seated on the couch together, Lilah expressed her concern. "Rose, you look so tired. Ben said you were getting a cold."

Rose shook her head and poured Lilah a cup of herb tea from a thermos. "Here, have a cup of Geneva's brew. She was convinced that it cured everything. No, I don't have a cold. That's just what I told Benjie to get him off my back. Lilah, I don't want to get up in the morning anymore. . . . You know why? Because every day that passes puts me one more day closer to Craig Kimball." She sighed and looked down at her cup. "I'm not going to make it, I'm afraid."

"You're stronger than you think you are, Rose."

"Not anymore. The nightmares are back. I worry about seeing him during the day, and at night he haunts my dreams."

"Have you thought about . . . maybe seeing somebody?"

"You mean, like a shrink? That's the first thing I did, but it hasn't done any good, and Ben hasn't been any help to me at all. He makes it worse, telling me that I have to face up to my problems and lick them. Nobody who's never been terrorized like that understands."

"What are you going to do?"

"I'm going to quit the show," she said softly.

"Oh, no! You can't do that!" Lilah protested vehemently. "Everybody's talking about you . . . and that song you sing over the credits at the beginning is so . . . fantastic. Without you that show would be nothing."

Rose smiled and replied ruefully, "Thank you for those kind, sisterly words, but it's just not true. It's a strong show with a well-known and solid cast. I'm really still the new kid on the block, in spite of the rise in the ratings. Maybe if this hadn't happened for a year or two—if I'd had a chance to really establish myself—but . . . ." Her voice trailed off regretfully.

"Rose, I've had a really silly idea floating around in the back of my mind. I'm almost embarrassed to suggest it . . ." Lilah began hesitantly.

"I don't suppose you're thinking of doubling for me in that episode, are you?" Rose asked with a laugh.

"That's exactly what I'm suggesting. Look, I brought the house down in a PTA skit once . . . and when Mary Ann used to be in the school plays, I always coached her on her lines."

Rose's doubting smile turned into a broad one as she listened to Lilah defend her suggestion. When Lilah finally came to a halt, Rose said, "You're serious!"

Lilah looked directly at her and said, "Why not? With a little makeup and a wig, surely I could fake my way through one episode, but if I don't, you're going to quit, anyway. What have we got to lose?"

"I haven't got anything to lose, but you sure as hell do. What about your husband . . . your family? You don't really think you can do this without telling somebody where you're going or what you're up to?"

"Nobody will ever know. Your face has been on the cover of every magazine in the supermarket in the past few months, and not one single person has even suggested to me that I might resemble you."

Rose threw her head back and laughed. "Good God, you're such an innocent! Nobody . . . nobody would ever make such a suggestion, even if I were the most beautiful woman in the world—which I'm not— because, *ma chère,* I'm black, don't you see? They'd be afraid you'd be insulted."

Lilah looked chagrined. "Oh, that sounds so . . . cynical, Rose."

"Not cynical, my dear, just very realistic, but okay, let's discuss the possibilities."

The sky had darkened, and it was almost six-thirty when Ben returned to interrupt their excited chatter as they planned their strategy. It was time for Rose to get ready to go to the set. Quickly the two sisters said good-bye and promised to talk on the telephone the following week when Rose returned to California. Lilah rushed downstairs to find a cab. Warren would be anxious and worried. It was after six o'clock.

When Lilah had gone, Ben looked closely at his beloved and said enviously, "I wish I could put stars back in your eyes like your sister can. What's her secret?"

Rose giggled and pulled away. "Don't you bother me now, Benjie. I have to hurry. Did you bring me something to eat?"

"Don't tell me you've got your appetite back too? I can't believe it."

"Be nice now, and maybe I'll let you in on it," she said coquettishly.

"On what?"

"Our secret."

"Why do I get a funny feeling that I'm not going to like this secret you and Lilah have hatched up?" he asked suspiciously.

"How could you not like something that makes me happy . . . and hungry?"

"Good question."

21

"**I**'D like to speak to Mr. Conway, please," Florence said into the telephone, speaking softly enough to shade her voice, hoping to disguise it from his secretary.

"I'm sorry, Mrs. Bennett, but he's still in conference. Would you like to leave a number where he can reach you?"

Annoyed that she had been so easily recognized, Florence's reply had a nasty edge. "No, but I'd like you to go into his office with my name written on a piece of paper saying that I intend to wait until he picks up."

"I'm sorry, but he's in private—"

"Please do as I say or I'll keep this line tied up until hell freezes over," she snapped. Florence had been getting the runaround from Warren's secretary for weeks, and she had been pushed about as far as she intended to be.

"One moment, please," the secretary said, and Florence found herself on hold. A good five minutes later the secretary's voice came back on the line and said, "Mr. Conway will be with you in a few minutes."

Five minutes later, when her eardrum was beginning to be numbed by jangling music, she heard Warren say, "All right, Florence. Just what's the idea of the scene with Sandra? She said you were getting abusive."

"Abusive? The witch doesn't know what *abusive*

means. If she pulls that little conference ruse on me one more time, I'll really get abusive. And what are you trying to do to your customers' ears with that music blasting at them, anyway?"

"What do you want, Florence? I thought we had things settled."

"Maybe you're satisfied with the arrangement, but I'm not." Her voice softened. "I miss you, Warren. I would never have agreed to not seeing you if I didn't need the money so badly. Now my car needs fixing, and I promised my sister I'd visit her in Florida, but I can't do both."

Warren sighed. "How much do you need, Florence?" he asked wearily, suspecting that this would not be the last time she would put the squeeze on him for more than the monthly sum she had reluctantly agreed to accept to end their relationship without telling his wife.

"Two thousand will do it, but it's more an exchange than a gift, Warren. I have something to tell you about Lilah, and it's worth every cent."

"What are you talking about?"

"I went to lunch with your wife yesterday, and she told me something very interesting. Of course, I swore on my soul and as her oldest and most trusted friend that I would never breathe a word to anyone."

"Good. Then maybe you should keep the faith, my dear. I don't intend to add spying on my wife to my list of sins."

"Warren, I'm going to tell you this out of the goodness of my heart. It's something you need to know, for the sake of your marriage. You are interested in preserving it, aren't you?"

"I'll meet you at the bar in the Carlton at five," he replied.

Florence was sitting and waiting in the dimly lit bar when he strode in and sat down at the table with her. She greeted him sweetly. "Warren, let's be friends. I still care for you, and the money means nothing to me.

I'd rather have you back." She looked into his eyes and put her hand on his thigh.

He pulled away. "Don't do that, Florence."

She leaned close to him, and her fingers continued their search. "You know you still want me, Warren."

"No, I don't, Florence. That's why I agreed to pay you blackmail."

"It wasn't my idea, Warren, it was yours, remember? And I know you're only doing it because you really love me and want me to have the same comforts your wife enjoys—nice clothes, a car, a little travel now and then—and speaking of travel, Lilah is secretly planning a trip . . . alone."

"Where?" Warren asked.

"She didn't say, and she's not exactly sure when. Sometime in January, she thinks. And she needs a cover. She intends to tell you that she's coming to Florida for a week or two with me, but of course she's going somewhere else." Florence's tone of voice was so smug and assured that Warren was convinced she was not lying.

"We just got back from a big trip to Europe."

"I know. She had a marvelous time. She said she particularly enjoyed the stopover in New York. Warren, tell me, was she alone much in New York?"

"No, we were together every minute," he lied, remembering the night that she had arrived at Le Cygne half an hour late, excited and starry-eyed. She had told him that she'd spent the afternoon at a concert by Vladimir Horowitz and that she was still stimulated and thrilled by hearing the world's greatest pianist. Although he had been a little puzzled by her lateness, he had accepted her story.

Florence watched him closely. Warren was so easy to read. His voice said one thing, but the expression on his face said something quite different. No wonder Lilah was looking for a little excitement somewhere else.

"She must be having an affair, Warren. What else

could be going on that would make it necessary for her to lie to you and take secret trips? Something very phony has been going on with her ever since she took that weird trip to New York with that trumped-up story about going shopping."

"Here's the deposit slip. I put a thousand directly into your checking account, but that's it. I promised to pay you fifteen hundred a month, and I'll do it, but don't come to me with any more stories about Lilah. I don't want to hear them," he declared emphatically, and got to his feet.

"Aren't you going to have a drink with me, darling? For old-times' sake?" Florence asked, trying to be as pleasant and charming as possible.

"I have to get home," he replied, and turned and left the bar.

Florence picked up her margarita, licked a little of the salt from the rim of her glass, and smiled. She had really ruined his day, his week, his month—his year—and, with a little luck, maybe even his life. It served him right for choosing that bitch over her. He deserved to be cuckolded . . . and blackmailed.

22

LILAH was sitting in the midst of packages and Christmas paper, trying desperately to finish wrapping the presents before it was time to leave for the airport. Mary Ann was coming home for the holidays two days earlier than planned because she had a cold. The telephone rang, and it was Rose.

"Lilah, honey, I'm so glad you're there. I had a real bad day today, and I needed to talk to you," Rose began.

"What's going on?" Lilah asked, and glanced at the clock. She would never finish the wrapping now.

"The word came down today. Craig Kimball signed the contract. He loves the script. They're sending out the press release tomorrow." She sounded miserable.

"We've got it all settled, Rose. Come on now, we'll pull it off, you'll see. I've been sticking to my diet, and I joined a health club. I'm looking terrific. What's your weight now?"

"I'm down to a hundred and five," she said quietly.

"Oh, no! You've stopped eating again, haven't you? You promised me you wouldn't."

"Now don't you start. Ben's bad enough. He's getting tired of my moaning and crying all the time. He got furious with me because I didn't act properly impressed when Revlon approached him about bringing out a new perfume called Lady Rose."

"My Lord, that's wonderful."

"Yeah, I guess so. They want me to do several TV spots for it. How're things going for Christmas? Have Matthew and Mary Ann gotten home yet?"

"Mary Ann's coming in today. Matthew will drive up day after tomorrow."

"That really sounds terrific," Rose said wistfully.

"What are you doing on Christmas?" Lilah asked.

"Oh, we're going to some parties here in Beverly Hills and in Bel Air. Ben said everybody invited us. I'd like to stay home with my feet at the fire, but Benjie says no . . . a star's got to be seen."

"Don't complain, Rose. There isn't a woman in the world who wouldn't change places with you."

"You think you can do it, Lilah?"

"As for the looks, yes, I'm sure I can. I just hope I can act well enough. I've been locked up in the bathroom reading that script every day, and although I've got the lines memorized, I sound awfully wooden."

"Don't you think you could get here a little sooner? Three days don't seem quite enough to get you ready."

"I feel the same way. Maybe I can talk Mary Ann into going back to school a day or two early. Let me see what I can do."

"Benjie got the wigs yesterday, and I must say they look just like my hair. Lilah, I really ought to have a recent photograph of you to remind us of things we might need to do."

"I'll stick one in the mail today."

By the time Lilah got to the airport, her daughter was already waiting at the curb, luggage in hand, looking about to cry.

"Mom, what took you so long? I've been waiting for ages," Mary Ann complained as she got into the front seat of the Cadillac.

Lilah pulled her beloved daughter close and hugged her. "I'm so sorry, honey. I had to go to the post office, and it was crowded, and the traffic was really bad. Are you feeling all right?"

"Not really. My nose is stopped up, and I haven't been able to clear my ears since the plane landed."

"You'll feel better when you get home and into your own room. Stella fixed your favorite vegetable soup."

Mary Ann reached over and squeezed Lilah's hand. "Mom, you'll never know how much I missed you—and Dad—and Matt. I'm so glad to be home."

"That's the way it's supposed to be," Lilah replied, and wished that Rose could meet her children.

Every day the burden of secrecy seemed to get heavier, and although she was frequently tempted to tell her husband everything, she knew she did not dare. Not yet, anyway. Not until the escapade in Hollywood was over and done with. Warren would certainly feel she was making a fool of herself. And he would probably be right.

23

Rose put down the telephone, and the tears started again. God, what was happening to her? For the past few weeks she seemed to be crying all the time. Here she had everything she wanted in life and she couldn't seem to find happiness in anything. And all because of that devil Kimball. Jesus, why had Benjie rushed out of here like a madman, just because she made some snotty remark to him about overexposing her?

She went to the intercom and buzzed for Mae. Clifton answered, "Yes, ma'am?"

"Did Ben say where he was going?" she asked.

"No, ma'am, he didn't. Your driver is here, waiting to take you to the studio."

"Tell him I'll be right down."

In the bathroom she splashed cold water on her face, and taking eyedrops from the medicine chest, she put them into her eyes. Within moments the swelling from her weeping had disappeared, and her eyes were large and bright and wide-awake again. She slipped the prescription bottle in her purse in case she needed it later, tied a silk scarf around her head, and pulled an oversize tan wool trench coat by Perry Ellis over her sweater and slacks. With a glance at the clock she hurried out the door. Damn, she was going to be late getting to makeup again.

On the drive to the studio in the Valley she lost herself in the script. She had three difficult and long passages to memorize for today, but the lines were complicated, and some of them didn't seem to make a lot of sense. God, what was wrong with the writers? Didn't they know that actors had to speak the lines and make them sound believable? Irritated, she pulled her red felt pen from her handbag and circled several offending words. She knew the director would be annoyed when she insisted on the changes, but she would stand firm. Damn, Benjie was supposed to do this stuff. Where in the hell had he gone?

Stan Selden, who was directing the episode of *Broadway* being filmed that week, was more annoyed with her lateness than she had expected him to be.

"We've been lighted and ready to go for twenty minutes, Rose. What took you so long?"

"They had to change the color of my nail polish to match the dress, Stan. Now you wouldn't want the smartly groomed Caymen Welles to appear on camera with red nail polish and a peach dress, would you, darling?" she said testily.

Stan shook his head wearily. "Rose, it's great for you to be a bitch on camera as Caymen Welles, but could you just be yourself when we're talking?" He moved closer to her and spoke softly. "Now tell me. Is there something wrong? You've been late three days in a row. Wardrobe says that your gowns don't fit because you're losing weight. Is there something I can do?"

For a brief moment Rose relaxed the poised and arch manner she had lately adopted to cover up the anxieties and fears that Craig Kimball had again brought to the fore. "Thanks, Stan . . . really, I'll be okay," she said, and then continued, "But for God's sake take a look at this script, will you? Who's the stupid writer who wrote those long-winded speeches for me?"

Stan's mouth twitched slightly as he replied, "Sis Thompson . . . you know, the gal who won three Emmies last year." He turned his back and walked away, leaving her feeling foolish and ignorant.

The crew went into an hour of overtime that day, and Stan blamed her. She knew she had ruined several takes by stumbling on her lines, and she could feel the disapproval of everyone around her. Though she tried to console herself with the thought that the other stars were jealous because she was getting all the media attention, in her heart she knew it wasn't true. Both of the other women in the series, Sheila Tandy and Beth Tyndall, had been successful themselves, with product endorsements and books published in their names. They were nice women, as well, and very generous.

When the long day finally ended, Rose got into the limousine and went directly home. If Benjie wasn't there, she would call up Monica Barnes herself and explain that she couldn't make the dinner party because she had had to work late. She didn't want to go, anyway. Who cared about the French ambassador?

Ben was waiting when she got home, and she was so happy to see him that her anger disappeared in a puff of relief. "Benjie," she said, and threw herself into his arms.

"How did it go today? Did you miss me?" he asked.

"I made it through the day, but promise you'll be there tomorrow. Stan's mad at me for muffing my lines."

"Don't worry about it. Last night's episode got a thirty-nine share in the overnight Nielsens."

"How come Stan didn't mention it today?"

"He didn't direct that episode. He's probably feeling the pressure, too, babe. I hope you didn't give him a hard time."

"I'm losing my confidence, Benjie. That's what's wrong. And I'm starting to act like Caymen Welles offscreen as well as on."

"Don't worry about it. When you and Lilah switch places, everybody will be so accustomed to your eccentricities that nothing she does will surprise them or make anybody suspect it isn't you. Now come on, let's get ready for that dinner party."

"Ben, I really ought to stay home and study my lines for tomorrow," she protested as she allowed herself to be led up the winding staircase.

"I'll help you in the car on the way over. Look, we'll only stay for dinner. I think you should make friends with the ambassador, and he'll be so grateful to have someone there who speaks fluent French. After all, France was very good to you when you were down, remember?"

"*C'est vrai.* Every happiness that's ever come my way started there," she admitted, "including meeting you."

"Good, then let's go. I asked wardrobe to send over that pink-and-silver beaded number you wore in the first episode for you to wear tonight."

"But it was so tight, I'll never be able to sit down in it," Rose protested.

"With all the weight you've been losing by fretting, you'll be lucky if it isn't too loose," Ben retorted.

"I talked to Lilah today. I asked her to come a couple days earlier."

"Good idea. Can she manage it?"

"She said she'd try. Benjie, why is she doing this for me?"

"I guess maybe she just wants to see what it would be like to be you . . . a star. Even for just a few days."

"But she's got everything, Ben . . . a home, a husband, a happy marriage, children she loves and whom she's proud of. She's a respected member of the community. She's got money and she's . . ." She paused and did not finish her sentence for a long moment.

Ben watched her and waited and then said softly, "She's white. That's what you started to say, didn't you?"

Rose nodded her head slightly.

They were now in the bedroom. Ben took her hand and led her to the bed. "Sit down here for a minute, baby. We need to talk about this."

"We'll be late, Benjie," she protested.

"Then we'll be late. I've got to tell you something, and it's important."

Obediently she sat down to listen. "I know color has been a problem for you, maybe even more so than it is for most of us, because without that mass of kinky black hair you look like one of them. But me, I'm black on the inside as well as on the outside. Always have been, always will be, and there's one thing I told myself when I was just a kid and getting called nigger and coon and jiggaboo and a lot of other shit down there in Tennessee." He paused. "Right then and there," he continued, "I pomised myself that never, never ever, not once in my life would I wish to be one of them. You understand what I mean?"

Rose nodded. "Sure, I know. That's why I need to have you around, Benjie, because that's the way I felt when I was growing up. It was just that—God, I hate to bring it up because I know it makes you mad—the experience with Craig Kimball screwed me up."

Gently he put his arm around her and drew her close. "I know, honey, I know, but he's done it to a lot of other young girls eager to get along in Hollywood, and believe me, he didn't care what color their skin was."

"You think I'm a coward for not wanting to face him, don't you?"

"Honey, I don't think you're a coward. I just think that if you forced yourself to do it, you'd be a lot better off emotionally than if you run away from him."

"He wants to destroy me, Benjie. I know it."

"Sweetheart, we're not sure he even remembers you. Besides, we've decided to give Lilah a go at filling in for you. Maybe it will work."

"God, I hope so, but if she blows it and the truth comes out about the two of us, it might hurt her family."

"Remember, it was her idea. Maybe she needs to do something for you . . . maybe she needs to do it for herself, but it might never happen, anyway. Who knows, maybe the old fart will have a heart attack or something and die before it's time to shoot the episode."

"Don't I wish."

"You wouldn't want to deprive your sister of her big chance to be a star for a week, now would you?"

"In a word, yes."

24

CRAIG Kimball sat under the bright lights of the makeup table in his bedroom while Maquita, the celebrated makeup artist, applied the last touches to his face.

"There, I think that should do it. Turn on the camera, Sudsy, and we'll have a look on the monitor," the young man with the slicked-back hair and tight white pants said. "When we see how you look on camera, we'll have a better idea, but I frankly think it's going to be fine."

Without saying a word, Craig Kimball swiveled his chair around as the bright lights came on, and he looked at himself on the monitor. For a long quiet moment no one said anything as they waited for the star's opinion, which was summed up in a word. "Shit. Is that the fucking best you can do?"

Maquita was tempted to say, "Yes, short of major surgery," but he refrained. He had tried to pass on this job, but there had been too much pressure, too much money offered. It was like trying to retouch the portrait of Dorian Gray. In response he asked, "What do you think's wrong, Mr. Kimball?"

"You're the expert. You tell me," Kimball said tersely, and then to Sudsy, "Get me a Scotch."

Maquita interjected, "If I might make a suggestion, sir, I think that perhaps you ought to stay off the booze until this show is finished. Alcohol causes fluid to be retained and contributes to that slightly bloated look around the eyes. It's very aging."

Kimball started to say something nasty, but one more glance at the television screen told him he'd better do everything he could. Sudsy decided that it might be the perfect time to suggest once more that he drop the whole thing. "Screw 'em, boss. You don't need to put yourself through this crap. Call it off. Tell 'em you've got artistic differences with the production."

"Screw yourself," Kimball commented, and then suggested, "Okay, now let's try some lifts at the jawline."

Maquita shook his head. "Your hair isn't thick enough to cover a lift. But have you ever thought of wearing glasses? A nice pair of oversize frames with slightly tinted lenses would mask the eyes a bit. What do you think?"

"Get my glasses," Craig ordered Sudsy, and the little man scurried to accommodate him. In moments he was back with a pair of rimless aviator-style spectacles, which the actor donned and stared into the mirror once more.

After a few moments, Kimball pronounced, "Yeah. I'll go with the glasses."

But Maquita suggested, "I think we ought to bring in an assortment of frames and find the best one. I think dark, heavy frames would look better."

Without taking his eyes off his television image, Kimball barked, "Do it, Sudsy. Get an optician over here as soon as you can."

"The tailor's going to be here in a few minutes, boss," Sudsy protested.

"Get the hell out of here and do as you're told."

As Sudsy left, Maquita began to repack his makeup case and prepare to leave, but Kimball stopped him. "Not yet, buddy, not yet. I want you to start all over, but this time, use a little darker base. And don't worry about trying to conceal that scar. Let it show. Just work on the other things."

As the makeup artist went resignedly back to work, a petite blond woman entered the room. Her expression was pinched with anger until she saw that her husband was not alone, and then a gentle smile lit her face.

"Craig! Oh, I didn't know we had company. Why, Maquita, how nice to see you again. What's going on in here?"

"Hello, Mrs. Kimball. We're just experimenting with the design for Mr. Kimball's makeup for his appearance on *Broadway*. How've you been?"

"Just fine. I didn't know you made house calls," she said.

"I don't. I'm so booked up that I don't have time, and I'm opening a new studio in New York, so I've been really busy," he replied.

"Well, it's certainly kind of you to take the time to come over here and help Craig. Would you mind doing my makeup for this evening while you're here?" she asked sweetly.

Maquita hesitated. If word got out, and it undoubtedly would, every customer he had would be furious that he had made an exception for her, and she wasn't even one of his regular clients. "I, uh, don't know how much longer it will be until I'm finished here."

With measured words she replied, "Then, Craig, darling, see that you give him enough time for me. Don't be such a perfectionist, dear."

"Get lost, Claire," Kimball said, but undaunted, his wife persisted, "When you're finished, I'll be in my dressing room waiting for you, Maquita. It's the third door down the hall, on the left. Don't forget we're going to a reception for the president at the Century Plaza at six, darling. Oh, by the way, I found the loveliest little diamond clip at Van Cleef and Arpels yesterday. They're holding it for me. I'd just love to have it to wear in my hair this evening. Shall I tell them to send it over?"

Without looking at her, Kimball asked, "How much is it?"

Giggling just slightly, she replied, "My goodness, I never ask the price when I see something I really like, and neither do you, Craig, dear." She waited for his answer, which came after a pause that was electric with tension. "Get it," he muttered.

"Isn't he just the sweetest thing? He spoils me terribly. He lets me have anything I want, don't you, precious? See you later, Maquita. Don't forget me, now."

Maquita hurried out of the mansion at five that afternoon, relieved to be out in the fresh air again. As he got into his Lamborghini to drive away, he reflected on the gossipy speculation about the marriage of Craig Kimball and the former Claire Mansfield Fordyce Clemson. What was so special about that little blond woman with the flawless complexion, bright eyes, and tiny teeth who had married and buried three millionaires prior to her alliance with the world's most popular movie star? Some said she had something on him, and others contended that the big star was really gay, which Maquita suspected was untrue. He was more inclined to think the old bastard couldn't get it up anymore and needed a wife to cover for him. Whatever. But of one thing Maquita was absolutely sure: Craig Kimball was making the biggest mistake of his career by appearing on television. All the makeup in the world could never hide the devastation that booze, years, and dissolution had wreaked on that once marvelous face.

He just hoped that word didn't leak out that he had designed the makeup.

25

"LILAH, how could you do a thing like that without asking me first?" Warren demanded angrily.

"I didn't know I needed your approval," Lilah retorted, wondering why he was making such a big deal out of her inviting Florence to stop in for a drink on Christmas Eve.

"I just don't want her around here tomorrow night. I want to spend a quiet evening alone with you and the children. It'll be too hectic at my mother's on Christmas, and we won't have another chance to really talk to them. Every other evening they'll be out gallivanting with their friends. Call her back and tell her it's not convenient."

"I can't do that. Besides, she's all alone. She hasn't got any family . . ." Lilah began.

"Let somebody else take care of her. With Stella in Alabama, you're going to have your hands full, anyway."

Realizing that he was absolutely right, Lilah admitted, "I know, but I honestly don't know what excuse to give her."

"Tell her we won't be here," Warren urged. There was just no way that he was going to permit Florence into the bosom of his family, especially on a holiday as important as Christmas. He was disgusted with himself for getting involved with her and having to buy her off. And it was probably all his fault for not being a better husband if, as Florence suggested, his wife was having an affair too.

"And we won't be here," he continued. "We'll go out to dinner. There's no reason for you to be drudging in the kitchen. I'll make a reservation at Samarkan . . . the kids will love it. You sit around big brass trays and eat with your fingers . . ."

Looking at him as if he'd suddenly sprouted a third eye, Lilah gasped, "Warren, are you serious? A Moroccan restaurant on Christmas Eve? Belly dancers instead of jingle bells?"

Warming to his suggestion, Warren continued. "Well, why not? Let's do something just for fun. Then we can talk . . . really talk to the kids. You won't be jumping up and down putting food on the table . . . doing dishes. Let's show them we're not a couple of old bumps on the log."

Overwhelmed by his rare burst of spontaneity and adventure, Lilah agreed to do what he wanted, but when she told Mary Ann and Matthew, they protested.

"That's the dumbest idea I ever heard. I want to sit in front of the fire and open our presents, just like we always do," Mary Ann protested.

"Yeah, so do I. Besides, if we're not at home, we'll miss the guys singing Christmas carols," Matthew added.

Finding herself now in the middle of a family crisis, Lilah rebelled. "Well, it's just too bad. I'm casting my ballot with your father. It's very seldom that he flies in the face of tradition, and frankly I don't intend to discourage him. We'll have an early dinner at Samarkan, and then we'll have dessert in front of the fire. Your father's Aunt Emily sent one of her special fruitcakes from Texas."

"Yuck, fruitcake," Mary Ann complained. "I hope there's some ice cream in the fridge to drown it in."

"Okay." Matthew grinned. "I'll go along on one condition. I get to put the money in the belly dancer's G-string."

Lilah had only one more hill to climb. She dialed

Florence, wondering why Warren had become intolerant of her presence in their house. She had invited her for drinks only because every other time she had suggested including Florence in any social activities, Warren had vetoed it.

When Florence answered the telephone, Lilah explained that Warren had suggested they eat out so that she wouldn't have to fuss with cooking.

"Well, that's unusually thoughtful of him, don't you think?" Florence commented.

Lilah could tell she was annoyed, and it disturbed her. She needed to keep on good terms with Florence until the trip to California was over. "I'm really sorry, Florence. You know I'd love to have you here with us."

"It's fine, Lilah. Most people don't want to be bothered with single women hanging around. Single men are desired guests, but women are a pain in the ass. There are just too damned many of us," Florence replied, and there was a lot of bitterness in her voice. She enjoyed making her friend feel guilty.

"Are we still on for January fifth?" Lilah asked, changing the subject. "I made our reservations on American, first-class. And I've got a deluxe room for you at the Beverly Wilshire Hotel. I understand it's beautiful."

"Lilah, aren't you going to give me even a little hint as to where you'll be? You know, of course, that I seriously suspect you're having an affair, for which I wouldn't blame you one iota, with that stick-in-the-mud of a husband you've got."

"It has nothing to do with Warren . . . and I'm not having an affair; you know me better than that. No, if you really want to know, I'm on a secret mission for the CIA. They want me to find out if those kids with the weird punk hairdos are really Martians trying to infiltrate our society."

"Okay, okay. Have your fun, but remember you promised to pay all of my expenses?"

"That's agreed, and I want you to enjoy yourself. I've taken some money out of my trust fund from my grandmother, so you can live it up. Just no merchandise on the hotel bill, okay?"

"I wouldn't do anything like that. Is the story still that you're going to visit me in Florida?"

"Yes, but I haven't broken the news to Warren yet. I'm waiting for the opportune time."

"Well, good luck. Suppose he says you can't go."

"Warren doesn't tell me what to do."

"Have a Merry Christmas, my dear. Call me when you have time. I'll be here, alone as usual."

"Merry Christmas, Florence." Lilah put the telephone down, glad to bring the conversation to an end.

Warren's suggestion that they go to a restaurant turned out to be serendipitous. Matthew and Mary Ann enjoyed the food, especially the b'stea, a flaky sugared crust with chicken and raisins inside. They all drank some of the sweet wine, and Warren was more relaxed than he had been in a long time. Lilah was surprised when he took her hand and held it while they watched the dancer, and she was startled when he held her fingertips to his lips and kissed them. His unusual public display of affection did not go unnoticed by their son and daughter.

"Say, Dad, looks like you and Mom are getting along fine without us," Matthew said slyly.

"Just because we're parents doesn't mean we still aren't lovers, Matt. I hope you're as lucky in choosing a wife as I was," Warren said.

Lilah was surprised at his candor. In all their married years she had never heard her husband say a word in front of their children that would indicate he'd ever touched her in a carnal way. She would have welcomed his words if they had come at another time, but now they made her feel even guiltier for deceiving him about her trip to California. As the dancer whirled around them to the beat of the drum, jingling the bells on her fingers, Lilah wondered what her family would say if they knew her secret. How much would their life be changed?

Later that evening, when the packages had all been opened and the house was quiet, Lilah and Warren were lying side by side in their bed when she felt Warren's hand gently caressing her back.

"I love you," he whispered. She turned toward him, and they kissed each other gently at first, and she reflected on how comfortable it was to be in his arms. Their lovemaking was tender and leisurely until her mind flashed onto the horror story that her sister had told her about the brutality of Craig Kimball. Suddenly she found herself ascending to a wild and long climax, and Warren joined her in his. When it was over, they held each other closely, saying nothing. Warren was pleased and satisfied, but Lilah nestled her head into his shoulder and fretted silently. How could she possibly have been fantasizing about being raped and brutalized? Good God, what was happening to her? Had she no shame?

26

ROSE looked up from the script she was reading and exclaimed, "Son of a bitch! Benjie . . . have you read this thing yet?"

Ben, who was lounging on the chaise in Rose's dressing room, did not look up from his copy of *Variety* as he replied, "No . . . haven't had a chance yet."

"Well, here, read it now. We've got a problem."

Ben was suddenly alert. He sat up and took the script from her hands. They were both silent as he scanned the pages quickly. "Jesus," he whispered.

"What do you think?" she asked, and there were deep furrows of worry between her eyebrows.

"Frankly I'm afraid of it," Ben answered, and got up to pace the room. "I'm not sure the heartland is ready for this, at least not in prime time."

"Ben, are they trying to knock me off the show? You know, public distaste could hurt the show and be especially damaging to me. Is this a deliberate setup?"

"It doesn't make sense. You've become the star attraction on that show. The public loves you. Why would they want to put you in that kind of a situation?"

"That kid looks like he's only thirteen or fourteen!" Rose fumed.

"He's actually nineteen years old, babe."

"Yeah, but his character is only a kid—and he's so white. I know some people think it's okay for an older woman to teach a young man, but that's not the story line here. I'm doing it only to get revenge on his mother. Ugh, I hate it, Benjie. The public's getting a little fed up with this sex stuff. I'm even a little worried about the scenes I've done in bed with white adults. This could very well be attacked as child pornography."

"You're right."

"What are we going to do?" Rose asked nervously. "After that big blowup about my not wanting to work with Craig Kimball . . . good God, Benjie, you don't suppose he's behind this, do you?"

"Now cut that out. Jesus, the way you talk, Craig Kimball knows all, sees all, screws all. No, I think somebody just got carried away. Bruce should be on the set. Let me ask him to come in here and explain it to us."

Ben left the dressing room immediately and returned with a tall, portly young man whose skin seemed to be stretched too tightly across his shiny pink face.

Bruce Stebbins was the man who had sold the concept of *Broadway* to the network and was credited with being its creator and producer. His boyish countenance had misled many into believing that he was naive, for although his demeanor was gentle and soft-spoken, he had the instincts of a cobra and was just as deadly when he was crossed.

"Okay, Lady Rose, what's the problem this time?" he asked wearily.

His attitude sent Rose into a fury. "Don't give me that long-suffering patient 'this time,' goddammit! This is only the second time I've complained about anything, and I think it's damned rotten of you to act as if I'm some kind of a problem star—"

"Okay, Rose, that's enough. We've got a situation that's a problem for everybody, not just you. I'm not sure Bruce will understand your concerns," Ben said smoothly, and then continued, "Have a seat over here there beside Rose, and we'll talk about it."

Bruce settled his bulk into the small boudoir chair to hear his star's latest complaint.

Before Rose could speak, Ben began. "Bruce, this script for next week's shoot calls for a love . . . uh, sex scene between Caymen Welles and Brian Webster. Don't you think that's a little risky?"

"What do you mean?"

"Come on, don't act so innocent, Bruce. Brian is a kid . . . and he's white. An affair between him and Caymen Welles, who by the way is black, might not wash with the American public. You should know that as well as I do. Who the hell wrote this stuff?" Rose interjected.

"Len Skinner. And I understand your concerns, really I do, but the idea was tossed around at staff meeting, and it's a go with everybody. Maybe if it had been one of those younger writers who had come up with the idea, we might have looked at it a little harder, but Len Skinner is no liberal, and if he thinks it'll be okay, I'm sure that it will."

"*Merde.* Of course, it's no skin off his ass if the public turns on me. I'm the one who has to take the risk," Rose snapped angrily.

"She's right, you know. Aren't you at all concerned about protecting her? The ratings have been sky-high ever since her first appearance," Ben insisted.

"That's completely true, but it's caused a bit of a problem for us, and that's why we brought in Len Skinner to write a few transition scripts for us. Frankly we weren't prepared for you to be the big hit that you've become, and let's face it, you're a problem for the writers. If the character of Caymen Welles is going to continue to get badder and naughtier with each episode, we've got to come up with more shockers. You can't be a sexy villainess without some outrageous screwing here and there. I really didn't expect to get this kind of complaint from you. After all, they've been doing this kind of thing in French movies for years."

"Yeah, man, but it's different in a movie theater than it is in somebody's living room," Ben interjected.

"I hope, for everybody's sake, that it flies," Bruce continued, "but if it doesn't . . ."

"Good-bye Caymen Welles," Rose finished. "I won't do it, Bruce. I'll walk off the show first. At least I'll be quitting while I'm on top and the public still likes me."

"Okay, Rose, that's enough! You're not walking off the show—not yet, anyway," Ben said.

The producer smiled. "Listen to him, Rose. He knows what he's talking about. It took Farrah Fawcett years to recover from walking off *Charlie's Angels*, ditto for Suzanne Somers and *Three's Company*, and they were . . . blond. Well, I've got to get going. Some of the network boys from New York are here visiting. Be very nice to them when I bring them over to talk to you later." He got to his feet and smiled broadly before walking out the door.

When he was gone, Rose threw herself down on the chaise angrily. "That bastard! I ought to walk off the show and tell the press that they wanted me to participate in child abuse on the screen and I just wouldn't compromise my principles. What do you think?"

"I honestly don't know. There's always the possibility that it won't create any kind of a stir at all. It's my guess that they expect it will, and they're counting on a stir of some kind to create publicity. The only problem is that you're the one who's going to take the heat if it blows up in their faces."

"Swell."

"I'm sorry, baby. I'm not doing so well taking care of you lately, am I?"

"Benjie, is there some chance that this episode could be shown before we start filming the one with Kimball?"

Ben shook his head.

"Too bad. Well, let's not worry about it. Look how the public embraced Archie Bunker, and that was a big surprise."

"Yeah, but unfortunately there were a lot of viewers who didn't see him as a bigot. They agreed with his prejudices and were happy to hear somebody say them out loud," Ben observed.

"Maybe so, but I'm going to go ahead and be daring about this. If I'm going out, I'm going out with a bang . . . hey, get it? I made a joke," she said, putting her arms around him and kissing him on the back of the neck.

Ben laughed and jumped to his feet. "Well, I'd better stop lolling around here and get going. I want you signed to as many endorsement contracts as possible before this thing hits the fan. Would you object if we move the filming of that commercial up a few weeks? The perfume company is eager to get it in the can so they can start using it while *Broadway* is on top."

"Be my guest. I'll work night and day from now until then. We'll start putting the money away for a rainy day. And I've changed my mind about playing Vegas. Take the Caesar's Palace thing and push it up to April," she said.

"Hey, you haven't got an act or costumes or anything yet!" he protested.

"Hell, all I need is a writer who can put out a few lines to string the songs together. What did I do in Paris all those years? Hire an arranger to do a couple of new songs to work around the old material and arrange to rent the costumes from the show. God, there are enough sequins and rhinestones in my *Broadway* wardrobe to do six shows."

"Great idea, baby. Great idea! The folks on vacation will love to see those dresses in the flesh," he exclaimed, and gathered her in his arms.

"Watch the makeup, honey," Rose cautioned.

"You amaze me, you know that?" he asked.

"Why?"

"Well, most of the time you're sweet and sensitive and kind of like a child who needs to be cared for, but every now and then you get pretty aggressive, like my old drill sergeant."

"Benjie, baby," she said, kissing him lightly on the tip of the nose, "a kid can't survive in the entertainment business and stay a kid . . . but I like having you take care of me, because you're so damn good at it."

"I got an idea."

"What's that?"

"I'm going to take that woman out for a drink . . . maybe even dinner."

"What woman?" Rose asked suspiciously.

"You know. What's her name . . . the watchdog. The one everybody hates . . . the censor."

"It's Rachel, um . . . something."

"Yeah. I think she might be interested in how this whole thing might look to middle America. I'll ask her to stay on the set that week."

Rose looked at Ben appreciatively and smiled.

"Benjie, I'm glad you're on my side," she said.

27

EVERYONE slept late on Christmas morning except Lilah, who got up early to clear away the mess of wrapping papers, boxes, and ribbons, and to prepare a hearty breakfast since dinner at Warren's parents' wouldn't be served until late afternoon. As she was cutting the wedges of grapefruit she suddenly found Warren's arms around her. What was going on? It was so unlike him to be affectionate outside the bedroom.

He kissed her on the neck and reached around and slipped a package into the pocket of her apron. "Santa came back last night while you were asleep and left this," he whispered into her ear.

Lilah held the small package, which had been beautifully wrapped in silver-and-red paper, and asked, "For me? Should I open it now?"

"It's Christmas, isn't it?"

They sat down at the table in the breakfast room, and she carefully pulled the paper off. Inside was a purple velvet ring box. Warren had never bought jewelry for her before. She looked up at him questioningly. "This isn't one of those solid-gold golf tees, is it?" she asked.

"Open it. What are you waiting for?" he urged.

When she lifted the lid of the box, shining up at her was a magnificent ring with a large center stone of a bright canary hue surrounded by diamonds set in gold.

She gasped, "My God, Warren, it's beautiful. It's the most beautiful ring I've ever seen!"

Her reaction was all that he had hoped it would be. "I'm glad you like it. I knew when I saw that diamond, I had to buy it for you. It reminded me of the color of your eyes."

"Good heavens, Warren, that's a diamond? It's so big!" she exclaimed.

"It's called a canary diamond because of the color, and it's almost six carats. It's an excellent stone. At least that's what the jeweler told me, and he's a very reliable man."

Lilah took the ring from the box and started to slip it on her finger but stopped. She handed the ring to her husband and said, "You put it on for me, Warren," and held out her hand. Warren slipped it on the third finger of her right hand. It fit perfectly.

Kissing him gently on the lips, she ran her fingers through his thick, wavy hair and tucked her head on his shoulder. Although she was tall, Warren towered over her.

"Thank you so much, darling," she murmured. "It's the loveliest thing I've ever owned." For a brief moment she was tempted to tell him about Rose, but she restrained herself. This was not the time. She must not spoil their holiday with what he would surely consider unsettling news, to say the very least.

Later, after they had all had breakfast together and everyone was getting showered and dressed for the trip to the elder Conways' mansion in River Forest, Lilah sat at her dressing table and contemplated her new bauble. In spite of its magnificence, it depressed her. It was cruel that Warren should choose this particular time to be thoughtful and generous. Why couldn't he have presented her with something uninspiring like a new putter or a leather golf bag, as he usually did? It would be so much easier to deceive him if he stayed true to form. For years she had wished he would be a little more romantic and less practical, but he had certainly picked a terrible time to start.

Studying herself in the dressing-table mirror, she held the ring next to her eyes. The color wasn't quite the same, but she was flattered that he saw a similarity. As she looked at the face that was so familiar, her secret surfaced again. Silently she ran the tip of her fingers along the narrow ridge that wound around the perimeter of her full lips. Why had it never before occurred to her that her mouth might have a Negroid quality? Why had she never suspected anything when she looked at her own olive-skinned, tall figure or compared herself to the photographs of her blond, petite mother? Why had she never questioned the striking diference between herself and her porcelain-skinned grandmother?

Above all, why was she not devastated by the revelation that her father was black? Why did she feel untouched, concerned only by the effect it might have on her children? Would she have had this much equanimity if Rose Wilkins had been some poor black lady who cleaned houses for the stars instead of being one?

"Lilah, I can't find my clean shirts. Do you know where they are?" Warren called from the bedroom.

"I put them in your chest of drawers. I sent them to the laundry because of Stella's vacation, and they folded them by mistake," she answered, now roused from her reverie.

As she eased on her panty hose and hastened to get dressed, she mused again upon Warren's sudden outbreak of generosity and thoughtfulness. Her grandmother's words of caution flitted through her mind: "Beware of spouses bearing extravagant gifts. They're probably just trying to salve a guilty conscience," and she laughed out loud. If there was one certainty in her life, it was Warren's faithfulness. Other men might cheat on their wives but not Warren. In spite of his attractiveness to women, he was far too prim and proper to do anything like that . . . ever.

When they returned that evening from the elder Conways', Lilah decided to bite the bullet and break the news about her planned trip. As soon as Matt and Mary Ann retired to their rooms to telephone their friends and gloat over their abundance of gifts, Lilah asked Warren if he would like a brandy. He declined.

"I'll pour one for you if you like, but I've got several early appointments tomorrow, and I'm full of eggnog."

"I'd like one. Want some tea . . . or decaf?" she replied. She knew she needed something to get her over the coming ordeal; lying was not easy for her. Her grandfather had often remarked that her mind was always perched on the tip of her tongue.

When they were seated in the living room, lit only by the twinkling lights on the Christmas tree, Lilah plunged immediately into the story she had rehearsed a thousand times in her mind. "Warren, I've decided to take a little vacation."

This is it, Warren thought, but he did not intend to make it easy for her. "Fine, where shall we go?"

"Not us . . . me. Florence is going down to Florida, and she wants me to join her there for a week or ten days. I know how she irritates you, but I enjoy her company. We've been friends for a long time. And I'm so tired of cold weather. Besides, we're together so much that I thought maybe we ought to have a little time . . . apart." She knew he was looking directly at her, but she could not raise her eyes to meet his and instead kept peering into her brandy snifter. She felt miserable. Warren did not deserve to be lied to.

"Is something wrong, Lilah? Are you upset with me about something?" Surely, he thought, if she knew anything about his transgressions, she would voice it now.

"Of course not, Warren. It's just that I want to lie on the beach and vegetate, that's all. Since we got married, we've never been separated for more than a night or two at a time, and it's always you who goes away on business. Just for once I'd like to take a little trip of my own. Is that wrong?" She finally forced herself to look into his eyes, and she was surprised at the misery she found there. Why would this be so painful for him?

"When are you going?"

"The fifth of January. Just for a week or ten days . . . that's all."

Quietly Warren got up and said he was going to bed. She did not follow him.

For a long time she sat alone, sipping her brandy and feeling wretched. Warren had been a wonderful husband and father. After her disaster in Moscow, Warren had been her salvation and her retreat. When the truth about her family was revealed, would he stand by her and love her as he had for the past twenty years? If she were really sure of his love and devotion, why had she not told him the truth when she first learned it?

As she climbed the stairs to bed Lilah began thinking about her coming adventure, and the cloud of depression and uncertainty suddenly lifted. She was doing this to help Rose, but there was no denying the urge she felt to taste the wine of celebrity. After all these years she would have a moment of stardom, and even though it wouldn't really be hers and it wouldn't be on the concert stage, it was going to be fun.

She must not let Warren's temporary unhappiness spoil things. After all, she was doing nothing wrong.

28

THE cast and crew of *Broadway* called it a wrap at seven o'clock on Christmas Eve. Ben was waiting in the limousine when Rose emerged from the studio, still wearing makeup and dressed in a pair of slacks and a sweater.

"*Mon Dieu,* Benjie, I wish we could call this thing off tonight. I'm exhausted." She let her body drop heavily onto the upholstered seat.

"I know, baby, I know, and I really feel awful dragging you out like this, but I don't think we ought to cancel at the last minute. Socializing is part of the business in this town."

"I know, I know. Pick up the telephone and call Mae and tell her to have the tub ready and lay out the red-beaded Oscar de la Renta for me."

He smiled and leaned over to kiss her forehead lightly. "It's already done."

She turned her large eyes on him in wonder. "Hey! How'd you know that was the dress I was going to wear tonight?"

"Elementary, my dear Ms. Watson, it's your favorite . . . and it's Christmas-red."

"Who else is going to be there?" she asked.

"I tried to find out, but nobody seems to know. Everyone I asked said they hadn't been invited. I even called Mavis Madden at the newspaper, and she said she wasn't going, either, and hadn't heard a word about it."

"That's strange. Kam Freedland never sneezes without calling up every newspaper in town to tell them about it."

"Maybe it's going to be very small and intimate, it being Christmas Eve and all," Ben suggested.

"Forget that. It might be small, but it won't be intimate. The Freedlands only entertain heavyweights. I told Stan where I was going, and he said I could now count myself as being in the *A* group of Los Angeles society . . . movieland-style, of course," Rose said.

"Interesting. I've always wanted to meet the old buzzard and see that mansion of his. You know, nobody knows for sure where Vance Freedland came from or where he got the money to start building his empire of shopping centers and office buildings. I talked to several newspapermen, and they speculate that his investment capital, which I understand amounted to millions, was all money that was laundered out of the rackets back East."

"How old is he?"

"Eighty at least, but he's only been on the Los Angeles scene for twenty years or so. He came out here, built that huge house in Bel Air, and then started handing out money to the local charities in big chunks, which is a sure method of buying his way into society here in L.A., or most anywhere, I guess. They tell me that anybody who ever turns down an invitation to one of his parties, no matter what the reason, gets wiped off his list and is never invited again."

"Guess we'd better go, then. By the way, Beth gave me a little tidbit of gossip today," Rose said, smiling.

"And what's that?"

"She told me they're going to have a different famous designer do the clothes for each show."

"What do you mean?"

"Well, it's super secret, but Oscar has agreed to start it off. Bill Blass is next . . . and so on. She said she wasn't sure, but she thought that Armani had also indicated that he was interested in participating."

"Wheeo, what a gimmick. It's great."

"Too bad I might not be around to enjoy it."

"What are you talking about?"

"There's too much stacked against me, Ben. Let's face it. First there's that business with me sleeping with Brian on the show . . . and then Craig Kimball. I want to believe that Lilah will carry it off, but—"

"Wait a minute. You're the one who was so positive Lilah could handle it. I was the one who said it wouldn't work. Don't you think it's about time you called the whole thing off and faced him yourself?"

"I'm giving it some serious thought, Ben. I really am. I'm not sure I ought to get Lilah involved in something that's so obviously my own personal problem. After all, what could the son of a bitch do to me in front of everybody?" she said, but the tone of her voice did not reflect the confidence of her words.

An hour later, dressed beautifully, Rose and Ben arrived in their limousine at a pair of very tall ornate iron gates brightly trimmed with colored Christmas lights. Their driver spoke into a microphone concealed in a large boulder. "Miss Lady Rose and Mr. Ben Frost," he announced.

"When the gates open, enter immediately and take the first turn to the right. Follow the road to the circle and drop your party at the entrance, then continue around and park the car at the carriage entrance. All drivers are to remain in their cars. A porter will bring you some refreshments," a disembodied voice commanded from the rock.

Suddenly the tension they were feeling disappeared as Rose and Ben laughed at the ridiculous talking rock. "Thus spake Zarathustra," Ben intoned mockingly.

The car drove up the tree-lined road to the top of a hill, and suddenly an enormous Georgian mansion loomed before them. A giant pine tree, covered with

lights, tinsel, and ornaments, reaching some forty feet
into the sky, stood in the grass-covered center of the
paved circle. As the car inched its way behind the
other limousines toward the long portico, Rose gasped,
"My God, Benjie, it looks like the White House!"

"So I see, except that it's bigger and more luxurious," he replied, "and since it's only twenty years old,
probably a lot more comfortable. I understand the art
inside is worth millions. Freedland's already hinted
that it will be donated as a museum when he and his
wife depart this mortal coil."

"Like Getty?"

"Maybe, but I don't think he's got that kind of
bucks."

"You don't think crime pays as much as oil?"

As they reached the portico a liveried doorman
helped them out of the car and directed them to enter
through the tall doors. They crossed the marble floor
and stepped through the impressive doorway into a
massive foyer, decorated profusely with Christmas gar-
lands and glittering lights. Rose was able to detect at a
glance that the paintings on the walls, in baroque gold
frames, were from the best of the French Impres-
sionist era, and she was truly awed.

A butler took her white mink coat and led them into
a large library where expensively dressed guests were
standing about holding brilliantly cut crystal glasses
and chatting softly. There was about the group an air
of quiet, which was unusual for people gathered together to consume spirits and celebrate the holidays.

Both Ben and Rose felt a little uneasy. "Are you
sure this is the right house?" Rose whispered, and Ben
replied quietly, "Beats the hell out of me. I think so,
but there's not a soul here that I know." "Me, neither," she remarked.

A butler offered them a drink from a tray of the tall
crystal champagne glasses, and Rose quickly took one.
Before Ben had a chance to taste his, she took a large
swallow and grimaced in surprise.

"Why are you making that awful face?" Ben asked, hoping that nobody would notice.

"It's ginger ale!" she said in a voice louder than she had intended.

Several people around them smiled knowingly, and a man remarked, "This must be her first time here."

A beautiful young woman with bright blond hair approached them smiling. Her gray chiffon gown barely concealed a voluptuously endowed figure. "Vance disapproves of alcohol. And tobacco," she said by way of greeting. "I'm so sorry. If it were up to me, it really would be champagne."

"Oh?" Rose replied, and smiled. "By the way, I'm Lady Rose, and this is my manager Ben Frost."

"Yes, I know. I'm Kam Freedland, and I'm glad you could come. I think you're terrific on *Broadway,* although I must admit I've only seen it once. We're out almost every night, and I don't get to watch television very often. Let me introduce you to a few of our friends."

Their hostess was just about to take them around the room when a tall, heavyset man lumbered toward them. He had the jowls and dewlap of a bassett hound, and his eyes were equally doleful. His voice, however, was high-pitched with a Capote-like whispery quality. "Well, well, how nice of you to accept my invitation," he said, taking Rose's hand and lifting it briefly to his thick and rubbery lips. "I am, by the way, Vance Freedland, and I see you've met my beautiful wife."

Rose was overwhelmed by the enormous size of the man. "How do you do? I'm Lady Rose, and this—" she began, but he interrupted.

"Ah, yes, Ben Frost, of course. Your reputation precedes you, Mr. Frost. I've heard about some of the deals you've been putting together for the beautiful lady, and I must say I'm very impressed. Now, come with me. It's time to go into dinner. The cocktail hour here is short"—he winked slightly—"for reasons I'm sure you already know, but you're in for a treat, nevertheless. My chef has outdone himself tonight, and the dinner shall be superb. Come, everyone, follow me," he said, and the group of about fifty people began to move out of the huge library where thirty-foot-high shelves were filled with leather-bound and color-coordinated books that looked as if they had never been opened.

A tall gray-haired woman leaned close to Rose and whispered in her ear, "The dinner will be spectacular, my dear, and he always has a precious little bauble for the ladies to make up for the lack of fine wines."

A look of amusement passed between the two women as the host beckoned to Rose and said in his strangely tiny voice, "My dear, I want to get to know you better, so I have arranged for you to sit beside me. Will you take my arm?"

Rose took his arm, and they led the way into the immense dining room, which looked as if it had been brought piece by piece directly from some European castle. One long table, richly set with brilliant crystal, heavy silver service plates, and china on which was emblazoned a coat of arms, stretched the length of the room. More than two dozen white-gloved waiters stood at attention, waiting to help everyone to be seated.

"This is my truly private party of the year, my dear," the host said to Rose confidentially as they proceeded slowly across the room. Rose looked up at the high-domed ceiling and was awed by its immensity and the brightly colored and embroidered banners hanging from stone battlements. She felt as if she were taking part in an Arthurian pageant. She was listening attentively to her host, however, and she asked, "Why is it so private?"

"Well, you see, Christmas is a lonely time for those like myself who were never blessed with children, and so every year I invite—from all over the world, I might add—those of my friends who have no offspring. I am honored that you and Mr. Frost have accepted my humble invitation to be a part of my family on this holiest of nights." His manner was courtly, and Rose smiled up at him warmly.

"I'm honored to be included, and I'm simply overwhelmed by the magnificence of your house. I see that you're an admirer of the French Impressionists, as I am."

"Ah, yes, so you noticed. I would like for you to come for tea some afternoon, and we'll walk through the house and examine them at leisure. It's like entering another world, a world of beauty and freedom from care. Would you like that, my dear?"

They had arrived at the head of the table, and without waiting for a response her host helped her into the chair at his right. He then settled his massive bulk into a huge chair that looked as if it had been purloined from the throne room of a medieval palace.

Vance Freedland devoted all his attention to Rose as he engaged her in a conversation about art collecting while they waited for the others to find their assigned places. When at last everyone was seated, without rising to his feet the host held his glass aloft and proposed a toast, "Welcome to my home, and a Merry Christmas to you all. Enjoy."

He lifted a glass of cranberry juice to his lips, and there was a murmur among the guests as they repeated the words *Merry Christmas* and took a drink of the bright red liquid that looked so much like wine yet tasted so different. Rose glanced down the table to see where Ben was seated and saw that he was near the center. She smiled and lifted her glass to toast him, but she was disconcerted by the expression on his face, which had turned as cold and frozen as his last name. She wondered what was wrong.

Suddenly the man who had been seated to her right leaned toward her and said very softly, "And so we meet again."

She turned quickly, carried back twenty years by the sound of the voice that had just spoken, and she found

herself staring into the time-ravaged face of the devil
who still dominated her nightmares.

"You!" she gasped in a voice just loud enough to
command the attention of those seated nearby.

Craig Kimball smiled the smile that had endeared
him to moviegoers for more than a third of a century
and replied, "My dear, I'm flattered that you remember me. I shall never forget you." As he spoke, he ran
his index finger lightly along the scar on his cheek.

Ben stared in horror at the woman he loved and saw
that she was about to shatter into a thousand pieces.
Without waiting, he got to his feet and rushed to her.
Gently he put his arm around her and lifted her to a
standing position as he murmured to his startled host,
"I'm sorry, but I'm afraid we'll have to go. We should
never have come, but Lady Rose thought it would be
rude to cancel at the last minute. She's been ill, and
I'd better get her out of here before she collapses.
Please accept our apologies."

Without waiting for a response, Ben moved Rose
out of the chair and away from the table. They were
out of the room before anyone realized exactly what
was happening. Rose's legs were so weak, they would
not support her weight, and so Ben half carried her
into the foyer. Quickly her coat was brought by the
attendant, and they rushed out to their limousine.

Rose was near hysteria, and Ben held her to stop
the shaking. "I was right all along. He's still furious
with me. He's going to kill me, I know it," she managed to whisper at last, through a throat already stran-
gled with fear.

"No, he's not going to kill you, but your fear of him
will. As soon as I saw the look on your face, I knew I
had to get you out of there."

Suddenly she burst into tears and pressed her face
into his shoulder. "What am I going to do . . . what
am I going to do . . . what am I going to do?" she
repeated hysterically, over and over.

Ben held her and patted her and tried to console

her, but she was totally shaken and unable to control the hysteria brought on by the sudden proximity of the man she most feared.

"Rose, baby, stop it! Pull yourself together now. Don't let him do this to you. You've got to fight it, honey, understand? If you give in to it, he'll have won. C'mon now, you haven't got anything to be afraid of. You're not a scared little teenager trying to make it in Hollywood alone anymore. You're a star. And you've got me. I won't let anybody hurt you . . . I promise."

An hour later Rose was lying in her bed. Ben had undressed her and given her a glass of champagne to wash down one of the tranquilizers he kept for emergencies. Feeling relaxed at last, she smiled up at him as he sat beside her gently stroking her forehead with a damp cloth.

"Thanks, Benjie. I couldn't make it without you."

"You're stronger than you think, honey. You're a survivor, remember?"

"You think that Vance Freedland will ever invite us back again?" she asked drowsily.

"Who the hell cares?"

"Benjie, that was the first time you ever saw Craig Kimball in person. What did you think?"

"I'm a little surprised."

"Like how?"

"Well, I know him only from seeing him on the screen. And up there he's funny and warm and amusing and interesting to watch . . . at least, he was when he was young, but in person he's different, totally different. Of course, maybe I'm just being influenced by what you've told me."

"How different?" she asked.

"He looks like he eats glass."

"He does, Benjie, he does," she said as her eyes started to close.

When he was certain that she was sleeping soundly, Ben left the room and sat down in the study with a stiff glass of brandy and thought about the evening behind him. His belief in a divine order was now more reinforced than ever. God had a good reason when he gave Rose a twin sister. Now it was up to him to do everything in his power to help her make the switch successfully. Rose's career in television depended on it. Suddenly he had an idea, and he wondered just how far Lilah was prepared to go in the coming charade, and if she would be willing to help him carry it through.

29

CRAIG Kimball sat in the Century City office of Vance Freedland and looked out toward the north at the mountains that separated the city from the Valley. It was a clear winter day; the sun was shining and the temperature was seventy degrees. Kimball was annoyed that he had been summoned here when he had intended to spend the day on his boat. Claire was occupied with her friends at a luncheon at the Music Center, and he had invited a group to come aboard the yacht to play a little poker.

The door opened, and Vance Freedland lumbered into the room like a giant grizzly and lowered himself into the oversize leather chair behind the highly polished mahogany desk.

"Jesus Christ, didn't you put on a clean suit before you came here?" were the huge man's first words.

Kimball was disconcerted. He was immaculately groomed, as always, in a navy-blue blazer and gray slacks. "What are you talking about?"

"Cigarettes . . . goddamned cigarettes. You reek of smoke and now, so does this room. Have you got any idea how nasty you smell?"

The actor was tired of being insulted. "Is that why you brought me here . . . to berate me about smoking? You know it's really none of your business what I do. Now get to the point. I've got friends waiting for me in the marina."

"I want to know what's with you and the little tar baby from that television show. You damned near ruined my party on Christmas Eve." Freedland's eyes narrowed to tight little slits, and it was obvious he was furious.

"There's nothing going on. She's just weird, that's all."

"Don't lie to me. You're the one who wanted her invited and asked to sit next to her. I thought you were just looking to screw her, but that's not it, is it?"

Craig Kimball clenched his fists together. He didn't want to talk about it, but he was afraid to lie to Vance Freedland. He owed him too much.

"It's old news. I met her when she was struggling to make it here in Hollywood. I gave her her big chance, but the little cunt turned on me and did this." He stroked the scar on his cheek.

"Why? What were you doing to her?"

"Nothing she wasn't enjoying," Kimball replied sullenly.

"Listen, don't give me that stuff. I know all about your encounters in Vegas. And I don't care. What you have to do to get your rocks off is none of my concern. But when you bring your little problems into my house, in front of my guests, then it becomes my business. Do you understand me? Now get your ass out of here before I decide to finish off what that little nigger started to do to you."

Kimball got to his feet and, hoping to recapture his dignity after the humiliating verbal assault, said, "Well, I'll look forward to seeing you at the Annenbergs' New Year's Eve party in Palm Springs. I understand that both the governor and the president are attending."

"Yes, I'll be there, but you won't. Send your regrets today. I don't want you around to remind me of the debacle you made of my Christmas party. And take a little advice. You'd better quit drinking so much liquor. That pretty face of yours is starting to look like the map of hell."

Craig Kimball hurried out of the skyscraper offices. His driver was waiting in the Rolls to take him to the boat, but he decided to go home and break the news to Claire before somebody else did. She was going to be furious.

As he rode, his anger at Lady Rose grew in its intensity. Now, more than ever, he had to find some way to fix that black bitch once and for all.

By the time his wife returned home from her luncheon, the aging actor was soused. Sitting in the large leather chair in his study, he had consumed glass after glass of Scotch, brooding on his problems, dreaming dreams of revenge, anticipating with dread his wife's reaction to being cut out of the party she considered the most important of the year.

"What are you doing at home? I thought you had a poker game scheduled on the boat?" she demanded.

"Didn' feel like goin'." He looked up at her and smiled. "Got a big surprise . . . we're not goin' to the Annenbergs'—" he began, but she interrupted him.

"What are you talking about? I've already bought a new gown. Of course we're going."

"No . . . we're not. I called 'em today and canceled."

Claire looked at the wreck of a man whom the public found so charming and debonair and talented, and wanted to throw up. God, how had she ever allowed herself to get trapped into a marriage with him? "Why would you do something as foolish as that?" she asked, and there was anger and menace in her voice.

"Decided I didn' want to go . . . thass all. Now fuck off."

"Don't use that kind of language with me. Now, you wanted to go to that party as much as I did. Why aren't we going?" She had changed her tactics and was speaking in a kinder and more reasonable tone of voice.

Kimball hesitated for a moment, then muttered, "Vance doesn't want us there."

Claire was startled. "Vance? What the devil has he got to do with . . ." Suddenly she remembered the scene at the Freedlands' dining room table. "Craig! Did you have anything to do with that woman leaving the dinner before it started? Did you know her?"

Her husband lifted his glass and drained the liquor. He held it toward her and said, "Pour me another."

"No. You've already had too much. Now answer my question."

"Go fuck yourself."

Claire walked toward him and stood glaring down at him. "Don't ever talk to me like that again, do you understand? We have an agreement, in writing, that you will treat me with respect at all times, remember?"

"Only in public, only in public. I can say any damn thing I want to you in the privacy of my"—he hiccuped—"home."

She stared at him with loathing and then whirled on her heel and left the room in a fury. Damn him! This was not the first time she had regretted getting involved with Craig Kimball, but it was getting close to the last. She had an agreement with him, and if he didn't watch out, he would find himself not only in the divorce court but in the deepest mess imaginable. All she had to do was blow the whistle on him and goodbye sexy movie-star image, hello, impotent old sadistic faker.

She paced around her elaborate and pristine bedroom, which her husband was never allowed to enter, pondering the problem. Her status would be seriously lowered if she didn't appear at that party. Everyone would assume they hadn't been invited. She picked up the telephone and called Kam Freedland, the young and beautiful actress who had given up her career to be the pampered darling of a rich and powerful man. Claire and Kam had a lot in common, except that Kam had to go to bed with her disgusting old man, a chore Claire had been spared.

"Kam, darling, it's Claire Kimball. I just called to

thank you again for that delightful party the other evening," she said, opening the conversation.

"Glad you enjoyed it. What did you think of the gifts Vance chose this year? I thought they were terrific."

"Absolutely spectacular. I couldn't believe it when I opened the package. Where did he ever find so many pairs of pearl earrings that big?"

"Mikimoto's in Tokyo has been working on it for almost a year. Vance just loves to do that kind of thing. So what's up?"

"I've got a little problem. Craig just told me that he'd canceled out on the Annenbergs' New Year's Eve thing because Vance didn't want him to go. Have you got any idea why?"

"God, can't you guess? Vance was totally pissed off about Lady Rose and her boyfriend walking out on the party, and I think somehow he blamed Craig. He said that she took one look at him and almost passed out. Vance had only invited her as a favor to your husband. That's all I know."

"Well, do you think it would look funny if I called and said that I'd like to go to the party by myself? After all, I have nothing to do with what goes on with my husband and some black actress."

There was a pause before Kam responded. "I don't know, Claire, although I'm sure Vance wouldn't like it. He totally disapproves of wives going anywhere without their husbands. He never lets me go to anything by myself. And that means I miss a lot of parties I'd really like to attend. Sorry."

"So am I. Well, Happy New Year, anyway. Maybe we'll be seeing each other again soon."

Claire put down the telephone, resisting a strong urge to throw it across the room. Damn men! She hated the bastards.

30

WARREN dialed Florence's number three times. The first two times he had disconnected the call as soon as he heard Florence's voice. On the third try, however, he said, "Florence, it's me, Warren."

"Thank God, Warren. Please say it was you calling the first two times. I get scared to death every time the telephone rings and nobody's on the line. Ever since my husband died, I worry about being set up by some maniac who knows I'm alone."

"I'm sorry I frightened you. Are you busy?"

"Not really. I was just doing my hair. I can't afford to go to the beauty shop," she replied. "What can I do for you?"

"I feel like such a fool asking you this," he said very softly, and then, "but I want to know where you and my wife are going."

"How much is it worth to you?" she asked after a long pause, and there was a trace of bitterness in her voice.

"How much do you want?" he replied, unwilling to degrade himself even more by bargaining.

"Is it worth resuming our relationship again, Warren? I'd rather have you than money, you know, even as poor as I am."

"Let's not go into that again."

Rebuffed, her voice hardened. "Since both you and your wife intend to use me, I think I should be paid for it. I want a thousand dollars for starters. If I uncover anything worthwhile, I'll want more, a lot more, especially if I find out exactly what she's up to. Agreed?"

There was a slight pause, and then Warren replied in a muffled voice, "Agreed."

"Good." Her tone was now brisk and businesslike. "We're leaving in the morning on American Airlines for Los Angeles. We'll separate at the airport there. She's booked me at the Beverly Wilshire Hotel. At this point I don't have any idea where she's going or who she'll be seeing, but it's very possible that I can do some sleuthing, especially if I can get her to keep in touch with me while we're out there."

"And she's given you no reason for this trip?"

"Not really. She just said she was feeling stifled and needed to be away on her own for a few days. I assume it's the same lame excuse she gave you."

"It must be the truth. I've never known her to lie about anything," Warren said, striving for conviction.

"Sure, and if asked, I'm certain she'd say also that her husband was faithful and true," Florence replied sarcastically.

"Florence, why are you so bitter?"

"Just go to hell!" she said angrily, and slammed down the telephone.

Warren had a strong urge to wash his hands. He felt dirty. Not only had he cheated on his wife, but now he was spying on her also. What a mess he had made of everything.

Feeling utterly miserable, Warren went into his study and sat down on the worn leather couch Lilah had chosen for him twenty years ago. He got up again and, pacing restlessly, went over to their wedding portrait, which was hanging on the wall beside his desk. He remembered how happy he had been the day Lilah accepted his marriage proposal. He had been so sure nothing would ever go wrong for him again.

As he walked through the darkened downstairs rooms

toward the kitchen, he thought how quiet and lonely the house was again now that Matthew and Mary Ann had gone back to school. He missed them. Was it possible for a man to suffer from the empty-nest syndrome, or was that the exclusive territory of women?

Suddenly Lilah walked into the kitchen carrying her empty coffee cup. "I thought you were watching TV. Would you like some decaf?" she asked.

"No . . . no thanks. I was just getting a glass of ice water. You go ahead and get ready. You have to get up early in the morning." He said it so wistfully that Lilah was touched. She put her arms around him, and for several moments they clung to each other.

"Come to bed . . . I need to hold you," he whispered huskily, and Lilah hesitated only slightly, thinking of all the things still undone. "I'll be right with you."

Their lovemaking was gentle and tender, and Warren tried to prolong it as much as he possibly could. When it was over, he did not withdraw but continued to hold her close until he at last fell asleep. Not wanting to disturb him, Lilah waited until his breathing finally became deep and regular, and then she slipped out of bed to finish her packing. She hated the thought that he was upset and depressed about her leaving, but it would be only temporary. Someday she would find the courage to tell him everything but not now, not yet. Nothing must spoil her trip.

31

BEN canceled all of their business and social engagements for three days after the encounter with Craig Kimball, not because Rose was so ill but because he figured he could use the incident to establish that she was not totally well, in case Lilah messed up during the filming of the series. He was now intensely committed to the plan the twins had concocted to prevent Rose from having to deal with Kimball. He even had begun to suspect, as Rose did, that Kimball had influenced the writing of the script to assure the maximum amount of physical contact between them. The incident at Vance Freedland's had convinced him the bastard still held a grudge.

When the series began filming again, Ben stayed close to the set, establishing that pattern so he could be at Lilah's side constantly when the switch was made. She was the linchpin in his plan, and if she couldn't perform the task properly, they would all be in trouble.

Rose was keyed up and excited the morning Lilah was scheduled to arrive.

"I just gave Mae and Clifton a couple of weeks off," Ben announced when she appeared for breakfast. "We don't need two more people knowing what's going on."

"Good idea. Maybe I ought to get out of town myself once Lilah starts working on the set."

"No way! You can't go trekkin' around the country. Somebody might see you," he declared.

"It might be a good idea if Lilah lived the part of being me all the time . . . just to keep her in the swing of things."

"I know it would be nice if you could get away for a little rest, but not now. Of course, Lilah has to think she's you, and we've got to help her."

Rose smiled and wrapped her arms around him. "You, on the other hand, better keep in mind at all times that she's not me," she said, and kissed him firmly and fully on the lips.

"Really?" he replied as he ran his fingers lightly down her abdomen into her soft, furry cleft.

She pulled away and looked into his eyes and said mischievously, "Ben, you ever hear any of those stories about identical twins suffering pain when the other gets hurt?"

"Yeah, but I never much believed it."

"Well, you'd better believe it, lover boy, because if I suddenly have an orgasm when I'm all alone here, I'll know that you've gotten confused and put your you-know-what you know where. So even if Lilah thinks she's me, I expect you to remember the difference. Understand?"

"Gotcha," he said softly, and held her close.

"We'd better get going. I want to get my scenes done early so I'll be here when Lilah's plane gets in," Rose said, gently pulling away, "much as I'd like to carry this on to its conclusion."

"You've just got to loop some lines today, right?"

"Right, let's go."

They were home just in time to send the limousine to the airport to pick up Lilah. As soon as she walked through the doorway, Lilah was smothered in a cloud of satin and lace and perfume as Rose threw her arms around her, exclaiming, "Lilah, *mon Dieu!* I can't believe you're really here!"

Although Lilah's eyes were dry, she was as moved as was Rose, who had tears streaming down her face.

When they disengaged, Rose said, "Let's go into the library for a visit alone." She took Lilah's arm and led her across the sunlit room to an area enclosed by greenhouse windows that looked out onto the garden and the swimming pool. "Come, *mon petit chou,* sit down. I've had a bottle of champagne chilled for us to celebrate our reunion."

Lilah settled herself into a white wicker chair uphol-stered in pink canvas covered with green ivy leaves. It was a bright and charming room, filled with palms and plants on the inside, which melded beautifully with the greenery of the garden.

As Rose poured the wine into the tall, thin flutes with stems of Lalique frosted wings, she remarked, "This is like a dream come true."

Lilah took her glass and lifted it in a toast. "To us . . . and to our first adventure together."

"Bonne chance . . . to us both," Rose replied. "We're going to need it." She sipped her wine and then said, "I asked Benjie to let us alone for a while so we can just talk about us. Tell me, what do you think of my house?"

"It's beautiful, but why do you call this the library? It has no bookshelves."

"Because I read here. If we decide to buy the place, I'll have shelves built along those walls over there. All of my beloved books are in boxes in the storage room. The people who own this house apparently don't read."

"Do you read much, Rose?"

"Mon Dieu, oui. Books have been my salvation. When I first left this country, I was very lonesome, and I found comfort in the pages of novels about home and love and romance. Then, when I was sing-ing in clubs and traveling, my only companions were my little books, because I trusted no one. Pretty soon I was reading French, which improved my command of the language. And now that I work in television, I

still have time to read while the technicians do their jobs."

"I never seem to find time to read anything except the newspapers and some of the magazines that come into the house every week. You make me ashamed of myself."

"Ah, but there is a difference, my twin. I live only for myself. You have a family, a husband, and a household to run," Rose protested.

"Not really. The children are away at school, and I have a very good housekeeper who also does the cooking. You've got Ben and a career to take care of," Lilah protested.

"Correction. Ben takes care of me. I don't take care of him. Now tell me everything about your children, your home, your husband . . . even your housekeeper. I want to know all about you. I must make up for the years we missed."

For more than an hour they talked and sipped champagne and nibbled at tiny buttered toast rounds on which they heaped spoonfuls of Beluga caviar with dollops of sour cream. They found themselves confiding details of their lives to each other, and they were so engrossed that twilight came and they took no notice of the darkening crepuscular light until Ben came in to tell them the time.

"It's almost six, and I've sent Steve to LaFamiglia to pick up some dinner for us," he announced.

"Oh, Lilah, *je le regrette beaucoup.* Come, I'll show you to your room," Rose apologized.

As they climbed the staircase Lilah was fascinated by the large portraits of Rose by Andy Warhol that lined the wall. They were identical except that each was done in a different color.

"Rose, those are beautiful!" Lilah exclaimed.

"I love them too. Andy did them in six colors for me . . . he calls them his *Rainbow Suite.*"

They walked up the frosty-green carpeted stairs, which were framed with white wooden balusters and a polished walnut banister, and into a room that looked like cotton candy. Lilah looked around in astonishment at the pale rose walls accented by white woodwork and white shutters at the windows, the white eyelet canopied bed with its pink chintz coverlet, the pink-lacquered vanity table, and the mirror etched in pink roses. "I hope you like pink," Rose commented dryly. "I think the owners of the house had a teenage daughter. Come downstairs when you're ready."

When Rose left, Lilah looked pensively out the window at the garden below. The lights had been turned on, and she could see that the camellia bushes were in full bloom. What a contrast to the grim winter still gripping her own garden at home. After a while she began to unpack, feeling completely at ease there in that candy box of a room, in the eternal summer of Los Angeles, and she hoped that her visit would not pass as quickly as this day had.

32

As soon as Lilah had climbed into the limousine that was waiting for her at Los Angeles International Airport, Florence began to worry that Lilah might disappear into the sprawling city and she wouldn't see her again. Quickly Florence knocked on the glass that separated her from the cabdriver. When he opened it, she said, "Listen, there's a twenty-dollar tip for you if you can follow that limo without him knowing we're following them, okay?"

"You been seein' too many cop shows on television, lady," he mumbled, but he pulled away from the curb and began to maneuver his way through the cars to do as she had asked.

They followed the limousine across Century Boulevard and onto the San Diego Freeway until they exited on Santa Monica Boulevard, though it was extremely difficult to stay with them through the heavy traffic. Suddenly they were surrounded by the stately homes of Beverly Hills, and the driver said over his shoulder, "If I follow them onto one of these side streets, they'll see us for sure, lady."

"Do the best you can," Florence ordered, and sank low into the backseat so that she couldn't be seen. "Just get me the address of the house where the woman gets out. That's all I want."

At last the limo pulled into a driveway, and the cab sailed past them with Florence now hidden completely from view. When it was done, the cabbie said, "Six twenty-five Beverly . . . now where?"

"The Beverly Wilshire Hotel. Is it very far?"

"No, ma'am. You could probably walk it if you were into exercise."

As soon as she was checked into her room and the bellman had left, Florence picked up the telephone to call Warren with her latest little tidbit of information. This was going to be fun . . . and profitable. It served that bitch Lilah right to have a spy on her tail. How dare she announce grandly that she wouldn't be in touch, even in an emergency, and what was even worse, she had ordered Florence not to return to Chicago until she called and gave her the signal.

Warren listened to the details of her trip without comment.

"I'll call you when I have more," she concluded, and slammed down the telephone.

She kicked off her shoes and settled down on the luxurious down couch, which was upholstered in rich brocade. She thought about unpacking, but what the hell. She would have a maid come in to do it for her. She would have her press her clothes, too, but first she dialed room service.

"What's a really good red wine?" she asked.

"We have a lovely Lafite, madame. It's a seventy-five," he replied, "or perhaps a Margaux or an Haut Brion . . ."

"Pick out something good and send it up. I'd also like a little snack."

"Would you like a cheese tray . . . or a plate of finger sandwiches?"

"Both," Florence replied, and put down the telephone. She smiled smugly. This was her chance to live in the style she deserved, and she had no intention of scrimping on anything.

33

CLAIRE Kimball perched on the edge of the silk lounge chair in her bedroom reading the morning *Times* and drinking a cup of tea. Her breakfast of dry whole-wheat toast, nonfat yogurt, and freshly squeezed grapefruit juice lay untouched on a small table beside her. As she finished reading Mavis Madden's column describing all of the important New Year's Eve parties about town, she crumpled the paper angrily in her hands and threw it as far as it would go, which was only about thirty inches from where she sat. She pulled the tiny gold half glasses, studded with real diamonds, from her face and got to her feet. She was filled with so much anger and loathing that there was certainly no room for food of any kind. She threw the embroidered linen napkin on top of the plates and yelled, "Cristinaaa-a-a-a!" at the top of her lungs.

A young Latino woman in a white uniform appeared at the door. "You call me, *señora*?" the woman asked.

"Get this tray out of here and get my tub ready. Is my black Chloe suit back from the dry cleaner's yet?" Claire asked in an annoyed and bitchy tone of voice.

"No, ma'am. Remember, I tol' you he said he not come this week. He take vacation for New Year. He bring everythin' back Monday, I think."

"Then find the Chanel suit . . . the white one with the full-length coat."

"The white blouse that match that suit is ruin. The red wine no come out."

"Shit!" Claire exclaimed, wanting to yell at her maid but knowing she'd better not. In Beverly Hills one didn't dare yell at good servants. There were too many people in the neighborhood eager and willing to hire them away.

She brushed past Cristina and went into the adjoining bedroom, which she had converted into a large closet. Quietly the servant followed behind her to help. Claire snapped on the lights and walked through the room filled with double rows of rods where her clothes were all hung on satin-padded hangers and covered with plastic bags. The blouses were hung together and arranged by colors; the same with dresses, suits, jackets, and skirts. The far wall was filled with shelves on which rested more than two hundred pairs of shoes, also arranged by color.

"Where's the suit I'm talking about?" Claire snapped.

The young woman walked quickly to the back of the room and emerged with it in seconds. She was Claire Kimball's personal maid, and she spent most of her time caring for her employer's extensive wardrobe. It was the best job she'd ever had, and although she could probably make more money doing general housework, at least she didn't have to scrub toilets or take care of someone else's brats anymore. Her own family of three boys and two girls caused enough aggravation as it was.

Claire began to rummage through the silk blouses, pulling them out of the bags and holding them up one by one next to the suit, trying to find a proper match. Dissatisfied with the white ones, she went to the colors, dropping the rejected blouses on the carpeting as she proceeded down the row. Cristina tried to scoop up the blouses as fast as they fell and return them neatly to the hangers so that she wouldn't have to iron them, but Claire moved too quickly. At long last she settled on a rich taupe Ungaro print. "This will do nicely," she murmured, and handed the blouse and the suit to the maid.

"Check these over carefully and make sure they look perfect." She moved to the shelves of shoes and chose a pair of off-white and taupe leather pumps. "Find the handbag that goes with these. Then call Roberto and tell him to have the car ready to leave at eleven o'clock."

In her dressing room she plugged in her hot rollers. There was no time to have her hair combed professionally. If she arrived at Vance's office any later than eleven-thirty, he would be gone for the day, and she didn't dare call for an appointment, because she simply could not afford to have him insist on talking things out by telephone. Unless she went into his office personally and groveled at his feet, they might stay in purgatory indefinitely. Purgatory, in Claire's definition, was not being able to attend any party that had at least six people from the most desirable and wealthiest group in town among its guests.

An hour later she stood in her large mirror-lined dressing room and appraised herself. She looked perfectly groomed. The blond hair wasn't terrific, but it looked nice and simple. She checked her eye makeup. Good, gentle but effective. She needed to project an image of rectitude and taste—good, conservative taste. Craig had once told her gleefully that Vance Freedland had described her as nothing more than a high-priced courtesan, and she needed to do everything she could to dispel that image in the old curmudgeon's mind. Besides, it simply wasn't true. She had never had one-night stands, and with this latest marriage, she didn't have to have sex at all. She was proud of the fact that with all her liaisons she had succeeded in being properly married every time. Of course, if that was his definition of a high-priced courtesan, she supposed she qualified . . . in diamonds.

As she picked up her handbag, which Cristina had dutifully filled with cosmetics, checkbook, credit cards, handkerchief, and glasses, she reflected on the only really bad decision she had ever made. Her present marriage.

Roberto, the handsome young man who drove for them and maintained their fleet of cars, tipped his hat and said, "Good morning, *señora*," as she hurried out of the house.

Claire looked at his dark, friendly eyes and smiled for the first time that day. "Good morning, Roberto. I'm going to Century City. Mr. Freedland's office. You know which building it's in, don't you?"

"Yes, ma'am," he said quietly, and helped her into the long, silvery brown Lincoln limousine.

As Roberto closed the door and walked around the car to get into the driver's seat, Claire sighed. Thank heavens she had lost her desire for men; otherwise, she would have been tempted to let Roberto service more than her cars. Life was less complicated and more comfortable as a celibate.

The chauffeur eased the car smoothly out of the driveway and down the winding hill toward the boulevard. Claire took her mirror out of her purse and checked her makeup once more. No matter how good the lights in her dressing room, the acid test was always out in the sunlight. Good enough but not great. It wouldn't be long before she'd need another little tuck around her eyes. Dr. Ed had refused to do it last year, insistng that she was courting trouble by doing it too often, but perhaps he'd reconsider now.

She snapped her purse shut and settled back in the luxurious seat to contemplate her strategy for the meeting ahead. Somehow she must convince the sanctimonious old walrus to forgive that prick of a husband of hers and let them back into the fold. After all, Craig was still the star of stars and they were in demand as honored guests at parties everywhere. It was unthinkable that Vance might make them turn down invitations to parties he was attending. She had to change his mind, because although Craig pretended not to care, she knew that being the center of attention was still the most important thing to him, and as for her, without her parties and her social life she might as well be dead.

She closed her eyes and tried to keep from frowning and deepening the tiny furrows between her brows. Damn, why had she ever agreed to that infernal prenuptial contract. Ten years! God, what an eternity that was. Ten years of being the dutiful little wife before the possibility of divorce without paying an awful price for her freedom. Not only was Craig Kimball a foul-tempered, impotent monster, he was also the cheapest man on two feet.

What kind of evil spell had he cast that influenced her to sign the document when her attorney had advised her against it? She had been beguiled at the prospect of having a wealthy and famous husband who would not expect her to service him in bed. She should have known that a man could never be kept in proper control without the weapon of sex. That was undoubtedly why Craig had turned out to be a much more recalcitrant mate than any she had had before. She had only her own stupid ego to blame. She had wanted to be the lucky woman chosen by America's idol, the biggest box-office draw of them all, the sex symbol against whom so many men had been compared and found wanting. Good Lord, what a joke.

The worst part of it all was that in spite of his wealth, she was forced to spend much of her own money to buy the things that made life worthwhile . . . designer gowns, jewels, exercise gurus, hairdressers. Her husband resisted paying for anything but the house expenses and the servants, and the monthly allowance he gave her was a pittance for a woman in her position. The cheapskate. If there was anything Claire hated, it was being forced to spend her own money.

Three more years. Just three more years. That was all it would take to fulfill the contract, and then she'd be home free and wouldn't have to wait for him to die.

The agreement would be null and void, and her attorney had told her that they could walk away with millions. With everything she had on him, Craig would never dare risk going to court. Then there was the will she had safely tucked away, in which she was named sole beneficiary. The best thing that could happen would be if the old lecher would die. She'd get everything he owned and would be able to do anything she pleased.

The limousine pulled up to Vance's office building, and Roberto helped her out of the car.

"I shouldn't be more than an hour, Roberto. Just keep watch for me," she said, and hurried inside. She stepped into the elevator and pressed the button for the top floor. The doors closed immediately, and the car began its swift ascent.

When the doors parted, a uniformed guard greeted her. "Whom do you wish to see, ma'am?" he asked in a tone that implied she had better have an appointment.

"Mr. Freedland, please. I don't have an appointment, but I'm sure he'll see me. Tell his secretary that Mrs. Craig Kimball is here."

The man continued to bar her exit from the elevator for another moment, but then he stepped back as the famous name sank in, and he said, "Mr. Freedland's secretary is down the hall. I'll show you where to go."

"That won't be necessary," she said as she brushed past him. "I know the way. I've been here before."

Quickly she made her way to the glass enclosure and opened the door. The secretary looked up from her desk and smiled. "Why, Mrs. Kimball, what a nice surprise . . . Mr. Freedland didn't tell me you were coming in."

"Hello, Charlotte. Happy New Year. No, Vance isn't expecting me. I was in the neighborhood and decided to drop in. He's here, isn't he? I missed seeing him on New Year's Eve, and I just wanted to say hello." There was an edge to her voice that sounded arch and a little fake, but she hoped the woman wouldn't detect it.

"Yes, he's here, but let me see if he's still in his meeting," she said, as a good secretary should. She got up from her desk and walked across the luxuriously appointed reception area. Gently she knocked at the door and then entered. Claire waited, ready to spring forward to the summons, but there was an awkward delay. After a few minutes, the anticipated feeling of humiliation began to crawl across her skin. She turned her eyes from the door and walked to the windows to look at the panoramic view of West Los Angeles and Beverly Hills. What a fool she had been to come here, only to be turned away like some poor beggar.

At last the door opened, and the rotund little white-haired woman came out smiling.

"Have a seat, won't you, Mrs. Kimball? He's on the telephone, but he'll be with you in a few minutes. Can I get you a cup of coffee?"

"No thank you."

"Tea, then? I have a few bags of Earl Grey that I keep for a pick-me-up in the afternoon," she asked, trying to be hospitable.

"That's very kind of you, but no thanks. I'm fine."

The secretary sat down at her desk once more and asked, "And how is that wonderful husband of yours? Just last night I watched *Heaven's Portals* on channel five. He was so handsome in that movie. You know, there's never been another star as big as he was. I always saw his pictures the first week they came out."

Claire smiled, but the smile was forced and looked frozen on her face. God, she was tired of the adulation of all those poor little ordinary women who thought the son of a bitch was a god. "Yes, he certainly was wonderful," she said, and hoped she hadn't put too much emphasis on the *was*.

"As soon as I read in *Variety* that he was going to appear on that show *Broadway*, I started watching it. I never thought much of it before, and especially not after that colored lady became the star, but when I found out Mr. Kimball loved it and was going to be on it, I started tuning it in every week."

"I never watch it myself. We're usually out on Tuesday evenings," Claire added, trying not to put the woman down.

Suddenly Charlotte's intercom buzzed, and she said, "He's ready for you now. Go right on in."

Claire got quickly to her feet and walked through the doorway into Vance Freedland's office. As she stepped inside she was struck once again by the sheer magnitude of the place. Except for his secretary's space, which was relatively small, and a bank of storage areas and rest rooms, Freedland had made the entire top floor of the building his own private office. Surrounded by walls of windows on three sides, his massive antique desk sat in the middle of the room. Large brass pots filled with exotic plants sat against the windows where they could drink in the light. The only solid wall was paneled in walnut and lined with bookshelves. There were several small groupings of couches and chairs, and the pale beige wall-to-wall carpeting was littered with skins of tigers, leopards, and zebras. A huge bear rug was spread in front of his desk. It looked as if a steamroller had run amok in a zoo and flattened the inhabitants.

Freedland did not get to his feet, nor did he ask Claire to sit down before inquiring about her visit.

"Now just what are you doing here, my dear woman?"

Startled by the directness of his approach, Claire responded in kind. She had long ago learned that it was wise never to kowtow too abjectly to bullies.

"I came here to find out why you made us stay away from the Annenbergs' party on New Year's Eve."

"I suggest that you talk to your husband," he replied sourly.

"He wouldn't tell me. So I'm asking you. At the time I agreed to marry him, I can't ever remember agreeing to accept the consequences of everything that he does. If you have a quarrel with him and you take action that affects me, I'm not going to sit back and take it quietly."

He lifted his eyes and stared directly into hers, and Claire knew how the animals lying under her feet must have felt the moment before he'd pulled the trigger. She did not look down, however, but met his gaze directly and firmly without appearing to be insolent.

"You've had too many husbands, my dear. You don't have enough respect," he remarked, but there appeaed on his face a hint of amusement.

"You're right, Vance. I've had one too many, and he was a mistake, but I've stood by him for almost seven years now. If I don't . . ." She paused to let the implication sink in.

"Don't be so foolish as to threaten me, my dear. I know the exact terms of your prenuptial agreement, and I also know that you won't do anything this late in the game to jeopardize your grip on Craig's estate," he said, his voice rolling and whistling as it made its way up through his fat-glutted chest and out of his throat.

"I . . . I'm sorry . . . you misunderstood me. I certainly have no intention of revealing anything that would . . . embarrass him. He's my husband, and it hurts me to see him cut off from social contacts. You know how important they are to him," she said humbly, and then added softly, "and to me."

The large head shook slightly, and the elephantine jowls quivered. After a long pause he said, "We all know that it would be very bad for him if certain things were to become public. It would not . . . serve anyone well. Now go home and tell him that I consider him sufficiently punished. I will expect both of you for dinner on the twenty-sixth at my home." He paused and took a deep, rattling gasp as his lungs pressed against the thick layers of flesh, trying to expand to get enough air for him to continue his speech.

"I'm sure you haven't forgotten," he continued, "that we are acting as a host for the Prince of Wales and his lovely Diana, who will be paying a visit to our fair city then."

Claire gasped at his sudden capitulation. God, she'd had no idea that her success would be so immediate and so overwhelming. "Vance, I can't tell you how much I appreciate—" she began, but he cut her off immediately and waved her out of the room.

"Go home now. I have work to do. Just tell your illustrious movie-star husband that he'd better not have any more surprises for me, and he'd damned well better behave himself from now on! And for God's sake, wear something tasteful, will you? No more of those thin things cut down to your navel." The laboring of his breathing added impetus to the threat in his voice. Claire knew it was time to take her leave as quickly as possible.

"Well, I must be going. Thank you so much for your kindness, Vance. I really appreciate your understanding, and we'll be delighted to be there on the twenty-sixth. If there's anything I can do to help . . ." She realized that she was jabbering like an idiot. "Give Kam my regards. Bye now."

She closed the door behind her, elated and disgusted at the same time. She had accomplished her goal, but she'd had to grovel to do it. With barely a good-bye to the secretary who had treated her so cordially, she strode imperiously past the guard and stepped into the elevator. As the doors closed, she hissed, "Go to hell, Vance Freedland," being careful, of course, not to say it too loudly.

34

AFTER a good night's sleep and an elaborate breakfast in her room, Florence called the concierge and
asked him to arrange a car and a driver for the day.

"Would you like a limousine?" he asked.

"Can it be charged to my hotel bill?"

"Yes, madam."

"I'll be ready at noon."

As she showered and dressed, her joy in the luxury
of the moment was tempered only by the realization
that it was all so damned temporary.

The long black limousine was waiting for her in the
porte cochere when she emerged from the hotel, and
the driver introduced himself as John.

"Well, hello, John. I want you to give me a sight-
seeing tour of the city, but first there's a street I'd like
to drive down. She gave him the address on Beverly
where Lilah had gone.

"No problem, ma'am. Any places in town you'd
especially like to see?"

"Not really. Just bring me back by six."

They cruised around the block where Lilah had
disappeared, but Florence saw no one except gardeners and maids walking dogs or pushing strollers with
babies in them.

After a drive that ranged from the beaches of Malibu to the downtown skyscrapers of Los Angeles, they
drove back toward Beverly Hills along Hollywood Bou-

ıevard. The chauffeur asked her if she wanted to stop at Mann's Chinese Theater and see the footprints of the stars, but she just laughed and said, "Not on your life." She had no desire to rub elbows with the strange people wandering the boulevard and was glad to be sheltered by the tinted windows of the limousine.

When they got back to the hotel, dusk had settled on the city. Florence asked the driver to circle Lilah's street a few times. On the third round she got lucky. The limousine that had carried Lilah away from the airport was sitting in the driveway, and the driver was standing beside it waiting.

"John," Florence said excitedly, "park the car so I can watch that house."

"Whatever you say, ma'am," he replied genially. "You want to be facing the house?"

"No, just pull up to the house next door. Then get out of the car and stand there as if you're waiting for somebody. I can watch out of the rear window."

After they had waited for about ten minutes, Florence became impatient. The light was diminishing rapidly, and the tinted car windows became difficult to see through.

Suddenly the front door of the house opened, and a man was silhouetted in the light briefly, but he hurried into the car before she could see what he looked like. Damn!

She went back to the hotel, determined to keep a better watch the next day. It took two days, however, before she saw any more activity at the house. After walking around and around the block, wearing large, dark sunglasses, a scarf on her head, and a dress that Lilah had never seen, Florence saw the car again. She approached the house very slowly, and saw a man appear at the door, hurry down the two steps of the porch, and cut across the lawn. He was tall, well built, and dressed in a superbly cut gray three-piece suit. He wore no necktie, and his white silk shirt was open at the collar. Just as he entered the car he looked up,

and Florence got a perfect view of his face. Before his
car had pulled out of the driveway, she had picked up
her pace and was hurrying back to the hotel to call
Warren. No wonder Lilah was being so damned secretive. She was involved with a man who was, for God's
sake, black! Florence shook her head in amazement.
Dear little old proper Lilah, of all people.

Warren took the call in his office. "Well, Florence,
how are you enjoying California?" he asked.

"I wasn't enjoying it much until a few minutes ago,
but let me tell you, I am now."

"Look, whatever you have to tell me, forget it. I've
changed my mind. I don't want to know anything that
my wife doesn't want to tell me."

"Oh, really? Well, too bad. We've got a deal, and
I'm not turning it off even if you are." Her voice was
clipped and stern. "For the past three days I've been
wearing out the soles of my feet walking back and
forth on the street where your wife is holed up, and I
finally got a line on what's going on inside."

"Look, I'll give you the money. Just forget whatever you saw."

"No way. Lilah's got herself a boyfriend all right,
and he's as black as the ace of spades. What do you
think of that? Do you suppose it's true that they're
better at sex than white men . . . hmmm, Warren?"

There was no response, and Florence said, "Warren, did you hear me?" There was still no answer, and
Florence jiggled the telephone until the operator came
on. "Operator, I was talking to Chicago and I got cut
off," she bellowed.

"I'll try to reconnect you, ma'am," the operator
replied. Florence waited impatiently for several minutes, until finally a woman's voice answered, and Florence recognized it as Warren's secretary.

"Sandra, this is Mrs. Bennett. I was just talking
long distance to Mr. Conway and we were cut off.
Would you please get him back on the line again?"

"I'm sorry, Mrs. Bennett, but Mr. Conway is not in the office," she replied firmly.

"What do you mean, he's not in the office? I was just talking to him two minutes ago!" Florence protested hotly.

"He's not in, Mrs. Bennett. That's all there is to it," the woman insisted doggedly.

"Listen, you go tell your boss to pick up the telephone now! Do you hear me?"

"It won't do you any good to yell at me. He isn't here, and that's that."

Florence heard a sharp click and knew that the telephone had been slammed down. The son of a bitch! Had he heard her news, or had he hung up before she'd gotten the words out of her mouth?

35

LILAH could stay in bed no longer. Although it was only six in the morning, she got up and put on her robe and slippers, ran a brush through her hair, and tiptoed down the stairs. The house was chilly, much chillier than she had expected it to be in sunny California. She needed a nice cup of hot coffee.

She snapped on the light in the large, well-equipped kitchen and set to work cleaning up the dishes from dinner the previous night. It took her just a few minutes to tidy up and set the coffee pot to dripping. The coffee was about ready when she heard a sudden thump. Muttering that paperboys in Beverly Hills were obviously just as irreverent as those in Illinois, she headed for the front door, trying to be as quiet as possible. As soon as she grasped the knob to pull the door open, bells and sirens began to pierce the quiet predawn silence. Lilah jumped back and slammed the door shut, hoping it would stop the clanging, but of course, it did not.

Ben came racing down the stairs with a pistol in his hand, looking wild-eyed and ready to defend his home, but the moment he saw the stricken look on Lilah's face, he realized what had happened. "It's okay, it's okay. You set off the alarm," he yelled above the din, trying to reassure her but not succeeding.

He ran to the entry hall and pushed a series of buttons on the wall, and the awful clamoring sound

was mercifully stilled. He then went to the telephone
and dialed a number.

"This is Frost . . . code number six-three-one-one.
False alarm. Sorry."

Lilah was still standing motionless at the door, her face
pale and her heart pounding. Ben set the gun down and
walked over to her and put his arm around her shoulders.
"Hey . . . don't take it so hard. I do it all the time."

"Oh, Ben, that scared the daylights out of me," she
whimpered.

"Yeah, that's the trouble. It only scares the good
folks. The thieves don't mind it at all. Just makes 'em
work faster. Come on, I smell coffee."

Lilah's hands were shaking as she lifted the cup to
her lips. After a sip she found her voice again. "I feel
like such a fool."

"It's my fault for not briefing you," Ben insisted.

"What do you think of our alarm clock?"

Lilah turned and saw her sister standing in the doorway wearing a rich ecru lace negligee. Her thick black
hair was pulled away from her face, which was devoid
of makeup and very pale.

"Rose, are you all right?" Lilah asked, concerned.
"You're so pale."

Rose and Ben looked at each other and laughed.
She settled herself at the table and poured a cup of
coffee. "My skin is lighter than yours because I rarely,
if ever, go out in the sun. You're tanned from playing
golf, true?"

"But you look darker than I do ordinarily," Lilah
protested.

"Courtesy of Elizabeth Arden. You see, when I
ran away to Europe, I was filled with hatred and
self-loathing, not because of my race but because of
what I had allowed to be done to me. I realized that
I had permitted it to happen because I didn't have
enough respect for myself, and I learned from Martin
Luther King that if you don't respect yourself, nobody
else will respect you, either. I vowed I would stop

being an imitation white. I would be what I was, proudly. A black woman. And so I dyed my brown hair black and used darker face makeup."

"That was a courageous thing for you to do, Rose," Lilah said, impressed.

Rose laughed and replied, "Not really. Black had begun to be fashionable. Besides, right after I got my hair frizzed with a permanent and had my eyebrows and eyelashes darkened, I got my first paying job as a singer. It was in a little cabaret on the Left Bank in Paris. They billed me as having *âme* . . . soul—and they loved me. I sang very sad songs, and the customers wept, and the more they would weep, the more wine they would drink, and the owner of the cabaret was ecstatic. They called me Tristesse."

"How fascinating," Lilah said softly.

"C'est vrai. By accepting my destiny I found my way. I thought I would never look back . . . until I learned about you. Now come upstairs to my bedroom while I dress." Lilah followed Rose as she hurried upstairs, chattering as quickly as she moved. "Take a look around my closet and get familiar with the clothes and the shoes and things this morning. At ten o'clock a manicurist is coming to the house from Long Beach to sculpt your nails . . . you know, put these long acrylic talons on. You've got to start getting used to them. Just cover your hair and say as little as possible. Ben will tell her that you have a migraine, and you can lie on the chaise while she works on you. If she guesses you're me, don't disillusion her. This will be your first test, okay?"

Lilah let out a nervous sigh. "So soon?"

Rose had slipped into a pair of tailored wool slacks, pulled on a heavy Irish cable-knit sweater and a pair of handmade leather boots, and then tucked her hair into a French angora turban. Lilah was impressed with every movement her sister made, especially with her regal carriage. If there was such a thing as star quality, her sister had been fully endowed. Was it possible that she could learn to transmit it too?

When she was ready to go, Rose pulled a cream-colored chiffon scarf from a drawer and handed it to her sister. "Cover your hair with this and put on the negligee I just took off. You might as well get used to wearing my clothes, *ma soeur*. Now I must go. Ben'll be here to pay the manicurist." She brushed Lilah's cheek with her lips and rushed from the room.

Lilah followed her out to the hallway, but Rose was already halfway down the stairs. Ben held the door open for her. She kissed him on the lips and dashed out of the house. Ben watched her leave, and then he looked up at Lilah and smiled.

"Come on down here and I'll check you out on the security system, although I won't leave until the manicurist arrives and gets started."

At five minutes past ten the doorbell rang, and Ben let the young woman in. Dressed in her sister's flowing negligee, Lilah peeked from the upstairs hallway, but when Ben and the manicurist started for the steps, she ran into the bedroom and stretched herself languidly on the chaise and laid a cold cloth over her eyes. It was her own little affectation and gave her something to hide behind.

Ben knocked gently at the door and said, "Honey . . . Doris is here. Are you ready for her to do your nails?"

Lilah managed to utter a whispery yes. Ben walked in and was startled to see her lying with her eyes covered. Stifling a laugh, he asked, "Are you sure you feel well enough for this?"

Lilah nodded her head and held out her hand dramatically. "I suppose so."

"Where did you get my name, anyway?" the young woman asked Ben curiously.

"A friend of mine told me to call you. She said that you were exceptionally good and used a special formula. My . . . uh, wife is an entertainer and needs long nails, but she'd had problems with them, so she wanted to try someone new."

"I'd better get started. It will take me a good two hours or more, especially if she wants them long."

"Yes, here's a picture of her hands as she used to wear them. She'd like that look again, all right?"

"No problem."

The woman opened her bag and set her paraphernalia on a little table that Rose had placed beside the chaise. Lilah wanted to watch but was afraid to take the cloth off her eyes.

"Honey, I have some errands to do," Ben said. "I'll call the service and tell them to pick up so you won't be bothered with calls. Why don't you try to nap a little? Remember, you have to be rested for our dinner party tonight. Bye now."

Doris took Lilah's hand and began examining her closely trimmed tidy unpolished nails. "Gee you don't look like you've ever had acrylics. Your nails are in perfect shape."

"It's been awhile," Lilah murmured, wondering in alarm just what was going to happen to her nails. She found out soon enough, as the manicurist began filing the tops of the nails to roughen them up to form a base for the substance. Shortly after that she felt a cold material hit her nail bed, and an awful odor permeated the room. Was it really supposed to smell this bad? She was afraid to ask and betray her ignorance, but she ventured a comment, "I hate that smell."

Doris laughed. "Really? I'm so accustomed to it, I don't even notice it anymore. Sometimes I worry that maybe it's rotting my brain cells or giving me cancer or something, but I love the work and I make good money. Besides, I can do it sitting down."

They chatted as she worked, and Lilah learned that she was supporting two daughters and that her husband had left her four years earlier. It took more than an hour for the product to be applied and sculpted on the nails, and then Doris began the long and arduous task of filing and smoothing. Lilah winced in pain several times, and she coughed frequently as the dust that was kicked up from the filing clouded the air.

At long last it was over, and Ben returned in time to pay the young woman. Before he did, however, Lilah said, "Ben, may I speak privately to you for a moment?"

"Sure . . . honey." He came into the room and closed the door behind him, sending the manicurist downstairs.

"Ben, how much are you paying her?" she asked, sitting up and staring in fascination at her hands, as if somehow they didn't belong to her.

"A hundred. I didn't want to use anybody in town. They're all tuned into gossip around here."

"Ben, I want you to give her an additional hundred from me. I'll pay you back, okay?"

"How come?"

"She's raising two little girls all by herself, and it's terrible work. All day she inhales the most awful smells and dusts, and I'm sure it's going to affect her health someday."

Ben put his arm around her and hugged her and gave her a kiss on the cheek. "Damned if you aren't two peas in a pod. My sweet lady is always helping strangers too. Sure, I'll give her whatever you want, but you can't pay it back, understand? Besides, I drop more than that for a lunch check at L'Ermitage."

"Really? Then give her three hundred. Giving is supposed to hurt," she said with a smile.

Ben laughed and saluted her as he reached into his pocket and pulled out a wad of bills. "You got it, baby."

When he had gone downstairs, Lilah went over to Rose's vanity table and sat down. She lifted her hands, now tipped with long slender nails that had been polished in a soft pink iridescent lacquer. She moved them around, back and forth across her cheeks, her face, and her lips, feeling very decadent. She tried to pick up a tiny brush to smooth out her eyebrows, but the nails got in the way, and she couldn't do it. When Ben returned to the bedroom, she was giggling.

"Oh, God, Ben, I'll never manage these things. I feel like such a klutz."

"Are you kidding? Rose tells me you have a golf handicap of eight . . . and I'm a twenty-three. Baby, you can't be a klutz! You're gonna do just fine. Now come on downstairs. I think we ought to start going over your lines. Rose will coach you on the acting, but I'll cue you for memorization."

"Oh, dear, here we go," she said reluctantly.

"Yeah, and let's start right there. Rose always says, '*Mon Dieu!*' Why don't you start using it too?"

"I never studied French in school, Ben. I signed up for Italian because the instructor was cuter."

"No problem. I understand it pretty well, and besides, I'll make sure that you don't get put in any difficult situations. I'll be by your side every second. Don't worry."

"*Mon Dieu!* No wonder my sister loves you."

36

CLAIRE was elated and eager to get home to tell Craig that they were out of the doghouse with Vance and could get back to living their lives again, but when she arrived at the house, he was gone. When she dialed Sudsy's number, all she got was his voice on the answering machine: "Hi, you've reached Sudsy, but I'm not home. Leave your name and number so I'll know who I'm not going to call back."

She slammed down the receiver. God, how she hated that nasty little bastard. She dialed the marine operator and was connected immediately to the boat. This time Sudsy answered in person, "Yo, ho, ho and a barrel of rum, suck my cock or I'll never come."

"This is Claire. I want to talk to my husband, you foul-mouthed little creep."

"Claire, ah, yes, Claire de Looney. Just a minute, I'll see if he wants to talk to you."

He dropped the telephone onto something hard, and the sound rattled in her ear as she heard him call, "Hey, boss, your ball and chain's on the wire. Whatcha want me to tell her?"

"Tell her I'll be home in plenty of time to get ready. I don't want to leave this hand now."

A moment later Sudsy came on the line and said insolently, "He's busy. He'll see you at home tonight," and without waiting for a reply he slammed down the telephone.

She was furious, and although she was tempted to dial the number again, she did not. It was useless. If Craig was playing poker and winning, there was no way that he would come to the phone to talk to her. Angrily she paced back and forth in the study, a lavishly decorated affair with walls of leather-bound books that the decorator had been careful to match with the suede couches. Claire was tense and miserable, her elation having evaporated with the phone call. Damn him. Damn his friends. Damn that boat. Angrily she threw herself into the Regency chair at the ormolu-laden French desk and picked up the telephone once more. She needed someone to talk to, and she began dialing, but halfway through the number she stopped and put down the phone so quickly that it seemed to be burning her fingers. No, she didn't dare. It had been three months since she had seen Mavis, but she had to keep her distance. She just couldn't risk doing anything that Craig might find out about and use against her. He would love to get rid of her, but as long as she remained above reproach as Craig's wife, there was nothing he could do to break their contract.

After a long time of frustrated musings and angry thoughts, Claire got out of the chair and went upstairs to her bedroom. She asked Cristina to draw a tub of water and then leave. When her bath was ready and she was alone again, Claire languidly removed her clothes in front of the mirrors and looked at her body with its white, smooth skin, firm breasts, and narrow waist. At the long, mirrored chest she pulled open a drawer and took an already rolled joint from an antique silver cigarette box. She lit it, inhaled deeply, and then stepped into the tub, letting her body slide down into the hot water until it lapped at her shoulders. She took another drag and held her breath while she turned on the jets that sent the water whirling and rushing around her, massaging her and relaxing her and sending her into a sensual haze. What fools her friends were for using coke instead of hash. She could never understand why they wanted those agitated highs when they could have mellow lows instead. '

After one final puff she put the joint out in the ashtray on the edge of the tub and slowly slid down in the water, opening her legs and positioning herself so that one of the jets sent its gushing water directly against her pudendum. With her eyes closed, she fantasized herself back on the couch in Mavis's studio, her legs spread wide as that tiny tongue flicked its way into all of her hidden pink places, finding out all of her secrets, and raising her to heights of ecstasy. Claire's path to orgasm took a sudden detour as she remembered the humiliation and the embarrassment of their last encounter.

Mavis hadn't told Claire that her daughter had returned from college and might appear at any moment. Why hadn't Mavis locked the damned door? God, Claire never would forget that girl's face as she stood frozen in the doorway, her expression a mixture of both astonishment and disgust. Claire had jumped up immediately to cover her naked body. Unruffled, Mavis had looked up and said icily, "Ava, darling . . . please. I've told you always to knock. Now leave us. I'll be with you in a few moments." The girl left, and although Mavis had wanted to continue, Claire refused. God, what a horror it had been. She had never felt so embarrassed in her life. She also realized how vulnerable she was. What had ever made her risk everything for a few moments of forbidden passion?

Claire was positive that she kept her tenuous hold on Craig only because of her knowledge of his weaknesses, as opposed to his perception of her own superior moral conduct. If he ever found out that she had been sexually active with anyone, particularly a woman, her seven-year investment would vanish. Craig had married her only because he wanted a beautiful and socially visible wife with a reputation above reproach, to provide a cover for his unsavory activities. Recently he had grown impatient with her demands, and she real-

ized he considered her an expensive albatross. She was
determined to outlast him, however, even if losing
Mavis was part of the price.

As if to prove she needed no one, she slipped her
fingers down into her vulva and began to stroke herself. At first the strokes were slow and gentle, but as
the minutes passed, they became more rapid and vig-
orous. She tried to concentrate, to fantasize again, but
it took a long time before she could feel her little clit
begin to get larger. She persisted, determined to come,
determined to be self-sufficient in everything, to need
no one. At last it happened, and her body arched in a
spasm of satisfaction that was intense and long-lasting.
When it was over, she continued, trying to force herself to another orgasm, just as Mavis did so successfully, but it was impossible. Her hand was getting
tired.

Frustrated, she stopped and tried to float in the
water to relax. After a few moments she opened her
eyes and looked at the clock. It was almost three.
Good, she would have an hour to nap before Armand
arrived to do her hair and her makeup. She got out of
the tub, dried herself, and smoothed a rich moisturiz-
ing lotion over her body, before slipping into a silk
nightgown. As she climbed into bed she heard a sound
in the next room and realized that Craig was home.
From the way he was thrashing around she guessed
that his valet would have a difficult time getting him
sobered up and dressed. Thank God she didn't have to
do it. There were a few compensations in her life. It
was just that sometimes they were damned difficult to
find.

37

Rose arrived home later than usual, exhausted from a long day of work. Ben had come to the studio to pick her up, but he had had to wait three hours while she did a scene with a new character on the show.

Lilah greeted them at the door, delighted not to be alone in the house any longer.

"Rose, you must be dead tired," she greeted her sister.

"*Mon Dieu!* Who ever said making movies was glamorous? I spent four hours wrestling on the couch with Norman this morning—I fell off five times—and three hours standing in front of a fireplace trying to look gorgeous while some young chick kept blowing her lines."

Rose had plopped herself down on the sofa in the living room and kicked off her shoes, demanding, "Benjie, I need a glass of champagne."

"Baby, I know you're tired, but as soon as dinner is over, you've got to work on Lilah's makeover . . . unless, of course, you've changed your mind and want to go to that ball tomorrow night yourself?" Ben said softly.

"Tomorrow night?" Lilah gasped.

Rose grinned. "*Oui, madame.* Tomorrow night you're going to make your debut. Benjie, darling, don't give me any trouble . . . just get the damned champagne. I don't have to report to the studio until ten in the morning."

Shaking his head, Ben went to the bar, opened the ornately carved wooden doors, and took out a bottle. "Yep, Lilah, you and I are going to make an appearance at the Beverly Wilshire Ballroom," he announced. "It's some charity or other. We don't have to stay long, so it'll be a good chance for you to make your first appearance as Lady Rose."

He eased the cork out of the bottle. "Want some?" he asked Lilah.

"Absolutely. Use a water glass," she replied. "I'm going to need it."

Ben shook his head. "Shame on you two."

When they finished dinner, Rose and Lilah went upstairs to Rose's dressing room. "Ben, bring those wig boxes from the hall closet, will you?" Rose asked.

"In a minute."

Rose had Lilah sit in front of the mirror at the vanity table. Quickly she ran her hands through her sister's short, wavy hair, which was streaked with both blond and a little natural gray. "Mmm, that feels good. I've had these tight permanents for so long that I'd almost forgotten what my natural hair feels like. When did you start streaking it with blond?"

"When I was a teenager at Camp Miniwanca, up in Michigan. Grams thought I needed a vacation from music, and that summer I spent more hours outside than I ever had. A girl in my cabin combed some medicinal peroxide into my hair, and it got sun-streaked. I thought it looked wonderful, sort of golden and outdoorsy . . . the California-girl look, you know. It made me feel very glamorous and blond. Anyway, I started doing that all the time . . . telling Grams, of course, that it was just the sun, and then the year I went to Juilliard, I had it done professionally. I've been a blonde, sort of, ever since."

"I guess every woman has wondered at one time or

another what it would be like to be a blonde. I know I
have."

Lilah smiled. "It's highly overrated. I was never
considered sexy. Most men I know want to prove their
manly superiority by beating me at golf rather than
hustling me into bed."

Rose laughed. "Are you really that good?"

"Where? In bed or on the golf course?"

Rose laughed again. "Very funny."

"I'm glad somebody appreciates my humor. My family never did."

"What about Warren?"

"He's a very serious person, too intense for his own
good, I'm afraid. I can't tell you the last time we had a
real giggle together." Her voice trailed away, and she
appeared lost in thoughts that were worrisome.

"Maybe something's bothering him."

"Not likely. Warren always has his life in absolute
control. He never forgets anything . . . he never makes
a mistake. He's an absolute paragon of virtue and
propriety."

"Sounds like somebody's talking about me," Ben
said as he arrived carrying two large pink boxes, which
he stacked on a chair. "Mind if I watch?" he asked.

"Out, Ben, out. When we're ready, we'll call you,"
Rose said, shooing him out of the room.

For two hours Rose worked on Lilah, tinting the
hair at her hairline dark and covering the rest with a
wig. Next she applied her makeup to Lilah's face and
handed her one of her negligees to put on. Rose took
a long, critical look at her creation, and then, taking
her sister's hand, led her across the room to the full-
length mirrors. Lilah gasped. For the first time since
the moment she saw Rose at the Plaza Hotel in New
York, the full realization of her identity swept over
her.

As if she had read her sister's mind, Rose said,
"And now, sister of mine, you have become a black
woman. Are you frightened?"

"I'm not sure," Lilah replied, and her voice shook slightly. She did not want to reveal the shock she felt and chance offending her sister.

"Let's go downstairs and see what Benjie has to say," Rose said, reassuringly taking her arm and leading her away from the mirror. The two sisters walked down the stairs and into the library where Ben was reading. As they entered, he looked up, and his jaw went slack. "Dear Jesus," he whispered as he got out of the chair and approached them. Neither twin spoke but stood quietly waiting for his assessment. He walked around them for a few minutes in silence, studying them carefully.

At last Rose said deceptively, "Do I look all right, Ben? Do you think I can pass?" There was a wicked gleam in her eye, and Ben knew he was being teased.

"Rose Baby, don't try to fool me. I know that's you."

"How do you know, Ben . . . how?" she asked.

"Lilah's still wearing that big yellow diamond ring on her hand."

"*Merde!*" Rose exclaimed in exasperation.

"I'm the detail man, honey," Ben said with satisfaction, "but I must admit you had me going there for a few minutes. Nobody would ever guess there weren't really two Lady Roses in this room tonight."

Lilah let out a long, shuddering sigh. "Well, what's next on the agenda?"

"I've asked Janine to come over here as a special favor to do my makeup for the party tomorrow night. She's expensive but terrific. She created the makeup for my character on the show, and she knows exactly what colors and shading to use."

"Does she know about me?" Lilah asked.

"*Mais non, ma chère.* She will think you are me. But don't worry. She hardly ever talks, and she gets very upset when her clients chatter while she's working on their faces. She says she doesn't like moving targets, so she's perfect for our needs."

"What dress should she wear?" Ben asked.

"Let's go and pick something out." The three conspirators went back upstairs to Rose's room where they chose a slinky white Jacqueline de Ribes gown with long sleeves. It was cut deeply in the front, draped to the side, and cinched with an expanse of pearls and rhinestones at the waistline.

"This should be perfect. Try it on, Lilah. Benjie, out of the room for a few minutes."

Ben got up and left the room quickly. Lilah took the gown gingerly and stepped into it. Rose tried to zip up the back zipper, but it was difficult, for the dress was tight. She persisted, however, and finally the zipper conceded defeat and closed.

"There . . . how's that?" Rose asked.

"Are my eyes bulging out?" Lilah asked.

"The dress is jersey and will give a little. Is it too uncomfortable?"

"I shouldn't have any trouble if I don't breathe."

"Damn. You'll never get into my costumes on the set. They practically paint them on me. Well, that settles it. We can't wait any longer. The final fitting for the show you're going to do is day after tomorrow. You'll have to go in my place and have the clothes fitted to you. Otherwise—"

"Day after tomorrow . . . oh, God!" Lilah exclaimed, suddenly aware that the moment of truth was bearing down on her.

"It's now or never. Do you want to back out?" Rose asked, and her voice reflected her fear that her sister might answer in the affirmative.

"No . . . no, of course not. Just be patient with me. I'm a little nervous."

Relieved, Rose touched her shoulder. "I'm so sorry I was deprived of all those years of knowing you, Lilah."

There was a soft knock at the door, and Ben stepped into the room. He saw Lilah in the tight-fitting gown and whistled, "Whee-ooo, sensational."

"Yes, but the dress is too tight. She's going to have to go to the studio day after tomorrow to fit the costumes. She's a few pounds heavier than I am."

"Are you scheduled to be on camera that day?"

"No, but of course there's always a chance that something could come up, but I say we risk it. What do you think?"

"It's fine with me. Okay with you, Lilah?"

"I'll do the best I can," she consented weakly.

"You'll be fine, and I won't leave your side for a minute . . . understand? I'll do everything I can to shield you."

Lilah said good night and went to her room. She stood in front of the mirror and stared at the strange figure trembling with anxiety and fear. Had Ben and Rose suspected that she had come within a hair of backing out?

38

WARREN settled down into his worn leather chair and picked up the latest copy of *Forbes* magazine. He tried to concentrate, but he found himself reading the same paragraph three times without having any idea what it said. Finally he put the periodical down and just stared out the window. Lord, he missed Lilah! What was she doing right now?

He looked at his watch. It was almost eight-thirty . . . about six-thirty in Los Angeles. She was probably dressing for dinner, but who was she going to have it with? He tried to erase the thought that she was being unfaithful to him, but the vision of his wife lying naked in bed with some faceless man kept insinuating itself into his thoughts, haunting him, punishing him. Thank God he had slammed down the telephone before Florence managed to fill his head with any other poisonous information.

Finally, unable to endure it any longer, he got out of the chair and walked into the living room where the piano seemed to loom like a ghost come back to haunt him and steal his wife away. Ever since the day it had been brought into the house, Lilah had been different. Although he hadn't heard her play it, he couldn't dismiss the thought that somehow the presence of the piano had brought about a marked change in her. Was it possible that she was still mourning the loss of her career after all these years?

He sat down on the bench and touched several keys. As little as he knew about music, he could tell that the tone was rich and mellow as the notes reverberated in the empty room. He hated the instrument, as much now as in his youth when it had dominated the life of the young woman with whom he had fallen so passionately in love. The piano had been a rival far more powerful than another young man possibly could have been, for it had made her seem aloof and self-assured, complete somehow, and markedly unlike all the other young women who mostly had marriage on their minds. Lilah had been entirely different from her friend Florence, who had tried desperately to interest him, in spite of the fact that he had not encouraged her in the slightest. In the wisdom of youth Warren had never once succumbed to Florence's enticements because he wanted only Lilah . . . and all Lilah had ever seemed to want was music and success and fame.

As he sat at his wife's piano he remembered the night that she had come home from Russia. He had tried not to take joy in her failure—no, actually that wasn't true. He had been ecstatic, elated, hopeful. He had called her on the telephone to utter patently false words of sympathy. To his delight she had asked him to come over and take her for a drive. She said she needed someone to talk to, and he hurried to her. As he drove, he listened silently while she poured out all of her misery: her disillusionment with her talent and herself, her bitter disappointment in having failed. And when she began to cry, he stopped the car so that he could put his arms around her and comfort her, euphoric that she had turned to him in her grief.

Then, almost without realizing what he was saying, words of love began to tumble heedlessly from his lips. He confessed all of his secret longings for her and begged her to marry him. He promised to love her and cherish her and protect her from ever knowing pain or disappointment again. With all the ardor and innocence of youth he vowed that he would create a life for her that would always be happy. He swore that she would be fulfilled and that she would never have regrets if she married him. Swept away by his love and his passion, she consented, pressing her body against the haven of his and promising that she would love him in return.

Often over the past twenty years he had felt a twinge of guilt for having taken advantage of her when she was at her weakest and most insecure, but he had squelched the notion. They had had a good life, he reminded himself again and again; he had fulfilled his promise to her. They had a happy home and two wonderful children. What more could he have done? Deep down, however, there was a recurring suspicion that Lilah never really had loved him as much as he still loved her.

Then what in God's name was he doing messing around with Florence? What had ever possessed him at the country club? He'd never, never been attracted to Florence, although she had been making secret suggestions to him for years. What foolishness had finally made him succumb?

He got to his feet and moved across the room, trying to walk away from the embarrassingly painful memory of his lust. If Lilah was having an affair, it was his own fault. Even if she didn't know about Florence, she was probably just trying to fill in the spaces in her life that apparently he had left empty. He thought his love for her would make up for the loss of her dreams. What a vain and egocentric ass he had been. He should have known that someday it would all catch up with him and he would lose her.

As he walked past the ebony piano on his way upstairs to the bedroom, he slammed the keyboard cover closed. "You miserable black beast!" he snarled at it angrily. "I hate you."

39

DRESSED in her Halston II gabardine pleated skirt and blouse from Penney's, Florence checked her appearance in the mirror. Not bad. She had been to the hotel beauty parlor every day. Charging it all to Lilah, she had her hair body-permed, woven in a tone-on-tone blond, and styled. Her fingernails were immaculately manicured, as were her toenails. She had a facial, a leg waxing, and her eyebrows tweezed. In fact, she had everything done that the hotel shop was able to do.

Now she was ready to go to the Polo Lounge in the Beverly Hills Hotel. Since it was early, she decided to walk. As she neared Lilah's retreat a limousine came barreling down the street and pulled into the driveway. She walked faster and was within twenty feet of it when the driver opened the door to help the passenger out. It was a woman, but Florence could not see her face, although she was certain it wasn't Lilah, for she had a mass of curly dark hair. As the woman hurried toward the house she called to the driver, "We won't be ready to leave until eight. Take your time eating dinner." She went inside quickly, slamming the door behind her.

There was something about the woman that struck a strange chord of familiarity. Where had she seen her before? Florence decided to return in two hours, hoping to get a better look at her then.

At the Polo Lounge, Florence was seated at a small table in the dark green room facing toward the patio area. A waiter appeared immediately, and she ordered a whiskey sour. She looked around, hoping to spot a movie star or two.

At the table across from her was a man with gray hair and oversize wire-rimmed glasses taking notes as he talked to an undistinguished-looking middle-aged man also wearing glasses. The man being interviewed looked vaguely familiar.

Two young women at the next table were noisily discussing an interview one of them had just had. Florence's antenna was tuned in to every word uttered, but they seemed to be speaking in tongues, for their conversation was littered with the jargon of the movie industry—words such as *biopic, grosses, pickups, opening soft, sweet deal.* It was a language decipherable only to readers of *Variety,* but Florence found it exotic and fascinating, and she stared at the brightly lipsticked young mouths from which the strange words tumbled so easily.

Suddenly the young woman sitting opposite her turned her big blue eyes, rimmed by thick globs of black mascara, on Florence and said, "Hi! You're from out of town, aren't you?"

Embarrassed at being caught eavesdropping, Florence laughed nervously and replied, "Why . . . yes, yes, I am. How did you know?"

A look of amusement passed between the young women as Blue-eyes replied perkily, "Just a lucky guess."

Florence looked again at the table across from her. The interviewer was leaving. "Thanks, Doc. This should be appearing in my Friday column. Nice seeing you."

Once more Florence returned to her guessing game now that she had a clue. "Doc" . . . did he mean doctor? Was he perhaps a dentist? She watched as the man signaled for the waiter and asked for his check.

"Yes, sir, Mr. Simon, I got it right here."

Florence put the two names together as he signed the bill and left. Doc Simon . . . Doc Simon . . . where had she heard that name before? Suddenly it came to her. Good heavens, that had been Neil Simon sitting just inches away from her . . . Neil Simon, the world's most successful and richest playwright. Of course, that's why he had looked so familiar. She'd seen him on Johnny Carson's show. Imagine that! Why, in person he didn't look like anybody at all.

Celebrity watching can become an addiction, and Florence was hooked. If that ordinary human being was Neil Simon, who else wonderful might be there right now in the same room with her? She ordered another drink. Well, she would really have some interesting things to tell at her bridge club when she got home.

The time passed quickly as Florence sipped on her cocktail and scanned the room, looking for another celebrity to add to her list, her self-conscious discomfort lost in the thrill of the hunt. The room got noisier, more crowded, more filled with smoke, but she was enjoying every moment of it. At seven-thirty she reluctantly paid her check and got up to leave. As he walked through the room her way was suddenly blocked by a man's bulky figure.

"You're not going to leave yet, are you, honey?" he asked.

Florence could see that the man's hairline was growing in small clumps and obviously had been plucked from the back of his head and transplanted to the front, then dyed a flat dark brown. He wore oversize tinted glasses, and the caps on his teeth were so large and white, they made her think of elephant tusks. Expensively dressed in a silk shirt over which he wore a soft Fendi leather jacket, he had tried desperately and unsuccessfully to appear younger than he was. When he took a drag off his cigarette, she noticed that he wore a heavy gold chunk of a ring studded with diamonds and a gold Rolex watch. He emitted a strong odor of expensive cologne.

"What?" Florence asked.

"I've been watching you sitting all by yourself over there. You're a pretty lady. Can I buy you a drink?"

Something about him intimidated her. "No thank you . . . really, I have to go. I have a—"

"Sure, I know. You already got another date. Okay, I'll let you go on one condition. You gotta promise to meet me here tomorrow night for a drink. Deal?"

She smiled. "Tomorrow night will be fine," she said, thinking it was the only offer she had had so far.

"No, no, no, no. You gotta cross your heart and hope to die," he said, flashing a bright, teasing smile.

"Cross my heart and hope to die," she repeated.

The man stepped out of her way. "That's much better. Now, tomorrow night. Don't forget. And who knows, I might even find a part in my next picture for you. You got good legs, kid."

In the cab on the way to Lilah's hideaway, Florence ruminated on her encounter in the bar. Was the man really a Hollywood producer? After all, if a titan like Neil Simon could look so insignificant, what kingdoms might that obtrusive and expensively adorned character command?

As they drew near the house on Beverly, a limousine pulled up and two figures appeared, silhouetted in the light streaming from inside the house. The first was the same woman she had seen earlier; Florence recognized the mass of curly hair. The woman wore a long white gown and a full-length white mink coat was draped over her shoulders. Florence was certain the man who followed was the same black man she had seen before. Tonight he was dressed in a tuxedo. The woman turned to say something to somebody inside, and as the light caught the glitter of jewels on the dress, Florence again sensed something familiar about her, although she could not see her face.

Damn! What a waste. Florence wished she had stayed at the Polo Lounge and talked to that producer more. She wondered if he really would be there the following night.

40

LILAH kept her eyes closed and her mouth shut as Janine, the makeup artist, worked on her face, silently smoothing on the base, the contour shading, the several colors of eye shadow, the liner, the mascara, and the lipstick. It took close to an hour, which Lilah found amusing. In all her life she couldn't remember ever taking more than five or ten minutes to apply a bit of moisturizer, a touch of makeup, a light brushing of mascara, and a quick swipe with a tube of lipstick. Good grief, it was just a face, not the Mona Lisa, and it would be all washed down the drain a few hours later, she reflected. Did Rose really feel that she needed all of this gilding, or was it just a ritual that people in the entertainment world performed as a matter of course? She wanted to ask the young makeup woman with the purple streaks in her hair and short black leather skirt, but she kept her silence. One stupid question could blow her whole cover.

At last it was done, and Janine spoke softly, "You can open your eyes now, Ms. Rose, and take a look." The girl spoke with a slight trace of a Southern accent, and although Lilah had expected her to be imperious, she was just the opposite. Young, sweet, and shy, in spite of her tartlike appearance.

Lilah opened her eyes to look into the mirror, and the same eerie sensation she had felt the night before came over her again. The reflection looking back at

her did not belong to her . . . it was her sister's face in
the mirror, looking strangely beautiful. It was odd, but
she had never before thought of herself as being particularly lovely of face, perhaps because she had been
raised in a culture that preached: Beauty is as beauty
does. Hard work and accomplishment were the values
that mattered. How often her grandmother had told
her that when she was a child.

She continued to stare intently at her reflection for
such a long time that Janine began to worry.

"Is there something wrong, Ms. Rose? Don't you
like it? I did it just the same as last time. I used all the
same colors . . . I keep detailed notes, you know."

"Oh, it's fine. Really, it's perfect. I . . . uh . . . just
had something else on my mind," Lilah responded
quickly, and then looked around for Ben. Where had
he gone? What was she supposed to do now?

"Mr. Frost went downstairs, I think. Want me to
get him?" Janine asked.

"Please," Lilah replied gratefully.

The young woman left the room, and Lilah returned
to the examination of her unfamiliar yet fascinating
image. Ben came in, and she felt relaxed. "Do I look
all right, Benjie?" she asked uncertainly.

Smiling, Ben replied, "You've never looked lovelier
. . . Rose. Take my word for it. Now I'll pay Janine
and get her out of here so that you can start getting
dressed. We haven't got much time."

As soon as Ben had escorted the young woman to
the door, Rose sneaked into the room. "Well, well, as
I live and breathe, the incomparable Lady Rose in
person. *Mon Dieu,* you look gorgeous . . . if I do say
so myself."

"Rose, I'm scared. My knees are shaking, and my
stomach's all wobbly."

"Calm down now, the first outing will be the hard-
est. You'll get used to it after tonight. Besides, I
expected that reaction, so I complained all day on the
set that I felt shaky and thought I might be coming

down with something. The young guy I was kissing wasn't too happy about it. He kept shoving vitamin C pills down his throat every few minutes and asking me if I'd had a flu shot." Rose laughed.

Lilah was too preoccupied with her own fears to be amused. "Now what?" she asked.

"Now take that scarf off your head, and we'll set the wig in place. The dye on your hair looks fine. Just comb it forward." She took the hairpiece out of its box and handed it to her sister. "Here, you'd better get used to doing this yourself. I might not always be here when you're getting dressed."

"God, don't say such a thing! Where would you be?" Lilah asked in a sudden panic. "Rose, you've got to be ready to fill in on a moment's notice in case I start messing up, you know that."

"Now listen, *mon petit chou,* you must stop thinking that you're going to fail. You're not! You're going to be fantastically successful and enjoy every moment, understand? In fact, you're going to have a lot more fun playing the big star than I ever had, because it's only an adventure for you, an interlude . . . not your life's work. Now think positively."

"You're right. Hand that thing here and let me have a go at it . . . which is the front?"

Half an hour later Ben, who was pacing back and forth in the entry hall waiting, looked up to see a vision in white standing at the head of the staircase waiting for him to become aware of her presence. Openmouthed, he watched as she proudly descended, dragging a white cape behind, her head held high, and on her face the haughty air of one born to royalty.

"Jesus," he whispered, "is that you?"

"Is it who, dummy? Close your mouth or you'll catch flies," Rose taunted from the landing above, a mocking tone in her voice.

Suddenly the austere vision cracked as Lilah dropped the regal pose and began to giggle. "Oh, God, Benjie, if ever I needed encouragement, that expression on your face gave it to me. Do I really look that good?"

"Baby, you look sensational. Now get back in character, Cinderella, your pumpkin awaits." As he opened the door for her he looked up and winked at Rose. "Get some rest, honey. And keep the bed warm."

The drive to the Century Plaza Hotel was brief, and as the limousine pulled into the line of cars waiting to drop off their passengers, Lilah's heart began to pound furiously. Her hands felt wet and icy. The car inched forward, and she became aware of the crowd of people at the hotel entrance, and saw the flashbulbs popping. "Ben, are those news photographers there? Oh, Lord."

"Just smile sweetly, but don't stop to pose. And pretend you don't hear any questions thrown at you. Hold on to my arm tightly. I'll steer you through them. Don't worry if I start shoving them a little. They're used to it."

"Is that what Rose would do?" Lilah asked.

"Yeah . . . sure," he replied, but without conviction.

"What would Rose do? Come on, tell me the truth. If I'm going to be her, I should try to do it right," she insisted.

"Rose always stops and throws out a line or two that they can use in their story . . . that's one of the reasons she's so popular, and why she's always on page one of the trash papers."

"Tell me what to say . . . let me have a go at it," Lilah insisted.

"No, it's too risky. Just do as I say."

Their limousine pulled up to the entrance, and a doorman opened the door. Ben slid out first and turned to help Lilah out of the car. Several voices yelled, "Hey, it's Lady Rose!"

Lilah emerged from the car to find herself the center of attention, with cameras being thrust at her and lights flashing in her face. She stood frozen to the spot for a moment, overwhelmed by her sudden taste of stardom. Then suddenly she smiled, and she felt herself become the star.

"Lady Rose, Lady Rose . . . over here . . . over here," the voices commanded, and she looked around, smiling regally at the mob of paparazzi, enjoying the moment. Suddenly someone yelled, "Say, Caymen, who're you gonna screw tonight?" referring to the character Rose portrayed on television.

Without thinking, the answer came in a voice that she barely recognized. "I don't know. I haven't seen the guest list." Her eyes twinkled, and she waved as Ben ran interference and hurried her into the hotel. Once inside the guarded door, Ben whirled her around and looked deep into her eyes. "Goddammit . . . are you Lilah or are you Rose?" he asked in a whisper.

Startled, Lilah looked back at him. "Ben, I'm not sure. We might have to get an exorcist before this thing is over. I feel like some outside spirit has taken over, and I'm on automatic pilot."

A couple approached them, and Lilah did not have to be briefed before they spoke. It was President Ford and his wife Betty. The former first lady said, taking Lilah's hand, "Lady Rose, I've just enjoyed your role in *Broadway* so much. Although I'm not able to see it all the time, I always have it taped, and I just forbid anyone to tell me what's happened until I can watch it myself."

Out of the corner of his eye Ben saw Craig and Claire Kimball emerge from their limousine and head their way. Quickly he took Lilah's arm and steered her in the opposite direction. There was no point in having any kind of a confrontation on her first night out, he decided, hoping that she was too involved with the guests immediately nearby to notice the Kimballs. As Ben and Lilah proceeded across the lobby and downstairs to the ballroom, a succession of beautifully dressed people stopped them to murmur greetings and congratulations on her success. Most of the faces were strange to her, but there were many that were familiar: Gloria and Jimmy Stewart; Veronique and Gregory Peck; Joan Rivers, who whispered to Ben that she wanted to schedule Lady Rose as a guest on her talk show; Anjelica Huston and Jack Nicholson. The smiling faces swam before her as in a dream. When at last they had a moment to speak alone, Lilah asked, "They all know me . . . er, Rose. Does she know them?"

Ben shook his head. "No, not really . . . not any more than you do. It's just that she's joined the club, you know. And now everybody knows who she is . . . and that's what's important."

A hand touched her elbow and a voice whispered into her ear. "Ah, it's so nice to see you feeling well again, my dear."

Lilah turned to find herself looking into the gargantuan mountain of flesh that could only be Vance Freedland. Surprised but maintaining her poise, she replied, "Yes, thank heaven, I'm feeling fine. And how are you?" Her mind raced ahead, trying to remember the details of the night as Rose had told her about them.

Concerned that Lilah might not recognize him, Ben interjected, "Well, how nice to see you, Vance. I hope you had a pleasant holiday season."

"Yes, yes, I did. Of course, my Christmas Eve party would have been much nicer if the pretty lady hadn't become ill and had to leave, but those things do happen, I suppose, although I must admit it was a first for me," he added pointedly.

The grungy old coot, Lilah fumed as she remembered everything Rose had told her, and the urge to strike back impelled her to retort. "And for me as well. That was the first time I've ever become ill in public, but believe me, you should be grateful that I got out as quickly as I did. I'm afraid I threw up all over the car and all over poor Ben. Intestinal flu, the doctor said. Your dinner would really have been ruined if I'd stayed five minutes longer."

Lilah smiled sweetly, assured that she had had the last word. When Freedland and his pie-faced young wife had moved on, Ben remarked, "Nasty, honey, nasty. I have a feeling our friend Vance will never mention that party again."

"I should probably have kept my mouth shut, but he irked me. It was extremely rude of him to say I'd hurt his stupid party."

"Are you always so outspoken?"

Lilah shook her head. "Occasionally. Am I making a mess of things, Benjie?"

"Good Lord, no. You're terrific. In fact, I wish that Rose would be a little spunkier sometimes. She tends to believe people are right when they're not friendly toward her. She carries a little too much guilt. But you haven't got any of that, have you?"

"Every woman has guilt. If God doesn't give us a healthy dose of it, our families will—not just parents but husbands and children. I've been more fortunate than most. Life hasn't kicked me around as it has my sister."

A waiter passed carrying a tray of glasses of champagne and offered it to them. Lilah refused because she was afraid of becoming even the slightest bit intoxicated, but Ben took two glasses and handed one to her. "Here, hold it and sip occasionally. No one ever saw Lady Rose pass up champagne, although I wish she would occasionally."

As they stood talking, others came up to speak to them. Lilah met Bruce Stebbins, the creator and producer of Rose's television series. Immediately he launched into a discussion of the next day's filming, because he and the director were at odds, and he wanted his star's opinion, hoping to win her to his viewpoint.

Ben tried to sidestep the situation. "Come on, Bruce, can't you let us enjoy ourselves for an hour or two without discussing business? We're not staying for dinner, you know. Rose got all gussied up just to make an appearance and give the photographers a few pictures, then she's going home to bed. So lay off her, will you? You and Stan fight it out alone. If she agrees with you, he'll be upset, and if she doesn't, you'll be pissed, but since I don't really care what either of you thinks, here's my opinion. You're both wrong. That script they're shooting is the most poorly written episode I've seen. You should have scrapped it and started over."

The two men eyed each other for a few moments. Stebbins was annoyed. "You're such a smartass, Frost. Where did you ever get the idea that you know more than anybody else in the world?"

Ben smiled and took Lilah's elbow to move her away as he replied with a sardonic smile, "My mammy done tole me . . . when I was in knee pants."

They walked away, and Lilah asked, "Aren't you afraid to antagonize him like that?"

"Lesson one in this business, my dear: When you're on top, you're expected to kick shit in everybody's face. And you don't have to worry about making enemies either, because as soon as you start slipping nobody will return your phone calls anymore, and it doesn't make any difference whether you've been naughty or nice. As Lombardi said, winning is the only thing."

About half an hour later the crowd began to move toward the tables. Ben whispered into Lilah's ear, "You're doing so well, we can sit down and have dinner if you want to, although I'm not sure who'll be sitting at our table."

"Would Rose stay?" Lilah asked.

"No, she wouldn't. You know how food bores her, and these things get stretched out quite a bit. It's noisy too."

"I'll race you to the car."

"Not in that tight dress, you won't."

"Good thing we're not staying. There's no room in this dress for even a tiny piece of lettuce, and I'm starved."

"I'll have the driver stop at Jacopo's and pick up a pizza on the way home," Ben suggested.

"I'm on a diet, remember? I'll have some fruit and cottage cheese before I go to bed."

As they drove home Ben took Lilah's hand and squeezed it. "You're something else, my friend," he said admiringly.

"So are you, Ben. I've never met anyone quite like you," Lilah replied.

41

CLAIRE was waiting impatiently when Craig finally made his way down the staircase. His valet had done a noble job of shaving him and putting him together. He had failed, however, to sober Craig completely, and the actor's attempt to light a cigarette as he walked down the stairs proved to be an impossible maneuver. He stumbled once, and Claire held her breath, viciously hoping he would fall and crack his rotten head into pieces. For a brief moment she had a vision of herself as the bereft widow of the great star, visibly grieved as she tried unsuccessfully to avoid the cameras on her way to his funeral. Craig recovered his balance, and the dream vanished in a blast of obscenity.

"What the fuck are you staring at?" he demanded as he reached firm footing on the marble entry floor, still concentrating on the lighter in his hand and not even glancing at her Galanos gown or her Armand hair and makeup.

Between clenched teeth she retorted, "Nothing, absolutely nothing! What the devil took you so long? I've been down here waiting for twenty minutes."

He took a deep drag from the cigarette and turned toward her. As he spoke, he deliberately blew the smoke into her face. "Good. That makes up for some of the hours I've spent waiting while you powder and pamper yourself. Now, let's go." Pulling himself together as well as he could, he turned disdainfully from her and lurched out the front door, leaving her to follow. He climbed into the limousine first and slouched down in the seat.

The chauffeur helped Claire into the car, and they drove off. Her lips curled in disgust as she looked at her husband. If the world could only know what a miserable bastard Craig Kimball was.

"I went to see Vance today," Claire announced without preamble.

"What the hell for?" Craig asked, feigning nonchalance, but she knew she had his attention.

"To get us out of the social purgatory you got us into, that's what."

"Did the old buzzard throw you out on your ass?"

Claire decided to toy with his curiosity a little. "You know, Craig, I've never understood this love-hate relationship you have with Vance. Behind his back you have nothing for him but contempt, yet in person you toady to him. I've been told that you were one of the people who introduced him to everyone when he first came to town. Why? Has he got something on you?"

Craig turned toward her and looked directly into her eyes for the first time that night. "My connection with Vance Freedland is none of your business." His voice dripped with contempt and finality.

Claire was not fazed. "I'm your wife, remember? What you do reflects on me, and I don't like it when things are going on that I don't understand."

"You want out? Okay, be my guest. You can walk away from this marriage anytime."

"I might do that, but remember that if I walk, I'll be carrying with me a very large bag filled with your dirty linen. I'm sure the press would pay plenty to know that the dashing and romantic Craig Kimball gets his rocks off only—"

He whirled toward her and grabbed her face in his hands. "Shut up. You hear me, cunt . . . shut up," he whispered ferociously, looking toward the driver to see if he was listening.

Claire clutched her heavy silver Judith Leiber minaudière tightly in her hand and, with one quick swing, smashed his wrist with it so ferociously that hundreds of the tiny rhinestones were dislodged from the purse. Diamond dust filled the air as the brilliants gently settled onto Kimball's tuxedo.

Wincing in pain, he let her go in order to examine the welt on his arm where she had struck him.

"Bastard!" she muttered. "This handbag cost two thousand dollars, and now it's ruined."

"Fuck the purse, you almost broke my arm," he exclaimed.

"I can't even open it to look at my makeup, which you've undoubtedly smeared. Keep your filthy hands off me . . . do you understand? I just might decide that your money isn't worth giving up the pleasure I'd get in destroying you. I'm not exactly poor, you know."

Kimball closed his eyes momentarily, trying to quell the disgust he felt for her and all the other filthy broads in the world. God, how he hated her. Where had he ever gotten the dumb idea that she was lady-like and gentle? Why had every woman he'd ever married turned out to be a monster? It never once occurred to him that he bore any of the responsibility for his failures in matrimony.

"I wish to God I'd never seen your face," he spat, turning away to look out the window. His other two marriages had been costly but possible to dissolve. This one, however, wouldn't let go. Claire was like an adder who had her fangs in him and was determined to hang on to the death. What had he ever done in life to deserve a bitch like this?

Claire finally managed to get the purse open, and checking her face in the mirror, she powdered over the fingermarks. Satisfied that no serious harm had been done, she settled back and continued the conversation as if nothing had happened. It was not the first time they had attacked each other, and it gave her a significant sense of satisfaction to know that she did not fear him physically, in spite of the difference in their size. In fact, in each of their brief encounters she had been the one to strike the telling blow. She wondered what his foolish fans would think about him if they knew that their idol was a physical coward.

"Well, for your information, Vance was charming to me," she said in a perfectly normal tone of voice. "He told me that he wouldn't dream of punishing me for your peccadilloes, and he apologized for keeping me from the New Year's party. He said he couldn't understand why such a nice woman would marry a creature as vile as you are."

"Bullshit. Vance doesn't like you any more than I do. He told me so. In fact, he told me I could find somebody a lot better than you to marry . . . that you were nothing but a high-priced whore," he said wearily. "I wish I'd listened to him."

"If that's what he told you, then he's a two-faced liar, because at our wedding party he told me that he was glad you were finally settling down and he hoped I'd be a good influence on you."

"Hmph . . . like the spider's a good influence on the fly," he muttered.

The limousine was pulling into the circle at the Century Plaza Hotel as Claire delivered her final thrust.

"Interesting that you should use that particular metaphor. I was just picturing myself as a widow in black. You're getting old, Craig, and the booze and coke are catching up with you. I can hardly wait to see what the public's reaction is going to be when they see that weathered and dissolute face of yours coming into their homes on television. I imagine it will be quite a shock." It was the second blow that had hit its mark in their brief ride together.

The car stopped, and the doorman helped Claire out. She started to walk toward the entrance, but Craig took her arm and pulled her back.

"Wait," he commanded sharply.

She looked up and saw the press crowding around a

celebrity. Curiously she stretched to her toes and immediately recognized the woman. "Why, it's your friend Lady Rose. Shall we go over and say hello?"

"No!" Craig barked at her. "Absolutely not!" His face had taken on a look of hatred and malevolence that even Claire found daunting. Craig took his wife's arm and maneuvered her around the fringes of the group and into the lobby without being noticed. Once inside, he dropped his hand from her arm and proceeded toward the downstairs bar. The import of the situation had not escaped Claire.

"Darling," she said softly, smiling and speaking in dulcet tones so that anyone watching would think they were having a nice, chummy conversation, "what's going on with you and the black broad? It's because of her that you're going to show that wrinkled face of yours on television, isn't it? Why? You'd better tell me. You know how I hate secrets."

"Mind your own business, cunt," he whispered sharply, smiling also, and presenting the congenial picture of a devoted husband.

"What you do is my business, you bastard, and don't forget it," she whispered back. "Your encounter with her kept me from the New Year's party, remember? And I want to be sure it never happens again."

Knowing that she would never give up, Craig snapped, "Then help me make sure that she doesn't see me . . . until I'm ready to see her, all right?"

"We'll discuss it later," Claire replied as they were approached by Jellie Beam, a writer who had been pursuing Craig for an interview about his comeback. Craig wanted nothing to do with her because she approached celebrity interviews as vigorously as if she were investigating malfeasance in public office.

"Damn it to hell!" Craig said under his breath, but smiled nevertheless, as the woman came near.

Jellie Beam was a living example of style gone awry. She was tall and lanky and tried desperately to dress fashionably, but since she had little to spend, she had to improvise. Her improvisations were slightly skewed. Tonight she wore a man's long silk dressing gown as a dress and a tiny flat pancake of a forties hat with a net eye veil perched atop her unruly red hair. Her large eyeglasses kept sliding down a bridgeless nose, pared down to a button by a cut-rate plastic surgeon.

Jellie was, however, unrelenting in pursuit of whichever celebrity she had targeted for dissection. Stars consented to be interviewed only because occasionally her insightful and meticulous prose was also highly complimentary. Celebrities were seduced by their own egos into believing that she would find them the exception worthy of her praise.

Not Craig, however. He did not intend to let her delve into his life or his psyche. There were far too many cobwebs in his closet. He smiled mechanically and tried to brush past her without speaking. Jellie never took umbrage at being ignored, considering it only part of her job. The less stars wanted her attention, the more important they became to her.

"Mr. Kimball, I'm so glad to see you. I can't seem to get your publicist to return my calls." She planted herself directly in Craig's path as she cooed to Claire, "Why, how lovely you look tonight, Mrs. Kimball. That gown is an Oscar de la Renta, isn't it?"

Enjoying Craig's discomfiture, Claire stopped to chat. "No, it's Ungaro," she replied.

"Of course. His gowns are so exquisite and elegant, just like you, Mrs. Kimball. You always look perfectly smashing. I can't understand why you haven't made the Best Dressed List. You're the most beautifully groomed woman in town . . . without exception. And you know, I see an awful lot of beautifully dressed women."

"Why, thank you, Miss Beam, for the lovely compliment," Claire preened. The canny reporter had hit the mark, for Claire was miffed that she had been slighted. No one devoted more time and money than she did on her clothing, and it was exasperating to be overlooked.

"Really, I mean it. Your profile has been far too low in the press. You know, I think it would be a terrific idea if I did a story on you also . . . not the two of you as a couple but individually. It would come at a great time for you, Mr. Kimball. I'd finish the research and the interviews in time for it to appear in print, just as you were doing your guest episode on *Broadway*. How about it? I could be at your house anytime you say. You name it."

Craig shook his head. "I'm afraid not. Besides, I never schedule interviews except through my publicist. You'll have to talk to him." He took Claire's arm and tried to pull her away, but she would not budge.

"Tomorrow morning will be fine," she said to Jellie. "Come to my house about eleven. Even if Craig doesn't want to talk to you, I will. It might be fun."

Jellie had what she wanted. "You're a peach, Mrs. Kimball. I think we're going to get along just great. I'll see you in the A.M."

"Plan to stay for lunch," Claire trilled as a furious Craig dragged her away.

"Have you gone nuts? I don't want that bitch in my house, much less messing around in my life, do you understand? You'll have to call her in the morning and cancel."

Claire pulled away from him and declared, "I will not! I'm sick and tired of living in your shadow. I didn't marry you to be invisible, you know. Besides, I'm not afraid of that dumb little scarecrow. I know how to handle her."

He shook his head. "You're an ass and you don't even know it. Nobody can handle the press. Sane people avoid them like the plague."

"You're a fine one to talk. You didn't get to be a star by hiding from publicity, now did you?"

"Yeah, but I don't need it now, and I don't want to have anything to do with that little bitch."

"Come on. You don't want publicity? Then why the hell are you going on that trashy television show?"

He stalked away from her and went to the bar to get himself a drink. Knowing that he would not bring one for her, Claire called a waiter and ordered a glass of wine. Then she looked around for someone to talk to. She saw Rosemarie and Robert Stack and headed their way.

42

THE day after her excursion to the Polo Lounge, Florence went shopping. She had noticed that neat little skirts and blouses were not fashionable in Beverly Hills. At Laise Adzer's she spent an outrageous amount of money for a dusty rose heap of gauze with an uneven hem, and an equally awesome price for a matching leather belt heavily studded with silver. After she found a pair of sandals to match, she hurried back to the Aida Gray salon in the hotel to have her neat little roller-set coiffure moussed and styled straight and severe.

She had been dawdling for an hour over her white-wine spritzer at the Polo Lounge when the producer arrived. He glanced at her briefly as he passed her table but proceeded on to the back of the room to join a group of men.

Damn, hadn't he recognized her? She looked down despairingly at all her expensive finery, which would never, never be wearable in her circle back home. Well, there was no point in letting all that money go down the drain, even if she had to risk making a fool of herself. She got up and walked toward the table where the man sat with his back to her talking, talking, talking.

Resting her hand lightly on his shoulder, Florence said, "Hi. We had a date tonight, remember?"

He looked at her blankly for only an instant, and

then smiled and replied, "We did? Well, if you say so."

He grabbed her arm with his huge hand and signaled to the waiter, "Hey, Paco, bring the lady a chair."

Immediately a chair was brought, and Florence found herself sandwiched between two men. The waiter brought her a drink, and the men went on talking. The only attention she received was from the producer's hand, which rested on her thigh and edged closer to the inside of her leg.

Florence tried to ignore the hand and concentrate on the conversation about points and breakouts and overheads. Finally the men ran out of deals to discuss, and one by one, each of them took their leave.

When they were alone, he turned to her and said, "You ought to get a new line, kid."

"What are you talking about?" she asked indignantly.

"Most of the chicks who work this bar are a lot more inventive," he said sarcastically, and took a swig from his glass.

Florence's insecurity flamed into fury. "How dare you insinuate . . . get your filthy hand off my leg and let me out of here." She tried to stand up, but he quickly moved his huge hand from her leg to her shoulder and pushed her back down on the chair. When he smiled, his huge teeth made her feel like Red Riding Hood discovering that the wolf was wearing her grandmother's clothing.

"Now don't get all excited, little lady. Let's talk this over in a nice, calm manner. Okay?"

"I've never been so insulted in my life," she protested, but she remained in her seat.

"Just take a swallow of your drink and relax. Look, I had too much to drink last night. My head felt like a watermelon this morning. And if I made a date with you and forgot . . . well, I'm sorry. I'm sorry about the hooker crack too. It's just that there's always a few of them around here in the evening looking for a little action." His voice had become soft and ameliorating.

Florence was mortified. "Oh, God, this is a strange town. I'd better go home before I get into real trouble."

"You're from out of town? Now don't tell me, let me guess. Nebraska, right?"

"You think I'm a hick, don't you? Well, I'm not. I'm from Chicago."

"Look, let's start all over. My name is Del—Del Gerstler. What's yours?" His arm was now across the back of her chair, and his manner and tone of voice had become warm and friendly and attentive.

"Florence Bennett."

"So, Florence, what brings you out here from Chicago?"

"My husband died last year, and I just thought I needed a little vacation."

"Where you stayin'?"

She told him she was at the Beverly Wilshire, and he said that he lived not too far away, in the flats of Beverly Hills. He confessed that he was married to Mayda Hastings, the faded star from the days of *B* movies, but it was an open marriage. They shared the same home and went to parties together occasionally, but not much else.

"What do you say we have some dinner?" Without waiting for her answer he called for the check and paid it from a thick wad of bills held together by a gold money clip. From the waiter's smile it was apparent that the tip had been a hefty one.

As they walked through the lobby of the hotel Del asked, "Anyplace special you want to eat?"

"Won't your wife be expecting you home?"

He laughed out loud. "Christ, no. With her I have to make an appointment a week in advance."

The parking attendant brought his shiny black Jaguar to the curb, and as they drove off Del said, "I'm gonna take you to a sweet place just a couple of blocks from your hotel. You like pasta?"

He was greeted warmly at La Scala, a smart restaurant in the heart of Beverly Hills, and taken to a comfortable booth. Wine was served immediately, and as she lifted her glass Florence asked, "Are you really a producer, Del?"

He threw back his head and laughed. "Everyone in this town is a producer. They don't necessarily produce anything, or they might produce shit, but they call themselves producers anyway."

"Well, what do you produce?"

"Anything I can, but I haven't had much luck lately. The studios are playing musical chairs with their executives, and every one of my projects has been scuttled by new administrations. Everybody's looking for a formula for success, only there just ain't one. It's a crapshoot. Sometimes you win, most of the time you don't. Want me to order for you?"

They ate black pasta with tiny scallops and thin white veal in a mushroom and tomato sauce and drank two bottles of Pinot Grigio. Florence felt light-headed.

It was well past ten when they left the restaurant and got into Del's car. Florence was sure the evening was not over.

Del drove down to Wilshire Boulevard, through the tall wrought-iron gates that sparkled with hundreds of tiny white lights, and into the concourse of Florence's hotel. He handed the keys to the parking attendant and asked her, "Which side are you on?"

She nodded toward the new tower, realizing that he intended to collect for the dinner, and she was ready to pay.

In her room Del made no romantic overtures but instead began to undress immediately. He was down to his boxer shorts, which were pale blue and monogrammed with his initials, when he went into the bathroom. Without bothering to close the door he urinated. Florence had finally begun to take her clothes off, too, but the mechanical coldness of it all bothered her. Even Warren had the grace to kiss her and make some attempt at being romantic.

After Del had finished in the bathroom Florence

went in, but she closed the door and locked it. Quickly she undressed and put on the lavender silk peignoir she had bought for her first weekend with her best friend's husband. She brushed her teeth and splashed some cologne on her arms and her thighs. Glancing in the mirror at her new, stiff straight hairdo, she sighed. She looked like a scarecrow.

When she wafted gracefully into the bedroom, trying to look as seductive as possible, Del was stretched out on the bed naked. His mouth was open, and she could hear a gentle snore. Good God, he'd gone to sleep!

Leaning over him, she examined the sleeping figure. People should never take their clothes off, she decided. He had been such an imposing figure in his Giorgio Armani silk jacket, and now he was nothing but a clump of used flesh. Between the freckles and the moles and the reddish blotches, the skin of his body was pasty white, contrasting sharply with the reddish and weathered texture of his face. His poor little prick lay helpless and soft on the wiry pubic hair covering his testicles. Amazing, she thought, how much havoc and ecstasy that wretched little organ had probably wreaked on women. For the first time that night she felt superior and in control. Del Gerstler, the big producer, was nothing but a man.

Florence sat down on the bed beside him and gently took his penis in her hand. She began to massage it to see what would happen. It stirred and began to grow in size, but he remained quiet. So absorbed was she in manipulating it that she did not see his eyes open, nor was she aware that he was awake until she suddenly felt his huge hand squeezing the back of her neck.

She tried to lift her head, but his grip was like a vise of iron. "Blow," he ordered her, "blow!" She cooperated as well as she could and tried to move her lips and mouth sensuously. He relaxed his grip slightly, and she slipped off the bed and onto her knees. Her back was hurting, and after a while she tried to lift her head, but he forced her down again. She did everything she could to satisfy him, but he seemed not particularly excited and nowhere near coming. She felt that she might pass out when suddenly he pulled her up and said, "Take off the gown."

Shakily she got to her feet and let the peignoir slip to the floor. He took her arm and pulled her down on the bed beside him. Quickly he was on top of her, spreading her legs wide with his knees so he could thrust his penis inside her. For a long time he pumped silently, showing no signs of emotion. She forced her thoughts to fantasy, deliberately romanticizing his brusque manners until she found herself beginning to flow with excitement that at last sent her into the throes of a climax. When that happened, he, too, came with a loud groan that sounded more like agony than ecstasy. When it was over, he rolled over on his back away from her. She put her arm across him and said, "Del . . . you haven't kissed me," trying in some way to salvage a shred of warm affection from the cold coupling.

He pushed her away. "I don't believe in kissing," he said. "It spreads germs. It's a filthy custom."

He swung his legs to the floor and stood up. "I think I'll take a shower and get this guck off me." Without a glance at her, he went into the bathroom, closed the door this time, and emerged fifteen minutes later, dressed immaculately.

"How long you gonna be in town?" he asked.

"Till next week," she answered.

"I'll call you. What's your name again?"

"Bennett," she replied softly.

"Oh, yeah . . . right." He opened the door and left.

Florence pulled the sheet tightly over her body and shivered. Good God, what had she become?

43

ROSE tied a silk Hermès scarf around Lilah's head and fashioned it into a turban that covered all of her hair except the newly dyed hairline.

"Voilà," she said when she had finished, "that should do it. You won't have to worry about makeup today, *chérie,* because you'll just be fitting the new costumes."

Sitting in front of the mirror in Rose's room, Lilah tried to cover her nervousness with humor. "With just a rag and a hank of hair the sow's ear becomes a silk purse. Oh, God, Rose, will I fool anybody?"

Rose gave her sister a hug. "You already have! Now, I'll stay close to the telephone all day. If anything goes wrong, just say you have a headache and need some fresh air. Benjie will whisk you home, and I'll go back in your place . . . okay? Just relax and let the designers stick pins in you. Probably the only problem you'll have is terminal boredom. Just concentrate on the clothes. And complain! I'm always complaining, so they'll expect it."

"Complain? Complain about what?"

Rose shrugged her shoulders. "Anything. The fit, the color, but most of all, the comfort. Move your arms around, walk, sit down. I never approve a gown unless it feels good. Costumes should help an actress give a performance, not hinder her, so don't let them hang something on you that constrains you in any way. All right?"

Lilah got to her feet. "Well, wish me luck."

"You'll be fine. Look how much fun you had pretending to be me the first time."

As they drove away, Ben took Lilah's hand and squeezed it. "Okay?" he asked. She nodded silently, but he could tell that she was tense. Perhaps this was the time to discuss his proposition and get her mind off the coming events.

"Lilah, if you don't pull this switch off, it won't hurt Rose or her career . . . you know that, don't you?"

"I don't know what you mean," Lilah replied.

"Yes, you do. The news that Lady Rose has a white twin sister would do nothing but give her a lot of publicity and make her more intriguing. You and your family are the only ones who might get hurt. Both Rose and I appreciate that."

"Don't remind me. Every night I lie awake in bed and worry about it, but something inside me won't let me stop. I don't know if it's guilt because I've had a life so much easier than hers . . . or maybe it's envy and I need to walk in her shoes and find out what it's like to be a star."

"You know it might just all be for nothing," Ben replied heavily.

"What do you mean?"

"I've been doing a lot of investigating into the shadier side of Craig Kimball. There's been a lot of whispering about him through the years, but no one ever came out and said anything bad about him, which is strange. I have a friend who works with the FBI, and he tells me that Kimball has strong ties to the underworld."

"Wouldn't something like that have gotten into the papers?"

"Not necessarily. My friend tells me that years ago there was a big cover-up involving one of the major studios. There was some kind of a rape, and Kimball was implicated. It never came to anything, because Kimball suddenly got married, but there was also an incident with a showgirl in Vegas who turned up dead after being seen on several occasions with him. The cop who found her was conveniently shot on a drug bust not long afterward."

"Do you think it's true?" Lilah asked.

"Given Rose's history with Kimball, yes."

"Your FBI friend told you all this?" Lilah asked, her fears about the day ahead of her forgotten.

"Yep, he said they began to investigate Kimball when it was learned that his name was on a list of investors in a casino in Atlantic City. Apparently somebody tipped Kimball off, because he withdrew immediately. I'm not scaring you, am I?"

"No, but why are you telling me all this now?"

"Because I want you to know just what you're getting into, and I need you to help me do something Rose couldn't pull off in a million years."

Lilah smiled but said ruefully, "I won't shoot him. I don't believe in violence."

Ben laughed. "Nothing like that. I just want to make sure that he lets her alone . . . from now on."

"That's why I'm here. What do you want me to do?"

The car was pulling into the gates at the studio as Ben said, "I want you to trap him into admitting what he did to Rose."

"How am I going to do that?"

"By pretending not to remember anything."

"That's all?" she asked.

Ben nodded. "Yep, that's it. I'm sure that Kimball will contrive to get you alone at some point. I'm sure that's why he insinuated himself into the production. He's been offered countless better roles in the past few years, and he's turned down every single one. I think he's holding a grudge, and he wants to frighten and intimidate her, which he's certainly managed to do very nicely. She's scared to death of him."

"Will you be nearby?"

"Every damn second."

"Well, I'll try. I'm not really afraid of Craig Kimball, in spite of what you and Rose have told me. I accept it intellectually, of course, but I don't have the emotional scars my sister has. I was never raped or brutalized by him—or anyone else, for that matter. Craig Kimball is just a movie star to me, one that I loved watching on the big screen."

As the car stopped, Ben made one last remark. "That's all I need from you. I'll take care of the rest."

He helped her out in front of a long frame building. "Where are we?" Lilah whispered.

"In front of your dressing room. See, over there . . . right there. Your name is on the door."

Lilah squinted in the bright sunlight and saw the neatly lettered sign on a door in the middle of the building. On the door next to it was Beth Tyndall's name, another star of the show. Quickly Ben escorted her inside, and Lilah looked around in disappointment.

"This is it?" she asked, her eyes quickly taking everything in. The room was small. There was a white couch, a brocaded chaise, a couple of small barrel chairs done in a dusty pink, a French provincial coffee table, and a small television set on a red Chinese cabinet next to the door. Two small windows covered with blinds of a coppery metal faced the wall next to the bathroom, which was mirrored.

Ben watched her face fall, and grinned. "Gorgeous, isn't it?"

"Uh, why, yes, sure," Lilah murmured.

"You know what Rose calls this place? Ben's Folly. I negotiated everything so carefully, but I forgot to include the dressing room . . . so this is what she got. The one next door isn't much bigger, but it's a lot nicer. Beth's agent had it put into her contract that she could choose the designer and have it done the way she wanted it. Rose's decorator was the prop department."

"I'm just surprised, that's all. I expected it to look like something in the movies."

"This is television, and although a hit show has some money to play with, they have to be more prudent about costs. We've also got a producer who tries to get everything onto the screen. He doesn't like to waste money on frills."

The telephone rang and Ben answered it. The conversation was brief, and as he put the telephone down he said, "That was Wardrobe. They're ready for you. Let's go."

They stepped back into the sunlight. "It's just a few steps from here."

They went into a big, newer-looking building and up the stairs to a large workroom. There were at least a dozen women working at sewing machines amid a clutter of fabrics and mannequins. A tall woman with gray hair, cut short and straight, called to them, "Good morning. I'm glad you're here early. We had to make that gown I showed you yesterday in a different color. The director said the fabric strobed and had to be changed."

As she talked, the woman briskly pulled a pale blue satin dress off a mannequin and held it out for Lilah to put on.

Lilah said good morning and turned hesitantly toward Ben. Was she supposed to undress right out here in front of the world? Ben caught her glance and nodded almost imperceptibly, annoyed with himself for neglecting to warn her that the wardrobe department was not concerned with modesty . . . and neither, usually, were the actors.

Lilah pulled off the heavy cotton sweater and stepped out of Rose's boots and slacks. What the hell, she thought. She wasn't exposing Lilah's body, it was her sister's.

"Garnet," Ben addressed the woman, pointedly saying her name so that Lilah would know who she was, "who did the designs for this show?"

The woman shook her head as she held the dress for Lilah to step into. "Well, they're Sevilla's designs, but

I haven't seen him once since we started cutting them, which is probably just as well. Most of his stuff wasn't makable, and I had to change everything. I think this using a different designer for every show is a bunch of hooey, and I told 'em so."

Lilah had the gown on, and Garnet was trying to zip it up, but the fabric would not give. It was too tight.

"Damn!" the woman said. "Somebody must have made a mistake when we cut it in this color. The lavender one fit fine. Good thing the seams haven't been trimmed yet."

True to his promise, Ben stayed close by and kept the conversation going, eliciting as much information as possible so that Lilah would learn what was going on.

When she put on a wool suit and it also was too tight, Garnet looked Lilah straight in the eye and said accusingly, "You're gaining weight!"

Lilah looked down sheepishly and softly murmured, "I've been on an ice-cream binge the last few nights."

"Ice cream!" Garnet exclaimed. "This doesn't look like ice cream." She squeezed the flesh at Lilah's waist and said, "Look . . . there's hardly any fat there at all. God, I never realized how muscular you were. Have you been working out with weights?"

Ben interceded. "You guessed it, Garnet. I put one of those Universal gyms into the house for myself, and my lady here has been using it more than I have."

"Amazing. These things fit her last week. Well, I'll just have to let 'em out, won't I? Now don't go starvin' yourself so they wind up hanging on you, okay? Bruce'll be down here on my back if you do."

"Don't worry about that. I promise to stay the same . . . at least for the next week," Lilah replied, and she winked at Ben.

They took a break at twelve for lunch, and Ben asked, "Do you want to try the commissary, or would you rather have me bring you something in the dressing room?"

"What does Rose usually do?" Lilah asked.

"It all depends on her mood. If she's feeling sociable, she goes to the commissary. If not, she lies down and reads. If I'm not here, she tends to skip eating altogether."

"Let's go. I need to test myself. Okay?"

They strolled slowly across the lot. Many people waved and said hi, but everyone seemed in a hurry and no one stopped to talk. In the commissary Lilah started to sit down at one of the chairs at the counter, but Ben pulled her back.

"Uh-uh, honey. Stars don't eat out here. They go into the dining room."

He led her to a large, high-ceilinged room that was filled with booths of various sizes, some seated two, others as many as ten. The walls were hung with huge film posters mounted on transparent glass and lit from behind. Waitresses in tan uniforms and sensible shoes scurried about.

Lilah saw no familiar faces as she looked around at the other diners.

"They're studio execs, I'm afraid. Not very glamorous," Ben explained, reading her mind.

"Oh, Ben, look who's coming our way," Lilah whispered.

Carol Burnett was walking toward them, followed by an entourage of men in navy-blue blazers and gray pants. As she arrived at their table she stopped and spoke to Lilah. "I want you to know that I think you're just wonderful as Caymen Welles, but they ought to have you sing more often. I heard you in a nightclub in Paris fifteen years ago, and I'll never forget the way you sang 'The Man I Love.' It made me cry."

Dumbfounded, Lilah could barely manage a soft "Thank you," but Ben picked up for her as he quickly got to his feet.

"I can't tell you how much that means to Lady Rose, Miss Burnett. She's one of your devoted fans. I understand you're preparing a special, and I want you to know that Rose will be happy to be included, if you want her."

A man standing behind the legendary comedienne stuck his hand out to shake Ben's. "Hi, Frost, my name's Culverson. Here's my card. I intend to hold you to that offer."

"Will you sing that song in a red dress?" Carol Burnett asked, and looked directly into Lilah's eyes, and Lilah answered, "Any color you want, Miss Burnett." A look of mutual understanding and admiration passed between them, and then the star and her retinue walked away.

Ben sat down and grinned. "Nice goin', honey. Rose will be tickled with this."

"You think so?" Lilah asked. "I feel awfully strange getting her involved in something she didn't know anything about."

"Hey, forget that. I can maneuver her out of anything she doesn't want to do."

"Oh, really? Then how come you couldn't get her out of appearing with Craig Kimball?" Lilah asked with more humor than sarcasm.

"Nobody's perfect. I admit that that was one I couldn't handle, but I know she'll be happy to do this. The part of Caymen Welles has been good for her because it brought her recognition and stardom, but she's always thought of herself as a singer. Her voice is pure gold."

"I know. I wish I could sing like she does."

"Did you ever try?"

"Yes, when I was a little grl, but that was a long time ago. I was always the one who sat down at the piano to accompany someone else. By the way, does Rose play the piano at all?"

"You're probably not gonna believe this, but she doesn't even read music. She just has a remarkable ear."

"So do I. When I'm listening to music, I can hear

any note that's even slightly off. I used to have my piano tuned every month."

The waiter came, and Lilah ordered a Jane Fonda, which was a raw vegetable salad, and Ben ordered an Esther Williams, which was a tuna sandwich.

As they ate, Ben asked, "Do you ever intend to play the piano again? Rose tells me you haven't touched it in twenty years."

Lilah shook her head. "No, that's a chapter of my life that's closed."

"Why would you throw fifteen years of your life away? Can't you play just for your own enjoyment?"

"I'm afraid it would be too depressing. You know, Ben, I actually thought about killing myself or running away so I'd never have to face my family and my friends after that ignominious defeat in Moscow. You see, I was brought up to believe that second best didn't count. Even my piano teachers drummed into me the need to be at the top. But they also told stories of good pianists who barely earned a living slogging along from one concert date to the next but never attracting a following or getting a decent recording contract. I didn't want to be like that, so when I failed, I made the decision to end the dream, once and for all."

"Well, I'm not sure I agree with that kind . . . uh-oh. Don't look now, but I think we're about to be attacked. Craig Kimball just walked in, and it looks like he's coming this way."

"What'll I do?" Lilah asked.

"Be sweet and charming . . . and act dumb. Pretend you've never met him before."

"I can't do that, Ben," she began to protest, but it was too late to argue the point.

Craig Kimball was accompanied by Sudsy, Bruce Stebbins, the series producer, and Stan Selden, who was scheduled to direct the segment in which Kimball was to appear.

As they came near, Bruce noticed Ben and stopped.

"Well, this is a surprise. Ben, Rose, I want you to meet Craig Kimball. Craig's a little concerned about the script, and he wanted to go over it with Stan."

Ben got to his feet and put out his hand to the aging star. "How do you do, Mr. Kimball," he said, and only Lilah noticed that his teeth were clenched as he spoke.

Kimball shook his hand and muttered, "Nice to meet you," and then turned to Lilah. "Well, Lady Rose, it's a pleasure to see you again."

Lilah smiled broadly and stuck out her hand to shake his as she gushed, "Why, this is a real pleasure, Mr. Kimball. I've been a fan of yours for years, and I want you to know how sorry I was about Christmas Eve. You must have thought I was just terribly rude to get up from the table and rush off like I did, but I had the worst case of intestinal flu or food poisoning or something. You're lucky I didn't throw up all over you on our first meeting."

Craig Kimball's eyes glazed over, and an expression of puzzlement inched across his face. Actor though he was, he could not mask his astonishment at the friendly greeting he had just received. Sudsy stepped forward and said, "Hi there, remember me, Rosie O'Girl?"

Lilah looked him directly in the eyes and replied, "No, I don't believe I do. Have we met before?" Her manner was so natural and friendly that it completely unsettled both men.

"Yeah, well . . . maybe not," Sudsy replied uncomfortably.

Bruce interjected, "Well, we've got to move along. Stan's got an appointment at three, and we need to get this script thing settled."

"What script thing?" Ben asked suspiciously.

Bruce immediately became defensive. "Don't get your back up, Ben. Kimball just had a few suggestions that he wanted to make to Stan, and I think we ought to take advantage of his expertise."

"Since when did a producer ever think an actor had

expertise?" Ben said coldly, his fake friendliness beginning to ebb.

"We have lots of expertise, don't we, Craig? These people behind the scenes just don't want to give us credit for having brains," Lilah said, smiling.

Both Sudsy and Kimball were numbed by her friendliness, but Ben continued to pursue his point. "If there are any changes in the script, I want to see them," he snapped.

"Ben, back down, will you? The changes are very minor, and they have nothing to do with Rose, understand?" And then very softly, he half whispered, "Craig just wants to make sure the camera angles are right for him."

Ushered away by the producer, the group moved on. Ben sat down again. Beads of perspiration had formed on his face.

"Jesus, I wanted to break the bastard's neck," he muttered, and took a long drink of ice water.

"Ben, he looks terrible. I would never have even recognized him."

"You were great, Lilah. That intestinal flu story is fantastic. It stops them cold."

"I've got to confess that it wasn't spontaneous. That one worked so well with Vance Freedland that I decided to use it again."

"Good show. We're gonna get him, Lilah . . . you and me, okay?" Ben said, and put his hand on her arm.

"I certainly hope so."

44

JELLIE Beam arrived at the Kimballs' residence feeling unsure of her welcome. Long experience with celebrities had taught her that they often had second thoughts about interviews, and Jellie was accustomed to being rebuffed. Even if she didn't succeed today, she had no intention of quitting. One way or another she was going to get to Craig Kimball, and Claire was going to help whether she wanted to or not.

The Kimball estate consisted of several acres in Holmby Hills. At the gates Jellie pressed a button on an intercom and gave her name, and the tall iron gates swung open. She drove her five-year-old Honda Civic up the narrow driveway bordered with tall trees and thick oleander bushes that shielded the house from the street. After she parked the car in a large concrete area in front of a six-car garage, she walked through a vine-covered archway to the front door of the huge house. She made notes of her impressions on a small tape recorder.

"The house is grand, although its architectural design is a mix of Colonial and California kitsch. It's huge and white, with a lot of well-manicured shrubbery. Must have at least two full-time gardeners. Kimball lives like the old stars did before the IRS. I see a chauffeur working on a Rolls-Royce in one of the garages."

She rang the doorbell, and a butler in a black, loose-fitting cotton jacket answered.

"I'm Jellie Beam. Mrs. Kimball is expecting me."

"Please come in," he said, and stepped back for her to walk past him. "Mrs. Kimball is waiting in the morning room. Follow me."

Jellie lagged a few steps behind so that she could record her impressions. "The butler's not English but correct and proper and undoubtedly expensive. Entry hall is imposing with its high ceiling. Staircase not very grand, but there are urns of fresh flowers everywhere, perfuming the air. Vivid colors, antique furnishings. Very quiet. The heels on my shoes are clattering on the highly polished marble floor."

She turned off the recorder as she was ushered into a bright room looking out toward a broad expanse of lawn.

Claire was seated at a small table drinking coffee and reading the morning *Times*. She was dressed in an exquisite mauve chiffon peignoir. Her makeup and hair were perfectly done, and she had limited her jewelry to pearl earrings and her engagement ring, a flawless twenty-carat pear-shaped pink diamond that she herself had picked out for Craig to buy as part of their arrangement. Looking up from the paper, she smiled and said, "Well, you're certainly prompt."

"I was afraid you might have changed your mind or forgotten," Jellie responded, taking a seat at the table.

"I never forget anything," Claire said.

"I'm going to quote you on that," Jellie replied.

"Good. That should make a few people uneasy."

"Do you mind if I tape our conversation, Mrs. Kimball? Some people are nervous about me doing it, but really, it makes for a lot more accuracy."

"I'm not afraid of the truth, Jellie, and please call me Claire. Now, how much of an interview is this going to be?"

"Let's get started and see how it goes. We'll probably need several days. I want to get a feel for what you do and how you live," she said, pushing her glasses up on her nose for the tenth time since she'd sat down.

"Oh . . . well, you mean you want to do one of those in-depth things. That might be interesting, but why me? Don't you usually just do that sort of interview on stars . . . celebrities, you know? I've never really done anything very exciting."

"That's not true. You're married to a man who's been idolized for years, especially now that his films are seen so often on TV. I think it's a mistake to overlook the woman chosen by this particular star to share his life. I've just got a gut feeling that you're a very special and interesting person and that you'll make a hell of a story." Jellie watched Claire closely to see how the pitch was going down.

Claire looked out the window at the huge lawn where she had held so many parties for charitable causes. Parties she had planned and presided over that had been attended by the great and the famous. She had helped raise millions for charity, and what had she gotten out of it? A brief mention in the society columns and, on rare occasions, a picture—usually out of focus—standing beside her famous husband. Nobody knew anything about her as a person. She turned back to the reporter and replied, "Turn on your machine. Would you like a cup of coffee?"

"Yes, please. Black," Jellie replied as she set the recorder on the table and aimed the microphone toward the exquisite Mrs. Kimball, already forming in her mind the title of the article, "High-Maintenance Woman."

"Let's start off with an easy question. How long had you known Craig Kimball before he asked you to marry him?"

"For many years, but very casually. We were both married to other people when we met on a cruise on Chuck Molina's yacht, right after the Cannes Film Festival. My husband at the time was Chase Stratton, who died in a plane crash a few months later."

"Who was Craig married to at the time?"

Claire hesitated perceptibly. It was a name that

Craig forbade her ever to mention. She wasn't certain about the circumstances of the divorce, but apparently it had been very messy. "Melissa Bedford," Claire replied without elaborating.

Jellie persisted. "Oh, that's right. Whatever happened to her?"

Claire shrugged her shoulders. "I believe she died."

"Wasn't there some scandal about her death?"

Claire was getting a little uncomfortable. "I really don't know anything about her. All I know is that my husband was very unhappy with her—she was years younger than he was—and it took him several years to get over the tragedy and heartbreak of that marriage."

"Yes, those May–December marriages often don't work out well. Would you care to comment on that? Especially since you've had a couple of them yourself."

Claire did not like the implication. "I wouldn't say that. There was never as great an age difference between me and my husbands as there was between that child and Craig Kimball." As soon as she had said it she wanted to bite her tongue.

"Exactly how old was she when she married Craig?"

"What does Craig's first wife have to do with me?"

"I want to provide some kind of a contrast between you and the unfortunate choices he made in his prior marriages, none of which lasted longer than two years, right?"

"That's true. Our marriage has far outlasted his others," Claire answered, somewhat mollified.

"How long after his divorce from his second wife, Bess Bellworth, did you start seeing him on a regular basis?"

Claire realized that she'd been sandbagged again. Obviously the little bitch knew the answers and just wanted to trap her into saying something stupid.

"A long time afterward . . . years, actually. Would you like some fresh coffee? Yours must be cold by now."

"Please. After your marriage you moved here into his house. He's had it for a long time, hasn't he?"

"Yes, he bought the property about forty years ago, but it never had been decorated properly. I'm responsible for the way it looks now."

"Well, it's certainly fabulous. What did it look like when you came here?"

"You can't imagine. Craig had never been interested in any room except the game room where he entertained his buddies, so the place was a shambles. I threw everything out and started over. I brought in a decorator from New York, and it took us a year to get it in shape. I'm extremely proud of the outcome."

"You should be. All of the pieces are genuine antiques, aren't they?"

"There's not a single reproduction in the house, and that's not true of a lot of the big homes in town."

"Really?"

"Yes, I can tell you about one tycoon who picks furniture out of antique catalogs and has them copied. There's not a single original in his house, but of course, he insists they are genuine."

"His name is?"

Claire laughed easily. She was on familiar and comfortable territory. "I won't go on record with that."

"Do you and Craig travel much?"

"Not as much as I'd like. Craig has never been interested in sight-seeing. Oh, every now and then there's a party somewhere—London or Paris—and he consents to go, but we always come home right afterward."

"But you have other homes, right?"

"Oh, my, yes. We have a place in the desert—Palm Springs—a cottage on the beach at Malibu, and a condo in New York, which is mine. Craig never goes there. He doesn't like to be too far away from the *Red Rose*."

"What's that?"

"His boat. She's the real love of his life. He spends more time there than anywhere."

"He's a real yachtsman, then?"

"Not really. He rarely takes it out of the slip. He just likes to entertain his friends there. They have poker games that go on for hours . . . sometimes days."

"You don't mind?"

"Heavens, no. Better there than having them here and messing up the house."

"You have your own activities to keep you busy, then?"

That was the question that Claire had been waiting for, and she launched into a long recital of her charity work, the balls she had chaired, the international dignitaries she had entertained, and the top-flight designers she had enticed to show their collections for Los Angeles charities. It was an impressive list, and Jellie had to turn the tape twice and listen patiently for cues to more important questions.

After two hours she saw that Claire was beginning to run down, and Jellie noticed her looking at her watch several times.

"Mrs. . . . Claire, maybe we should continue this on another day, if that's possible. I'd like to come back with a photographer to take a few pictures."

"Fine," Claire replied.

"I need to go over the tapes and see if there's something missing. What would be a good day for you?"

"Well, tomorrow?"

Jellie hedged. "I really won't have the material digested that soon. How about Friday?"

"Friday it is. Same time?"

"Great, and maybe you should have a few different outfits picked out. I'd like to have the photographer get you in several poses, in different parts of the house. Maybe a suit you'd wear to a meeting, and something casual, and perhaps a formal gown. Do you suppose your husband would agree to pose in a few pictures with you?"

Claire frowned. "I don't know, but I'll certainly ask him."

"Is he here now?"

"He slept on the boat last night, but he'll be home later this afternoon."

As she drove home Jellie thought about Kimball's first wife, Melissa Bedford. She smelled a story there. Claire had been noticeably uneasy talking about it. Jellie decided to go to the morgue at the *Times* and see what she could find. She also had gotten a glimpse of the dark side of the Kimball marriage. The next time she was in the house, she would ask for a tour. Maybe she'd find out if they slept in the same bed, which she doubted. Craig Kimball's wife was definitely not one of his fans.

Jellie was elated to be on the trail of the kind of story she had sensed might be a real shocker. A star she'd recently interviewed had made an interesting gaffe when he was commenting on the suicide of a veteran character actor who had secretly been his lover.

"I told him not to cross Craig Kimball . . . I told him he'd never work in this town again, but he wouldn't believe me." Right after the actor had said it, he begged her to forget it. He told her he would be ruined, too, if it got out that he'd said such a stupid thing. She assured him she wouldn't use it. Not yet, anyway. The story she wanted was how a superstar like Craig Kimball could ruin someone else's career so handily. Where the hell would he get the power?

45

Rose went to the studio the next day to finish filming the episode she had been working on, leaving Ben at home to coach Lilah on her lines one last time. While she waited for her call to the set, Rose sat in her dressing room poring over the notes she had made each night since Lilah had arrived.

There was a knock at her dressing room door, and when she opened it, looking up at her was Kimball's strange little sidekick, Sudsy. The shock sent her into a near panic attack. She might as well have opened her door to a cobra, coiled and ready to strike. Afraid that her voice would crack and reveal her agitated state, she merely stared at him mutely.

"Hi, Rosie. How's tricks?"

Rose closed her eyes and told herself that this was not her enemy. When she opened them, she said in a very soft voice, "I have a migraine, uh, Mr., uh," deliberately allowing herself to stutter over his name, as if she couldn't remember. Do what Lilah did yesterday, she admonished herself: Act dumb.

"Sudsy . . . everybody calls me Sudsy. Don't you remember me?" His eyes bored into hers, demanding that she give him some sign of recognition, which she refused to do. Determined to protect the cover of ignorance that Lilah had manufactured, Rose smiled faintly and replied, "Um, I don't . . . oh, yes, I'm so sorry. We have met, haven't we?" she began, and he smiled triumphantly as she continued, "Yesterday in the commissary. What can I do for you, Mr. . . . Sudsy?"

Sudsy did not reply. He just looked at her, but she held her ground, determined to outwait him. She knew how discomfiting silence could be. In the end it was Sudsy who backed off, "Oh, nothing, just stopped in to say hello and renew an old acquaintance."

She smiled faintly at what she presumed to be a joke. "Well, thank you. I'm sorry I can't invite you in, but I promised the director I'd rest between takes." She backed inside and slammed the door. Collapsing on the couch, she thought that if that little ape could turn her into a wet noodle, what would Kimball do to her? Thank God for Lilah.

They wrapped the shoot at nine that evening, and she hurried home to tell Ben and Lilah of her successful encounter with Sudsy.

"Son of a bitch!" Ben exclaimed, annoyed at Kimball's gall in sending his shadow to intimidate her.

"It's over, Benjie, relax. I handled it fine. Of course, they had to do six takes of the scene I was in right after that, but on the whole I think I held up pretty well, don't you?"

"Are you sure you still want to make the switch? You could probably handle it yourself, Rose," Lilah said.

"No way, sister, no way. Besides, the costumes for the next episode are being fitted to you, remember? Get me a drink, Benjie. Don't just stand there with the veins on your neck bulging out like that."

After dinner Rose suggested they all retire early, since she was tired and Lilah would need a good night's rest.

When Ben and Rose were alone, he took her in his arms and held her tightly. "I'm not protecting you very well, am I, baby?"

She gave him a long, tender kiss and whispered, "Benjie, just knowing that you love me is all the protection I need." She nestled her head under his chin and continued. "I never loved anybody before you. Never. Most of the time I slept with men who could help me in some way, but you came along and changed everything. You were stronger and brighter and gentler than any man I'd ever known. Geneva said my daddy was like that too."

"I knew the moment I saw you singing in that club in Paris that I wanted you all for myself. I'll never forget the blue silk dress. Man, I was knocked out by the way you looked and the way you sang," Ben said, tilting her chin up so he could look into her eyes.

"Benjie, it wasn't a blue dress. The spotlight was blue," she teased. "The dress was white."

"It was too blue. I wish you'd kept it."

"How come you waited so long to send that note backstage?"

"The bartender told me you never dated customers. It took me three nights to figure out that he was after you himself."

"Benjie, no matter what happens, remember that I love you. I'll always love you," Rose said, clinging to him. For a long time they kissed and hugged each other affectionately, and when they finally joined their bodies, moving in harmony, Rose felt herself transported to a higher, more sublime level of feeling than she had ever known before. Throbbing with the intensity of emotion and fulfillment, she wanted to tell him about the joy she felt, but she could not. How could she reveal to him that the other times, while filled with love, had also been shaded with pretense?

The next morning, when Lilah and Ben were ready to leave for the studio, Rose put her arms around her sister for one last hug of encouragement. "You'll do fine now, 'Lady Rose,' understand? Just don't go setting some high standard that I can't possibly live up to when I get back . . . uh, on the set."

"That's the least of my worries. Pray I don't freeze

when the director says 'action,' " Lilah replied with a nervous laugh.

"Don't worry about it. Some of my best scenes the director wanted to do over, and some of what I thought were the worst he loved. Now, Ben, you call me as soon as she finishes her first take and let me know exactly what happened," Rose demanded.

Ben gave Rose and hug and a kiss and said, "Right. I'll keep you posted."

Standing at the front door, Rose watched until the limousine was out of sight, and then she went back into the house and raced up the stairs. Quickly she got into the shower, and when she finished toweling herself dry, she went into Lilah's room. From the closet she took Lilah's beige tweed suit with a loose-fitting jacket, a brown silk blouse, and matching shoes and handbag. Back in her own room, she donned a new wig, and suddenly she was no longer Lady Rose. She looked at her fingernails and realized she did not dare trim them until the telephone call came in. If she had figured it right, that should be around twelve. Stan Selden was an efficient director, and he took great pride in keeping to the schedule.

When the clock struck noon and she still hadn't heard anything, she decided that since there obviously had been no major calamity, she could risk packing the suitcase.

Again she went into her sister's room and, feeling a twinge of guilt, took Lilah's suitcases and packed her sister's clothes. She took everything except Lilah's cosmetics and her medicine and her money, and left a note that she had written earlier.

The telephone call from Ben came at one-fifteen. "Honey, how're you doing?" he asked.

"Forget about me, how's Lilah doing?"

"Fine, just fine. She was a little nervous in the first take of that scene with Beth, but she got it right on the second. In the next setup she did it on the first take. Selden's pleased that everything's going well, so it would be a relaxed set if it weren't for that prima donna Kimball, who's been raising hell with makeup."

"Whee-o, am I glad I'm not there."

Suddenly Ben said, "Say, I gotta go. Kimball just came out of makeup, and he's headed toward Lilah. I'll call you later and tell you what happened."

"You can tell me about it when you get home. I'm going to take a nap. I love you. Don't ever forget that."

Before she left, Rose placed the note she'd written to Ben on his pillow. She had had a much more difficult time writing it than she had Lilah's. She just hoped he would understand.

46

FOR hours the next day Jellie sat with her eyes glued to a screen, looking at microfilm in the newspaper's reference room. She noticed that Craig Kimball was often photographed in the company of Vance Freedland. The most recent picture had been taken in December, the earliest over twenty years before. Interesting. She decided to see what she could find out about the fat man.

Jellie was frustrated at the paucity of real information about Freedland. The only place he ever seemed to get coverage was in the society columns, for his endless parties and for his generosity; or in the real estate section where he was frequently named as a principal in the buying or building of shopping centers and office buildings, all of which were apparently clean, conservative deals. At least, there was nothing to indicate anything to the contrary. Every mention in the paper described him merely as a wealthy investor, philanthropist, or benefactor. He had appeared on the scene in Los Angeles twenty years ago but from where?

At closing time Jellie got back into the elevator. Perhaps one of the reporters in the newsroom could tell her something. She walked through the aisles of computer terminals and wondered what the old reporters would think of a newsroom now, where no copyboys raced about with sheaves of papers in their hands. She saw several reporters hunched over their keyboards, but she passed them all, hoping to find an older man around somewhere.

At last, in the corner, out of the main work area, she found a reporter who looked to be in his late fifties. He was lighting a cigarette and staring at the screen of his computer.

"Hi," Jellie said, "can you give me some advice?"

"Sure, advice is something I've still got lots of. Nobody seems to want any of it anymore. Here, have a seat."

Without revealing that she was not a staff writer, Jellie sat down and said, "I'm trying to get a lead on a story about a man named Vance Freedland. Have you ever heard of him?"

"The big guy who hands out money like it's going out of style? Sure, who hasn't?"

"Yeah, that's him. From what I know, he came into town from nowhere about twenty years ago. Apparently he's got big bucks. Where does it come from?"

"Why do you want to know? Who put you on the story?" he asked pointedly. "You don't work here, do you?"

"No, I don't work here. I'm a free-lance writer," she admitted, "and it's not really him that I'm interested in. I'm doing a story about Craig Kimball, and I thought I saw a connection there."

"Well, well, you are an ambitious little girl, aren't you? Yep, there's lots of things around this town that everybody knows but nobody ever prints in the paper. Why are you on to Kimball? You tryin' to follow that old story about him bein' connected to the mob? Forget it, kiddo, better men than you have tried and failed."

"What do you think?"

"You're Jellie Beam, aren't you?"

"How'd you know?"

"Why don't you start investigating somebody worthwhile? You're a good reporter. Don't waste your time chasing movie stars and rock stars. What happens to them doesn't matter, because they just don't count in the scheme of things. Turn your attention to somebody important. Shine your spotlight on someone who's doing something that could hurt."

"Well, don't you think the public has a right to know about the stars they idolize? Don't you think we ought to expose celebrities for what they really are?"

"Not in our society, kiddo, no way. Let the public have their Mick Jaggers and Bruce Springsteens, the Pete Roses and Reggie Jacksons . . . and the Craig Kimballs. Why? Because they don't matter, that's why. They'll last a few years, and then somebody else'll come along. No harm done. That's what makes this country different. We only idolize people who don't matter. The time to worry is when we start making heroes out of our politicians, but that's not likely to happen . . . not in my lifetime, anyway."

"Okay, that's your theory and it's fine, but I don't agree with you. Maybe John Belushi would have cleaned up his act and lived if the world had known what a dopehead he was."

"That was his problem, not society's." The older man was enjoying the discussion.

"Suppose Craig Kimball decided to run for the Senate?"

"He won't."

"Why? Why won't he?"

"Because he doesn't give a damn about politics. And besides, the press would then start to care about him, and it would come out that he was the only son of a mob leader in Philadelphia named Karoffska, who was killed in a gang war fifty years ago."

"You're kidding? All of his bios say he was raised in New York City."

"Nobody believes the crap the studios used to put out."

"He is connected, then?"

"As I said before, so what?"

"What about Freedland? What do you think?"

"Well, he donated a quarter of a grand to the Music Center, for starters; and he's been pumping money regularly into every other good cause in town. Besides his big—and I mean big—real estate holdings, he's also been quietly buying stock in a number of companies, good solid companies. Not huge amounts at one time but small, inconspicuous sums spread out over long periods of time."

"You think he's fronting for people who might want to take over these companies?"

"No way. He hasn't concentrated on any one company. If you want my opinion, I'd say he's laundering money, turning it from illegal gains to legal investments. But don't quote me, kiddo, because there's no proof . . . none. Everybody guesses but contrary to popular thinking, we don't print guessing games."

"Has Freedland pumped money into any political campaigns?"

"He's too smart for that. He's the slickest operator in town."

"Okay, then why would he be involved with Kimball?"

"What the hell's wrong with Kimball? He's a respected and venerated star, not just here in Lotusland but all over the world. He's made a lot of movies, most of them not great, but he was always terrific. He was an actor who rose above his material, as they say."

"But I understand that he's not very nice. He's gotten in trouble several times when he's been drinking."

"Yeah, he's a mean drunk, I'll grant you that, but his public never cared. It just made him more exciting, I guess."

"Have you ever met him?"

"I've covered a few things where he's been, but I never knew him. I'm just a lowly hack, grinding out copy with hardly a byline to my name."

"Why do you suppose he's making a comeback in that television show?"

"Because old actors never die, they just go to series television . . . or run for president."

"Why do you suppose he retired, then?"

"Well, I'd guess if he did make a mistake in his career, it was his need to be the leading man . . . always. He just couldn't make the transition to being a character actor. His ego got in the way. Look, kiddo, this has been fun, but I have to finish this story and get home. I'm taking my grandson to a Laker game tonight."

"Well, thanks a lot. I never got your name," Jellie said.

"It's not important. I'm an anonymous source. Let's keep it that way," he said, and turned back to his computer.

Jellie hurried to the parking lot and got into her car. She had been doing her research all wrong. What she needed to do was talk to some people who had been around town a long time. What she wanted to know hadn't been printed in the papers . . . yet.

47

LILAH'S only difficulty during her first makeup session at the studio came when the young man doing her face complained, "My goodness, what's wrong, Miss Rose? Your eyelids are quivering so much, I can't get the line straight."

Ben interceded. "I told her not to drink that second cup of coffee. It always gives her the shakes."

"Really, now," the man agreed.

As they walked back to the dressing room Ben held her cold and trembling hand.

"Ben, I hope I can go through with this. I'm really getting cold feet."

"And cold hands," he teased, and rubbed her hands vigorously to get the circulation going.

When they were alone in her dressing room, he tried to reassure her. "You're going to be fine. Once you get out there and do it, you won't be so scared anymore."

"I hope you're right . . . God, I hope you're right."

The dresser, who was an attractive young woman, arrived to help her into her first costume. When she was finished zipping and buttoning, she asked Lilah if she was comfortable.

"Yes, I'm fine, Linda. Are they ready for me yet?"

Ben replied, "The assistant director should be calling any minute. You can go now, Linda. I think this is the only costume she's scheduled to wear today, right?"

"Yes, it is, Mr. Frost. If you have any problems, Miss Rose, just call me."

Lilah looked out the window and longed to be out in the fresh air. Suddenly the telephone rang, and she knew it was time. Her heart pounded, and when she looked at Ben, she reminded him of a deer facing the teeth of a tiger.

"Hey, now," he said firmly, "don't forget that you're Lady Rose, star. Stand up straight. Let's go. Stan gets furious when the actors dawdle."

Taking her arm, he escorted her to the soundstage. As they picked their way through the tangles of equipment and crew and cable, Lilah tried to smile and return the greetings of everyone they passed. It was obvious from the cordiality around her that Rose was popular. Ben never once forgot to call each person who approached them by name.

When they arrived on the living room set of Caymen Welles's extravagantly decorated New York penthouse, Lilah looked around and tried to get her bearings, but she was in a panic; all the lines she had so diligently memorized had evaporated into thin air.

Stan Selden walked toward them and greeted her with, "That dress looks great in that new fabric. Let's get this scene going, okay? I don't want to waste much time with the regulars because I have a nasty feeling I'm going to have problems with our guest star . . . so let's run through the action. Rose, stand over there in front of the desk. Look over toward camera and then toward the door. I want a slow appraisal of Beth, very hostile and superior . . . okay? Don't hurry the line. Beth, stand there with your hand on the door but look back over your shoulder at Rose. Cheat it a little so the camera can see your face better. Ready now for a run-through. Action."

Lilah did as she was told, and for a long, long minute she looked haughtily at Beth, but the lines wouldn't come out. At last the director said, "Too long, Rose. Say the line a lot sooner."

Desperately Lilah tried again, but she couldn't remember the line. When the director finally said, "For
God's sakes, Rose, say the damn line!" Rose dropped
her pose and turned to him and said, "I would if I
could remember what it was."

"Jesus, Rose, what's wrong? You're the only one
around here who always knows her lines."

Without missing a beat, Lilah replied, "Well, I guess
it's just my turn to be forgetful."

"Read the line!" Stan ordered, unamused.

The script supervisor intoned without expression,
"Stay out of my way . . . or you'll be sorry. I intend to break that husband of yours, one way or the
other."

When she heard the words, Lilah was relieved. Of
course. It was such a simple line. What was wrong
with her?

Wearily the director asked, "Are we ready now?"

"Ready," Lilah said softly.

"Let's go for a take. Cameras ready? Roll. Action."

Lilah did the long, hostile glance and then said the
line, putting as much menace and threat into it as she
could. After the director said "Cut," he commented,
"One more time. And Rose, you're too hostile. Be a
little cooler and more in control. Okay?"

When the take was over, Stan said it was fine, and
Lilah looked over at Ben, who winked and made a
small inconspicuous circle with his thumb and index
finger. They went immediately into a second setup,
which Lilah did perfectly.

The director told her he'd be ready for her next
scene shortly, when suddenly a gofer came running
toward them.

"Mr. Selden, Mr. Kimball says you're to come to
the makeup room immediately."

"What's wrong now?" Stan said, and his voice barely
concealed his exasperation.

"I don't know, sir. Kimball's pissed about something."

Stan hurried to the makeup room, and Lilah moved to where Ben was standing.

"You were great," Ben said softly.

"I wasn't great, but was I adequate enough not to arouse any suspicion?" she asked.

"You were a lot better than adequate."

"Well, it didn't exactly take a lot of emoting for that line. What's going on with the big star?"

"From what I understand, he brought all his own makeup with him, but the head makeup man says it's too dark for the lighting. He wants to do it his way. He's an artist, you know, and Kimball's in a snit."

"What's going to happen?"

"Well, if I know Stan Selden, he'll try to work out a compromise, and if that fails, he'll give in. It doesn't mean a damn to him how Kimball looks."

"But won't it look funny if he shows up darker on camera than I do? After all, I'm the one who's supposed to be black."

"Yeah, Kimball will realize his mistake when he sees the tape, and then he'll have to beg Stan to do it over. Okay if I leave you for a minute to call home and tell our friend that everything's going great?"

"Go ahead. I'll be fine. Tell her if she wins an Emmy for this show, I get to keep it six months of the year."

Ben arrived back on the set just as Stan Selden emerged with his guest star, who looked pleased that he'd prevailed. Stan strode toward Beth, had a hurried conference with her, and they began the scene that had just been interrupted.

Craig Kimball approached Lilah, and as Ben backed away slightly, she greeted the star with a smile and said, "Well, hello again. Did you get everything straightened out in there?"

"No problem. No problem at all. I just hate for these young faggots to tell me they know more about making up my face than I do."

"I wouldn't think they'd presume to tell you what to do. After all, you're the one who's been looking at your face in the mirror every morning for all these years. You should know more about it than anybody else does." Since she smiled sweetly and did not emphasize the phrase *all these years,* Kimball was not sure whether he had been insulted deliberately or not.

The assistant director asked them to take their places for their first scene together. Lilah glanced over at Ben, and he winked reassuringly in spite of the fact that he was as nervous and apprehensive as she was.

"Rose, I want you sitting there on the couch with a glass in your hand. In the master shot I want you holding it close to your lips and looking over it at him as he walks toward you and sits down. Your eyes are to make and hold contact—this is an important meeting—and you're both determined to dominate the other. Craig, walk across the room and sit down across from her. Hold the locked glance for a beat and then say the line, 'How do you do, Ms. Welles.' I want to set up a nice counterpoint between the banality of the words and the smoldering feelings between these two powerful people . . . understand?"

Lilah nodded and hoped the glass in her hand wouldn't shake too much. Craig Kimball moved to his mark.

"Okay, let's run through it once with the camera and see what happens," the director said.

At the word *action* Craig Kimball was the consummate professional. It was almost as if a switch had been flipped inside him that turned off the person he was in real life and turned on the star. As he walked across the room, moving with the slightly slouched walk that was his trademark, he was compelling, and Lilah had no trouble fastening her eyes on his. This was the star she remembered, and he had no resemblance at all to the creature her sister knew.

He spoke the line perfectly, sensuously, threaten-
ingly, and when it was done, the director called out,
"Cut. That was perfect. But let's do it again to see if
there's something more we can get out of it. Rose,
that slight tremble in your hand was an inspiration . . .
keep it in, but I'd like you to lift your eyebrow just
slightly. You're fascinated and attracted to this powerful tycoon, but you're not afraid of him . . . got it?
Now, let's expand the scene here a beat. After he says
his line, Rose, I want you to respond very sexily with,
'I do very well.' This is a battle of the titans, okay?
Let's go, then. We're on a roll."

The second take went perfectly, and they moved
directly into the conversation between the two, which
was sexy and loaded with innuendo. Kimball was thoroughly professional, although when it was over, he
insisted on watching the takes, which the video had
duplicated. When he saw the color of his skin on the
monitor, he did not throw a fit as everyone had expected him to. He just turned to the director and said,
"I was wrong about the makeup. Can we fix it and do
it again?"

The director, who was always pressed for time and
rarely ever agreed, could not resist the star's unusually
humble plea, and he consented. With Craig Kimball's
appearance, the show had become more than just a
weekly installment of a series for Stan, and he felt a
resurgence of the old desire to get things as perfect as
he did when making features. Kimball said thanks,
hurried to the makeup room, and was back within
fifteen minutes. They did the scene in one take, and
everyone was happy.

Except Ben. He didn't want to stand there and
admire Kimball. He didn't want to be won over by
that old star charisma. He hated him. He wanted to
keep on hating him so that he could make sure the
bastard never hurt his Rose again.

Lilah rehearsed each scene with Craig several times

and she stumbled on her lines occasionally, but when the camera rolled, everything went smoothly. Lilah realized that she was being carried along by a real pro, and she was impressed with his skill.

At the end of the day they were still on schedule, and the director was elated. "Great work, everybody. See you in the morning."

Craig moved toward Lilah and said, "Well, that was fun. I'm looking forward to tomorrow."

"You're just wonderful, you really are. I've never worked with someone quite so . . . talented," Lilah said, looking around for Ben. It was one thing to be on the set saying lines she had memorized, but it was quite another to be writing her own dialogue.

"Your . . . friend doesn't seem to be here. Would you like to come to my dressing room for a drink? I really would like to get to know you better. What do you say?"

"I'm afraid not tonight. Maybe another evening when I'm not quite so tired," she said, backing away.

"When? What night?" he persisted.

"Uh . . . let's see . . . uh, tomorrow or maybe the next night," she replied, feeling backed into a corner.

"Tomorrow it is. I think it would be nice to get a little better acquainted before we get in bed together for our big love scene, don't you?" He leaned close to her and said insinuatingly, "We want it to look very real, don't we?"

Lilah looked over her shoulder and was relieved to see Ben striding toward them, followed closely by Sudsy. "Oh, here's Ben. Well, I'll let you know tomorrow about that drink. I'll have to see if we can make it."

Ben looked like a thundercloud as he approached them, and Sudsy chirped, "Thanks a lot, fella. I appreciate the help."

Taking Lilah's arm, Ben hurried her away. When they were out of earshot, she asked, "What were you doing with him?"

"I was being set up. I knew it, but I went along. He asked me to walk over to the commissary with him and talk to some reporters. They weren't there, of course, so I knew that Kimball had told him to get me out of the way. What happened?"

"He asked me to his dressing room for a drink. I said no, but he insisted on tomorrow night. What'll I do?"

"I think you ought to go."

48

IT was a cold, blustery day at the Chicago airport, and
snow flurries caressed Rose's face as she got into a
cab. She gave the driver the address of Lilah's house
in Winnetka, and as the car moved through the traffic
she got her first glimpse of the area where her sister
had grown up.

At last the cab turned onto a street lined with bar-
ren trees and large, solid houses, each set in the middle of what appeared to be huge lots. How different
from Beverly Hills, she thought, where big houses
were nestled together on small pieces of land and
surrounded by walls, like chocolates in a box of candy.
There were no walls or fences here.

The cab pulled off the street onto a circular driveway in front of a large two-story brick house.

"This is it," he said.

She paid the fare, and he carried her bag to the
door for her. As he drove away she rang the bell,
shivering slightly. There were keys in her purse, but
she wasn't sure which was the right one. Better to
have Stella let her in. Several minutes passed, but
there was no answer. She rang again. When there was
still no response, she dug into her purse for the keys.
The second key she tried worked, and the big green
door opened for her.

She stepped into the hall and called, "Stella? Stella?
Are you here?"

The house was quiet. She carried her bag inside and closed the door. What could have happened to the housekeeper? She was fairly certain that this was not her day off.

The stillness of the house testified to its emptiness. The only noise she could hear was the hum of the blower on the furnace, and the house felt warm and comfortable. For half an hour she strolled cautiously through the rooms, orienting herself. When she got to the master bedroom and saw that the king-size bed where Lilah and Warren slept had not been made, she knew that for some reason or another she would not have to deal with Stella, at least not for the time being.

She carried the suitcase upstairs to the bedroom and unpacked. Carefully she hung her sister's clothes in the closet, and as she did so, she familiarized herself with its contents.

Lilah obviously had money, but it was surprising how few clothes she owned. They were of good quality, of course, but for the most part, unexciting, classic, wool pleated skirts and cashmere and shetland wool sweaters. A couple of suits . . . one Adolfo, one David Hays, and a few Ralph Lauren separates, an Anne Klein dark green wool dress, and a black velvet cocktail dress that had no label made up the rest. Lilah had several pairs of boots, probably needed for the winter, and the shoes were sensible Ferragamos and Julianellis. Hmm. How dull compared to her own designer-stuffed closets.

Rose changed into a pair of wool slacks and a sweater, fairly certain that was how Lilah would dress around the house. The pants were big on her, but she pulled the waistline tight with a leather belt.

Downstairs in the kitchen, after a bit of shuffling around, she found a box of tea bags. She put some water on to boil and fixed herself a large mug of tea. Then she went into the living room to relax. She passed the piano and felt a momentary sense of loss.

What a waste of talent and effort. Why had Lilah given up so easily?

Before settling down, she went into Warren's study and picked up the pictures of Matthew and Mary Ann that rested on his neat and uncluttered desk, and again she felt melancholy. Lucky Lilah, to have such beautiful children.

Suddenly the clanging ring of the telephone startled her out of her reverie. She stared at the instrument on Warren's desk as it rang a second time and then a third, undecided if she should answer it or not. On the fourth ring she picked it up and said, "Hello," in a very low voice.

"Mom? Mom, is that you? Are you all right?"

"Yes, yes, I am," she finally managed to reply to the caller, who obviously was Mary Ann. "How are you?"

"I'm great, but you sound a little weird. I hope you didn't get that cold I had at Christmas."

"Just a little hoarse, that's all," Rose replied, but she did not have to worry about further conversation. Lilah's daughter had called to talk, not to listen.

"Mom, guess what? My roommate didn't come back to school."

"Oh?"

"That's the bad news, now here's the good news. Marie Langtry moved in with me . . . remember, I told you about talking to her."

"Why, yes," she replied, faking it.

"Her father's the president, or something, of the stock exchange, you know. Well, her brother drove her back to school, and I met him, and guess what?"

"Don't tell me . . . you're in love." Rose couldn't resist. The answer was so patently obvious.

"Well, not quite, Mom, but close . . . very close. He's a sophomore at Princeton, and he's the most gorgeous guy you've ever seen. He's at least six-two. He's their top tennis player. He's got curly blond hair and the cutest little freckles on his nose."

"Sounds wonderful."

"But here's the kicker, Mom. He likes me. Can you believe it? He stayed over for dinner and we talked and talked. Marie went to bed and left us alone. He's invited me to the Valentine party at his school next month. It's destiny, I can just feel it."

"Don't get too carried away," Rose counseled, trying to be wise and motherly.

"He's coming here again next weekend . . . just to see me. Marie's all excited about it. She said I'm the first friend of hers he's ever shown an interest in. Isn't it exciting?"

"Very."

"Mom, I was really ready to quit this place when I came home at Christmas. Thanks for talking me out of it. Gotta rush. Tell Dad hi."

The conversation was over, but it left Rose with a poignant feeling of emptiness, as she wished for one brief moment that she had been talking to her very own child.

Rose sat in a wing chair, looking out at the bleak and dark landscape and comparing it to the rich greenery of a winter day in Los Angeles. The trees were stripped bare, their stark branches poking holes in the sky, allowing the tiny snowflakes to escape and flutter to the browned and dead grass of the lawn, where they touched and disappeared. Shivering, she took a big gulp of the hot tea to warm her body.

Suddenly she heard a noise from the back of the house. Was it the wind or was it the sound of a door being opened? Cautiously she got up and walked as silently as possible through the hallway toward the kitchen. She felt a sudden blast of cold air. My God, the door was open.

Nervously she called out, "Who's there?"

A surprised voice replied, "That you, Miz Conway?"

Fairly certain that it was Stella, who had finally come home, Lilah moved more quickly. This would be her first test, and she was anxious to see if she'd pass it.

"Stella, is that you?" Rose called.

Wrapped in an old black wool coat with a frayed mink collar and a bright wool babushka tied around her head, the black woman put down her battered luggage and said, "Gosh, Miz Conway, I didn't expect you back so soon. Mistuh said you'd be gone mebbe another week."

Rose smiled and began the carefully constructed story she hoped would explain everything. "I know, Stella, but as you can see, I haven't been feeling well. I caught some kind of a bug down there in Florida, and I couldn't keep a thing in my stomach. I lost a lot of weight and decided I'd just better get on the plane and get back home quickly."

"Sho' did get skinny, ma'am. You okay now?"

"It might take a few days to get back to normal. How have things been here?"

"Okay, I guess. I been gone since las' week. Mistuh gave me a coupla days off, and I went to visit a friend." Stella's manner was so defensive that Rose realized she was too worried about having been away herself to question her mistress's sudden reappearance.

"Well, I better get movin'. If I'd known you was gonna be back home, I'd'a gotten here a little sooner. You gonna be eatin' here tonight?"

"I think so. I must call Warren," Rose said, and left Stella mumbling at the prospect of throwing together a dinner without having had time to shop or prepare for it.

In Warren's study Rose found a leather book of telephone numbers. She located the bank's number and dialed it, but when a woman answered, she panicked, realizing she'd neglected to find out his secretary's name. She would have to bluff. She asked, "Who is this?"

"This is Sandra, Mr. Conway's secretary. Who did you want to speak to?"

"Oh, Sandra, your voice sounded different. Have you got a cold?"

"Who is this?"

"Why . . . uh, Lilah . . . Mrs. Conway," Rose replied. "Don't tell me my voice sounds strange too. Maybe we have a bad connection."

"Oh, I'm sorry. Mr. Conway will be so happy to hear from you. I'll ring him."

Rose's heart beat faster as she waited for him to pick up the telephone, and when she heard his deep voice say, "Lilah, where are you calling from?" her knees began to quiver so violently that she had to sit down quickly.

"Warren . . . hi. I'm calling from home," she said weakly.

Warren's sense of relief was palpable. "Home? Well, that's wonderful. I'll clear up my desk and be on my way immediately."

Now it began. She hoped he wasn't too discerning or critical. "I told Stella we'd be home for dinner. I . . . I haven't been feeling well since I left. I picked up some kind of a flu bug, and I'm having a few problems."

"What's wrong?" His voice was filled with apprehension. He sounded like such a nice and caring man.

"Nothing, really. A week of rest and good plain cooking should have me back to normal in no time at all."

"I'm on my way," he said tersely, and the call was over.

Rose replaced the receiver and hurried up the stairs to check her appearance. She had had stage fright before, but never, never like this.

Half an hour later, as she sat in the den staring at the news on television, she heard the door to the garage slam and knew it was time for the biggest performance of her life. Would Lilah rush to meet Warren? Would she hug him and kiss him the way she hugged and kissed Benjie? She'd do it that way, the way she found most natural. In this charade she would have to rely on her own feelings and instincts and trust that they were close to her twin's.

She got out of her chair and walked down the hallway, and suddenly there he was . . . this strange man whom she would have to treat intimately and with affection and care. He was so much bigger than she had expected and so much handsomer than his pictures. As she hurried toward him he opened his arms for her and held her close. She could feel love and warmth and affection flowing from him, and she responded to it, feeling like an interloper in an embrace that was meant to be shared by two people who loved each other deeply.

Warren held her tightly for a long, long moment, and she felt a terrible sense of guilt when she heard him say in a voice filled with emotion, "I'm so glad you're back." Breaking the almost unbearable intensity of his greeting, she reached up and kissed him on the mouth quickly and laughed, "My goodness, I must go away more often. I missed you too."

Suddenly he put his hands on her shoulders and moved them down her arms, and the look of relief on his face switched immediately to concern. "My God you're skin and bones! How could that happen in such a short time?"

"Isn't it wonderful? I've always wanted to have one of those skinny bodies like the models, and presto . . . one long bout of stomach flu and look at me!" She laughed and pulled away from him. "Warren, take your coat off and come in here and sit down, and I'll tell you all about it. Now, don't get upset. I'm fine. Really I am."

"Well, you don't look it. I'm going to call Dr. Bob in the morning and take you right over there to have a complete examination," he said forcefully.

"Give me your coat, and let's go relax by the fire. I haven't started it yet, so you'll have to do it."

"Good idea. Take the chill off the room," he said, handing her his topcoat. "Would you like to have a drink . . . or maybe you'd better not have any alcohol. . . ."

"No, it's all right. Um, but the doctor said to stay away from hard liquor. A glass of wine or champagne before dinner is fine."

"Champagne?" Warren asked quizzically.

Rose laughed. "He was a very expensive doctor."

"Well, we haven't got any of that, but I think there's some Montrachet left. I'll put a bottle on ice."

"Good idea. Let's celebrate my homecoming."

"I can't think of a better reason to celebrate."

As they talked, Rose stood holding the heavy coat on her arm, waiting for him to go into the other room. There were two doors in the entry hall, and she wasn't sure which one was the coat closet. She certainly couldn't take a chance and guess wrong.

He looked at her and smiled. "You changed your hair," he said.

"Do you like it?"

"It's okay, but I like the old way better. Those bangs cover up your face too much."

"It was just an impulse. It'll grow back soon," she said, brushing her hand across the bangs she'd had to cut on the wig to cover the hairline and make it look more natural.

As soon as he was out of sight, she pulled open the door on the left and sighed with relief. Thank God she had waited; it was the powder room. She opened the other door and put his coat on a hanger in the closet. So far, so good. Now she had to go in and talk him out of taking her to the doctor.

Cautiously finding her way through the rooms, she found the den again, the cozy walnut-paneled room with its print sofas, television set, and bookshelves. The fire was already blazing, and Warren stood twirling a bottle of wine in the bar sink, which he had filled with ice cubes.

He took two stemmed glasses out of the cabinet behind the bar, opened the wine, filled the glasses half

full, and then carried them to the couch where Rose
had settled.

"To us," he said, and lifted his glass.

"To health and happiness," she responded, trying to
avoid his eyes, which seemed to be searching for something in hers. What did he want?

After they had sipped the wine a bit, he said, "Now
tell me everything. I want to know all about your visit
to . . . Florida."

"There's not much to tell, because I got sick right
away. At first I thought it would go away in a day or
two, but it didn't. Florence got worried and called the
doctor. He did all kinds of tests but couldn't find
anything. He finally decided it was probably a virus
and would take time to go away."

Warren's eyes narrowed immediately when she mentioned Florence's name, and it unbalanced her. She
was sure Lilah had told her that Warren believed she
had gone to Florida with a friend named Florence.

"I see," he said coldly. "And did Florence come
home too?"

Rose had a sneaking suspicion she had dug herself
into a hole because she had no idea where the hell
Florence was. "There was no reason for her to come
home because I was sick," she replied evasively. "By
the way, I talked to Mary Ann this afternoon. She was
all giggly and happy with school now. It seems she's
got a new roommate who has a handsome brother at
Princeton. She says she's in love."

Rose could tell that Warren was not really listening
to her chatter. He got up to refill his glass, and she
could tell he had other things on his mind. When he
finally joined her on the couch again, he stared into
the fire for a long time, and there was an awkward
silence in the room. She had to say something. It
would be unnatural for her to pretend there was nothing wrong when he was so obviously distracted.

"You really mustn't worry about me, Warren. Be-

lieve me, I'm going to be all right in a few days . . .
just as soon as I get my strength back."

Suddenly he turned to her and said, "Lilah, please
don't lie to me. I just can't stand it."

Good grief, what had she gotten into? "What do
you mean, Warren?" She felt as if she had fallen into
the ocean and didn't know which way to go to find the
surface.

"You haven't been near Florida. You went to Los
Angeles."

"What?" she asked, afraid that if she said more, she
would lose all control of the situation.

"You concocted the whole story and enlisted Florence's help, but why? Why did you go to California?
You don't know anyone out there, do you?"

"Who told you I'd gone to California?" she asked,
cursing her impulsive scheme to find out what Lilah's
life was really like.

Warren said nothing, but there was a noticeable
droop of defeat in his shoulders. It was obvious he
didn't want to tell her.

"Warren, since you've accused me of lying to you,
I'm entitled to know," she persisted.

Without looking at her he said, "Florence. Florence
told me everything."

Sacré bleu! Why would Lilah's friend betray her?
What kind of a woman was she? Certainly no friend,
more like a vindictive or jealous . . . That was it: The
bitch wanted to cause trouble between Lilah and
Warren.

"When did you talk to Florence? Warren, is something going on between you two that I don't know
about?" she asked, taking the offensive. Let him do
the explaining.

"She was just telling me, as a friend . . . that's all,"
he said lamely, wishing to God he had never brought
the subject up.

"Why would you take her word? Do you have any
reason to believe this woman more than you believe

your wife?" Whoops, better get out of the third person. "More than you believe me?" she corrected herself.

Warren looked thoroughly miserable. "She telephoned me from Los Angeles and said you'd separated at the airport. She said she'd followed you to a house in Beverly Hills and that you'd told her that you wouldn't see her while you were there."

"And I suppose she suggested that I was probably having an affair? She did, didn't she?"

Warren nodded his head.

"Do *you* think I went to California to see some man?"

He looked down into his glass and murmured, "If you say you didn't, I'll believe you." The tone of his voice, however, told her he wouldn't.

Mon Dieu, why didn't I stay in L.A. and keep my nose out of other people's business? Rose fumed. Here she was in the middle of probably the biggest crisis her sister's marriage had ever had, and she didn't have a script to guide her. She didn't even know who the characters were or what were their motivations. God, send in the writers!

"You know, a very wise old woman once told me that people often justify their sins by saying that everybody else did it too. That's why so many politicians are corrupt . . . they claim it's fine to be on the take because everybody else is, and that's why so many people accuse their spouses of infidelity . . . because they've been guilty. Is that true, Warren? Have you been getting it on with Florence?" Good grief, Lilah would never use a phrase like that. She corrected herself, "I mean, Warren . . . are you having an affair with her?"

"I was. I'm not now," he replied contritely.

Rose turned away, angry and disgusted. Was every man in the world a bastard except Benjie? Or was she being fooled, too, just the way her sister was fooled by this upright, solid citizen? She sighed and wished she could walk away, but she knew she had to play the scene to its conclusion.

"How long has it been going on?" she asked.

"It only happened a couple of times."

"Only . . . only a couple of times? How considerate of you," she said, a sarcastic edge to her voice. Her anger was real, as real as if she had been the one betrayed.

"I can honestly say that I never wanted to get involved with Florence. Never. I was a bit down. I remember thinking that there ought to be more to life. Anyway, ever since her husband died, Florence had been calling me on the telephone to ask for advice. I tried to help her as much as I could because I knew how alone she was. One evening I stopped at her house to have her sign some papers, and she told me that she'd been in love with me since we were kids. She said that the biggest disappointment of her life had been when I'd married you and not her. God, I never even dated her, Lilah."

"But you were flattered," Rose said quietly.

"I guess. She asked me to stay. She said she needed someone to hold and make love to her, and she cried."

"And you slept with her only because you felt sorry for her, right?" She tried not to sound bitter, but she wasn't successful.

"No . . . no, not that time. It happened on Fiesta Night . . . at the club. I'd had too many margaritas, celebrating your winning the club championship, remember?"

"Where was I?" Rose asked curiously.

"You left me alone and went into the women's lounge to settle that handicap dispute between Jenny and Merle. You must have been gone an hour or more."

"And?"

"Well, Florence asked me to dance with her. And I did. She pressed her body close to mine, and she told me she wanted me. I . . . got aroused, and a few minutes later I found myself out by the large tree near the second tee. And, uh, I did it.''

"Weren't you afraid someone would see you?"

"We stood up against the tree. Sure, I was afraid we'd be seen, but that made it more exciting, somehow. Anyway, it was over pretty quick.''

"But it wasn't over, was it, Warren?"

"I wanted it to be, but Florence insisted that we . . . carry on. She didn't actually threaten me, but the implication was always there. I took her with me on a couple of business trips, but it wasn't any good. I didn't want to be there, and I especially didn't want to be there with her. Finally I agreed to buy her off. I've been giving her money to leave me alone.''

Rose got up and walked over to the bar and refilled her glass. If the poor bastard only knew that this was merely a dress rehearsal and that he still had to tell his real wife the dismal story. She sat down again. "Warren, you haven't been paying her to leave you alone . . . you've been paying her not to tell me. Isn't that true?"

"Yes, but not entirely. You see, there's more. I paid her to tell me what you were up to.''

"That's sick, Warren. Well, let me tell you that your wife did not go to California to have an affair!" God, there was that damned third person again.

Warren had not noticed it. "Then why did you go?"

"I can't tell you because it's not my story to tell, but you can believe me, it was nothing like you imagined. Well, this has been some homecoming," she exclaimed, and got to her feet. She didn't know what else she could say, and she needed time to think. "Let's have dinner.''

"What are you going to do . . . about our marriage?"

"It's much too soon for you to ask that question."

Rose went into the dining room, and Warren followed. They spoke very little, and when dinner was over, Rose insisted on watching television. By the time the late news came on, she had made her decision. The least a wronged woman could do was insist on sleeping alone for a while.

"Warren, I'd like for you to move into the guest room until I've had a chance to sort things out."

"Lilah, we promised never to go to sleep angry . . . and we never have. Please, can't we talk it over some more?" He was humbling himself, and Rose had no wish to humiliate him although she still did not have the right to forgive him. That was up to Lilah.

"I must have some time alone. That's the least you owe me," she declared.

"If that's what you want." His eyes searched hers, but she looked down. If eyes were indeed the windows of the soul, she didn't want him peering through hers and discovering that she was not the woman he thought she was.

After Warren had taken his things and moved to another room, Lilah went up to the bedroom and locked the door. Well, things were in a mess, but some good had come out of everything. At least she had found a way not to share his bed, a problem that had almost kept her from embarking on this adventure. Not only that, but now she wouldn't have to sleep in the damned wig.

49

THEY were comfortably settled in the backseat of the limousine on their way home when Lilah asked, "Okay, Ben, why do you want me to meet with Craig Kimball alone? What can it possibly accomplish that's worth the risk of his seeing through my impersonation of Rose?"

Ben leaned forward to make sure the window between them and the driver was securely fastened and the intercom shut off, before he said, "I need your help. I didn't want to ask for it until I was sure you were going to be able to carry off the deception, and I certainly don't want Rose to know anything about it."

"I'm listening."

"Well, as you know, I was opposed to this scheme at first. I felt that Rose needed to face Kimball and get it over with, to prove to herself that he was no longer a threat to her. But once I saw for myself how she reacted to him, I realized she couldn't handle it. Now I want to get him off her back and off her mind."

"How are we going to do that?"

"By giving her a weapon she can use against him if she ever wants to. Something that will make her feel less vulnerable." Ben opened the compartment where the bar items were usually kept and pulled out a small black box. "With this," he replied. He opened it to reveal a tiny tape recorder with a small jewellike microphone. "We're going to wire you for sound."

"Hmm, that's very interesting, but suppose Kimball doesn't cooperate?"

"I think it will work if you just pretend not to remember anything about your prior encounters with him. I'm hoping that you can get him to reveal how he terrorized her. Think you can do it?"

Lilah hesitated. "Well, I suppose if I can pretend to be Lady Rose in front of a zillion people, I can certainly pretend not to remember anything about an encounter I never had," she said with a laugh.

"You're sure you're not afraid of him? At all?" Ben asked.

"No, I'm not. As a matter of fact—now please don't ever tell Rose I said this—but after today I find it very difficult to connect him with the horror stories I heard from my sister. He's so damn smooth and professional, and he really is an extraordinary actor."

"Let's say he's an extraordinary personality who's managed to give the illusion that he's acting. Every character he's ever played on screen has been basically on one note, but what he does he does better than anybody, and he's shrewdly avoided any parts that would stretch him too much. He knows how the public wants to see him."

"You'd know more about that kind of thing than I would. Okay, when should we tackle him . . . tomorrow night?"

"It's as good a time as any," Ben said, replacing the box in the compartment. "Tell him you'll be happy to have a drink with him but only at the studio. Don't agree to go anywhere with him, understand? He's probably only a toothless tiger these days, but let's not take any chances."

"Do you really think that Rose will feel safer if she has this tape? It doesn't seem like much to hold over him."

"It all depends on what you can get him to say. If you can get him, in fact, to be a witness to the crimes he committed against her, she won't worry so much about no one ever believing her side of the story."

"Are you going to tell Rose about it?"

"Not until after it's over, and then only if we're successful in getting something worthwhile on the tape. If we try and fail, it will only make her more sure than ever that the son of a bitch is omnipotent."

When the limousine pulled into the driveway at the house, Ben jumped out of the car immediately and rushed toward the front door without waiting to help Lilah out. It was obvious that he was upset about something.

"What's wrong, Ben?" Lilah asked apprehensively as she followed him toward the front door.

"The lights are out. Rose always turns on all the lights when she's home alone, and the place is completely dark," he replied, agitated. Lilah looked up at the windows, hoping to find a glimmer of light somewhere to indicate that there was life in the house, but she could find none.

Without ringing the bell, Ben thrust his key into the lock and opened the front door. Switching on the hall lights, he turned off the burglar alarm's insistent buzz and called, "Rose! Rose! Are you all right?"

He charged from room to room, turning on lights, but she was nowhere to be found. "Maybe she fell asleep," he said, and rushed up the stairs to the bedroom. His panic had now affected Lilah, too, and she found herself racing from room to room with him. He stormed into their bedroom, with Lilah just steps behind him, and when they saw that it, too, was empty, a terrible dread descended on them both.

"Ben! Look! There's a note!" Lilah exclaimed.

Ben snatched it up, ripped open the envelope, and took out the sheet of pink stationery with its embossed rose in the upper corner. He read what Rose had written but then was quiet, and Lilah had to restrain her curiosity. He sat down on the bed and read the note again. On the third reading, he read it aloud.

My darling Benjie,

Please forgive me for not taking you into my confidence, but if I had, you never would have let me go, and I had to do this. It's not often that one has a chance to be somebody totally different . . . not just in a play but in real life. I hope you'll understand and will help Lilah realize how much this adventure means to me. I need to know what it would have been like if Geneva had given me up instead of her, and since Lilah's getting the chance to find out, I figured it was only fair that I should too.

I hope neither of you is mad or hurt, especially you, Benjie. I love you more than anything in the world.

All my life I never really knew who I was. Maybe being Lilah for a few days will help me find out.

All my love,
Rose

When he stopped reading the letter, Lilah sat down beside him and put her hand over his sympathetically. They remained that way for a few quiet minutes, and then Ben asked, "Why did she have to do this, Lilah?"

"I don't know, Ben, but I wish she'd talked to me before she did it."

"What's she gonna find out? What the hell is she going to find out?" he said, and his voice was bitter.

"Well, for one thing, she's going to find out that she hasn't missed much. My life is nice, but it's going to seem very dull to her. Too bad she didn't believe me."

"You're just as upset as I am, aren't you?" Ben asked. "And you should be."

"I have no right to be angry with her for wanting to see for herself. God knows I was anxious enough to find out what it would be like to be her. Ever since I first learned the truth of my background, I've also wondered 'what if?' but darn it, she should have talked to me first. If she was determined to do it, at least she should have gotten my help so she'd've had a better chance of pulling it off safely."

"Damn, I'm sorry, Lilah," Ben said, "and I hope you won't hold it against her if she screws up."

Lilah let out a long, quivering sigh. "Maybe I'm overreacting. After all, what's the worst that can happen? Warren will know the truth. It's just that I wanted to tell him myself . . . and it looks now like I waited too long."

"Everything's going to be fine. Rose is a great actress and a quick study. It's gonna work," Ben said, trying to reassure her.

"I hope so. Ben, I'm going to take this wig off. It's giving me a headache. Why don't you send out for some dinner. I'm not really Lady Rose, you know. I need to eat."

Ben stood up. "Sure, what would you like?" he asked, glad to have something to do to relieve the tension.

"Just no more pizza, that's all," she replied as she went into her room and shut the door behind her.

As she sat down at the dressing table to remove the hairpiece, she saw the note Rose had left for her. She ripped it open and read her sister's apology for not confiding in her. Rose promised to be both discreet and chaste and asked Lilah to kiss Ben good night but let him tuck himself in. Lilah laughed and put down the letter. She wondered just how Rose planned to rebuff Warren's amorous advances without revealing herself. She wondered why she wasn't jealous. Perhaps because she trusted Rose, just as Rose trusted her.

The only thing that really concerned her was what Warren's reaction to the reality of her birth would be. Would he still love her? Would their marriage be the same? The fear that she had managed to repress made its way to the surface. She hadn't told him because she really didn't know how he would feel. Strange, but she might very well know more about her sister than she did about the feelings and prejudices of the man who had shared her life for twenty years.

Late that night, long after she had said good night to Ben and gotten into bed, Lilah lay awake, staring into the darkness and thinking about Warren. Was it her fault that they had lived together all this time without ever really knowing each other? How could a marriage produce two wonderful children, yet leave their parents emotionally unconnected?

Lilah buried her face in the pillow and tried to put it out of her mind. It was all too uncomfortable to think about, especially the thoughts of Matthew and Mary Ann, for they were the ones whose lives would be most seriously affected. Or maybe not. Their world was not, after all, the same as hers. She hoped it was better. Perhaps tomorrow, if she had some free time, she'd call them just to hear their voices.

She closed her eyes tightly and tried to force herself to get some rest so that she would be able to cope with the day to come. She had enough on her hands here in Hollywood without worrying about what was going on elsewhere.

Still, she did wonder what the sleeping arrangements were back in Winnetka that night.

50

MAVIS Madden had been the most influential society columnist in Los Angeles for ten years, and if there were some skeletons in the closets of the local glitterati, Jellie Beam was sure that Mavis would know where they were.

"Hi, this is Jellie Beam. Ask Mavis if she has time to have lunch with me today. If not lunch, then maybe drinks, okay?" she said to one of the columnist's young assistants.

"I'm sorry, but Miss Madden is writing today, and she doesn't want to be disturbed. If you have any news for her column, I'll be happy to take it down for you."

"Look, young lady, tell Mavis to pick up the damn telephone or I'll call in all my juicy little tidbits to the *Times*," Jellie said curtly. There was only one way to treat officious little sidekicks, and that was with as much menace as possible.

"One moment, please," the young woman replied, and exactly three minutes later the husky voice of Mavis Madden came on the line.

"Okay, Jellie, this had better be good. I'm working against a deadline," she snapped.

"I need a favor, Mavis . . . and it's your turn. If you'll recall, I was the one who clued you on the Davis—"

"Yes, yes, I remember. So what do you want?"

Mavis Madden's exquisite good looks, taste, and

family background had made her welcome in all the important homes of the city. She had become a star columnist as well, accustomed to dealing with only the rich and the powerful, who fawned over her in their desire to have their names mentioned as frequently as possible in her column.

"I need to talk to you. I'm doing an in-depth story on Craig Kimball. What can you tell me about his relationship with Vance Freedland?"

"Nothing everybody else doesn't know."

"Come on, Mavis, you can do better than that. All I need is a lead or two . . . I'll track it down myself. You owe me that, Mavis, after all the—"

"I can't be seen with you in public, Jellie. If the people I write about suspected I was helping you with your muckraking, it would do me irreparable harm. Come over to my house at ten tonight. I'll be packing to go to Monaco, and we can talk then."

"I'll be there." Jellie looked at her watch. It was almost noon. She tried to reach Claire Kimball but was told that she had a luncheon engagement at the Bistro. Disgusted, Jellie thought that all those broads ever did was spend money on their hair, their bodies, and their clothes, and occasionally throw a charity ball that would give them another excuse for spending money on gowns and hairdressers. One of these days she was going to write a story describing them as they really were. She would call it "Deeply Superficial." Now that was a satisfying oxymoron. She gloated as she placed her empty coffee cup in a sink filled with dirty dishes.

She listened to the tape she had made during the Claire Conway interview, hoping to pick up something she might have missed the day before, but the only really interesting thing was Claire's reaction at the name of Melissa Bedford, Kimball's first wife, and her strange death. Surely Mavis would know something about that. Jellie could remember only the most perfunctory mention of it in the newspaper clippings she had perused the day before.

She dialed the reference room at the *Times*. It was busy. It was always busy. She kept dialing until finally she got through.

"I'm looking for some information on a woman named Melissa Bedford. She died twenty-five or thirty years ago."

"Any reason for more than an obit on her?" the young man asked.

"Yes, she was Craig Kimball's first wife."

"I'll see what I can find. Call back in an hour. Ask for George."

"No!" Jellie yelped into the telephone. "I might never get through again. Your line is always busy. Can't you do it while I hold?" There was no answer, and Jellie realized the line was dead. It took her two hours to get George back on the line.

"What did you find out?" she asked, paper and pencil in hand.

"Not much. She was married to Kimball in 1955. The studio said she was eighteen, but her mother said she was only sixteen at the time."

"What's her mother's name and where did she live?"

"Blanche Brodsky. L.A., no address given. The girl was divorced from Kimball after less than two years of marriage. She died six months later. Unidentified studio spokesman said Kimball was too broken up to talk about her. Died of natural causes on December 24, 1957, at Sunshine Sanctuary, a small convalescent hospital in Glendale. That's it."

After a call to information confirmed that the hospital was still operating, Jellie dialed the number and asked to speak to the director.

"Mrs. Childs? My name is Patricia Carter, and my mother died at your hospital in 1957, a few months after she gave me up for adoption. I'd like to have a look at her records, but my attorney tells me I'll have to petition the court under the Freedom of Information Act. Since it was all so long ago, I was hoping perhaps you would dispense with that formality and just let me see them."

"We have a policy of keeping our patients' records confidential. This is a private facility, you know."

"But this happened almost thirty years ago, and I'm sure that there's no one living who would be affected by it now."

"I'm sorry, but rules are rules," the woman said, although Jellie sensed a certain weakening.

"May I have your full name for the subpoena? I guess I'll just have to go through legal channels," Jellie said, trying to sound regretful.

"Subpoena . . . what for?"

"You're the person in charge, aren't you?"

"Look, Miss Carter, I don't have time for subpoenas. My husband and I bought this hospital just two years ago, and he died last month. I'm having a difficult time managing everything, and I don't have time to go to court. Why don't you just stop in and we'll talk it over."

Jellie tried to keep the excitement out of her voice. "This afternoon?"

There was a short pause before Mrs. Childs agreed. "This afternoon at three. Give me her full name and I'll see what I can find."

"It will be listed under the name of Melissa Bedford or Brodsky or Kimball. I'll be there at three, and I can't tell you how much I appreciate this."

Jellie slammed down the telephone before the woman could change her mind. Bingo! *Subpoena* was a magic word. It had worked for her before. How people did hate to be dragged into court.

A conservatively dressed Jellie sat primly at Miss Childs's desk, waiting as the woman looked through a folder.

"I have the records here, but there isn't very much to tell. What are you looking for?"

"Everything I can find out. You see, I've inherited a great deal of money from my adoptive parents, but I'm all alone. I was hoping there might be some clues as to whether or not my natural mother had any living relatives."

"All I have here is that your mother, Melissa Jean Bedford, died of an overdose of sleeping pills on December twenty-fourth in 1957. She was admitted as a chronic alcoholic on August eighth of the same year by her ex-husband, whose name was Arthur Karoffska. A newly hired orderly admitted procuring the pills for her in return for a large sum of money. He was fired, of course. Her body was claimed by a woman named Blanche Brodsky, who was her mother."

"Is there any other information about my grandmother?"

"I'm afraid not."

"Is the name of the man who gave her the pills in there?"

"No, only that he was dismissed and reported to the police." She closed the file, and it was obvious she would be forthcoming with no more information.

"Christmas Eve," Jellie commented, and felt a real pang of sadness for the young woman whose life had ended on that holy night.

Jellie drove home at twilight. *Natural causes, my ass,* she fumed. Where the hell were the reporters when studios were giving out nothing but self-serving shit?

51

AFTER a night of tossing and turning and terrible nightmares from which she awakened with her heart pounding as she groped across the cold, empty sheets, vainly trying to reach Ben, Rose awakened to a still, dark emptiness. It was only six A.M., and she shivered. *Sacré bleu,* it was freezing in here. Warren must have turned off the heat. These Midwesterners must have very thick blood, she decided. This was the last night she was going to bed in a thin silk nightie. Surely Lilah had a flannel gown tucked away somewhere and a pair of heavy wool socks.

Inching back the thick down comforter, she reached for Lilah's velour robe. She pulled it off the chair and onto herself as she stepped into a pair of slippers. Quickly she dashed into the bathroom where she turned on the hot water in the shower. What she needed was a good, long session with the scalding water to thaw out her skinny body.

An hour later she emerged from the bedroom dressed in a cashmere turtleneck sweater, a shetland cardigan, a pair of panty hose under the wool tweed slacks, and over those she added a pair of wool socks. The only shoes the socks would fit in were a pair of brown loafers.

She had done her makeup and wig with care, and she was generally satisfied with her appearance, but she was too tense, too worried about making a slip to relax and enjoy her adventure. Was her sister having the same problems?

She heard the furnace fan going and realized that the house was beginning to warm up. Perhaps Stella was up and fixing breakfast. As she started downstairs to get a hot cup of coffee, she heard Warren's voice. She turned and saw that he looked haggard. He must not have gotten any more rest than she had. Why did she feel so sorry for him? He deserved a good boot in the britches, she thought, or at least something to bring some life to this terribly formal relationship he and Lilah had.

"I've got an early breakfast meeting this morning, Lilah. Tell Stella I won't be eating here," he said, and she could tell that he was trying to recover some of the dignity he had surrendered the night before. *Pauvre diable.* If only he knew how safe the information about his indiscretion was with her. Without knowing it, he had had the satisfaction of getting the whole thing off his chest without the consequences, for she would never be able to tell Lilah.

"Will you be home for dinner?"

"Yes, unless there's some reason you'd prefer that I not . . ." he began uncertainly.

"I'll have Stella fix something special." She hoped she hadn't sent a signal of forgiveness, because she didn't have the power to do that, nor did she want to. The sleeping arrangements were perfect.

Warren smiled hopefully. "Great idea. I'll bring home a bottle of good wine." He walked down the steps toward her and took her in his arms, but all she did was present her cheek for a quick peck.

"What time do you think you'll be home?" she asked coolly.

Warren stepped back. "The usual. I'll call you if there's any change."

"I'll see you then," she replied, and headed toward the kitchen, leaving him to put on his topcoat and go out the door alone. She was unaware that Warren was as rebuffed by that gesture almost as much as he was by being evicted from his bed. Lilah always saw him off. He considered it bad luck if she didn't.

Warren tried to lift his spirits on his drive to the office, but nothing seemed to work. Lilah was home, but she seemed more distant and aloof than ever. Of course, what did he expect after the ugly confession he'd made?

At the office he was distracted, concerned only with getting his meetings out of the way so he could get home for dinner on time. Just before lunch, however, he took a call that gave him the diabolical pleasure of retaliation.

"Mr. Conway, long distance. Mrs. Bennett is calling from Los Angeles, person to person. Will you accept the call?"

"By all means, put her on," he replied. He was going to enjoy this.

"Hello, Florence. What's new?"

"Not very much, Warren. Although I've been haunting that house she disappeared into, I haven't seen Lilah, and she hasn't called me. But that's not what I called about. Warren, do you think you could send me next month's allowance a little early? I've been having a lot of expenses out here. . . . God, everything costs a fortune in Beverly Hills, and I've met this—"

Warren had listened until the urge to blast her out of her complacency overwhelmed him. "No, Florence, no money. Not from me. Never again."

There was a shocked silence on Florence's end, and then she retorted bitterly, "What are you talking about? We have an agreement, or have you forgotten?"

"I've told Lilah everything."

"You're lying, Warren. How could you possibly tell Lilah anything when you don't even know where she is?"

"Lilah came home last night."

"She's home?" Florence asked incredulously. "She wasn't supposed to go home until next week!" Her voice climbed the scale until it reached a thin shriek of surprise and anxiety.

"Lilah's here, and everything's fine, in spite of what I did," he lied. "I'm sorry for everything, Florence, and I blame myself for what happened. Now, I don't think we have anything to say to each other, not now, not ever again."

"Wait, Warren, don't hang up, please. Lilah promised to pay my hotel bills here. If she doesn't, I'll really be in a mess. I haven't got the money for this kind of place," she wailed, fear pinching at her vocal cords.

"That's between the two of you. Good-bye, Florence."

"Wait just a damn minute, Warren! If Lilah's at home, then I presume you know the reason she was out here staying in a home with a black man. Tell me, was it all as innocent as our little affair?"

Although she did not realize it, her arrow had struck home. Warren continued, a little hoarsely now, "Good-bye, Florence. We have nothing more to say to each other ever again." He replaced the receiver and got up to leave. As he passed his secretary's desk he said, "If Mrs. Bennett ever calls here again, tell her I'm not in."

He walked out into the cold air, and although his car and driver were waiting for him, he waved them away. He needed to walk and think. The previous night, he had spilled out his insides to his wife, and as usual, she had given him nothing. He was tired of writing love letters and getting postcards in return.

52

FLORENCE put down the telephone, utterly shaken. What in heaven's name would she do if Lilah refused to pay the enormous hotel bill she had rung up? With her hands trembling, she dialed the front desk and asked for the cashier.

"This is Mrs. Bennett, Florence Bennett. I understand that my bill has been prepaid by a Mrs. Lilah Conway. I might be checking out today, and I wondered how it had been arranged."

The cashier said she would check it out and call her back. As she waited, Florence paced the room, with visions of meals and massages, champagne and caviar, haunting her. God, what a fool she'd been not to make sure that everything was taken care of in advance. Ten minutes later the telephone rang, and she snatched it up.

"Mrs. Bennett, I'm afraid there's been some kind of a mixup. Mrs. Conway signed a credit-card receipt, but it covers only the room rate and taxes for two weeks. She probably intends to cover the other charges with another receipt when you check out. When are you planning to leave?"

"I'm not sure. I'll have to get back to you on that. Thank you for the information."

As Florence put down the telephone she felt herself begin to shake uncontrollably. If Lilah knew everything, she might very well refuse to pay for anything at all. The smart thing to do would be to check out today and let the whole two weeks' room rent go toward paying for everything else. It probably wouldn't cover it, but at least she wouldn't be running up any more bills. Damn, where would she go? She had no choice. She'd just have to pass up the dinner party with Del tonight, forget about glamorous Hollywood, and go home.

On the other hand, perhaps she ought to call Lilah and find out if Warren was telling the truth. Feeling she had nothing to lose, she picked up the telephone and called Chicago.

"Lilah, what's the idea of going home without calling me and letting me know? We had an agreement, remember?"

Rose was momentarily confused. She must make it a point not to answer the telephone anymore, she decided.

"Who is this?" she asked.

"What do you mean, who is this? This is Florence, remember? You left me stranded here in Beverly Hills, in case you've forgotten."

Suddenly the picture came into focus. Ah, yes, Lilah's two-faced friend. "Florence, of course. How did you know where I was?"

"I talked to Warren this morning. I hope you didn't believe all that drivel he fed you."

"What are you talking about?" Rose had to play for time. Good grief, she'd left one soap opera for another.

"You know what I mean. Warren took advantage of me. That's the real truth, no matter what he said. There I was, just a poor helpless widow, vulnerable and lonely, and he used that to—"

Rose shook her head in amazement. This woman had enough gall to float a battleship. She wished she could meet her.

"I have nothing to say to you, Florence, nothing at all. Now good-bye." Rose was anxious to end the conversation, but Florence was not.

"Wait just a minute! We had an agreement. You said you'd pay all my expenses at the hotel here, and I found out that you'd only arranged to pay my room charges. What do you plan to do about the other expenses?" she demanded.

"Other expenses? What other expenses?" Rose asked incredulously. What a pushy bitch! She'd been screwing Lilah's husband, and now she wanted her bills paid.

"Meals, the beauty shop, you know. It amounts to quite a bit."

I'll bet it does, Rose thought, but she said, "Forget it. I'd never have gotten involved with you at all if I'd known what was really going on, and you've got a lot of nerve to expect me to pay for anything!"

Florence's aggressive tone shrank to a whimper. "Please, Lilah. You know I don't have that kind of money. You got me into this fix. I was only trying to help you deceive Warren . . . as a friend."

"Sure you were. Well, if you haven't got the money to live the good life out there, then I suggest you cut your losses and get on a plane and come home."

"Lilah, I can't. I've met this producer, and he really likes me. Last night he took me to a big party in Bel Air, and he's invited me to another one tonight. I don't want to come home now when things are looking up. Please help me. I promise not to put another cent on the bill if you'll just take care of what went before . . . and the room charges, of course."

"Florence, you're something else, you really are."

"For old-times' sake, Lilah, give me this one chance—"

"For what, Florence? What are you going to get out of some producer out there? A couple of parties? A roll in the hay? You're a crazy lady." Rose caught herself. Lilah probably never would talk like that.

"Okay, maybe I'm crazy, but if I come home now, I'll never know. I'll tell you what. If you'll pick up the bill, just what's already on it, and nothing else from now on, I'll tell you something important."

"And just what is that?" Rose asked, curious to know what she was hinting.

"Will you pay the bill?"

"It depends on what the information is. If it's really important, yes, I will."

"Good. I know where you were staying. I followed you there; I've been watching the house and reporting to Warren. I told him that you were staying there with a man . . . a black man."

There was a long silence on the line until Rose finally said, "And is that all?"

"That's all."

"I'll pay," she said quietly, and slammed down the telephone.

When the call was over, Florence threw herself onto the bed. What a relief. She would have to be extremely careful about money or she might have to go to work, and that would be a real calamity. There was nothing she could do at her age, except perhaps clerk in a department store, and wouldn't *that* cause all the tongues at the country club to waggle?

After a while she got up and showered and dressed. She would have to return the outfit she had worn the night before to the store again and exchange it for something else. It wasn't going to be easy, but perhaps, if she spent a little more, a very little more, they'd let her get away with it. She really needed to look great tonight.

Two hours later Florence was back in her room with a new black wool dress after a miserable scene in the store. She had succeeded in exchanging the dress she had worn to the party the night before for a more expensive one, but it had been an embarrassing ordeal. The manager obviously was on to her, but Florence had held her ground, insisting the dress had not been worn.

Since she could no longer afford the luxury of room service, she had stopped at Nate 'n Al's delicatessen and bought herself a sandwich for lunch. With it she drank lukewarm tap water, now that even ice was beyond her means. When she was finished, she rolled her hair in hot rollers. No more pampering in the beauty salon, either. What a shame. She had been having such fun.

Del was only half an hour late. Although he was smartly dressed in a well-tailored dinner jacket and crisp white shirt, he wore glasses with a darker tint than usual, and his speech was a little slurred. She noticed that he stumbled slightly as they stepped into the elevator.

"Are you all right?" she asked.

"Couldn' be better," he replied, and they had no more conversation until they emerged into the night air and Florence found herself being helped into a long silver limousine. She was thrilled. "Del, what a nice surprise. Did you get this just for me?" she asked coyly.

"Naw, couldn't drive. Had too much to drink this afternoon," he replied thickly, and slumped down into the seat and closed his eyes.

"Del . . . Del, are you all right?" she asked anxiously, but there was no reply. He was either sound asleep or dead.

The driver spoke to her on the intercom. "There's a bottle of champagne back there in the refrigerator . . . or you can mix yourself a drink if you'd like, ma'am. It's going to be a long drive."

"Where are we going?" Florence asked.

"To Santa Barbara."

Florence took out the bottle of champagne and tried to open it, but the cork wouldn't budge, so instead she poured a little gin into one of the crystal glasses, filled it with ice, and settled back to think about the day just past. God, she'd had better ones. She hoped the party would be more fun than the one the previous night. Del had been so busy working the room, he'd had practically no time for her at all. And in spite of the energetic sex, he still had not kissed her.

By the time they reached their destination, Florence had come to a decision. Del was obviously interested in her or he wouldn't have taken her out three nights in a row. If he would just sober up, she'd ask him if he'd like for her to stay in Los Angeles. She had nobody to go home to in Illinois, anyway, and even though Del was married, he was better than nothing. Surely he would be able to get her a job at one of the studios or at a television station. She could rent her house back home until she found out if she could make it here or not. She could always go home if she didn't. What did she have to lose?

53

JELLIE pulled her car into the narrow driveway and set the brake so that it wouldn't drift down the hill. Mavis had bought the house in the Hollywood Hills years ago because it had both history and character, and she had put a lot of money into preserving its original Art Deco design.

Mavis's daughter answered the door. "Are you Jellie?" the young woman asked as she let her in.

"You must be Mavis's daughter, Ava, right? I thought you'd gone away to school," Jellie replied to the cool, young, blond woman, who was remarkably poised.

"I did, but New England was a poor choice for a California girl. I'm at UCLA now, studying communications."

"Going to work with your mom?"

"Maybe."

Ushered into the starkly white, black, and chrome living room, pristine in its steely elegance, Jellie chose a black patent-leather chair and settled down to wait. She looked around and wondered where Jean Harlow was hiding. Suddenly the lady of the house swept into the room. Jellie had to admit Mavis was gorgeous. Petite and slim, she wore her shining black hair flapper-style, short and very straight, parted deep on the side, and swept across her head like a helmet. She wore a purple silk dressing gown and high-heeled silver mules and held a long black cigarette holder. She looked as if she had been designed by Erté.

"What's up, Jellie?"

Jellie inclined her head toward Ava, but Mavis shrugged her shoulders as she sat down and signaled her daughter to do the same. "Don't worry about Ava. I tell her everything."

"Well, I've done an interview with Claire Kimball. Not that I'm much interested in her—"

"She'd sell her soul for publicity, you know . . . the right kind, of course." Mavis laughed.

"I'm basically interested in her husband."

"Who isn't? He's still the star of stars, bastard that he is."

"You don't like him, I take it?"

"Hardly. He spilled a glass of red wine down the front of my white satin Oscar de la Renta at a dinner party one night simply because I asked him a question he didn't want to answer."

"What was the question?"

"It was very innocent. I asked him how he'd gotten that scar on his cheek."

"What did he say?"

"Not a word. He just poured wine on me. Of course, he apologized profusely and insisted it was an accident, but I knew better. I keep my distance. I think his wife is a fool to stay with him, but I'm sure she's hoping to outlive him and collect his money."

"What's his relationship with Freedland?"

"You know the answer to that, don't you?"

"Not really. There are rumors that Freedland has some ties to the mob and so does Kimball. What do you think?"

"It's a delicious rumor, and I'm sure it's true, but it's not what you'd call news."

"But there's never been anything written about it that I can find," Jellie protested.

"And there won't be. Don't waste your time. First of all, it won't be published because there's no way you can document it, and secondly, if it did ever manage to get into print, you'd be finished in this town."

"Why? Surely you don't think he'd have me rubbed out?" Jellie asked in a mocking tone.

Mavis laughed her light, tinkling laugh of genuine amusement. "No, of course not. It's just that nobody would talk to you anymore. You'd be an outcast. People would be afraid to go near you. Craig Kimball has connections to everybody in this town, one way or another, and he's not afraid to use them. He's vindictive and mean, and he has an aura of power that's been enhanced by countless nasty little rumors, which are probably true. Remember Charles Hammond?"

"Vaguely. Wasn't he a singer or something?"

"Right. He started out as one of Kimball's cronies, and then he fell from favor."

"How?"

"Against Kimball's orders he signed a contract to sing at a club in New York that Kimball was boycotting for some silly reason or another. When the contract was up, nobody else would hire the guy. Hammond did everything he could to get back into the great star's good graces again, but no dice. They found him in an alley with his wrists slit."

"He killed himself?"

Mavis shrugged her shoulders. "It was listed as suicide, but my sources in the police department told me that the alcohol level in his body was so high, there was no way he could have done it himself."

"Why would anyone kill a drunken singer, for God's sake?"

"I told you Kimball was vindictive, didn't I?"

"How can he get away with this stuff? This is, after all, the United States," Jellie protested.

"Who said Craig Kimball lived in the United States? Dearie, he lives up there, in the rarefied air of superstardom, not down here with us mortals."

"Well, well, Plato, when did you become such a philosopher?" Jellie asked sarcastically.

"It comes with the territory. Don't ask me why the public decides to elevate some people into the stratosphere of superstardom, I don't know. Mind you, I don't envy them. It can be an isolating, lonely experience, and many of them can't handle it. Most of those who live in the realm of the gods are quite miserable. Look at poor Elvis."

"Maybe, but it's not like it used to be. Superstars are just people. They shop, they eat, they get married and divorced, they get sick and die . . ." Jellie protested.

"What do you want from me, Jellie?"

"First of all, I want to know the story of Melissa Bedford's death."

"What do you know about that?"

"Nothing. Nothing at all. Continue."

"You'd better never attibute this to me, Jellie. Understand?"

Jellie nodded.

"*The Red Rose,* Craig Kimball's first big film, was nominated for an Oscar but he was ignored, so he was furious at the Academy. He refused to attend the ceremonies and instead went out on a drunken spree. He and his cronies picked up a group of high-school girls who were coming out of a late movie. One of the girls was a pretty little thing named Melissa Bedford."

"So that's how they met."

"In a manner of speaking. Apparently they lured the girl to Kimball's house, where they all had their way with her."

"They raped her?"

"Exactly. She escaped and went home after the booze knocked them out. The next morning, her mother and her father took her to the police, where she told all. She was a bright little girl, and she remembered everybody's names, the address, et cetera, et cetera. The sergeant who talked to her put in a quick call to somebody, and within the hour Momma, Poppa, and

Soiled Baby were whisked out of the station in a limousine and hauled off to meet somebody," Mavis continued.

"Who is 'somebody'?"

"Anonymous. It was a long time ago, and don't ask who told me. Just rest assured that it was a very reliable source. Anyway, the girl's parents would not settle for money. They wanted justice. Their little angel had been sullied."

"So he married her and made it legitimate? Are you kidding?"

"It was different then, my dear, very different. Melissa's parents were from Europe, and for them, lost maidenhead could not be repaired with money."

"Jesus. They gave their little girl to her rapist."

"Nicely put. Kimball was furious, but he did what he was told. He wasn't a superstar yet, and his budding career could have been squashed by the studio . . . and would have. He married her, all right, but can you imagine what her life was like after that?"

"But eventually he divorced her, didn't he? I mean, she killed herself after the marriage ended. Maybe she was in love with him."

"Hardly. Kimball's cronies were afraid she was going to die from the drugs he was feeding her or from the beatings. I understand he's a real gorilla in the boudoir."

"He should be strung up, not idolized."

"Nobody ever said life was fair."

"Do you think she was murdered?"

"I don't think anything. I know there was a collective sigh of relief when she was buried, and I also know that the man who supposedly slipped her the pills was never prosecuted."

"Jesus Christ! Is this story generally known around town?" Jellie asked incredulously.

"Not really. He's had no trouble with his other wives, and he's getting a little long in the tooth now. If there have been other instances, they've been well covered up."

"Do you think he abuses Claire?"

Mavis laughed. "No way! That marriage is a business arrangement. He's never touched her."

"What do you mean?"

"He wasn't getting enough kicks with the whores in Vegas, so he started having his buddy Sudsy bring him young guys from the Strip."

"He's gay?"

"No, but he's into the S and M thing. Anyway, one of them shook him down for some heavy money. It seems Kimball got carried away and did some serious damage. The guy struck back by sneaking some snapshots of our hero in action. It took some heavy muscle to square it all away."

"What happened to the kid who put the squeeze on him?"

Mavis shrugged. "Who knows. He just got lost in the jungle as so many of them do. As a result, Craig was told to shape up and get himself a wife, a nice, socially acceptable matron, and start living up to his public image. Kimball's movies are a valuable part of several studio's libraries. Besides, nobody in the industry would want to see a legend like him destroyed. It makes everybody look bad."

"Anything else I should know?"

"None of this is worth anything but a *tsk-tsk* over coffee, and you know it. Don't you think if it were publishable, I'd do it myself?"

"Not for a minute," Jellie hooted derisively. "You wouldn't want to get those lovely manicured hands dirty. You're too comfortable traveling with the set you write about. Acceptance at their swell parties is more important to you than any story."

"Jellie, go to hell. It's none of your business what I do," Mavis said, but there was more amusement than anger in her voice.

"Mavis, we've known each other a long time. You're too smart not to know that the day you lose that column is the day your telephone will stop ringing, and then you'll be just about as popular with your fancy friends as I am. Would you come back to real reporting, Mavis? Help me nail this guy?"

Mavis lit a cigarette and got to her feet. "Take my advice, Jellie, and pick on somebody your own size. Craig Kimball is out of your league. Now get lost. I've got work to do."

As Jellie drove home through the night she had the terrible feeling that she had just glimpsed Dante's Inferno, and she felt like hell.

54

"**H**OW about dinner after we're finished tonight?" Craig asked Lilah as they waited for the technicians to adjust the lighting. The first scene of the day would be an easy one, since Lilah had no lines, just reaction shots as Craig spoke what had turned out to be almost a soliloquy. Rose and the writers had done an excellent job of throwing most of the dialogue and the emoting in the episode to everyone except her character, for which Lilah was extremely grateful.

She smiled slightly, being careful to hold her position for the lighting crew. "How nice of you to ask, Craig, but I'm afraid I can't make it tonight. We could have a drink together in my dressing room if we finish early enough. It will give us a chance to get to know each other a little better. Then perhaps we can have dinner another night."

She had spent two hours the previous night thinking up those lines, and she hoped they would be effective. Even though she had told Ben she was not afraid of Craig Kimball, she was more apprehensive about the encounter than she wanted to admit. She had also suggested to Ben that it might be easier to bug her dressing room than for her to try to manipulate a hidden tape recorder.

Speaking in his sexiest and most persuasive voice, Craig Kimball said, "I've got a better idea. Why don't you come to mine . . . alone? We can't really get to know each other with that manager of yours hovering over us every minute."

Lilah smiled seductively. "Ben has an appointment at the record company late this afternoon, and then he's meeting with my publicists. He won't be back until it's time to pick me up for the dinner party."

The actor smiled and raised his brows, "Ah, well, in that case, I'd be delighted. I drink Scotch."

"So does Ben," she said, and turned away quickly to stifle a nervous giggle that was threatening to escape. Ben, who was standing not far away listening, was delighted with her strategy. Without waiting for the scene to be shot, Ben hurried back to the dressing room to get everything set up for taping. He was happy to be busy and involved so that he could try to forget that his lover was thousands of miles away impersonating a white man's wife.

The day's shooting turned out to be a disaster. The director was not happy with the way the scenes had been written, and he insisted that dialogue be added here and there for his star actress. Lilah found herself speaking lines she had not learned, and she lost her confidence and her composure. She spoke the new lines hesitantly, moved awkwardly, and could not seem to hit a single mark on cue. Everyone was annoyed with her for slowing down the production.

Worst of all, Ben wasn't around to give her support because he was busy getting ready for the taping. More than once that day Lilah wished herself back home in Illinois. She was in over her head, and surely somebody was going to figure out that she was a faker . . . or worse, they might start thinking that Lady Rose was an overhyped and unprofessional actress.

At six o'clock the director called it a wrap.

"That's it, everybody. Rose, you'd better get to bed early tonight. We're going to have to do three extra setups tomorrow to catch up. Try to pull yourself together. Another day like this and we'll all be in trouble." Stan's voice reflected his exasperation with her clumsy performance.

As Lilah walked from the set Craig tried to follow her to her dressing room, but she needed to talk to Ben and recover her poise. She felt totally unhinged by the day's filming and didn't have the confidence to begin another charade without a moment's respite.

"It's been a rotten day, Craig. Give me a few minutes to get out of this costume and into something comfortable. I also have to return some telephone calls," she began, but he didn't seem to be paying attention.

"Okay. I'll just fix my own drink and wait for you," he replied, continuing to move toward her dressing room.

She put her hand out to stop him. "No! Really, I must have a few minutes to myself. If it's too late for you, we can do this another time. As a matter of fact, maybe it would be better if—" she started to protest, but he acquiesced immediately. It was apparent that he did not want to be put off another day.

"No problem. No problem at all," he said, backing off. "What do you say I come over in a half hour or so? That will give me time to change, too, and take this makeup off my face."

"A half hour will be fine," she said tersely, and hurried to Rose's dressing room, hoping that Ben would be there, but all she found was a note on her mirror: "It took some doing, but everything's working. I'm alone in the makeup room next door listening and recording every word. When you read this, just say something. If you don't see me in two minutes, you'll know I'm hearing you fine."

Lilah smiled and spoke very softly. "Ben, it's been a miserable day, and I hope I haven't messed things up too badly. Cross your fingers that I play the role of Lady Rose better than I did Caymen Welles today."

As she got out of her costume and slipped it on a hanger, she noticed that Ben had arranged a silver tray with a chilled bottle of champagne, two crystal glasses, and an iced server of caviar beside a plate of crackers. She laughed and teased, "Ben, don't tell me I'm going to have to open the bottle myself." She chatted as she got dressed in a pair of slacks and a sweater. It made her feel a little better to know that Ben was only a few steps away and could hear every word that was said.

Unfortunately, although the tape recorder was recording every word she said, Ben was not hearing it. He had been diverted by the appearance of the show's director and producer.

Quickly stepping outside the makeup room to talk to them, Ben closed the door behind him so that they would not see the recorder.

"What the hell is going on with her, Ben? She's been acting as if she's never seen a soundstage in her life."

"She'll be fine. All those changes you made in the script probably threw her, that's all. You know, I really think it's a bad idea to do that—" he began defensively, but Bruce wouldn't accept his excuses.

"That's what being a professional means. You have to be able to handle it. You know that, Ben. And, in all truth, she usually does fine. She wasn't herself at all today."

For a good twenty minutes the conversation continued, with Ben lamely trying to assure them that everything was going to be fine but not being particularly successful.

"Look, Ben," Bruce finally said, "let's have a little candor here. It's Craig Kimball who's shaking her up, right?"

"Why do you say that?" Ben asked suspiciously.

"Look, we're not stupid. Everybody knows she was upset about having him on the show. Why?" Stan demanded.

"It's fun to stand around and gossip about the overpaid and uncooperative actors, guys, but I've got to go. We'll talk about this again tomorrow if you're still having problems, but I predict everything will be fine."

Ben walked away, hoping they would leave so that he could get back into the makeup room.

Ten minutes later, however, he was still waiting for them to move when he saw Craig appear at the door to Rose's dressing room. As he watched her open it and let Kimball in, Ben noted the time. If his way was still blocked in ten minutes, he would just have to barge in on them and to hell with the tape. He didn't dare leave Lilah alone with that bastard. Finally Bruce and Stan began to move away slowly, and Ben surreptitiously made his way to the door of Rose's dressing room. He stopped to listen but heard only quiet, casual conversation. Relieved, he moved toward the makeup room and was about to enter when a voice stopped him.

"Hey, hey, old buddy. Whatsa matter? You forgot to put on your lipstick?" Sudsy asked.

Ben whirled on him. "Don't ever sneak up on me like that again!" he snapped.

Sudsy raised his arms in mock surprise. "Hey, cool it, old man. I wasn't sneakin' up on you. You were the one who was listenin' at the door. Whatsa matter . . . you don't trust your broad with the big romantic star?"

"What are you doing here?"

"Same as you, fella, waitin' for that little tit-a-tit in there to be over . . . and it looks like we might have a long wait. Want to have a drink?"

"No thanks, I've got some reading to do. I'm going to wait in the makeup room."

"Good idea. I'll wait in there with ya."

Annoyed, Ben rasped, "Find your own place to wait and leave me alone."

"This joint don't belong to you, fella, even though you prance around here sometimes like it does. If I want to go in there, too, then you can't stop me."

Ben was stymied. If he went inside, Sudsy would undoubtedly follow him and see the recorder. He had to find some way to shake the clown off his tail.

"What's with all the sudden togetherness, Sudsy?

You and I have nothing to talk about, okay?" Ben's manner became more reasonable.

"That's not a very friendly attitude, you know. I was just tryin' to be nice," Sudsy said with a slight whine.

"No, you weren't. You were just doing what you were told to do, weren't you? Didn't that bum you work for tell you to keep your eye on me so that I didn't bother him while he was pitching Lady Rose?"

"Why would he do that?"

"Don't ask me . . . you know him better than I do."

"He just don't like bein' intruded on when he's got somethin' goin' with a dame. That's all, buddy. And whatever he wants, it's up to me to see that he gets it."

"What makes him think he can get something going with Lady Rose?" Ben asked pugnaciously.

Sudsy grinned nastily. "He's just bein' friendly, I guess," he replied, but he emphasized the word *friendly,* and there was a leer on his face.

Ben ignored the remark and continued moving closer to the door to Rose's dressing room. Since he was obviously not going to be able to shake the little ape, he would just have to be as near as possible in case Lilah needed help.

Inside the dressing room things went much more smoothly at first. Unaware that Ben was not monitoring the conversation, Lilah's performance was considerably better than it had been on the soundstage earlier.

"Are you always so punctual, *mon cher?*" she asked, purposely using a French phrase the way Rose did.

"Not unless I'm going to do something I really want to do," Craig Kimball said, flashing the smile that had worked for him on the screen a thousand times. He settled himself on the couch.

"I thought I told you I like Scotch," he complained when he saw the champagne on the table.

"I'm sorry, but it's been a bad day, and I'm afraid I forgot. Surely you won't object to a little Dom Perignon.

I promise to be better prepared the next time." Lilah tried to emphasize the word *next*, but he seemed not to be paying attention. He pulled a silver flask out of his breast pocket, opened it, and poured several ounces into the tall crystal flute. He then took some ice out of the champagne bucket and filled his glass.

"There, that's better. I really hate that expensive soda pop. It's a woman's drink."

He lifted the glass and drained half of it and then quickly replenished it. Lilah watched apprehensively, suspecting he would be more difficult drunk than sober.

"Craig, you've implied that we've met before, but you're wrong. I could never forget meeting you. Why, I've been a fan of yours ever since I was just a little girl," she said, spreading some caviar on a cracker and offering it to him.

He refused the caviar with a shake of his head and took another swallow of the Scotch. Lilah nibbled at the cracker and watched him closely.

When he put the glass down, his eyes narrowed.

"Let's cut the crap. I don't blame you for trying to pretend it never happened, but we both know it did, and I've got this damned scar on my face to prove it." The silken quality of his voice and manner switched to an accusatory tone. "Don't you know that you never hurt an actor's face—never—no matter what happens?"

Disconcerted at his sudden change in demeanor, Lilah began to struggle with the champagne cork in an attempt to appear nonchalant and avoid looking into his eyes. The damn cork would not give.

"You must have me confused with somebody else. I have no idea what you're talking about." Lilah tried to keep the expression on her face genuinely perplexed.

She looked up and saw that he was watching her with the hooded gaze of a snake.

"Very well, if that's the game you want to play, it was on the set of *Star Bright*, remember?" he asked.

Lilah shook her head. "I don't think I ever saw it."

"Lucky for you. It was the only bomb I ever made,

and that was your fault. The studio recalled the prints
and destroyed them."

"My fault? What are you talking about?"

"You not only cut up my face so that half the
picture had to be shot from my worst side, but they
were forced to recast your part in a hurry, and the
singer they replaced you with had no tits and no talent."

Lilah laughed nervously and continued to wrestle
with the bottle. Suddenly it gave way with a loud pop,
and the sparking wine spilled out and drenched everything on the tray.

"Goodness, I'm making a terrible mess here," she
apologized as she dabbed nervously at the wine with a
cocktail napkin.

Kimball took another swig of his whiskey and agreed.
"You have a knack for doing that."

Lilah poured herself some wine and asked with false
cheeriness, "What could you possibly have done that
would make me angry enough to slash your face? I've
never hit anyone in my life, and I disapprove totally of
violence—"

Kimball, whose voice had taken on a surly and
insulting tone, interrupted her. "I don't care what you
say you are now, but twenty years ago you were an
ungrateful little nigger. I gave you your first big break,
a shot at the big time. You knew what was expected of
you in return."

"What was expected of me, Craig? Did you treat
me any different than you treated white actresses?"
Lilah asked, trying to retain her composure.

"Look, you were nobody. You were lucky I wanted
your body at all. Women all over the world would pay
to have me screw them. You just didn't have enough
sense to appreciate that."

"That was the price I had to pay for the part?
Really? Providing sex for you, wherever and whenever
you wanted it—in your dressing room or at night in
your house in Malibu, all night, every night—and then
having to go to the set each morning, exhausted,
humiliated?"

"You do remember, don't you?"

"No, not at all. It's just a story that I've heard from other actresses you've abused."

"What are you talking about?" he demanded, and there was a look of crazed fury in his eyes.

"You'd be surprised at the stories going around town. Tell me, what was different with me than it was for any of those other young girls you beat and abused with . . . Coke bottles?" Although her voice was controlled, she could feel her hands begin to tremble. Suddenly her identification with her twin sister became exquisitely real, and she felt as if she had been violated by the creature sitting beside her. The emotion was so strong that she could no longer look at him.

"No difference. The other ones had better sense than you did. They knew they had to put out or else. But you, you black bitch, you were the only one who ever turned on me, and believe me, I did a lot less to you than I've done to others. I was easy on you. You were lucky to get out of there alive."

"I didn't give you that scar. You've got me confused with some other actress. You shouldn't drink so much."

"You can lie all you like, but I can prove it happened. I've got a witness who was there. Sudsy took me to the doctor after you sliced up my face with that piece of glass."

"It's my guess that you fell down in one of your drunken stupors and hurt yourself, Mr. Kimball. You'd better leave now, before your wild accusations make it impossible for us to work together."

Suddenly Lilah realized that he intended to intimidate and demoralize Rose to the point where she would walk away from the production and anger everyone in the studio and at the network.

"I haven't finished with you yet," Kimball said, pouring the rest of the whiskey into his glass.

Lilah got to her feet. "Maybe not, but I'm certainly finished with you. Now get out of my dressing room, Mr. Kimball."

"You're a dumb broad. Always have been, always will be. Don't you know that nobody crosses me?"

"I'm not afraid of you. And there's nothing you can do to get me to leave this production, do you understand? I know that's what you're up to, but it won't work," Lilah snapped, and there was rage and hatred in her voice.

Suddenly the snake struck as Kimball's hand whipped across and grasped Lilah's wrist, pulling her back onto the couch.

"Let go of me," she demanded, loud enough for Ben to know that she was being accosted, unaware that he could not hear her.

"Come on, you can remember it if you try hard enough. Now think back. You were lying on my bed with your legs tied. You loved that, didn't you? All women want to feel like they're being taken against their will, don't they now?"

His voice had grown husky and low, and Lilah sensed that he was getting excited just talking about it. "Remember the bottle, Rosie? I was giving you an extra-special thrill with that bottle. Whores like you need something like that, don't you. When you've had so many cocks, just another one doesn't do it anymore, does it? You need something bigger and harder. But you were a bad little cunt, hitting me in the face with that decanter. Don't you know I've had people killed for less than that? You'd better be afraid of me, Rosie. I can be the boogeyman when I want to."

Lilah steeled herself to listen, letting his dark, moist breath creep along her skin, hoping that Ben was getting everything on the tape.

"Let me go or I'll scream for help," she insisted, trying to pull her arm from his iron grip.

His grasp on her wrist tightened. "Don't threaten me, you cunt. Everybody's gone now. It's just you and me, and I'm gonna give you a little something to prod your memory." He grabbed her around the neck and tried to pull her toward him, but she reacted defensively and fiercely. Reaching up with her free hand, she grabbed his face and sank her long acrylic fingernails into the wrinkled and paper-thin flesh under his eyes. Because she was an athlete, Lilah's grip was strong and painful, and Kimball let go of her instantly, jerking his head back from her lethal grasp. He screamed as her nails raked his skin and left long, bloody scratches on the cheek above the old scar.

At the moment he heard Kimball's cry Ben stormed into the dressing room like an angry tornado, but he was too late. Craig Kimball was already vanquished, and the actor rushed out the door, eager to get away from the vengeful woman.

"My God, did he hurt you?" Ben asked anxiously.

"No, but he wanted to." Although Lilah appeared calm, there was a quiver in her voice as she continued, "God, Ben, I hope I didn't mess things up for Rose. I didn't intend to hurt him, but I couldn't help it. When he grabbed me, I just reacted. I hope I didn't scratch his face too badly."

"No kidding?" Ben asked gleefully. "You got him in the face? Well, I'll be damned. Just like your sister."

Lilah headed for the bathroom. "I feel so . . . dirty. I've got to wash my hands."

"That's the way he made Rose feel, and she's never really felt clean since the day he touched her."

Ben went to retrieve the tape to make sure it was securely in his possession. When he returned to replay it, Lilah insisted he use the earphones.

"Ben, I don't ever want to relive that scene again."

When he had heard it all, Ben sat for a long time without speaking, a grim look on his face. Finally he said, "The guy's nuts."

"Tell me, but is the tape any good?"

"It's better than good . . . it's great, but I wish you hadn't had to go through that. It must have been terrible."

"You know, for a few minutes there I felt that I really was Rose. It was very strange."

"That's what being a good actress does to you. You start thinking like the character you're playing."

"It was more than that, Ben . . . more than that."

As they walked toward the car Ben said, "Let's call Rose. I want to talk to her."

"Not now, Ben. First thing in the morning after Warren has gone to the office," Lilah suggested. "I'll bet she's bored to death and ready to come home."

"And you, Lilah, are you ready to go home too?"

"When I'm finished with what I set out to do."

"You still upset with Rose?"

"Are you?"

"Not a chance. I can't ever stay angry with her. She makes life too interesting. What about you?"

"Warren is so remote and involved with his work, he'll probably never suspect a thing."

When they were settled in the limousine, Lilah asked, "What are you going to do with the tape, Ben?"

"Well, first I'll have several copies made, and then I'm putting the original in our lawyer's safe. Then . . ." He paused, and there was a wicked gleam in his eye. "Then tomorrow I'm going to mail a copy to the big star. It'll no doubt ruin his day. I just wish I could see his face when he hears that remark about having people killed. Lilah, you were brilliant. Rose never could have done what you did."

55

WARREN handed Rose a glass of red wine. "I thought you might need something to warm you up, so I went ahead and opened the Bordeaux. Are you okay?"

Rose accepted the glass and took a long swallow. "Of course, why do you ask?"

"I was worried about you. It's not like you to be late. Stella said you went shopping."

"I did. Do you like my new outfit?" There was a bright fire crackling in the fireplace, and Rose moved close to it. She was wearing the chocolate-brown cashmere skirt and sweater she had bought on her shopping trip, and although it fit her perfectly, it was bulky enough so that it concealed her thinness. Usually she didn't wear dark colors, but the blond streaks in her hair made a difference.

"The clothes are nice, but why did you come home in a cab?" Warren asked.

"You must have been watching out the window for me."

He nodded. "The weather took a bad turn, and I was worried—all that snow and wind. Where's the car?"

"I got a flat tire. I left it at a gas station. They'll bring it back in the morning."

"Those are new tires."

"I, uh, probably picked up a nail or something.

They were really busy. It was too cold to wait." Rose didn't want to admit that the snowstorm had frightened her so much that she'd left the car at a gas station and hailed a cab.

"When I heard the weather report on the news this morning, I called Brenda at the travel agency and told her to book us into the Mauna Kea Hotel in Hawaii for a vacation. Okay?"

The expression on Warren's face was so naked and hopeful that Rose looked away in embarrassment. Did her sister have any idea how much the man loved her?

Rose groped for an appropriate response. "It . . . uh, sounds lovely. When were you planning to go?"

"I told her to make the reservations as soon as possible. Will you go with me, Lilah? We can play golf every morning and swim every afternoon. Remember the mai tais at the beach bar . . . with the orchids in them?"

She tried to hedge. "It sounds like a lovely idea, Warren, but won't you need time to get squared away at the office? And I probably ought to look into getting a few resort clothes . . . for both of us."

"I'll be ready to go day after tomorrow. We have to attend the Rotary Club dinner tomorrow night, remember? I'm in charge of the program, you know, and I was lucky enough to get Josh Petrone to fly out from Los Angeles to be the guest speaker. He's invited us to fly back to the Coast with him on his company jet. I thought you might enjoy that. We can spend the night in Los Angeles and fly from there to Hilo. What do you think?"

Rose was cornered. "This is all so sudden. I need a few minutes to think it over."

"Please . . . go with me. Let me try to make things right between us again. Our marriage is the most important thing in my life, and I just can't let it slip away because of some silly—"

Rose stopped him. "Don't. Please, Warren, don't do this . . . not now. I need a few days, that's all, and then we'll talk. You know, *mon cher* . . . dear . . . I learned when I was just a little girl that it was best to let things simmer on the stove for a while. That way the bad feelings get boiled away. I just need time. You don't have to take me to Hawaii."

"But I want to take you there. Let's work this out together. I love you, Lilah. I've never wanted any other woman but you. That idiot wasn't me."

"All right, Warren. If the reservations come through, we'll go," she agreed quickly. She couldn't bear having him expose his emotions so nakedly to her. She felt as if she were eavesdropping on a very intimate relationship.

"Great, and you'll go to the dinner with me tomorrow night?"

"Of course. Now, let's eat. Stella's fixed something special. Bring the bottle of wine."

Warren was quietly ebullient at dinner, and he did most of the talking, making plans for the trip, telling her to forget about clothes, saying they'd shop for what they needed in Hawaii. Rose listened with just half her attention. God, now what was she going to do?

That night as they prepared to go upstairs to bed, Warren asked, "Do you still want me to sleep in the guest room?" He looked so wistful and boyish that she wanted to take him in her arms and promise him that everything was going to be just fine, but of course she could not do that. She reached up and kissed him lightly on the lips and said, "Let it simmer, Warren. It will give us both something to look forward to in Hawaii . . . like a second honeymoon, okay?"

Disappointed, he nodded and watched her go into their bedroom and close the door. Rose felt sorry for him.

She locked the door, however, and got ready for bed. Before she turned out the light, she set the alarm for two A.M. It would be midnight in Los Angeles, and Ben and Lilah surely would be home then. She was going to need help out of this one.

56

THE party was over. The last limousine had pulled away with the last guest, and Florence was alone, stranded in a strange mansion in Santa Barbara. For the last two hours she had been searching futilely for Del. She had gone to the rest room, and when she returned, he had disappeared, and so had the limousine that brought them there. God, what had happened? Del was a little drunk, but everything had seemed fine. Had she said something to anger him? Going into the library, she found a woman conversing with a butler who was tidying up, and she approached her.

"How do you do? I'm afraid I need your help. It seems that I've become separated from my escort, and I . . . don't know what to do."

"My dear, how terrible for you. Who were you with?"

"Del Gerstler. We got separated during the cocktail hour. Are you by any chance Mrs. Van—"

"Vandeventer, yes. This is my home, and I'm afraid I don't know Mr. Gerstler. Please, come with me into the library and I'll ask my husband. What is your name, my dear?"

"Florence . . . Florence Bennett. I'm from Chicago and I'm staying at the Beverly Wilshire Hotel."

"Oh, my goodness . . . so far away." They walked into the library where a tall, good-looking man with thick white hair sat at a desk. He got to his feet as they approached him.

"Fritz, dear, this is Miss Bennett. It seems she came to the party tonight with a Mr. Gerstler, and he apparently left without her. Do you know him?"

The man looked at Florence with distaste, and after a brief pause he said, "Yes, I met Mr. Gerstler early in the evening. I'd talked about investing in a movie project of his, but when I found out that he was the scoundrel who produced that piece of filth *Lovenest,* I asked him to leave my house."

"He's left this poor woman stranded," his wife protested.

"You should be more particular about the company you keep," the man snapped. "Have Beeler call her a taxi."

Florence was aghast. "No, I don't have enough money to pay a cab to take me all the way back to Beverly Hills. I'm just a widow, here on vacation from Illinois," she exclaimed.

"How long have you known this man?" Vandeventer asked her.

"I just met him. A friend of my late husband's asked him to show me around a bit. My goodness, I feel like such a fool," she said.

The man's face softened and he said, "I'm sure you're not the first person this man has victimized, my dear. Phyllis, tell Beeler to have Martin drive her back to her hotel."

For a long time that night Florence stared at the ceiling from her hotel bed and wondered if had she been born under an unlucky star. Not once in her life had she ever caught the brass ring. She had wanted Warren; she had had to settle for George. She had wanted money and social position; she had spent her life always making do. Life was so unfair.

When morning finally came, she called the airline and moved up her reservation to the next day. She had only one more thing to do in Los Angeles, and that was to see Del Gerstler again and find out why he had bothered with her at all. She dialed the telephone number he had given her and left her name with the answering service.

She spent most of the morning packing her things. She was just about to take a walk and find a place to have a hamburger when the telephone rang. It was Del.

"Flo . . . real sorry about walkin' out on you like that. I just got so steamed at that guy, I gave him the finger and got out of there as fast as I could. How'd you get back?"

"As Blanche DuBois said, 'A poor widow has to depend on the kindness of strangers,' or words to that effect."

"Who the hell is Blanche DuBois?"

"One of Tennessee Williams's ladies. Actually, Mr. Vandeventer was kind enough to have his driver bring me back to the hotel," she said, suppressing the animosity she felt toward him. After all, he was what he was, and he made no pretenses. He didn't even kiss a woman before he screwed her.

"Look, I'm real sorry. How about if I take you to dinner tonight to make up for runnin' out on you like that?"

"Dinner would be fine, but early. I'm leaving L.A. in the morning."

"I'll pick you up at seven and we'll eat Italian over at LaScala Boutique . . . okay?"

"Whatever," she replied wearily.

To her surprise Del arrived only a half hour late, and they walked the few blocks to the casual little restaurant adjacent to the fine, expensive one where he had taken her on their first date. When they were settled in the red leather booth, sharing a carafe of red wine, Florence looked at Del in his expensively tailored sport coat, tight gabardine trousers, and silk monogrammed shirt and asked, "Why, Del? Why did you even bother with me?"

"What do you mean? You're a nice lady . . . that's all."

"No, that's not all. I'm okay, but I'm not your type. I'm not flashy. I don't have a million dollars. My figure has seen better days, and although I was fairly pretty when I was young, I'm past forty. Why me?"

"I like you. You're different from these chicks out here who've been around and seen everything and done everything . . . that's all," he said, but there was an evasive look in his eye, a look she didn't understand.

"God, how I wanted to believe that. You know, yesterday I actually thought we might have something for each other. I was going to ask you to help me get a job out here. I was going to stay in California—can you believe this—because I was seriously thinking of chucking my life and my friends and my home and doing something exciting . . . all because of you."

"Hey, look, I told you I was sorry about last night."

"So you said, but if you're really sorry, then tell me the truth. Tell me why you took me out. And no more baloney, please."

"You don't want to know," he said, staring into his wineglass.

"Ah, but I do. And don't worry about hurting me. You've already hurt and humiliated me. So go ahead. For once in your life be honest."

"You're not the first."

"I'm not the first . . . what?"

"The first little old lady from Iowa."

"I don't understand."

He twirled his glass and stared at it as he spoke. "I've been around a lot, you know, with women. I've had the clap twice, syphilis once, but antibiotics took care of that. Then this other stuff came down the pike, except this is different . . . it kills you. For a while I thought, well, maybe it was time to hang up my gun, so to speak. You can't trust anybody in this town when it comes to sex. A lotta guys, you know, swing both ways . . . and a chick could pick up something from one of them and pass it on. So I quit screwing around with the young girls around here, and I started hanging out at places where the tourists come to see the real Hollywood."

"I don't understand," she murmured, mystified.

"I laid down some rules for myself, see. I only sleep with dames who've been here less than a day or two—a lot of these gigolos are AC-DC, you know—and I didn't want to mess around with anybody who'd maybe messed around with one of them. And I made sure to sleep with them on consecutive nights, so they couldn't get anything else going in between."

There was a long silence while she let the almost incomprehensible information sink in. When she finally made sense of his motives, she looked at him and said, "Well, I've got to hand it to you. You really have life figured out for yourself. Now let's order dinner. I need to get to bed. My plane leaves early in the morning."

"I guess this means we're not gonna, you know . . ."

She laughed bitterly. "Sure. Let's have one for the road."

They ate a delicious dinner of salad made with shredded mozzarella, lettuce, and salami, followed by spaghetti with a thick red meat sauce, and finished off the meal with cappuccino and cheesecake. They drank a lot of red wine and laughed and talked like old friends who knew each other's shortcomings and accepted them.

Later, at the hotel, after they had had sex and Del was dressing, he said, "You know, I'm really sorry to see you go. You're a swell chick. It's not many women that you can be honest with, you know that? You're somethin' else."

This was the moment Florence had been waiting for all evening. There was a mean glitter in her eyes as she replied, "You're right, Del . . . I am something else, and I'm surprised that a guy with as much smarts about women as you think you have didn't figure it out right away. Other men I've slept with have. You see, I'm not really your little old lady from Iowa. I'm more like your little old nymphomaniac from Chicago. At least that's what my shrink calls me. And I've had a lot of sex here in California. Why, I've screwed every bellboy in this hotel . . . I get great room service . . . and I've cruised the bars in the afternoons. I know it's a risk, but I can't seem to control myself. Just last night I repaid the nice young man who drove me home with a quickie."

She tried not to smile at the shocked expression on his face as she continued. "So, you see, your game plan was original, but it's as full of holes as your head."

"You cunt!" he said hoarsely.

"Exactly," she said with a smirk. "Who knows, maybe I've given you something to remember me by."

He drew back his arm to swing at her, but the triumph on her face stopped him. He turned and stalked out of the room, slamming the door behind him.

Florence got out of bed and headed for the shower. It wouldn't wash the filth off her soul, but at least it would get rid of all traces of that lecher. She almost wished that the story she told him had been the truth.

57

CLAIRE Kimball was just about ready to leave for a dinner party at her friend Betsy's when she heard her husband in his bedroom yelling for his valet to call a doctor again. Thinking Craig might be ill, she knocked on his door. "Craig, is something wrong?" she called.

"Mind your own business!" he snapped, and did not open the door.

Raising her eyebrows slightly, she went back to her own room. She hoped the bastard was sick and dying. She finished putting the last touches on a fingernail that she had chipped while pulling up the zipper on her dress. As she waved her hand about to dry the polish, she studied her reflection in the mirror. Satisfied that she looked perfectly wonderful in her new gray silk Oscar de la Renta gown and her long strand of black pearls and matching earrings with diamond drops, she went to her fur closet to choose a wrap. She was trying to decide between the lynx coat and the white mink jacket when Craig burst into her room holding a wet washcloth to his face.

Startled, she asked, "What happened to you?"

"None of your goddamn business! Where the hell can I find that plastic surgeon of yours? I need him right now!" he bellowed.

"How would I know? You'll have to call his service, I suppose," she replied coldly. "What happened? Did some cat try to scratch your eyes out?"

"Call your doctor for me. I need him now!" he ordered, and stalked out of her room.

Claire hesitated. She had no desire to help the bastard, and if it had been a life-threatening problem, she wouldn't have, but obviously it was only his face he was worried about. With a sigh she dialed the number of the doctor who had done such a beautiful job on her eyes. It would be nice to talk to Dr. Ed again. When she gave her name to his answering service and said it was an emergency, the call was put through directly to him.

"Claire, I hope nothing's wrong," the doctor greeted her.

"I'm fine, it's my husband. He's had some kind of an injury to his face, and he's storming around the house like a raging bull. Could you possibly come over right away? I'd consider it a very special favor."

"What kind of an injury is it?"

"I really don't know. He's got a washcloth on his cheek, and he's too upset to talk."

"Hasn't he ever had care from another plastic man?"

"Well, if he had, he'd certainly never admit it, at least not to me."

"May I speak with him, please?"

"Just a moment." Claire put down the telephone and went to Craig's door and called: "Craig, please come into my room. Dr. Everson is on the telephone and wants to talk to you."

The door was wrenched open, and Craig brushed past her and rushed into her room. He picked up the telephone and said, "What's all the fucking delay? I need to see you here right now!"

With extreme patience the surgeon replied, "I have to know what kind of injury you've sustained so I'll know what kind of preparation I need to make."

Craig hesitated before answering, and when he did, he saw his wife's lip curl in wry amusement. "I, uh, had a little argument on the set, and the damn bitch clawed me on the cheek with her fingernails."

"Was there much blood?"

"No . . . well, some."

"I think you ought to meet me at my office. The one thing we must watch out for is infection. Fingernails can carry a lot of bacteria."

"I don't want anybody to know about this. Can't you come here?" Craig protested.

"Look, Mr. Kimball, if those wounds get infected, the scarring could be very serious. Of course, if you'd like to call someone else—"

"Where's your office? I'll be right there."

Craig repeated the address and slammed down the telephone. As he brushed past his amused wife Claire murmured with a smirk, "The black bitch nailed you, hmm?"

"Go fuck yourself," he snapped.

"That's more than you can do," she snapped back.

Claire went into her room, pulled the lynx coat from its hanger, and walked slowly through the house and out the front door just in time to see their limousine and driver, who had been waiting to take her to the dinner party, pull out of the gates carrying her husband to the doctor's office. Infuriated, she charged back into the house and ordered the butler to bring her Mercedes out of the garage. God damn that son of a bitch! Now she would have to drive herself to the party, like any ordinary slob.

It turned out to be an interesting dinner with a number of guests from New York, but as with most dinner parties in Beverly Hills, it ended fairly early. Claire was the first to leave. She was uncomfortable driving alone wearing furs and jewels, particularly at night. When she entered the house, she saw the light on in the library and went in to see how her husband was feeling. Craig was slouched in a large brown leather wing chair holding a brandy and reading a script.

"Is everything all right?" she asked noticing that there were no bandages on his face. She moved closer to see what damage had been done.

Without looking up at her he muttered, "I'm fine."

"Did he have to take stitches or anything?"

"No. He said they were just surface scratches and should be healed in a week."

"Will you be able to work?"

"I've already talked to the director. I told him I had a fight with my wife and got a little scratched up. He said he'd shoot me from the side."

Claire was furious. The last thing she wanted was to have a reputation for being a brawling, clawing wife. "That was a rotten thing to do. Why in the world would you drag me into one of your nasty little affairs?"

"I figured you ought to be good for something. God knows you cost enough."

Claire flounced out of the room and went to bed. How she hated him!

She rose early the next morning and showered before her hairdresser and makeup artist arrived. Jellie Beam was coming at eleven with a photographer to take pictures for the article, and she wanted to look perfect. The florist delivered several elaborate flower arrangements for the living room, where she planned to have the pictures taken. At eleven-thirty Jellie arrived, flustered at being late.

"I'm so sorry, Mrs. Kimball, but my photographer got stuck at a fire. He'll be here soon. I hope you're not in a hurry."

"No problem. Would you like coffee?"

"I'd love some. Do you mind if I turn on the recorder so that we can get a few more questions in while we're waiting?"

"Not at all."

The coffee was brought, and when they were alone, Jellie asked the question she had been working on all night. Mavis had given her an idea, and she just hoped it didn't backfire and get her kicked out. "Mrs. Kimball . . . do you know the real story about your husband's first wife, Melissa Bedford?"

Claire was instantly on the alert. "What do you mean, real story?"

"Well . . . do you know the circumstances under which she met and married your husband and how she died?"

Suddenly Claire's curiosity was piqued. She had the feeling that this reporter might give her something of value to hold over Craig Kimball, but she remained very cool. "No, I can't say that I do. I heard she had a drinking problem."

"Well, suppose we make a little trade. I'll tell you everything I've found out if you'll give me some honest answers about your husband's background."

Claire smiled. "What could I possibly tell you that the whole world doesn't already know? Craig has been one of the most exhaustively covered stars in Hollywood."

"You don't know that he's the son of a mobster named Karoffska, who was murdered in a gang war?"

"Stories are always being made up about superstars like my husband," Claire said evenly.

"Look, Mrs. Kimball, don't worry about the interview. I promise to write the story about your clothes and your charities and your beautiful home, but I'd also like to know more about your husband. I think there's a story to be told about him that's been lurking in corners and alleys for years. Just last night I found out that he'd been forced to marry Melissa Bedford after he and his pals raped her, and that she died of a drug overdose in a hospital. . . ."

Suddenly Claire was intensely interested. The information very possibly could rid her of the need to kowtow to Craig Kimball. She wanted the details, and she made Jellie a proposition. "Jellie, I'll answer any question about my husband that you ask. But only one."

Figuring that something was better than nothing, Jellie told her everything she had heard. When Jellie finished her report, Claire questioned her sources. "Where did you find this out?"

Jellie told her about her visit to the hospital where Melissa had died, and then added, "Mavis Madden filled in the details."

Claire was on the alert again. "How well do you know Mavis?" she asked, wondering jealously if perhaps they were lovers.

Jellie responded in a manner that convinced Claire they were not. After all, what would pristine, delicate Mavis see in this rumpled heap of rags with dirty fingernails?

"I've known Mavis for years. She used to be a good reporter until she got to be a famous columnist," Jellie said with a hint of disdain in her voice.

The doorbell rang, the photographer had arrived, and the rest of the afternoon was given over to posing. When the photographer left, Claire tried to dismiss Jellie as well, but the reporter was not ready to go.

"Mrs. Kimball, we've got a deal. You haven't answered my question yet."

Claire steeled herself. "Very well. What did you want to ask?"

"I want to know what connection there is between your husband and Vance Freedland."

Claire smiled. "Jellie, that's almost too easy. Why didn't you ask me something hard? Vance is one of Craig's nearest and dearest friends."

"And?"

"That's all. They're just friends. Now, if you'll excuse me, I have another appointment. It's been a pleasure meeting you." As Claire walked out of the room she called back over her shoulder, "The butler will show you out."

Claire went into her room and locked the door, shivering with apprehension. Damn. Thank God she had dismissed Jellie before she had revealed anything to her about Vance Freedland. Many dark insinuations about the man from her husband had taught Claire that Vance was not one to have as an enemy.

She picked up her private telephone and dialed Mavis's number. Why hadn't it ever occurred to her to quiz the columnist about Craig? And now that she had that juicy little tidbit about Melissa Bedford, there was no reason not to resume her relationship, discreetly of course, with Mavis. She felt a twinge of excitement as she waited for her lover to come to the telephone.

58

THE telephone awakened Ben from a sound sleep, but the voice he heard brought all of his senses to alert.

"Benjie, what are you doing asleep at midnight?" Rose asked.

"Rose, baby, are you all right?"

"Do you miss me?" she asked.

"You know I miss you . . . wait, no I don't. What the hell's the idea of walkin' out like that on your sister and me without sayin' a word?"

"Benjie, it was an itch I had to scratch, but *mon Dieu,* I should have just used calamine lotion."

"What do you mean? Is everything there all right?"

"I walked into a real mess. Now don't you tell Lilah, but that husband of hers confessed to me that he's been having an affair with Lilah's best friend, which worked out just fine with me, because it gave me an excuse to lock him out of the bedroom."

"What did you intend to do in the first place, sleep with him?" Ben asked.

"I was sure I could figure something out. Now he's acting so contrite that I feel sorry for him."

"Don't get carried away," Ben remarked dryly. "Only Lilah has the right to forgive the bastard."

"You think I don't know that? How's everything going there?"

"Great. Lilah and Kimball had a little tiff last night

after work, and she got mad and scratched the hell out of his face." His words were spoken with studied casualness.

"You're kidding, right?"

"I'm kidding not, but what do you care? You're busy out there being a white woman. Tell me, does it feel any different?"

"No, it doesn't, but I'm going to a Rotary Club dinner tonight. It should be the big test."

Ben laughed out loud. "Jesus, I can't imagine Lady Rose going to a Rotary Club dinner."

"Hell, Lady Rose isn't going—Lilah Conway is—and you'd better keep these little distinctions in your mind. That lady in my bed isn't me, remember?"

Ben's manner went from teasing to very serious. "Don't worry about that. Your sister is one of the finest women I've ever met, and I've got nothing but respect for her."

"Benjie, now you're really making me jealous. What's going on there?"

"Last night she helped me set Kimball up. She got him to admit to a few things that could be very damaging to him, especially in light of all the rumors that have floated around about him over the years. And I got it all on tape. I don't think you'll have anything to fear from him anymore."

"Ben, did you put her in some kind of danger? You must have, or she wouldn't have had to scratch him. How could you do that?"

"I didn't intend for things to go as far as they did, but she's fine. She's a tough lady, Rose. I don't think she's afraid of anybody."

"Ben, you were supposed to take care of her!" Rose accused.

"Will you stop with that? It's all over. I've got the tape. Aren't you happy about that?"

"I guess it just hasn't sunk in, Benjie. How's Lilah doing on the set?"

"That's where we've got problems, babe. They

changed a lot of her lines, and she's not doing too well. Everybody's kind of down on her because they're falling behind schedule."

Rose was annoyed. "Well, *tant pis* on them!" Suddenly she had an idea. "Ben, listen to me. Warren and I are flying to L.A. day after tomorrow. He insists on taking me to Hawaii to work things out. Call Lilah in sick today and tomorrow, and I'll be there to take over."

"What about Kimball? That big love scene hasn't been shot yet, and if you come back, you'll have to do it yourself. Can you handle it?"

"I don't know, Benjie, but I can't see any other way out of this mess I've gotten us all in." The conviction was drained from her voice as she imagined herself touching Craig Kimball again.

"What do you want me to tell Lilah?"

"Don't tell her anything about Warren. Just tell her that you told me about the tape, and that I feel confident enough to carry on for myself, okay? I'll call you in the morning, same time, and tell you what time we'll be in. *Bonne nuit, mon cher.*"

Ben spent the rest of the night tossing and turning and trying to decide the best and most effective way the tape could be used. At dawn he picked up the telephone again and called the show's producer.

"Bruce, sorry to get you up like this, but we've got a problem. Rose's been up all night with the flu . . . and a fever. I don't think there's a chance in the world that she can make it to the set today. Can you shoot around her?"

"Jesus Christ, Ben, are you sure? I really don't want to go over schedule on this one. That damned contract we've got with Kimball will penalize the hell out of us."

"What can I say? She's sick. I haven't got any control over it."

"Okay, okay . . . but promise me that if she starts feeling better later today, she'll come in."

"Sure, sure I will . . . but don't count on it."

Whistling to himself, Ben donned a bathrobe and went down into the kitchen to fix himself some coffee. This was one morning he intended to read the paper leisurely. He might as well let Lilah sleep.

By eight o'clock he had finished the *Times* and *The Wall Street Journal* and was just beginning to thumb through the latest *People* magazine when Lilah came rushing into the room, clutching her bathrobe around her.

"Ben, my God, why didn't you wake me? We'll be late!"

"Whoa, turn it down to simmer. Sit and have some coffee. You've got the day off."

"What do you mean?" she protested. "I have at least three scenes scheduled for today." She sat down, however, and looked at him quizzically.

Ben poured the coffee and told her about Rose's call, omitting the part about her husband's infidelity. When he finished, Lilah got to her feet.

"I'm getting dressed to go to the studio. And, Ben, I hope you'll come with me."

"But I've already called you in sick. You can't—" he protested.

"Oh, yes, I can. I can stumble through one or two more days. I really don't want to quit until I've done what I set out to do."

"But, Lilah, you did what had to be done. If you hadn't been so terrific last night, I never would have been able to make that tape—"

"That's not what I meant. Ben, for most of my life I've been looking in the mirror and seeing a failure and a quitter. I don't ever want to see her again, understand? Now, I need you on the set with me, but if you won't go, I'll have to do it by myself. This time I'm going to finish what I started."

She turned on her heel and rushed upstairs to dress.

They arrived at the studio only an hour late, and Stan Selden, the director, greeted her joyously.

"Sure you're feeling okay?" Stan asked.

"Not really, but the show must go on. Just be patient if I'm not in top form, will you?"

"No problem. They're setting up for the encounter at the door. I want to get through the entire schedule today so that we can set up the bedroom scene for tomorrow in the afternoon," Stan said.

"Why are you moving that scene?" Ben asked suspiciously.

"I don't want to push my luck too far with Mr. Big."

"Why? What do you mean?"

"He came in with his face clawed this morning, and we have to shoot everything from one side. I want to get all his scenes in the can before something else happens to him, that's all," he said sourly.

"So, if all goes well, he'll be finished tomorrow, right?" Ben asked.

"You got it, Frost," Stan said, and lowering his voice, he added, "Frankly I'll be glad when this episode is finished. Everything's been out of kilter since Kimball's been here. Everybody's tight as a drum . . . even me." He sighed. "It's probably all in my imagination, or maybe I'm just underwhelmed at working with a superstar, now that I know what he's really like. Anyway, I hear through the grapevine that the network has commissioned the writers to do the first six episodes for next season featuring his character."

"You're joking, I hope?" Ben asked, alarmed.

"Don't tell Bruce I told you, because they wanted everything settled before Rose found out. Which is a damned rotten way to treat somebody who's done as much for this show as you have, honey."

Stan looked at Lilah, who turned away and declared flatly, "I'd better get into makeup."

An hour later the set was lit and Lilah was in makeup and costume, but Craig Kimball was still not ready. He and the makeup staff were in the midst of another heated discussion.

"You little fag, I told you to be careful with that scratch, and now it's bleeding again!" Kimball bellowed, loud enough for everyone to hear. The crew muttered among themselves, snickering and making obscene gestures, and the producer hurried in to arbitrate the dispute. It took another fifteen minutes, but finally Kimball was ready. As usual, the makeup artist was in tears.

Although Lilah tried to avoid Kimball's eyes, it was impossible once they had taken their places and were ready for a run-through. There was a delay while a light was adjusted, and Craig snarled under his breath, "I won't forget you for this. The score isn't settled."

Lilah shut her eyes so that she wouldn't have to look into his. For the first time in her life she was experiencing an overpowering sense of hatred. She had grown up attending church, believing in the presence of God and some good in all men. Her trip to Hollywood had taught her something else. To her dismay she found herself filled with anger and hatred toward another human being, to the point that she wished him serious harm, and although she was not afraid of Craig Kimball, she was afraid of her own feelings. The previous night she had dreamed she was swinging her nine iron, but instead of taking a divot, she was snapping off Craig Kimball's head . . . and laughing.

The director called for action, and they ran through the scene smoothly. The day before, Lilah had felt awkward and insecure, but not so today. She was propelled by a need not to fail.

"Okay, that was fine," Stan said, "but, Rose, take it easy, will you? Tone it down, both in voice and in intensity. You're inviting the guy into your house for a tête-á-tête, not challenging him to a duel."

"Who says?" she muttered through clenched teeth, just loud enough for her costar to hear. He was startled at the hostility evident in her comment.

"Don't challenge me, bitch. You'll lose," Craig snapped.

"Oh, really? I could swear it was you who left last night bleeding . . . not me."

"Can we get on with the scene, please, or would you two prefer to chat?" the director asked, aware that they were talking but unable to hear what was being said.

"We're ready," Lilah stated, and the scene was filmed. When it was over, they went to their dressing rooms to change and wait for the next scene to be lit.

Ben came into Lilah's dressing room, and he was in a fury. "God, I feel like punching somebody out," he exploded when the door was closed.

"I know exactly how you feel. I've just—how do they say it—uh, drawn first blood, and God forgive me, but I want more. I hope that when that bastard kisses me, I can keep myself from biting off his upper lip."

"Go for it, baby. That would solve all of our problems," Ben replied wearily, and sank to the couch, suddenly feeling defeated.

"Don't give up, Ben," Lilah said, and sat down beside him. "He hasn't won yet."

"Yes, he has. Rose will never be able to go on with this show, and I wouldn't want her to. It would be just too tough to have to face him on a daily basis. No career is worth that."

Lilah, who had begun to see her own life in a new perspective since she had assumed her sister's identity, said, "Oh, but it is, Ben, it is. You can't ever give up doing what you want to do. I realize now that Rose has got to face him . . . tomorrow, the day after, and the day after that. She mustn't back away like I did."

"You'll have to convince her of that. I don't think I can."

"Well, some good comes of everything. If all goes as Stan hopes it will, we'll be finished with Kimball's scenes just in time for Rose to come back and take over."

"This hasn't been easy for you."

"It hasn't been hard, either, Ben. I've had a great time and I've learned a lot."

"Such as?"

"Well, for one thing, being a star isn't all that glamorous. Frankly, I'd go crazy if I had to be cooped up in a little dressing room like this for days on end waiting for the sets and the lights to be ready. Making movies is a lot like watching cement harden."

"Television moves fast. You should see what it's like on a feature film . . . now *that's* cement. When I was acting in Italy years ago, each film felt like a life's career. Nobody ever expected the damn things to get finished."

Lilah was called back to the set. As Ben walked with her, she said, "You know, Ben, I've loved being with you both, but I really miss my family. I've felt strangely disconnected from them all since I came here. I'm eager to see Warren and the children again."

Ben wondered how she was going to handle the news of her husband's infidelity. It was a damned shame. Lilah deserved better.

59

ROSE spent the day going through Lilah's clothes and trying to pack things her sister would need in Hawaii. When that was done, she looked for something suitable to wear to the Rotary dinner. She had no idea what would be appropriate—a simple wool dress, a suit, a cocktail dress . . . what? At four o'clock she was still in a quandary, and although she had asked Stella her opinion, the surprised expression on the housekeeper's face told her that she had made a mistake in asking. Obviously Lilah had never sought Stella's opinion on anything, particularly fashion.

Finally Rose settled on the basic black wool, but when she put it on, it looked wretched. The fitted waist drooped down to her hips, and the belt was narrow and caused the fabric to bunch up when she tightened it. Suddenly a terrible thought occurred to her. Suppose it was black tie?

Feeling a bit frantic, she called Warren's office. Surely his secretary would not think it strange if she asked her.

"Hi, this is Lilah . . . um, how are you today?"

"Just fine, Mrs. Conway. Your husband just left for home."

"Already?" Rose asked with a touch of panic.

"Um, do you know if the dinner tonight is black tie? I'm not sure if my husband's dress shirt is back from the laundry."

"Oh, doesn't Stella do his shirts anymore?"

Good grief, now what? she thought, but covered herself quickly by saying, "Oh, yes, but the pleated shirt needs special care."

"Oh, my. Well, I hope you have it. Yes, the dinner is black tie tonight. The annual evening meeting always is. As you know, the rest of the meetings are at lunchtime."

"How stupid of me! Well, I must rush and check on that shirt. Bye now!"

Rose slammed down the telephone and hurried to Lilah's closet. Damn, there wasn't a long gown anywhere to be found. She must hang them somewhere else. Taking off the black wool dress, Rose slipped on a robe and hurried downstairs to talk to Stella. She would just have to risk the maid's thinking she had suddenly lost her mind. She knocked on her door.

"Stella, I know this sounds strange, but I can't seem to find my long dresses. Do you have any idea where they might be?"

Stella stood in the doorway looking at her skeptically. After a while she asked, "You okay, Miz Conway?"

"I'm fine. Why do you ask?"

"They's in that special lined closet in Mary Ann's room. You know, the one you built out onto the side porch for her."

Rose laughed nervously. "Oh, right. I completely forgot about that closet. Thanks, Stella. I've got to hurry."

"Ma'am, I know this ain't none of my business, but I think maybe you ought to let Dr. McIntyre have a look at you. You just ain't seemed yourself since you come home."

"I'm fine, really. We're going to Hawaii tomorrow for a vacation, and I think that's just what the doctor ordered. When I get home, I'll be my old self again," she said, amused at her own joke.

She dashed up the stairs, hesitated, and then barged

into the first room on the left. Nope, that must be
Matthew's room. It still had a slight odor of old tennis
shoes. She went into the next room, which was obviously Mary Ann's, with its four-poster bed and doll
collection in the bookcases lining the walls. She found
the cedar-lined walk-in closet and checked through a
number of formal gowns hanging from a high pole.
Most of the gowns were frilly pastel dresses, probably
from Mary Ann's debut the year before.

Only two of the long gowns could possibly be Lilah's.
Rose pulled them down and carried them into the
bedroom. With a sinking heart she looked over both
of the dreary dresses and groaned. Dear God, did her
sister really wear these tacky things? One was a beige
crepe dinner dress that would have been fine if she'd
had a smashing Judith Leiber belt to brighten it up.
The other was a simple navy-blue silk with a wide
white organdy collar. Too summery.

Disconsolately she thought about faking a migraine,
but Warren would be disappointed if she copped out
on his big evening. She held the beige dress up to her.
It might fit. Without stopping to cover her wig with a
scarf, she quickly slipped the dress over her head. She
buttoned several of the tiny cloth-covered buttons that
ran all the way down the front of the bodice. Not great
and a little saggy, but it would have to do.

She looked at the clock. God, it was after five and
she hadn't even showered. Without thinking, she pulled
the dress off quickly, but one of the little buttons got
caught in her wig. Try as she might, she could not
untangle it. At last she tottered out into the hallway
with the dress covering her head and yelled, "Stella!"

Suddenly she heard Warren's voice at her elbow
say, "You look like you need help."

Rose's heart sank. Dear God, send him away, she
prayed silently, but instead she said, "Oh, it's nothing.
My hair got caught on a button. Would you ask Stella
to come up and help me out of this dress?"

"Here, let me help you. Have you forgotten how
nifty I am with zippers and buttons?"

She tried to back away, but since she could not see where she was going, she was moving perilously close to the steps. "No, no . . . I can do it myself," she protested. Suddenly her foot stepped out into thin air, and she lost her balance and began to fall.

"Watch out," Warren shouted, and grabbed at her, catching the wig and the dress, all of which suddenly came loose in his hands. Once she was free of the dress, Rose managed to grab the banister to stop her fall, but she sat down hard, her legs sprawled out in front of her.

"Good God!" Warren exclaimed, looking at the figure lying spread-eagle on the stairs below him. The woman he had thought was his wife was a creature wearing a nylon wig cap covering, for God's sake, black hair! He looked so shocked and perplexed and funny standing there with the wig in his hand that Rose couldn't help giggling as he gasped, "What happened to your hair?"

Pulling herself up, she stood before him clad only in her bra and panty hose. Funny how destiny had a way of wrenching things out of one's grasp. Oh, well. She put out her hand to shake his. "How do you do, Warren. I'm your wife's twin sister, Rose."

Warren was in a state of shock. Words failed him completely. It was simply not possible for him to absorb such a bizarre and incredible turn of events. Either Lilah was losing her mind or he was losing his! For a long time he just stood there staring at the wife-like apparition before him.

"I think we'd better talk," Rose said calmly.

60

ROSE was seated on the chaise in the bedroom, wrapped in a robe, her long, curly black hair falling free, released from the confines of the wig.

Warren had not once taken his eyes off her as she related in detail the story of twin sisters who had been separated at birth, one to be raised black, the other white. When she was finished, he said nothing. Rose was nervous and very uncomfortable.

"Warren, for heaven's sake, give me some kind of reassurance that I haven't messed up my sister's life. Or, God forbid, have I?"

Warren shook his head. Words could not express his astonishment, anger, hurt, and humiliation, feelings that were also colored with disbelief. Was it possible there were really two Lilah's? All he could manage to say was, "It's too incredible. I think I'm looking at my wife, talking to her, but I'm not. In spite of the hair, I can't seem to make the distinction. Are you sure you're not Lilah having a mental breakdown of some kind?"

"I'm not Lilah, Warren. I'm her identical twin. Believe me. I'm Lady Rose. And does it bother you that I'm black?"

"My God, I have no idea! Give me some time to get used to the idea that there are two of you before I have to start dealing with that," he hedged. His eyes narrowed suspiciously. "Why didn't Lilah tell me about this herself?"

"Warren, I know you're upset, but please try to see this from her perspective. She probably was worried about how you'd feel about our father, although I'm sure she intended to tell you everything eventually. I know that once she'd decided to impersonate me, she was afraid you would disapprove, and that was one of the reasons for her waiting to tell you. You know, she was really intent on doing this, not only to help me but also to find out what it was like to be a star. Do you realize your wife has a lot of unfulfilled dreams?"

"God, how well I know. For twenty years I've felt guilty for encouraging her to quit . . . giving her a way out." There was a hint of bitterness in his voice as he wondered if his well-ordered life would ever be the same. "I need a drink. Will you join me . . . Rose?" And suddenly, having said her name, she became real to him. She was Rose now, not his Lilah anymore.

"I'd love it," she replied.

Downstairs in the den, Rose sipped on her gin and tonic and watched Warren closely, wondering what was really going on inside his head. Finally he spoke. "I don't understand how you can be identical twins and one be white and the other . . . not."

"I guess you might say I'm culturally black, Warren, just as Lilah is culturally white. Our skin is the same color, but I dye my hair black and she bleaches hers blond. I've been raised to think and feel black . . . and she's been raised to think and feel white. Who's to say what we are?"

After a long, awkward silence, Rose blurted out, "Warren, say something, please! I know you've been thrown off-balance, and I feel just awful about that. If I hadn't been so damned arrogant and curious about Lilah's life, it never would have happened. All you'd have had to worry about was your wretched affair with that woman. Oh, *merde!* I never should have said that, it was cruel. But do you have any idea how concerned I am that I might have messed up my sister's marriage . . . and her life?"

"It's your fault that you're black?" he asked sardonically.

"No, damn it, that's not what I meant. I only meant that if it hadn't been for me you'd have never known about anything," she snapped.

Warren took a long swallow of the stiff Scotch he had poured for himself and replied, "I believe in the truth, Rose, even though you might not think so after that miserable story I told you last night. I believe that lies and duplicity will destroy you. I'm just sorry that Lilah didn't trust me enough to tell me herself, but I'm happy about one thing: At least now I know she wasn't making secret trips from one coast to the other to rendezvous with another man."

Suddenly the clock struck six, and it galvanized Rose into action. "Good Lord, I'd better hurry and get dressed or we'll be late for that Rotary dinner."

"You mean you still intend to go?" he asked in surprise.

"I came here to find out what my sister's life was like, and I've never been to a Rotary Club dinner. Besides, I'm not ready to quit being Lilah just yet . . . unless, of course, you don't think I can . . . pass."

For the first time that evening Warren smiled. "Lady Rose, I suspect you can do damned near anything you set your mind to."

As soon as Warren left the room, Rose began to turn herself once more into Lilah Conway. She tried not to think about what Lilah's reaction would be when she found out what had happened.

Dressed in the beige dress, Rose walked downstairs to meet Warren, who wrapped a dark mink coat around her shoulders.

"Will your friends suspect I'm not Lilah?" she asked nervously.

"Don't let this upset you, but I can't believe that you fooled me. As much as the two of you look alike, the differences are obvious to me now."

"Like what?"

"We really should be on our way, or we'll have to traipse through the entire dining room to the head table."

"The head table?" Rose asked in alarm.

"Yes, I'm a vice-president and in charge of the program tonight. That's why it was important for me to be there."

"*Sacré bleu!* That's more than I bargained for."

"Not really," he said encouragingly, taking her arm and guiding her toward the car. "Sitting at the head table isolates you a bit from the crowd. Nobody will really be able to inspect you close up."

"Inspect me? I feel like a piece of horseflesh," Rose replied, but her tone was bantering and not angry.

"You know what I mean."

When they were in the car and on their way, Warren described the differences he now was able to see. "You walk differently, that's the most noticeable distinction. I can't believe I failed to see it immediately."

"How so?"

"Well, Lilah strides, like she knows where she's going and doesn't want to waste any time getting there. You amble . . . and sway . . . like you hear music and you're walking to the rhythm. Are you?"

"I'm always listening to a tune in my head. What else?"

"Obvious things, like the hair. Now that I know it's a wig, it really looks fake, especially around the neckline where it sticks out when you tilt your head down. And your hands . . . they're whiter than Lilah's. Why is that?"

"Because she plays golf, and I never, ever go out in the sun. Ben calls me his hothouse flower."

"Tell me about Ben."

For the rest of the drive Warren listened as Rose detailed her love's virtues. How he had changed her life, given her a whole new career, and made her happy. When she finished, Warren commented somewhat ruefully, "It's too bad your sister didn't have someone to support her as you did."

"Why do you say that? She has you and two wonderful children. She's been very lucky."

"Maybe, but I did everything in my power to keep her away from music, even though I knew it was important to her."

"That was her decision, not yours," Rose responded emphatically.

"Maybe, but I moved in on her at the most vulnerable moment of her life, and I knew exactly what I was doing. You see, I fell in love the moment I first saw her, but wrapped in that cocoon of music of hers, she was unreachable and nothing like the other girls I knew."

"Her music was part of her, Warren, and one of the reasons you were attracted to her. Has it ever occurred to you that without her music she's not the same person she was then?"

Warren was thoughtful. "Maybe, but I've always feared that if she ever went back to the piano, I'd be shut out again, and there'd be no room for me . . . or our family."

"People need more than careers or achievement. They need love too. Ben's more important to me now than my career, but I'm lucky I can have them both."

They arrived at the hotel just as everyone was moving into the grand ballroom for dinner. Warren guided Rose through the crowd carefully, addressing friends by name so that Rose had only to smile and echo him. When they got to the dais, he introduced her to Josh Petrone, the powerful banker who had flown all the way from Los Angeles to be the guest speaker for his friend and colleague.

"Josh, you remember my wife, Lilah, don't you?"

"I certainly do, and it's a pleasure to see you again. The last time we met was in Florida . . . at the Boca Raton—"

Warren interceded, "That's right. Lilah took first place in the women's golf event, remember?"

"I sure do. I especially remember the women threatening to enter you in the men's tournament next time so that some of the other women would have a chance at first prize. Tell me, what's the secret of that magic swing of yours? Everybody was talking about it. They said you had it grooved perfectly on every shot."

Warren interceded, "Let's not talk golf—"

Rose, however, interrupted. "The answer is music, Josh. I hum a little tune in my head just as I start, and I listen to the rhythm as I swing."

Warren looked at her sharply, wondering where she'd gotten such an odd notion.

"What's the song?"

"That's my secret," she said, and smiled. "Everybody has to swing to their own tune."

"We'll have lots of time to talk on the plane tomorrow. Maybe I can persuade you to hum that tune for me."

"Maybe," Rose said, and smiled. "I'm looking forward to the trip."

Rose was seated next to a man with an extraordinary talent for eating and speaking in a concerted rhythm so that one didn't interfere in the least with the other. She picked at the chicken breast with its pale gravy and withered vegetables and tried to listen, but most of his conversation was so far removed from her life and experience that she couldn't relate to him at all. Then he said something that captured her attention and sent her adrenaline soaring.

"It's a damn shame, that's what it is. I don't care how many federal holidays they dedicate to some damn coon, I told my employees that if they wanted the day off next week, they could do it without pay. Damn politicians always catering to the nigger vote."

It had been so long since that word had been used in her presence that the sound of it startled her. "I beg your pardon?"

"Oops, sorry. I'm not supposed to call 'em that now, am I?" he smiled, and winked conspiratorially.

Rose had a strong urge to dump her gravy-laden plate into his lap, but she refrained. Rose Wilkins might be able to do that, but Lilah Conway would not. Instead she looked at him coldly and turned away. She wondered how many times in her life her sister had listened to insulting remarks and said nothing. How could people assume others to be in sympathy with their bigotry?

The pink sherbet in its little glass dish had melted, and the speeches droned on. Rose had tried to listen, but her mind was filled with Peggy Lee's song, "Is That All There Is?" It was time Lilah stopped wasting herself and her talent and got back to her music. It wasn't too late. It was never too late. But first, Rose decided, she must convince Warren he had nothing to fear from Lilah's music, and secondly, she had to help both of them over this crisis. Lilah had a good marriage, but she needed more from it, and so did Warren.

In the car on the way home Warren praised her performance. "You were great, Rose. Say, where did you ever get that business about the music and the golf swing? It was inspired."

"Lilah told me about it," she said, surprised that he hadn't known. *Mon Dieu*, didn't those two ever talk to each other?

61

LILAH was in makeup and waiting to be called to the set when the telephone in her dressing room rang. Since Ben was outside talking to the producer, Lilah answered it and was startled to hear her husband's voice.

"Uh . . . Rose . . . Lilah?" he said in response to her hello.

"Warren, is that you?" she gasped, startled and bewildered.

"Lilah, I know everything," he said softly.

A cascade of emotions washed over her, and suddenly she felt as if she were drowning in them. Had her sister betrayed her? Had Rose told him everything . . . everything?

"Warren, I don't know what to say," she murmured.

"Look, we can't talk now . . . not on the telephone. I just want you to know that it wasn't Rose's fault. It just happened."

Her pulse raced as she asked, "Where are you?"

"Here in Los Angeles. We just arrived at Rose's house. She was upset when she found out you had continued working. She's on her way to the studio."

"She can't come now!" Lilah gasped. "Somebody might recognize her."

Warren laughed. "I don't think so. She looks just like Lilah Conway to me—well, almost. Anyway, she

363

wanted you to call the gate and arrange a pass for Lilah Conway. Lilah, why didn't you tell me?"

"Oh, God, Warren, I'm sorry, I really am. But this is no time to talk about that. Why is she taking the risk of coming here now?"

"She said it was time for her to face Kimball. She thinks if she can get through the bedroom scene with him, she won't be afraid anymore."

"It's too late. I'm all ready and waiting for them to call. She's not even in costume or makeup yet."

"Can you delay—" he began, but she cut him off when a courier knocked at the door.

"I've got to go, Warren. I'll call you back."

As Lilah followed the young woman out the door toward the set, she looked for Ben, who was nowhere to be found. Stan was waiting for her, anxious to get on with the scene.

She turned to the courier and quickly whispered to her to have the gate admit her friend Lilah Conway.

"Good, you're ready," Stan said, taking her arm and leading her onto the set, where she climbed onto the huge bed covered with ice-blue satin sheets. She reclined on a stack of lace pillows, and the prop girl slipped the twenty-five-carat cubic zirconia ring on her finger and placed a lucite breakfast tray in front of her. A white telephone was set on the bed close to her hand, and she picked it up for the scene to begin. Stan wasn't happy with a shadow on her face, and as she waited for the adjustments to be made she tried to concentrate, but it was almost impossible. Why had Rose found it necessary to tell Warren everything?

Stan complained about the type of telephone, and they had to wait while the prop person secured a more exotic instrument. Twenty minutes after she settled into the bed, twenty minutes in which she had managed to stew and fret and worry about everything in her life, the director was ready for Lilah to begin the scene, the stupid, irrelevant scene she had to perform while her life and her family disintegrated.

"Okay, Rose, hold the telephone in your left hand and pick at the food on your tray with the fork in your right hand as you talk on the telephone. When the door bursts open and you see Craig, don't say good-bye until the receiver is halfway down to its cradle. Focus your eyes straight into his. Telegraph to the camera that this is a sizzling hot, very intense moment. Let us see that you're ready and waiting for him to hop on your bones . . . okay?" Stan instructed.

Lilah nodded in agreement, trying to concentrate, trying to obliterate everything except this scene, this moment in time.

"Ready. Let's go for a take without a run-through. See if we can get some nice, spontaneous sizzle. You ready, Craig? Open the door when I give you the signal. And cheat toward her left shoulder so we don't see the scratches on your face."

"I'm ready," Kimball said with a leer that indicated he was eager to get on with it.

"Okay, quiet on the set . . . let's go."

The assistant director called, "Quiet . . . roll cameras."

The sound man affirmed. "Rolling."

Stan said, "Action."

The set suddenly grew very still. Lilah poked at the food with her fork and smiled as she said her lines into the telephone. "I'm not sure I want to do that . . . no, really, Charles, I mean it this time." Suddenly the door burst open, and Craig stood there warding off a maid who was trying to stop him. The two actors stared into each other's eyes for a long moment, and then, as the director signaled with his arm, Lilah said, "Close the door as you leave, Maribelle." The maid backed from the room and closed the door, and Craig began a slow and insinuating walk toward the bed.

Lilah expected the director to yell "Cut," but he didn't, and Kimball kept moving toward her. Suddenly, with one fast movement, he unbuttoned his jacket and let himself drop toward her. He whipped back the sheets that were covering her and snatched her into his arms. My Lord, she thought, what was he doing? Startled and mesmerized by the pace and the fervor of his maneuvers, Lilah allowed herself to go limp so that she could be gathered into a crushing embrace. Their eyes locked into each other's, and their mutual hatred arced between them like electricity. Suddenly the gossamer thread that separates the passions of love and hatred snapped, and she surrendered herself, much as the beauteous Lucy had surrendered to Dracula's lethal embrace, knowing that it would destroy her but unable to resist the rapture of the moment.

The cameras continued to film, the crew was fascinated by the highly charged sensuality before them, but just as Craig clamped his mouth down hard upon Lilah's, he also let the full weight of his body press down upon her. At that instant she felt a sharp, excruciating pain at her hipbone, a grinding pain so intense that her body contorted and tried to repel it, but his grip was like steel, and he pressed himself into her even harder.

Lilah tried to turn her head away to scream, but he moved one hand to the back of her neck and held it so tightly that she could not get her mouth free. She began to struggle, but moving made the soaring pain at her side worse. The director let the scene continue, for it appeared to be sexy and urgent—perhaps too urgent—but he figured that the editors could cut it wherever necessary.

"Just like two lions in heat," Stan murmured to the script supervisor with satisfaction.

Suddenly Craig released her and with a yelp leapt backward, clutching at his buttock. "You bitch!" he screamed.

Lilah sat up, and there was blood on her mouth where her own teeth had cut into her lip from the pressure of his mouth on hers. Clutching her side, she shrieked at him, "You hurt me!"

She got out of the bed and moved toward him, still holding the fork that had gained her release. She looked as if she might kill him with it if she wasn't stopped. Finally coming to his senses, the director stepped between them, shouting, "Cut! For God's sake, cut! What the hell is going on here?"

"Look under his jacket . . . he's wearing something!" Lilah cried accusingly. She tried to move toward him, but Craig backed away, buttoning his jacket about him.

"Nothing! I've got nothing on! Keep away from me, you shrew! How dare you jab me with that fork! It's a good thing it wasn't sharp enough to do me any real harm."

"I wish it had been a knife. I would have run it right through you," Lilah responded furiously. Ben had just arrived on the scene, and he crept up silently behind Craig and, with one lightning movement, grabbed the actor's arms and pinned them behind him. "Stan, check him out!" he ordered.

"Don't you touch me, or you'll never work in this town again!" Kimball warned the director, who hesitated. But Lilah did not. She rushed forward and yanked open his coat to reveal a large silver belt buckle that was decorated with numerous protuberances, all of which had been filed to razor-sharp points, a piece of equipment designed for a sadist.

There was a loud gasp from the crew as everyone turned from the belt to stare at Lilah. Hesitantly she looked down to see small spots of blood seeping through the satin gown and forming a stain at her hip.

"Jesus Christ!" Stan gasped.

Ben pulled Kimball's arms tighter and muttered fervently, "I'll kill you for this!"

Bruce Stebbins had arrived on the scene just in time to witness the unveiling of the belt and the wound. "Let him go, Frost! You hear me? I'll take care of this. Now, everybody back to your places, and if I read about this in any of the newspapers, including the

Enquirer, none of you will ever work for me or this network again!"

He turned to Lilah. "Rose, I can't tell you how bad I feel about this. I'll get a doctor to your dressing room right away. Frost, take care of her. As for you, Kimball, you'd better get back to your dressing room and lock the door before one of us forgets who you are."

"Don't tell *me* what to do, asshole! It was an accident, pure and simple. Can't you see that?" he snarled, and haughtily walked away.

The producer turned to the director and snapped, "Stan, for God's sake, how did you let that happen?"

"I didn't see the damn thing. He hid it under his coat. The bastard's sick."

"Christ! Has he put us on the spot," Bruce moaned. "Maybe this will convince the brass to jettison him."

"It's not our fault."

"Yeah, well, Rose can sue the hell out of all of us, the network included, if she wants to. Has somebody called the doctor yet? And for God's sake, get the legal office on the telephone and tell Dick Trask to get his ass over here as fast as possible."

Just after the two men walked past a mound of sound blankets, the pile moved slightly. When she was sure that no one was looking, Jellie Beam extricated herself from the dusty things and looked around cautiously before darting toward the exit. She had bribed her way onto the set, hoping to see or hear something of interest, and she had hit the jackpot.

Ben rushed Lilah into the dressing room and was startled to find Rose sitting at the dressing table applying her Caymen Welles makeup. She had taken off the wig and combed out her natural hair.

"Jesus, what are you doing here?" he asked sharply.

"Well, that's a fine welcome, Ben Frost," she began, and then she saw the red stain on Lilah's gown and gasped. "My God, what happened?"

"That son of a bitch nailed her with a belt buckle!"

"Mon Dieu!" Rose exclaimed, and helped Lilah to the couch. "Has somebody called a doctor?"

"I'm fine, Rose. It hurts, but I don't think it's serious. I've had worse injuries skiing," Lilah assured her.

"But it's bleeding . . . oh, Lilah, why didn't you wait till I got here? Didn't Warren tell you I was on my way?" she wailed.

"It was too late. I had to go on."

Suddenly the door burst open, and Craig Kimball walked into the room, furious and ready to complete the mayhem he had begun. His momentum was brought to a sudden halt when he saw the two women. Everyone was frozen in place for one horrible moment, and then Kimball exclaimed, "Good God! There are two of you bitches!"

Ben grabbed Craig's arm and propelled him out of the room. "Hey, man, you're outa your mind! When the doctor gets here, I'm gonna have him take a look at you and tell him you're seeing double."

Horrified, Rose and Lilah looked at each other. "What are we going to do?" Lilah asked.

"You're going to have to be Lady Rose a little longer. Sorry, Lilah. I'll hide in the closet while the doctor's here. When he leaves, I'll become Lilah again and get the hell out before anybody else sees me. Ben can bring you home. It was a stupid mistake for me to have come here."

"But suppose he tells somebody?"

"Don't admit anything! Like the man said, he was seeing things. He's not in a position for anyone to believe anything he says now."

Lilah was taken to the hospital where an examination revealed severe contusions and several lacerations. At the request of the network the attending physician insisted that she remain overnight, and over her objections Ben agreed.

When she was settled into bed in one of the VIP

suites at Cedars Hospital, she asked Ben why he had refused to take her home.

"No sense taking any more chances than we already have with you, and besides, it's good strategy, Lilah. I want everybody to worry. God, I'm sorry as hell that I let him hurt you, but now that it's done, we've got to use it to our advantage."

"What happened when you dragged him out of the room?"

"I just held on tight until I found his little buddy, Sudsy. I told him about the attack with the killer belt and said I thought Sudsy should watch his boss closely, because he was seeing double and apparently had gone over the edge."

"And Sudsy accepted that?"

"Strangely enough, he did. He led Kimball into his dressing room and said, 'Thanks, fella. I'll take it from here.' It's a damn good thing nobody else saw the two of you together."

"I guess Rose got out without being recognized."

"I sure hope so."

"Ben, I can't stay here overnight. I just can't," Lilah moaned.

"Why not?"

"I'll have to sleep in this miserable wig, that's why. And I'll have a monster headache in the morning."

"No problem. The doctor told me he'd prescribed some pain medication for your side. It should help with your head too," he said, and grinned.

"Swell."

"Nobody ever said acting was easy," he teased gently.

"Ben, where did he ever get that hideous belt buckle?"

"Probably one of those S and M shops. They've got a lot of weird stuff in them, and I've got a feeling he does a lot of shopping there."

"Ben, Warren knows everything."

"I know. I was in the dressing room when Rose arrived, and she told me the whole story. That's why I wasn't there when that bastard hit you with the hardware."

Tears began to form in her eyes. "I need to talk to my husband," she said softly.

"Lilah, everything's okay. You haven't got anything to worry about."

62

"WELL, this is a surprise. Long time no see, darling," Mavis cooed into the telephone.

"It has been a long time, Mavis. Can we have dinner together tonight? I need to see you," Claire asked nervously.

"Can't tonight, darling. I have to be at that celebrity tribute to Lucille Ball. Surely you're going to be there, of course."

"I'm afraid not. My husband never goes out at night when he's working. Besides, he hates tributes, especially to other actors."

"Do I detect a slight note of dissatisfaction in Hollywood's dream marriage?" Mavis asked with a hint of spite in her voice.

"I need your advice. I've just learned something very important, and I thought perhaps you might help me put it into perspective." She hesitated and her voice lowered. "I've also missed you . . . terribly."

"I've missed you, too, Claire. Why don't you come over for tea. We can talk privately. About five, all right?"

"I'll be there."

Claire arrived exactly at five and was disconcerted at being greeted by Ava, whom she had not seen since that humiliating moment when the girl had caught Claire and her mother making love. If Ava remembered, however, she did not let on. She served tea and they conversed awkwardly until Mavis finally breezed in. Although she had been rushing around the entire day, Mavis's appearance was perfection itself. Dressed in her trim little black Chanel suit with ropes of pearls and gold chains, she looked as meticulously chic as the society matrons whose names filled her columns.

"Darling, how good to see you!" Mavis exclaimed, and they hugged each other briefly. "Ava, sweetheart, get rid of these cups and bring us some sherry. It's a chilly, damp day, and I need to thaw out."

When they were at last settled with glasses of the bright amber liquid in their hands, Mavis told her daughter to leave them alone and to inform anyone who called that she was not available. She lifted her glass and toasted. "To us, darling, and the renewal of old friendships. Now, what's on your mind?"

"Mavis, you know how miserable I am with Craig Kimball."

"Yes, you've mentioned it a time or two," Mavis replied sardonically.

"You're the only person I've ever confided in. Let me tell you what I've just found out." She launched into the story of her husband's first wife that Jellie Beam had told her. Mavis listened, amazed at how swiftly the story had come full circle. When Claire was finished, she asked, "And you want me to tell you how best to use this information to force Craig . . . to do what?"

"To let me lead my own life, to see whomever I choose to see without fear of being cut off from the marriage or the inheritance I was promised when I sold myself into this loathsome alliance," Claire said heatedly.

"I see." Mavis sipped her sherry, and after a long, pensive moment, she asked, "How much is it worth to you, Claire?"

"What do you mean?"

"Don't be coy, my dear. You know exactly what I mean. You don't think I live in the manner I do on the puny pittance I get from my column, do you?"

"Why, I never thought—" Claire began.

"Of course, I tell everyone that I'm an heiress from Upstate New York, but that's as phony a background as most of the ladies in this town have. Now, my dear, this is my proposition. You go home and continue to be the good little wife, nothing more. Let me do the rest. When I get things worked out for you, I'll tell you. And then, when you inherit all of that money, I want ten percent."

"What do you intend to do with him?" Claire asked suspiciously.

"That's my business. Is it a deal?"

"Ten percent of Craig Kimball's estate could go as high as a million dollars . . . maybe two. I don't know exactly."

"Actors are always worth less than we think they are—in more ways than one—but ten percent is a small amount, considering what you will have. Now, if we have an agreement, we must have it in writing."

"I'm not sure I want to get involved in this. Suppose I sign my name to some paper giving you ten percent and he suddenly drops dead with a heart attack. Do I still owe it to you?"

"Yes," Mavis said evenly. "On the other hand, you might suddenly slip up and get kicked out on your pretty little ass, then neither of us will get anything. Do you want some time to think it over?"

"No, I don't know what you have in mind, but draw up the paper and I'll sign it . . . with a time limit. If everything is still as it is six months from now, however, the deal's off."

"Fair enough. Six months is more than enough time. As you know, I'm a very fast worker. Now, shall we seal it with a kiss?" Mavis asked.

"Your daughter's in the house," Claire replied nervously, but the thought of Mavis's expert and velvety touch sent a quiver of longing deep inside her.

"I've had a lock put on my bedroom door. Come, I must be dressed by seven, and I hate to rush."

The two women rose from their chairs and moved without touching toward the bedroom to make love. Claire felt a rush of anticipation as she glimpsed their reflections in the mirror-lined hallway. Mavis was beautiful . . . and so was she.

Later, after Claire had gone, Ava informed her mother that Jellie Beam had called and left her number. "She was furious because I wouldn't awaken you. She said it was extremely important."

"I hope so," Mavis replied, dialing the number quickly and hoping that Jellie had something interesting and usable to tell her about Craig Kimball.

"Mavis, is there something going on between Craig and Lady Rose?" Jellie asked. "And if not, then is it a habit of his to torture and maim his leading ladies?"

"Not unless he married them. What are you talking about?" Mavis asked, intrigued.

"Look, I'm going to tell you something in confidence. Ordinarily I'd never share this with another reporter, but I know this kind of story would never appear in that fancy column of yours, and I need your help. I want to blow this asshole out of the water, and I can't do it by myself."

"All right, Jellie. I may know something more, but I don't want to be associated with the story in any way. Do you understand? It's got to be just between us. If the story flies, however, I want half your take, all right?"

"A deal." Money had never been Jellie's motivation. "Now, what have you found out?"

"I bribed my way onto the set of that television show Kimball's filming just to watch, and did I ever get an eyeful." She went on to describe in detail everything that had happened during the belt-buckle incident. When she finished, Mavis's reaction was guarded. "You're not going to write that story, are you?"

"Not without finding out what he's got against that singer Lady Rose, who, by the way, was taken to Cedars, where she still is."

"Was she badly hurt?" Mavis asked.

"I don't think so. She managed to stab him in the ass with a fork to get him off her. I didn't get a close look at her side, but I saw the buckle, and it was lethal."

"The son of a bitch!" Mavis exclaimed bitterly.

"Yeah. Now what do we do?"

"Let me see what I can find out. I'll get back to you shortly." Mavis slammed down the telephone and rushed into her bathroom to shower and dress for the evening. This was one party she had to make. Vance Freedland would be there, and she needed to talk to him as soon as possible.

Just before dinner was served, Mavis made her way through the throng of glitterati to stand beside the great hulk that was Vance Freedland. As soon as he saw her, he ended his conversation with Angie Dickinson and turned all his attention to the columnist.

Standing together, the two looked very much like a mouse and an elephant, especially as he leaned toward her so that she would not have to shout up at him.

"Vance, my dear, I have something very important to talk to you about," Mavis said as softly as she could in the midst of the large and noisy crowd.

"I'm all ears, my dear," he replied.

"No, not here. It's very complicated . . . and private." She did not stipulate time or place. Vance would make that determination.

He looked at her thoughtfully and then said, "Can it wait until tomorrow, or is it more urgent than that?"

"It's something you need to know."

Vance smiled graciously. "Then, my dear, I hope you will do my wife and me the honor of riding home with us in our car. My wife likes to retire early, so we can talk then."

"I have my own car. I'll follow you."

"Very well. I hope you enjoy the program. And, by the way, my wife is entertaining a group of ladies who are organizing a function for the Music Center. I'll have her secretary call you and give you the details, or, of course, you are always welcome to join them."

"May I bring a photographer?" she asked, using the magic words.

"Kam would like that."

Satisfied that her mission was on countdown, Mavis began to move through the crowd, noting the names and the faces and chatting with those she considered important enough to write about, although her mind was awhirl with her own plans. What a fool Claire Kimball was, first to have sold herself into slavery to Kimball without even knowing what the exact price was, and now, to agree to pay ten percent of an unknown figure was the height of stupidity. Claire needed someone to watch out for her. Everyone knew that Craig Kimball was gloriously wealthy. He might even have an estate that approached sixty or seventy million. He had been one of the first actors to take a percentage of every picture he made. He might be vain and evil and sadistic, but he had had extremely good guidance in his business affairs. He was also known to be as penurious as Scrooge, spending money only on himself. Everyone who knew him well assumed that Claire spent a lot of her own money on her clothes and jewels, but Mavis had no quarrel with that. The more he was worth, the better she would make out. She had been trying to put away a little nest egg for the future, in case the paper ever found out that she was accepting gratuities, but she hadn't been very successful. Her expense allowance was ridiculously low, and it was important to her to appear to be the equal of those about whom she wrote.

But now that she was on the verge of not only appearing to be one of them but actually joining their ranks, she must not make any mistakes. She would call her attorney in the morning and have him prepare the papers immediately. If things went as fast as she expected they would, that paper would have to be signed and witnessed immediately.

*   *   *

Mavis waited in the huge book-lined library at the Freedland mansion and hoped she was not overplaying her cards or making a fatal miscalculation. Vance Freedland was not the huge teddy bear that he appeared to be. He was a powerful friend and a dangerous adversary, and she had been careful never to arouse his anger. She only printed items about him that he approved, and contrary to established practice, she always read the exact wording to him and changed it if he asked her to. She hoped they had a tacit agreement to be allies, although she had been careful never to ask anything of him, nor did she intend to do so now. She just prayed he did not suspect what was behind her little gambit.

At last Vance lumbered into the room, and Mavis was amused to note how the spacious library diminished in size as his great body moved into it. He lowered himself into the huge leather chair that was scaled to fit his posterior, and without preamble, he asked, "What do you want to tell me, Mavis?"

She was careful to choose her words so they could be interpreted to his liking. "I've come into some interesting information about a man whom we all admire and who is a particular friend of yours . . . Craig Kimball."

"Go on, Mavis. It's getting late," he said with little apparent interest.

"I know for a fact that there've been a lot of stories about him whispered around town, but they were all just gossip. There's never been any real verification of any of them, until today," she began.

His tiny eyes, which were barely visible buried as they were in the loose folds of flesh, narrowed even more. "What happened today?"

"On the set, in front of dozens of cast and crew members and a newspaper reporter, Mr. Kimball deliberately injured Lady Rose. She was taken to Cedars where she was admitted. I have no idea how badly she was hurt."

"Who was the reporter?"

"Jellie Beam. A free-lancer. She's a strange little duck, but she's tenacious and an extremely good reporter. She's been doing some digging around about Kimball lately. She knows about his Melissa, but her focus is to try in some way to tie him to you, not just as a friend but as a . . . business associate."

Without questioning her story, Vance asked her, "What did Craig do to the woman?"

She described the belt buckle's sharp protrusions, and as she spoke, the room began to fill with a silence that became suffocating when her story ended. At last the venomous stillness was broken by a bilious grunt as Vance pulled his great body out of the chair to dismiss her.

"Thank you, my dear, for bringing this directly to me. I know you only had Mr. Kimball's welfare in mind. After all, he is truly one of the greatest stars of all time, and I understand your wish to protect him. I know for a fact that he is not well. Rest assured that I will see that everything is taken care of, and I won't forget your kindness. Would that all of your colleagues were so honorable. Good night, my dear." The courtliness of his words did not mask the menace floating just below the surface.

Mavis left the house and drove home, but her hands were shaking. Vance Freedland scared the hell out of her. His words indicated appreciation, but she had also detected contempt. To hell with it. It was done, she couldn't take it back. She hoped it wouldn't backfire on Jellie, but those were the risks of the game.

Vance called his attorney as soon as Mavis left his presence. "Grant, get out of bed and get over here. We've got to talk." He slammed down the telephone and rang for the butler.

"Bring me a pot of hot water. Put some lemon and honey in it. Mr. Weathers will be here shortly, and then you may go to bed," he ordered.

Since he lived only a few blocks from the Freedlands, Grant Weathers arrived within minutes. Although it was late at night, he had taken the time to put on a dark gray suit with a fresh shirt and a necktie. Vance Freedland was a man to whom the proprieties of life were extremely important.

When the lawyer had heard Mavis's story, he asked Vance, "What do you want to do? I'm not sure we can keep this thing quiet. Too many people saw it."

"We'll have to defuse it. Tell his publicity agent to put out the word that he's been trying to work in spite of being ill . . . very, very ill."

"Is he going to recover?" the attorney asked.

"That's in the Lord's hands, not mine. Just make sure that nobody sees him or talks to him from now on . . . nobody. We may have to admit him to that private hospital in Arizona for a while," Vance replied.

"He's not going to go without a fight. You know how difficult he can be."

"I don't think we should let his sickness destroy the beautiful reputation he's enjoyed for so many years. I'll have Sudsy bring him over here tonight so that I can talk to him."

"What about the reporter? The one who saw it all."

"Get her out of town . . . find her a job she won't be able to turn down: Paris, Rome, Nicaragua."

"Reporters aren't easy to handle, you know that."

"It's your job. Do it."

"What about Craig's wife?"

"I'll take care of her."

"And Mavis?"

"I want her off the paper. I can't believe she actually had the nerve to come directly to me about controlling Craig Kimball. Who does the little slut think she is?"

"You know we can't push a big newspaper like that around, and it would be very dangerous to try," Weathers cautioned.

"Of course it would. That's why you're going to call

Tim Jordan on the telephone on Monday and tell him she's been shaking down people all over town to get their names in her column."

"They'll want proof."

"You've got canceled checks, haven't you?"

"They'll know I set her up."

"Doesn't matter. They'll want to sweep the whole thing under the rug. Gossip columnists are expendable. Now, it's past my bedtime. Good night."

"What about Lady Rose?"

"Don't go near her. She was Kimball's target, not ours. Colored stars don't last long, anyway. In a year or two nobody will even remember her name."

When Vance Freedland was alone again, he picked up the telephone to find out why Sudsy hadn't called him immediately about the belt-buckle incident.

"I've had my hands full," Sudsy wailed. "He's really actin' crazy. I had to wrestle the keys to the gun cabinet away from him, 'cause he was threatening to blow that black chick away the next time he sees her. You should hear some of the wild things he's sayin'. He's been puttin' away the booze pretty good."

"Bring him here. I want to talk to him," Vance demanded.

"He's too far gone. Besides, I don't think I can handle him in the car."

"Then make absolutely certain he doesn't leave the house, and above all, keep him from talking to anybody, understand? Not tonight, not tomorrow morning. I want you to call the producer of that show and tell him in confidence that Craig is very ill and that you've called the doctor."

"Whatever you say. Anything else?"

"It won't be long now, Sudsy."

"Right."

63

JELLIE was exasperated. She had been calling Mavis every fifteen minutes all day long, but her answering machine was always on. Finally, at four in the afternoon, she reached her at the office, but Mavis was busy writing her column and impatient.

"Make it quick, Jellie. I'm working against a deadline," Mavis snapped.

"I've been trying to call you all day. You promised me some information in exchange for that story I gave you last night, and I need to talk to you now," Jellie insisted.

"That stupid fairy tale you gave me last night? I checked it out and nobody saw anything of the sort. What are you trying to pull on me, Jellie?"

"I was there! I saw it with my own eyes," Jellie protested.

"Then I think you'd better clean the lenses on your glasses, my dear, because you're seeing things."

"Just why is Lady Rose in the hospital then?"

"The producer said Rose had collapsed on the set because of some kind of virus. She got hit by a bug, Jellie, not by Craig Kimball's belt buckle!" Mavis feigned irritation and contempt.

"Baloney! Can't you tell a cover-up when you see one?" Jellie was frustrated beyond belief.

"A reporter is supposed to look for the truth, not make it up. Craig Kimball is not the monster you think he is, and you'd better be careful about pursuing a vendetta against him. What the hell did he ever do to you, anyway?"

"What's with you, Mavis? Have you forgotten that story you told me about his first wife?"

"I have no idea what you're talking about. I can't remember ever discussing that subject with you."

Furious, Jellie slammed down the telephone. There was no use talking to that bitch anymore. She sat down at her typewriter, as she always did when anger welled up inside her, and tried to write it out. Her opening line was, "Is there human life on the planet of the superstars," and for hours she wrote the story that she had been tracking so assiduously. She omitted none of the sordid details accumulated about Kimball's life and career, which she cleverly combined with veiled references and rumors, dropping hints but skirting libel. She created a portrait of a legend run amok. She finished it at about four in the morning, and while she drank her tenth cup of coffee she reread it with satisfaction. It was the best thing she had ever done, and even if it never saw the light of print, she felt better for having written it.

She slept until ten, and then she dressed and headed for the office of the newspaper that ran most of her stories.

In Dave Sinclair's office, Jellie sat and watched as he read the story. When he was finished, she asked eagerly, "What do you think, Dave? Is it any good?"

The editor took off his glasses, rubbed his eyes, and then said, "Jellie, it's brilliantly written. Frankly I had no idea you were such a talented writer. It's thoughtful and perceptive, and you've dissected the character with exquisite precision. You've also delineated a lot of things that're wrong with our society and the way we make heroes out of assholes and vice versa."

As he talked, Jellie began to see herself as a writer, a real writer, not just a Hollywood hack, and when he paused, she exclaimed, "Thank God, I was so afraid you'd turn it down."

"You're not listening, Jellie. I *am* turning it down. Not because it's not good, not because it's not true . . . we just can't take a chance on it. It's not as if he were the president or something. He's just some dumb movie star, and what he does is basically . . . irrelevant. He's not worth the risk of a lawsuit."

"Jesus, Dave . . . please, think it over, will you? The public would eat it up."

"Forget it, Jellie. You did a good job, but nobody's gonna touch it. You haven't exactly uncovered a new toxic-waste dump or a guy stockpiling nuclear weapons. You've written a thoughtful treatise on the evils of superstardom, using one of the biggest as an example. Craig Kimball is growing old, but he still has a lot of admirers. I don't want any problems with him . . . or any of his friends."

"You're afraid of him! Right? You know he has mob connections," she accused.

"Look, you don't take big risks without the possibility of a big gain, and your story is back-room gossip and rumor and just not very important. Sorry."

Jellie got to her feet. "Maybe. I'm going to shop it around, anyway."

"Take my advice, Jellie . . . don't show it around town. You never know who might take exception to it and cause you trouble." His tone of voice was serious.

"You think some of his friends might try to waste me?" she asked with derision.

"I doubt it. But somebody might very well steal it for a novel. I know I'm tempted." Dave grinned, and Jellie gave him a finger as she walked out the door.

She went home and wrote the kind of society-matron story she had told Claire Kimball she would do. It would sell easily if she made it glitzy enough, and she needed the money. She thought about Dave Sinclair's advice and wondered if she should take it. She really was getting sick of the Hollywood scene.

Late that evening she got a call from Dave Sinclair, offering her a position in their London office.

"Dave, where did this come from?" she asked suspiciously.

"From me, stupid. I said you were too good a reporter to write the crap you're doing, and when I found out there was an opening, I put my ass on the line for you. So . . . will you take it?"

Jellie hesitated. It was all too pat . . . too coincidental . . . too easy. Was it possible that even Dave was not immune from persuasion?

"Well?" he demanded impatiently.

Jellie knew she was being manipulated, but a strong instinct for self-preservation told her she really had no choice. It was time to leave town.

"Et tu, Brute . . . how much does it pay?" she asked.

Later, in the early morning hours after a restless night, Jellie remembered the remark Dave had made in jest about writing a novel, and she wondered if perhaps that might not be the way to tell the world her story. A novel could tell it all and more. By the time dawn appeared, she had conceived a title, as well as a plot on which to hang the story. *Up Above the World So High*, a novel by Gilda Beam.

It wasn't going to be easy, because she had never tried writing fiction, but it was better than leaving the story completely suppressed and untold. London would get her out of the scene here and give her some perspective too.

Having made the decision, she went to sleep.

64

***

BRUCE Stebbins stood at the foot of Lilah's hospital bed and remarked, "My God, this room looks like a mobster's funeral parlor."

"This is nothing. Most of the bouquets went down to the pediatric ward. After the story hit the eleven o'clock news last night, there was a big run on roses," Ben replied.

"Are you feeling all right now?" Bruce asked. "I can't tell you how sorry I am about what happened."

"Did you have to lie, Bruce? I really would have preferred that you'd said I'd gotten injured on the set," Lilah protested, just as Ben had instructed her. "If the truth leaks out, you're going to make us all look like conspirators."

"You're probably right. It's just that we needed to get something out fast before people started speculating. Now, I expect you to back us up on this."

Ben interceded. "We're not giving out any statements, but we're not going to lie, either. Not until we find out what you intend to do about that viper."

"Let's calm down now. I haven't had a chance to talk to him personally yet, but I'm sure it was just a thoughtless mistake on his part. I can't believe that he really intended to hurt Rose."

"And I suppose you still believe in the tooth fairy! Don't treat us like idiots. You've heard the rumors about that guy, and yesterday proved they were true," Ben protested.

"Look, I'm going to have a talk with him, and Stan and the writers are going over the script to see if there's some way we can finish shooting their scenes separately, but if we can't . . . ."

"No way. Lady Rose will never appear on a sound-stage with that bastard again. And if . . . if you try to force her, we'll go to court and sue the skin off your ass! You want to see the holes he punched in her? Do you? I'll see that you get a copy of the pictures I had taken this morning," Ben said, declaring war.

"What do you want from me, Ben?" Bruce asked stonily.

"We want that episode scrapped. We want him gone—forever—from this series."

"I can't do that. We've got a contract with him," the producer replied, and his tone of voice had taken on a distinct whine.

"Tough shit," Ben snapped. "When you talk to that son of a bitch, tell him that if he tries to enforce that contract, we're going to the district attorney and nail him for assault with intent to do severe bodily harm. The belt buckle might even be considered a deadly weapon."

"Aren't you getting a little carried away, Frost?"

"No! I want him carried away . . . far away and out of sight. Do you understand me?"

"I'll see what I can do, Rose. I should have taken my mother's advice and gone to medical school." Bruce smiled ruefully. "Get well. I'll get back to you on this as soon as I can."

"Twenty-four hours, Bruce. There was a crime committed here."

When they were alone again, Lilah grabbed her side as she began to laugh. "Ben, that was a marvelous performance. You must have been a wonderful actor."

Ben grinned. "Not was, Lilah, am. A little rusty, maybe, but still got the old juice."

The telephone rang, and Ben picked it up. He smiled and said, "Here, you can talk to her yourself."

"Is it Rose?" Lilah asked, but Ben shook his head and handed her the telephone.

"Are you all right? I've been so worried about you. I wanted to talk to you last night, but Ben said there were reporters all over the place, and he was afraid someone might hear us." It was Warren, voicing his concern.

"I'm fine. How about you?"

"I'm okay. How soon will you be coming home?"

"In a little while, I think. I love you," she whispered into the telephone.

"Thank God you're all right."

Lilah closed her eyes as she put the telephone down, trying to hold back the tears that were forcing their way out.

"Are you okay?" Ben asked, and took her hand in his.

She nodded her head but couldn't speak.

"Go ahead, honey . . . shed a few tears. You've got a right."

"Please, Ben, leave . . . I've never been able to cry in front of anybody," she said as a sob rose in her throat.

"I'll be right outside."

When the door closed behind Ben, Lilah let the tears and her tightly held emotions flow. For the first time in her married life she realized how much Warren's love meant to her, and she wanted to be safe in his arms again.

65

"WHO the hell was that?" Craig Kimball snarled drunkenly, and Sudsy whirled around with the telephone in his hand.

"Uh . . . it was Vance. He heard about the little fracas on the set today, and he just wanted to know what was going on."

"So what'd he say?" Craig muttered as he poured himself another Scotch on the rocks.

Sudsy shrugged his shoulders. "So what could he say?"

Carrying his drink, the actor stumbled to the leather couch and let his body fall into it. "I bet the old lard-ass was pissed, wasn't he? Did ya tell him I found out there were two of 'em? I walked into her dressing room, and there they were, big as life. What'd he say?"

Sudsy avoided making eye contact as he busied himself in the bar refrigerator looking for a beer. "About what?"

"Don't give me that shit. You know about what." His laugh came out in a satisfied snort. "The buckle, what else?" he patted the heavy piece of metal at his waist.

"You shouldn'a done that to her . . . not in front of all those people."

"Them . . . I didn't do it to her . . . I did it to them . . . both of them," he declared boozily, and then

389

stopped to think about what he'd just said. Confused, he added, "Wait . . . I must've done it to one, not both." He shook his head to clear it and then returned to the more comfortable exercise of berating Sudsy. "Besides, I don't want you tellin' me what I should or shouldn't do, you pissant. What do you know about anything . . . you haven't even got any balls." Heaping insults on the little man's head was a cathartic ritual. Sudsy was his whipping boy, his court jester, his aide-de-camp, his slave. Degrading him was as natural and satisfying as breathing.

Sudsy, on the other hand, was approaching the saturation point. Although he was too smart to get himself into trouble, he was not above needling Kimball. "Yeah, well, the crew was sayin' that the buckle was really a steel brace you needed to help you keep it up because you can't do it on your own anymore."

His dart landed where it was aimed. "Who said that? Who? Tell me his name and I'll see that he never works in this town again!'

"Take it easy. He was nobody. It was a joke, that's all. You know how the crew likes to poke fun at the actors. Everybody gets it, one time or another."

"Get me another drink," Craig demanded, throwing the glass at the little man, who ducked and permitted it to hit the stone fireplace and shatter.

The study door flew open, and Claire stood in the doorway, glaring at her husband.

"That was a piece of Baccarat you just smashed. Sudsy, how many times do I have to tell you not to let him use the crystal when he's drinking! Use those plastic glasses under the bar," she ordered.

"No! Stars don't drink out of damn plastic glasses." Craig tried to pull himself to his feet, but he could not. His knees buckled, and he slumped to the floor. Sudsy and Claire looked at him, and Sudsy jerked his head toward the other room. Claire followed his lead, and the two tiptoed out of the room.

"He's a sick man, Claire. You ought to be nicer to him. Try to be more understanding."

"Sick, my foot. He's drunk. I wish he was really sick. I wish the old fool would have a heart attack and die!"

"You know, my sainted mother used to say, 'Never wish anyone harm . . . it just might fall on you instead.' "

"Is the story about the belt buckle true?" she asked.

"Where'd you hear about that?"

"None of your business. Are they going to keep it out of the newspapers?"

"What difference does it make to you?"

"I'm his wife. Everything he does reflects on me."

"You shoulda thought about that before you married him," Sudsy retorted insolently and turned on his heel, leaving her to fume in the hallway. He went back to his boss and fixed him another drink in an expensive glass. This drink, however, would be his last for the evening, for Sudsy had emptied two Seconal capsules into the glass before he filled it with Scotch and ice.

At nine o'clock the next morning, when Sudsy went into the study to answer the telephone, he had to step over his employer's sleeping body. He had decided the night before that he was finished dragging Craig Kimball up the stairs to bed.

"Is he still asleep, Sudsy?" Vance Freedland asked.

"Out like a light."

"Wake him up. His attorney just called to tell me that unless he withdraws on his own, the network will tear up his contract and release the truth. They also threatened to sue for the time and money they wasted filming an episode that has to be scrapped to keep that black woman from suing them. I told the fool to stay away from that situation," Vance fumed.

"He won't go quietly, Mr. Freedland. He's gonna make a big stink, I'll tell ya that."

"The jackass. What do you think we ought to do? You're the one closest to him."

"I think we ought to do whatever is needed to protect his name and his reputation as the star of stars."

There was a long silence while Vance seemed to be pondering the problem, and then he made his decision. "You're right. Perhaps we've waited too long. He's become his own worst enemy. Make certain that nobody is called except Dr. Walters."

"Don't worry, Mr. Freedland. I'll take good care of him. Just like always."

"You've done well, Sudsy. Don't make any mistakes now."

Sudsy put the telephone down and walked upstairs to his room. From a box hidden on the back shelf of the closet he took out a Baccarat glass that had been carefully wrapped in a linen handkerchief to protect Mrs. Kimball's fingerprints, just in case something went wrong.

Holding the glass with the handkerchief, he emptied the contents of a small vial of liquid into it and carried it down to the study where he filled the glass with Scotch. He then sat down on the couch to wait for the actor to awaken and demand his last drink. Sudsy was in no hurry. He had been waiting for this moment for twenty-five years.

66

LILAH paced back and forth in the hospital room like a caged lion. Ben had promised to be back by noon to take her home, and she hadn't heard from either Rose or Warren for hours. Where was everybody? Had they all forgotten about her?

At last she went to the telephone and called Rose's house. Warren answered.

"This is"—she had started to say "Lilah" and remembered that Ben had told her to be discreet—"me. Where's Ben? He was supposed to take me home this morning. The doctor's already been here and released me."

"Good morning, me. Calm down. Ben got an early call from the network this morning. They asked him to come in for a little discussion. I'm sure he'll be there as soon as he can."

Warren's ability to be calm and controlled in almost any situation was maddening at times.

"I'm just so anxious to see you and get back to . . . the way things were," she said.

"I've got . . . something to tell you," he said softly. "In fact, we have a lot to talk about." The tone of his voice was more serious than usual.

Lilah panicked. Had everything between them changed? In the cold light of morning, had he suddenly decided that he couldn't live with her ancestry?

"You sound so gloomy," she said, and there was a question in her voice, a begging need to be reassured.

"I don't want to upset you, but we can't discuss this now. It will have to wait until we're together. I'll see you in a little while."

She put the telephone down and felt worse than ever. Where the devil was Ben? She wanted him to take her out of this mess right now. She was tired of being a star. She was sick of pretending she was somebody she wasn't, and she needed the reassurance of Warren's devotion. Being a celebrity without the satisfaction of having achieved it herself had turned out to be a hollow experience. Fame without a personal feeling of accomplishment was nothing.

A nurse peeked into the room and said, "My, we are ambitious today, aren't we? How's the pain? Does it hurt much when you move around?"

Lilah's hand automatically flew to her side. Good grief, she had almost forgotten all about it. "Better, much better, thank you."

"I'll be bringing your lunch tray in shortly. Anything special you'd like to drink? Milk, juice, coffee . . ."

"No . . . well, maybe some tea."

The nurse disappeared, and Lilah sat down on the bed just as Ben came rushing into the room with a paper in his hand.

"Get your clothes on, sugar pie. We're going home in triumph," he announced with a broad smile.

"What's going on, Ben? Where've you been?" she asked as she lifted herself from the bed and moved toward the closet.

"It's all over. We won!"

"Already? What happened?"

"Bruce talked to Kimball's attorney this morning, and I don't know what he said, but a few minutes later the lawyer called back and said that the big star was ill and wouldn't be able to finish the episode. He also said that Mr. Kimball was upset, because he'd never in his life walked out on a show before, and he'd pay them back every cent he'd received. He also gave the network permission to make all the announcements, since Kimball was too ill to speak for himself and would be unavailable to the press until he was well again. Can you believe it?"

"It's too good to be true!" Lilah proclaimed with gleeful disbelief.

"Oooh, don't say that! It scares me. Now, get dressed and we'll get outa here. There's a couple nice folks waiting for us at home."

Lilah had her final taste of celebrity as she was being wheeled out to the limousine. There were several reporters and one television crew waiting to throw questions at her.

"Lady Rose, Lady Rose . . . is it true that you had a fight with Craig Kimball on the set and he knocked you down?"

Ben answered for her. "Absolutely not. She had a touch of the flu, and she got dizzy under the lights and fell."

"When will you be back to work?"

"I'm not sure. Perhaps tomorrow or the day after. Really, I'm feeling just fine now," Lilah responded.

"What was it like working with Craig Kimball? Is he as terrific as ever?"

"It was an experience I'll never forget. After all, he's still one of the great ones, isn't he?" With that answer she took Ben's hand and moved from the wheelchair to the backseat of the limousine. Ben followed, and the driver pulled away from the curb swiftly, leaving the press people behind.

"Great answer, Lilah. He really is one of the great ones. In fact, he's the biggest bastard of them all, and this town has more than its share of them. Well, now that it's just about over, are you glad?"

"It's an experience I wouldn't have missed for a million dollars, and I wouldn't do it again for ten million," Lilah said with a chuckle.

"Really? I thought we had a good time. Was it as bad as all that?"

"No, but I found out who I really am. I'm Lilah Conway, housewife, mother, golfer. And I'm happy with it."

"What about Lilah Conway, musician? Whatever happened to her?"

"She's locked up somewhere inside me, Ben, and I don't know where the key is. Right now I have more important things to worry about."

"I talked to your husband, and he seems like a really great guy. You'll work it out."

"I hope so, Ben. I hope so."

When the car pulled into the driveway of Rose's house, Warren came out the door to meet them. He seemed about to gather her in his arms, but he pulled back when he saw her. Chagrined, Lilah, too, held back.

"Warren, what's wrong?" she asked softly.

"That wig . . . those clothes . . . I don't know who you are," he said softly.

"I'm your wife, Warren, that's who I am." Tears filled her eyes as she looked up at him. He took her into his arms, closed his eyes, and kissed her gently. "So you are," he whispered into her ear.

With their arms entwined, they walked into the house together. As soon as they were inside, Rose swooped down on them and gathered them both into her arms. For a long time they clung to each other.

At last Lilah reached up and pulled the black wig and wig cap from her head. "I've got to sit down. My knees are all wobbly."

Suddenly everyone was solicitous. Warren helped her to the couch, Ben kneeled at her feet and took off her shoes so she could lie down, and Rose brought her a glass of ice water.

The two sisters looked at each other, and a smile of understanding and love passed between them.

Rose knelt beside Lilah and put her head on her shoulder.

"I'm so sorry Craig hurt you, Lilah."

"It's nothing, Rose . . . really. I'm just glad that everything worked out all right."

67

RAYMOND Anthony Walters, M.D., knelt over the figure of Craig Kimball, movie star, with a stethoscope pressed to his chest. After a few moments he looked up at the two figures hovering over him—the short, ugly ex-clown and the chic, cool blonde—and announced sorrowfully, "I'm afraid we've lost him."

"Oh, yeah?" Sudsy said.

"Are you sure?" Claire asked.

"Yes, I'm afraid his heart finally gave out. I warned him to go easy on the cigarettes and the alcohol, but he wouldn't listen. Mrs. Kimball, did you and Mr. Kimball make any, uh, prior arrangements?"

Claire looked puzzled. "What do you mean? Oh, for a funeral home? No, no, but . . . I think we should call Forest Lawn, don't you, Sudsy?" She was barely able to restrain her exultation.

"Sounds right to me. Why don't you do it, Mrs. Kimball? Let's get him out of here as soon as possible."

Nodding her head, she hurried away. When they were alone, Sudsy spoke softly to the doctor. "They won't do an autopsy, will they?"

"There's no reason to, especially since I was here at the moment of expiration. Besides, I have a complete record prepared that will attest to a long-standing and extremely serious heart ailment." The corner of his mouth twitched slightly. "He asked me to keep it a secret so that his fans wouldn't know."

The hypocrisy of it all brought joy to the soul of the old clown. The only organ in Craig Kimball's body that didn't work right was his dick, Sudsy thought, but he said, "Then you'll sign the death certificate. No problem?"

"No problem, but I suggest that you have him cremated without delay."

"Oh, yeah, sure. I can't remember how many times he told me to do that. He said he wanted people to remember the star up on the screen, not the stiff in a casket. I'm sure his wife will be more than happy to see that you're well compensated for your speedy arrival. It's lucky you got here just before he passed on."

"You didn't call the paramedics?"

"Not a chance. He made me promise never to call anybody except his own personal physician. He was pretty paranoid about his privacy, you know," he replied with a sly grin.

"I understand," Dr. Walters intoned unctuously.

Later in the evening, after the mortuary had picked up the body for cremation and the lawyer and publicity agent had been notified, Sudsy knocked at Claire's bedroom door.

"I just wanted to tell you good-bye, Mrs. Conway," he began when she opened the door and looked questioningly at him.

"I'm sorry if I ever said anything to upset you, but I was just tryin' to be a friend to your husband. No hard feelings, I hope."

"You miserable little lecher. If I never see your face again, it will be fine with me. Now get out of my house and stay out," Claire commanded him.

Sudsy smiled. "But it ain't your house, Mrs. Kimball . . . not anymore. It's part of the Craig Kimball Trust now, and everything he owned has gone into that trust. The money's gonna be used to fund scholarships for drama students in colleges all over the world.

Craig Kimball's name is never gonna be forgotten. Ya see, I'm one of the trustees."

Claire's mouth dropped open. "You're lying! I've got a copy of Craig's will in my jewelry safe. He left every last cent to me," she protested. "It was all part of our agreement."

"Sorry, Mrs. Kimball. That will you have is as useless as yesterday's newspaper. He tricked you. The only regret he had about deceiving you was that he wouldn't be around to see the expression on your face when you found out about his big joke. He wanted me to be sure to tell you all about it on the day he died."

"That's impossible!" she squealed.

Sudsy shook his head. "He had a new one prepared two years ago. He asked me to give you a copy on the occasion of his demise." He handed the document to her with a smirk.

As a bolt of lightning in the midst of a summer storm suddenly makes everything bright and clear for a brief moment, Claire knew in an instant that what Sudsy was saying was true. "I'll break it," she announced flatly.

"You don't want to try that, Mrs. Kimball. He left you a monthly income of twenty grand, which you'll automatically lose if you initiate any action to contest the will. Take my advice, don't do it. He covered all bases. Ask your attorney. See you at the funeral."

He turned and walked jauntily down the stairs, a free man at last.

Claire went into her room and threw herself on the bed. She wanted to scream and yell and smash things, but she knew she had been beaten, and she hadn't enough energy to waste on anger. She had gambled and lost. Well, twenty thousand wasn't much, but with the money she already had, it would allow her to live in relative comfort and luxury. She hated the thought of losing the house, but what the hell? At least she wouldn't have to put up with Craig anymore, and she still had the distinction of being the great star's widow.

At least that should keep the invitations coming and her name in the columns. She had had the last laugh on him, anyway. She had outlived the son of a bitch.

The important thing now was to plan the funeral. It would have to be big and glamorous since it would be covered by all the media. She would contact the White House and see if the president would attend, and then, perhaps, the French embassy. Surely they would send someone important. After all, Craig Kimball had received the Legion of Honor, and he was a star of stars, and everybody who was anybody would be there.

Claire went to her desk to begin making notes. She would call the caterer first thing in the morning and arrange a lovely reception here at the house. She must make a list of all the movers and shakers in the community and have her secretary call to invite them personally. As soon as her maid got here in the morning, she would go through her closet and find something smashing and suitably mournful to wear.

When she was finished making her plans, she picked up the telephone to call Mavis to tell her the news. Thank God Craig had kicked off before she had signed that damn paper or Mavis would probably expect to collect ten percent of her allowance. At least he had done one thing right.

68

BEN and Rose went upstairs to their bedroom to leave Lilah and Warren alone in the living room. Rose threw herself down on the bed, and every movement of her body expressed worry and frustration.

"What the hell's wrong, Rose?"

"I'm so worried, Ben."

"About what?" he asked, stretching out beside her and putting his arm across her solicitously.

"Mary Ann called while I was in Chicago. I talked to her as if I really were her mother, and it was wonderful." Her voice quivered with emotion as she tried to explain her feelings. "She's found a new beau . . . he's handsome, has blond hair, and has freckles on his nose. What do you think will happen to that relationship if Lilah tells her children the truth about us . . . about me?"

"Her children have a right to know."

"I don't want to be responsible for causing Lilah or her family any more trouble than I already have. I've never seen her children, but I love them as if they were my own. Maybe Lilah and I will have to sacrifice our own relationship to protect them. The world is a cruel place, Ben."

He drew her close to him. "God, I love you, Rose. I can't imagine living my life without you. Promise you'll always stay with me."

As his lips gently touched hers, she whispered softly, "Promise."

Downstairs the conversation was off to a slow and awkward start.

"I'm sorry, Warren," Lilah began, "I really don't know what came over me. Looking back now, I can't believe that I deceived you as I did."

Warren said nothing, and when she started to speak again, he got up from the couch where they were sitting and went to stare out of the window so that he wouldn't have to look into her eyes.

"You see, in the beginning I was caught up in the mystery and excitement of having a twin, and then I was afraid your feelings toward me might change if I told you about my father. I just kept putting it off with one foolish reason after another. Then this scheme of my changing places with Rose came about, and I convinced myself I had to lie to you or you'd stop me from doing it. I just hope you can find it in your heart to forgive me for not trusting you."

"Don't, Lilah . . . don't. I'm the one who should ask for forgiveness," he said, his voice hoarse with emotion and his eyes fastened on the camellia bushes under the window.

Misunderstanding the meaning of his words, Lilah hastened to explain further. "I know you're worried about the children and their children, Warren, and so was I, but I talked to a genetic counselor, and there's no problem. Unless they also marry a person of mixed parentage, their children will be just like them."

"For God's sake, stop it, Lilah!" Warren stilled her in a tone that was sharp and commanding. After a long, tense silence he spoke again.

"Please don't explain or humble yourself any further. I'm not worth it."

Lilah looked away. Was it possible that her world would be shattered here in the midst of all this luxury and beauty? Would there be pieces of her hopes and dreams scattered about, making a mess on the Oriental rug? For twenty years Warren's love had been a constant, taken for granted and underappreciated until

now, when it was about to be torn from her. She
steeled herself, determined to come away with her
dignity intact, if nothing else.

At long last Warren found the words to express his
feelings. "I've had two days to think about everything,
and I'll admit I was upset for a while. God, what an
insidious emotion prejudice is. It eats away one's reason. Then I remembered how beautiful and intelligent
and talented you are . . . and the bright and perfect
children you gave me. And your sister Rose. God, she's
amazing. No, the problem is not you, Lilah, or Rose
or the man who was your father. The problem is me."

Lilah's voice showed her nervousness as she said, "I
don't understand."

"In spite of the fact I've been through this once
before, I can tell it isn't going to be any easier. You
see, when I thought Rose was you, I told her everything. It was bad enough the first time, but it's worse
now that I know how innocent you were and how
rottenly I've behaved." He turned from the window
and looked at her intently.

"You see, Lilah, I was the one who was really
deceitful, not you." He paused momentarily, and then
the words came out in a rush. "I had an affair with
Florence. Don't ask me why . . . I don't know. I have
no excuse. It was short, unpleasant, and costly. I've
been paying her money not to tell you." By the time
the last word was said, his voice had dropped to a
whisper.

"Florence?" Lilah gasped and said no more until
she had heard him out. Warren sat down in the chair
next to the couch and told her everything.

When he was finished, he asked, "Can you ever
forgive me?"

Stunned by the almost incredible story, Lilah at last
managed only the briefest of questions. "Why?"

"Frustration, or maybe because I've been madly in
love with you most of my life."

"That doesn't seem like a very good reason to have
sex with my best friend," she remarked ruefully.

"Not unless you take into account that I've never felt that I'd gotten anything back from you. Oh, I know you've been a good wife and mother, and I tried to be content with that, but you never let me see the passion I knew was somewhere deep inside you . . . the fire I used to see when you were at the piano. Don't get me wrong, I never blamed you, Lilah. It's not your fault that you didn't love me as much as I wanted you to. I blame myself for taking advantage of you at the most vulnerable moment of your life. Maybe under other circumstances you might not have consented to marry me at all. . . ."

Lilah had recovered her composure. "You sell yourself short, Warren, and besides, that's ancient history. Tell me how you feel now that you know who I am."

"I knew the moment I kissed you out there on the lawn that nothing had changed."

"Would you have fallen in love with me and married me if you'd known about my father then?"

"I can't answer that question. If I said no, then I'd be denying you, Matt, and Mary Ann and everything we've shared together as a family. If I said yes, it would probably be a lie, because I fell in love with the girl you were then, not some hypothetical other. Yesterday exists only in our memories, and we can't change it. I only know that I loved the girl you were then, and I love the woman you are now."

Lilah joined him at the window and slipped her arm into his, feeling secure once more. Together they looked out at the bright green lawn, the camellia bushes blooming pink, red, and paper-white among waxy, dark green leaves, and Lilah thought with longing of the winter view from her own living-room window with its bare boughs and withered grass. After a long silence she said, "I'm sorry I wasn't a better . . . a more loving and passionate wife, but I wonder if maybe through the years I might have unwittingly blamed you for taking my music away."

"It was you who ran away from your music. All I did was give you a place to hide."

Lilah held his arm tightly and rested her cheek against his shoulder and she tried to put into words feelings she had long suppressed. "That's true, but ever since I learned about Rose and her accomplishments, I've been thinking about things that for years I avoided because they were too painful to remember. In some strange way I believe that when I renounced the piano, I lost contact with my soul. A violinist once told me that music is like God . . . invisible and untouchable but with beauty, intelligence, and grace and with the power and majesty to give us a glimpse of heaven. Perhaps when I renounced it, I lost the spiritual part of me, the part with the passion."

"Lilah, can we start all over again?" he asked.

She turned and looked into her husband's eyes and smiled, shaking her head. "I don't want to start all over again. I want to go on from here, from a place of understanding and awareness . . . and above all with honesty. I love you more than I ever loved music or the piano, Warren, and I'm sure now that even if I had won at Moscow, I would have found my way back to you eventually."

"Can you ever forgive me for Florence?" he asked, afraid that he had imagined her words and that they were only his long-held wish fulfilled.

"If you'll forgive me for not trusting you enough to tell you about Rose."

He took her in his arms and held her closely. "You are the only love of my life."

Ben and Rose emerged from the bedroom sometime after and called down the stairs, "Ready or not, here we come!"

When they were all gathered in the living room again, Warren said, "Rose, I think we ought to go on to the hotel and let you two be alone for a while."

"Couldn't make it on the couch, huh?" Rose teased, and they all laughed self-consciously.

"No, it's just that we ought to call the children before it gets too late and tell them we're leaving for Hawaii tomorrow," Lilah explained.

Rose's manner suddenly turned serious. "What else are you planning to tell them?"

"You mean, are we going to tell them about their wonderful new aunt?" Warren asked. "Not by telephone, no, but we've always been open and honest with them. I see no reason to change that."

There was concern and anguish in her eyes as Rose said hesitantly, "Just promise me you won't move too fast. Think about it and make sure you're doing what's right for them."

Lilah looked at her sister quizzically. "Why are you so upset, Rose? Surely you don't want us to lie to the children, do you?"

Ben spoke up. "She doesn't want to be responsible for bringing any kind of unhappiness to your family." His voice was low, and it was obvious that he was trying to explain Rose's fears but that he did not share them.

Lilah looked at the distress on her sister's face, and after a long pause she replied, "You once told me that Geneva said it was a sin that blacks had been denied their history. Because of a lie, you and I were separated for most of our lives. Perhaps it will complicate their lives somewhat, but life wasn't meant to be easy, and I'd rather make a mistake by telling them the truth than to err by lying."

"For my sake, don't rush into it. That's all I ask."

"We won't do anything to harm them, Rose. I promise you."

After a quick, tearful embrace of farewell, Rose said to her sister, "I love you, Lilah."

"And I love you, too, Rose. I'll miss you terribly."

"Take care, sister. Take care."

69

Christmas Eve

ROSE was in a dither as she rushed through the house, checking to make sure that everything was in perfect order and as she had planned it. A huge tree thick with white flocking and trimmed with red-and-silver roses dominated the living room.

"Benjie, turn on the tree lights and make sure they're working. I want them to twinkle," she ordered.

"Rose, will you relax? Look, they're twinkling perfectly."

"I've never been this nervous in my life."

"I'd never have guessed," Ben remarked dryly. "Would a drink help?"

"No! Did I hear a car?"

Ben laughed. "I don't think so, but I'll check."

He went to the front door and opened it. "Rose," he called, "you were right. They're here."

Rose raced toward the door, stopping only briefly at the mirror in the hallway to check her appearance. She sped past Ben and out the doorway, and within seconds she and Lilah were in each other's arms for the first time in almost a year.

Warren, Matthew, and Mary Ann got out of the limousine and observed their mother's emotional reunion with her twin. At last the sisters broke apart, and Warren took his turn at hugging Rose and shaking Ben's hand.

Lilah spoke first. "Rose, I want you to meet your niece and nephew. Matt . . . Mary Ann, this is Rose."

With great composure Rose reached out to shake their hands as she said very formally, "You have no idea how happy I am to meet you both."

"Hi, Aunt Rose," Matthew said, and when she heard those words, she could no longer restrain herself. She gathered both of the young adults into her embrace and burst into tears of joy.

"Rose never does anything halfway," Ben remarked to Warren as they walked toward the house.

That evening after their first dinner together they sat under the tree and opened gifts. Matt and Mary Ann were overwhelmed with the gold Rolex watches and miniature television sets Rose gave them.

"It's too much, Rose," Warren protested.

"Hush up, brother-in-law. I've never had a family to buy Christmas gifts for before. Let me be!"

"Aunt Rose, Mom said you'd let us visit the set while we're here," Mary Ann said. "Can we?"

Rose winked conspiratorially at Ben and said, "Well, when I heard you were coming, I got an idea. So I talked to Bruce—" she began, but Ben interrupted her.

"Talked, no—needled, yes," he commented with a grin.

"I talked to Bruce—he's the producer—and we've got a scene coming up day after tomorrow that both of you can be in. No lines, understand, but I'll make sure you're on camera. What do you think of that?"

"You're kidding?" Matthew asked.

"Your Aunt Rose would never lie to you, honey. It's all set."

"You mean, like with makeup and everything?" Mary Ann asked eagerly.

"With makeup and everything, honey child," Rose assured her. "Your boyfriend should get a kick out of seeing you on the tube. By the way, how is he?"

"I don't see him anymore," Mary Ann replied, and dropped her eyes.

Matthew muttered, "The guy was a creep." There was an awkward moment in the room as Rose looked up into the eyes of her sister, who also looked away.

It was Warren who broke the awkwardness of the moment. "Ben, how about giving me a refill on the eggnog."

By the time all the gifts had been opened, Rose had regained her ebullience. "Now, Lilah, go wash your hands in hot water and meet us in the library."

Lilah was bewildered. "What for?"

"You told me you always warmed your hands before you played the piano. Now do it."

Five minutes later Lilah joined the rest of the family in the spacious room where she and Rose had spent their first hours together in California and saw her family gathered around a new, brilliantly polished ebony Steinway grand piano.

"Rose," she gasped, "my God, what an extravagance!"

"I'm rich, remember? Now sit down and show me what you can do," she commanded. "By the way, there's a Pianocorder inside that piano. I want you to cut some tapes for me, and when I get lonesome, I'll just turn it on and close my eyes and pretend you're here playing for me."

Lilah sat down, adjusted the bench, and ran her fingers lightly across the keys. After a few minutes of practice she turned to her family and said, "Tonight, in front of this very prestigious audience, I intend to exorcise an old ghost. When I went to Moscow, the first composition I played was Cesar Cui's Causerie Etude in F Major, Opus forty, Number six. I was going to dazzle them with my daring. It's a difficult work, and in their wisdom few pianists tackle it. Anyway, when I started playing again last spring, I decided to master the damn thing, once and for all. So here goes."

She turned back to the piano and began to play with assurance and strength. She handled the intricate fingering brilliantly, and one did not need to be a music critic to sense that Lilah was in command of the instrument and the music. Rose and Ben were enthralled by her performance.

All too soon Lilah struck the last chord and whirled around triumphantly to receive the adulation and approval of her loved ones. She had given the finest performance of her life for them.

There was a hushed silence, and then Rose spoke. "My God, Lilah, you're a genius. You stayed away from music for twenty years and you can still play like that?"

Lilah and Warren smiled at each other, and Rose detected a connection that had been missing before. "I'm playing better now than I ever did when I was young. Age, maturity, and my family have given me a better understanding of the music. I could feel it the first time I sat down at the piano—the day we returned from Hawaii—even though my fingers were stiff and my technique rusty. I practice long hours, I take lessons three times a week, and I love every bit of it."

Warren added proudly, "Sergei, her instructor, thinks she'll be ready for a small, private concert next year."

"You're going to do it, aren't you?" Ben asked.

They answered in unison but not in agreement. Lilah said, "No," but Warren said, "Yes," and went on to say, "I think she should. She keeps saying she's expending all this effort just for her own satisfaction, but I know that's not enough. Everyone needs a goal of some kind. If she won't arrange it, I will. Of course, I'm not exactly sure how to go about it, but I'll find a way."

"Warren, I think you're enjoying this as much as she is," Rose teased.

"How can I not? She tells me she plays only for me," Warren said, smiling and taking his wife's hand.

Matt and Mary Ann excused themselves and went back to the living room to admire their gifts and permit the adults to talk alone.

"Has the music interfered with your golf game?" Ben asked Lilah.

"You bet it has. She can't beat me anymore," Warren said with a wicked smile. "She's lost the calluses on her hands too."

"Can't have everything, I guess, Lilah. Say, I've made arrangements for the three of us to play at Bel Air the day Rose takes the kids to the studio. Would you like that?" Ben asked.

"Warren would love it, but I personally want to go back to the scene of the crime. I still can't believe we actually got away with that outrageous charade. When I look back on some of the things that happened, it seems like a dream. Have you seen Vance Freedland since Kimball died?"

"Only at the funeral. He spoke very cordially to both of us," Ben replied. "I got the feeling that he was relieved to have Kimball out of the way. Warren, how about taking a look at my new clubs and telling me if I paid too much." The two men headed for the garage, leaving the sisters alone.

"You didn't tell me you went to Craig's funeral. Whose idea was that?" Lilah asked.

"Mine. I wanted to be sure he was really dead. Pretty ghoulish, wasn't it?"

"Any more nightmares?"

"Occasionally, but not often enough to bother me. Life's too good. I have more success than I've ever dreamed of, more money than I can spend, a man I love, not a soul in this world to fear, and now I have a family. Lilah, tell me the truth, are the twins accepting this? I mean, what did they say when you told them about me?"

Lilah chose her words carefully. "They were shocked, curious, interested, very grown-up about it, and intrigued at being related to a big star. Hollywood is a